ARTEMIS
AWAKENING

JANE LINDSKOLD

A Tom Doherty Associates Book • New York

ARTEMIS AWAKENING

Copyright © 2014 by Obsidian Tiger, Inc.

A Tor Book
Published by Tom Doherty Associates, LLC
175 Fifth Avenue
New York, NY 10010

www.tor-forge.com

Tor® is a registered trademark of Tom Doherty Associates, LLC.

ISBN 978-0-7653-7082-2

Tor books may be purchased for educational, business, or promotional use. For information on bulk purchases, please contact the Macmillan Corporate and Premium Sales Department at 1-800-221-7945, extension 5442, or write to specialmarkets@macmillan.com.

First Edition: May 2014
First Mass Market Edition: April 2015

Printed in the United States of America

0 9 8 7 6 5 4 3 2 1

Tor Books by Jane Lindskold

Through Wolf's Eyes
Wolf's Head, Wolf's Heart
The Dragon of Despair
Wolf Captured
Wolf Hunting
Wolf's Blood
The Buried Pyramid
Child of a Rainless Year
Thirteen Orphans
Nine Gates
Five Odd Honors
Artemis Awakening

To Jim, still my favorite archeologist and historian

ACKNOWLEDGMENTS

Many thanks to my agent, Kay McCauley, for striking the spark that lit the fire.

Thanks also to my first readers—Jim Moore, Bobby Wolf, Sally Gwylan, and Julie Bartel. Your thoughtful responses helped me feed the flames.

Thanks to my editor, Claire Eddy, who provided excellent comments. She helped me see where the fire had burned too high and needed to be damped—as well as where I should shift some coals to give the tale warmth.

I'm grateful to my friend Cale Mims for taking the time to turn words into pictures. These definitely helped with the evolution of the cover art.

The quotation in the "Interlude" at the conclusion of chapter thirteen comes from the works of Paul Stamets, noted mycologist. Thanks to Michael Wester with whom, on a tour of UNM's medical library, I came across a display featuring this material. It was one of those magic moments when creative thoughts jell.

And ever, and always, to my husband, Jim Moore. Thanks for being there when there wasn't even a fire, for blowing gently on the sparks so they'd catch, and for constant attention so that the flames neither ran out of control nor guttered out.

Finally, thanks to all those cats, great and small, who contributed to my enduring love for all things feline.

From the white tiger cub at the National Zoo that I petted when I was very small to the pumas at the Rio Grande Biological Park to all those domestic cats who have domesticated me—you've provided tremendous inspiration.

ARTEMIS AWAKENING

I

Crash Landing

A falling star! What luck!

Adara the Huntress froze in place, watching as a thin white line with a heart of fire grew into a wider streak that rushed earthward at an incredible speed. She frowned thoughtfully.

It must be huge to be visible in daylight.

The moment the streak vanished below the tree line, the ground trembled. A crashing louder than any thunder caused Adara to press her hands protectively over her ears. In the glade around her, spring pale leaves shook and dry needles showered from the evergreens.

Immediately, Adara sent out a mental cry. Sand Shadow had been ranging near where the star must have hit. The puma should be unharmed—Adara would have felt her death or pain.

Sand Shadow, did you see where it fell?

The image that came in response placed the puma atop a cluster of boulders, looking down where dust and steam fountained up from a narrow ravine. The puma had not yet mastered the art of linking her senses to those of her partner, but Adara received the impression that something smelled very bad—acrid and bitter, like nothing in nature.

Wait for me.

Adara's thought was a suggestion, not a command. Though the untutored took comfort in the idea that hunters commanded their demiurges, the truth was that who commanded whom was more a matter of the personalities involved than of any automatic superiority of human over beast.

However, although Sand Shadow would be the first to assert she took orders from no one, Adara sensed that this time the puma was content to watch and wait.

I'll be there as soon as I can, Adara promised, not so much in words as with an image of her booted feet carrying her closer to the rising column that marked the star's grave.

As Adara raced to join Sand Shadow, she speculated as to what they might find. Certainly something that had struck down with such force would not have been melted to nothing by the heat of its passage. That meant there would be a treasure to retrieve.

Best would be one of those pieces of iron ore the smiths valued. Next best would be one of those strange things the seegnur had left swirling in the currents of the sky. These curiosities weren't as useful as iron, nor as valuable, but Bruin knew those who collected such artifacts. Even if Bruin could not trade an artifact for as much as he could for iron, Adara's find would gather favors for them both.

Adara loved her mentor and knew he would be pleased if she found an artifact. She was considering how favors might be more valuable than goods when she felt a flash of astonishment from Sand Shadow. The puma focused hard, carefully shaping a new image. Adara gasped and redoubled her pace.

Down in the dust and steam, something was moving.

He hadn't meant to crash the shuttle. That was Griffin Dane's first thought upon coming to, hanging upside down in his restraining harness with his pulse thundering in his ears.

His second thought was that his first had been incredibly stupid. No one ever *meant* to crash. Crashes by definition were unintended. His third thought, how he supposed that in some cases a crash might be intended—as in certain sports or forms of combat—died half-formed as Griffin became aware that the thudding noise in his ears was not solely his pulse.

A grinding, grating sound mingled with the thudding. Those sounds almost certainly meant that—despite the force with which the shuttle had impacted *terra firma*—Griffin's ship was sliding. Sliding probably did not mean anything good either for him or for the ship and its irreplaceable contents.

With efficiency born of frequent and meticulous practice, Griffin set about getting himself out of the crash harness. The shuttle had landed top down. Griffin flipped over so he could walk on the ceiling-turned-floor. Even though he landed lightly, he felt the shuttle slide in response to the shift in balance.

Unstable, Griffin thought. *Still, if I move slowly, I can grab some supplies. There's an emergency kit in the locker near the exit hatch. I'd better get my excursion pack, too . . .*

He moved, first stepping, then—when even that small motion started the shuttle jolting along again—lowering himself so that he could slide on the decking. Sweat stood out on Griffin's forehead by the time he reached the exit hatch. When he tapped the release on the locker, nothing happened. Next he tried the airlock. Nothing.

Nothing, that is, except another of those sickening surges of motion and a sound like hail falling. Claustrophobia—a ridiculous sensation for a starship pilot—hit Griffin.

If I don't get out of here fast, I'm going to be buried alive. Equipment won't do me any good then. Out first. Gear later.

The airlock was equipped with a manual override.

Frowning when each jerk of the lever jolted the shuttle, Griffin forced the heavy levers through their prescribed patterns. He'd been worried something like this power outage might happen, but he hadn't thought it would occur so soon.

Maybe I didn't crash the ship after all, he thought. *Maybe it was crashed for me. Still, I thought I had the shuttle systems sealed. I followed the protocols . . . Maybe what happened was just an accident.*

Focused as he was on these unsettling speculations, Griffin could hardly believe what he saw when he finally slid the airlock door open.

An enormous tawny lion crouched on a steep, crumbling talus slope only a short distance from the shuttle. When the wild cat saw Griffin, its fanged mouth opened in a snarl, its dark-tipped tail lashed, and its shoulders tensed to spring.

⁂

A human male! Sand Shadow was too flustered to send more than the most minimal image. *Within the fallen star!*

Adara put on a burst of speed and arrived at the same rocks upon which the puma had stood moments before. She looked down. The stranger remained crouched within an opening in the surface of his strange vessel—for vessel it must be.

His eyes, which he held fixed on Sand Shadow, were wide and well made, their color a warm brown. His hair, which was mussed and cut much shorter than that of any man of Adara's acquaintance, was golden fair with darker undertones. His skin looked as if it never saw the sun.

He's afraid of you, Adara reproved Sand Shadow, and felt the puma's pride that this was as it should be. *Yes. At most times I would agree most heartily, but this time . . . That thing is sliding on the talus, sliding more with every motion the man makes. If the man does not*

*get out soon, he will be carried with it. I do not think he
will live if he does.*

Sand Shadow acknowledged the sense of this. With a
flick of her long, heavy tail and a frolic of her hindquar-
ters, she bounded away. The man stared after the puma,
obviously eager to escape, but afraid lest any movement
on his part bring the great cat back.

Adara called out to the stranger, pitching her voice
so that it would carry, but hopefully not frighten the
man.

"Hold still! I'm going to throw you a line."

At the sound of the voice, Griffin started, causing the
shuttle to jolt downward, jarring against something and
jamming to a halt. He heard footsteps crunching on the
gravel slope above him. A piece of rope snaked down and
landed near him. Then the footsteps retreated.

"The rope's anchored to a tree," a confident, female
voice said. The words were spoken with an accent like
but not identical to that in the induced language lessons
Griffin had brainloaded in preparation for this trip.

Leaning out from the shuttle, Griffin grabbed hold of
the rope. Even that controlled motion proved to be a mis-
take. The precariously balanced vessel broke loose from
whatever it had been resting upon, then began to plum-
met downward. Hands tight around the rope, Griffin was
jerked free from the vessel, then smashed flat onto his
face. Despite the red flash of pain, he kept a tight grip on
what had become his lifeline.

The landslide poured over Griffin, scouring his exposed
skin, blinding and half-smothering him, causing him to
gasp and wheeze as he struggled against being carried
away by the terrible stream that flowed over him.

The cascade was beginning to subside to a trickle when
Griffin became aware that the rope was pulling from his

fingers, burning the tender skin of his palms. Almost too late, he realized that his yet unseen rescuer was attempting to haul him up. Although his palms were raw and his fingers ached, Griffin clamped down and felt the rope tighten in reply.

A muffled cry of exultation rewarded his effort. The pulling became stronger. Inch by inch, Griffin was hauled from beneath the earthy debris. When his head broke the surface, he gasped for air. What he drew into his lungs was so full of dust and grit that he choked and coughed, but it was air.

The accented voice spoke again. "Hold tight. We're going to start pulling again."

Although his tortured hands protested, Griffin did as he was told. He was aware that any attempt on his part to kick or roll might restart the landslide. Even this slow tugging caused pebbles to trickle by, their rattle and hiss sounding like the warning of a venomous serpent.

When at long last the ground beneath him was stable, Griffin rolled to his feet. He was bruised all over and bleeding in several places. Nonetheless, he refused to give even the slightest wince. Although he was the odd scholar in a family of warriors, still he was a Dane of Sierra and he had his pride.

A Dane of Sierra who will need a miracle or two if he is ever to see Sierra again. Still, who ever said pride was a reasonable thing?

As soon as Griffin was certain his footing was secure, he located his rescuer. She stood beneath the trees higher up the slope, the rope that had saved him still caught in her hands. Griffin had expected a woman—the voice had told him that much—but he had not expected a woman anything like this one.

She was tall—perhaps a hand's breadth shorter than he was, and he was counted a tall man. Her hair was the shining iridescent black of a raven's wing, her eyes a deep amber gold. Both went well with skin tanned golden brown. She was attired in soft leather trousers and a long-sleeved shirt. Her feet were booted.

This woman was not lovely in the soft, drawing-room fashion Griffin had been taught to admire at the university, but was slimly elegant in the manner of one of those handmade knives his brother Siegfried collected.

Griffin thought his rescuer must be as deadly as a blade as well. At her waist was sheathed a hunting knife. Over one shoulder she wore a quiver holding grey-and-white-fletched arrows. Near to hand was the hunting bow that fired those arrows. She studied him quizzically, then began coiling her rope.

"Are you a seegnur?" she asked in her oddly accented Imperial. "I think you must be, for I have never seen a vessel like the one that you came from. Yet, there are tales of such vessels in the lore."

Griffin considered. Her words held an archaic flavor, but he could understand most, all but the most crucial. What was a "seegnur"? It was not included in his language induction vocabulary. He decided on a partial answer.

"My name is Griffin Dane. I am very grateful for your aid. Without it, I fear I would now be dead."

"Quite likely," the woman agreed with dry practicality. "Your boat—I think that was some manner of boat?—is quite wrecked, yet I think it is made of harder stuff than flesh."

"Wrecked?" Griffin repeated in disbelief.

He labored uphill so that he could see into the ravine. The shuttle had continued its slide in a nose-first, upside-down fashion. All but the stern was buried beneath a considerable amount of sand, gravel, and rock. A few trees, ripped from their roots by the force of the landslide, poked out of the debris, mute witnesses to the violence of the event.

"Well," he said, "I'm certainly not getting it out of there."

"Now that your vessel is broken, will you fly away then?" the woman asked. "The lore says the seegnur could fly."

"I'm not sure what a 'seegnur' is," Griffin admitted, "but if I am one, I certainly cannot fly."

"Not all the seegnur could," the woman said, and Griffin realized her words were meant to be comforting.

He forced himself to look away from the wreck of his shuttle. The woman had seated herself on a rocky outcropping large enough that the mountain itself would need fall away before it went anywhere. The puma had reappeared and was resting its head in her lap. Griffin estimated that the creature was something like nine feet long from nose tip to tail tip, a formidable animal indeed. He also noticed that it wore a series of copper hoop earrings in one rounded ear.

"You are Griffin Dane," the woman said. "I am Adara the Huntress. This is Sand Shadow. She apologizes for frightening you before, but she did not expect the shell of your vessel to open in that manner."

The way in which Adara said "the huntress" made quite clear this was a title, not a merely a professional designation. Here was someone who, at least in her own assessment, was a person of importance. Griffin bowed slightly from the waist, rope-burned hands pressed against his thighs.

"I am pleased to meet you," he said. He noticed the puma's ears flickering back and added quickly, "And Sand Shadow as well."

The puma's eyes narrowed, but in the relaxed manner of a cat well pleased rather than in annoyance.

Does she understand me then? Griffin thought. *I remember tales that some of the animals on Artemis were genetically engineered so that they might provide a greater challenge. Could this be one of their descendants?*

He longed to ask but decided against it, at least not

until he knew these two better. They were his only hope of survival and he dared not offend them.

"Adara the Huntress," Griffin said, "my ship may indeed be wrecked, but I believe I can get back inside it and retrieve a few things that would be useful. I already owe you my life. May I impose upon you for further assistance?"

Adara looked at him and her dark amber eyes crinkled in a smile of appreciation.

"You speak very prettily, seegnur," she said, "but I think both courtesy and request come from the heart. We will help you. Let us wait to make certain the landslide is well and truly ended. Meanwhile, I can take you to a stream that runs with clean water and offer a cut from a somewhat lean but still quite tasty haunch of venison."

"I will accept your kind hospitality, lady."

Feeling the ache of his stiffening muscles, Griffin toiled up the slope to join his rescuer. Then he followed Adara and Sand Shadow a short way to where a south-facing hollow sheltered a pocket-sized mountain meadow. The promised stream splashed and gurgled along one edge, pooling at the lowest point before overflowing and continuing its way down.

"I will fetch the venison," Adara said. "Sand Shadow will guard you while you bathe, lest some wandering creature decide you may be edible after the dirt comes off."

She chuckled as she vanished into the shadowed pines. The puma settled into a sunny patch of thick grass and yawned, once again displaying a magnificent array of fangs.

Griffin contemplated the pool. Although the sun was pleasantly warm, he knew that this high up the water would be very, very cold. However, there was no avoiding this bath. He was filthy, and Adara the Huntress did not look like someone who would respect a request for heated bath water.

Though in the days of old, he speculated as he peeled off his coverall, *certainly hot springs or such would have been available. The Imperials—I wonder if that is what Adara means by "seegnur"—liked their comforts. Of course, if the springs were artificially heated, they would now run cold.*

Griffin thought of his shuttle as he had last seen it, mostly buried beneath dirt and rock. If he could get into it, he could retrieve a comm unit and contact his orbiting ship, but what if he couldn't get in? As Griffin stepped into the stream, the cold water was not the only thing that made him shiver.

When Adara returned, she found Griffin Dane much cleaner, although his hair was still dripping wet and his lips were blue with cold. For the first time, she got a good look at his attire unsmudged by debris. This proved to be a one-piece garment, colored two-toned green. Although it had been through a landslide, it showed not a single rip or tear, nor even as particularly dirty.

More evidence, she thought to herself, *that Griffin Dane is a seegnur, even though he does not seem to know the word.*

The twitch of Sand Shadow's ears and flick of her tail told Adara that the puma had found the man's bathing quite amusing. Images of Griffin combined with those of a fluffed and splashing robin showed the determined fashion with which the man had tackled the icy plunge.

Adara chuffed at the cat. *You might have offered to dry him.*

He would have died of fright.

Adara considered, then thought apologies. *You're right.* She turned to Griffin Dane.

"I have a towel you can use to dry your hair," she offered. "I'll make a fire. Sand Shadow should have done so, seeing how cold you are."

Griffin Dane accepted the cloth gratefully and immediately began to tousle the darkened gold of his wet curls.

"Sand Shadow should have made a fire?" He looked about for the puma.

"She has gone to get some wood," Adara said, scraping the ground clear and arranging a circle of river rock around it. Next she used flint and steel to strike sparks into the dry pine punk she shook from a small bag on her belt. "Something she could have done before. Like all cats, Sand Shadow goes from activity to purest indolence with great speed and enthusiasm."

"Oh?" Griffin said.

His tone invited Adara to say more, but she ignored the hint. She wanted to know why, after so many generations—Bruin said that something like five hundred years had passed—a seegnur had returned to Artemis. She wanted to know what had brought this Griffin Dane here. The lore had always been mixed regarding the seegnur. Some tales presented them as wise and talented. Some as grasping and cruel. This seegnur seemed neither wise nor particularly talented—although he had shown courage. Nor did he seem cruel.

Still, Griffin Dane might be minding his manners because he needed her aid. Best to wait and watch and learn. Was he alone? Part of a larger excursion party?

Adara fed her flickering flame with dry grass, then a handful of twigs broken from a scrub oak near at hand. She saw Griffin Dane move to the fringe of the hollow, carefully concealing the stiffness of his battered body. When he returned, he brought with him a dried pine bough.

"Will this help?" he asked.

She smiled up at him. "It will. I wonder where that lazy puma has gone?"

"I could go look for him," Griffin Dane offered. Adara

admired his offer, because Sand Shadow was right. Griffin Dane was afraid of the great cat. "Or I could mind the fire so you can look for him."

"Her," Adara said. "Sand Shadow is female. I think she will call if she needs help but, if she continues slow, I may take you up on that kind offer. In the meantime, are you injured? I have an ointment that is very good for bruises."

She saw Griffin Dane consider denying his injuries, saw, too, that he ruled this to be stupid bravado. Faces and bodies were like game trails. The signs were subtle, but could be read by one who learned the marks.

Bruin, who had been Adara's teacher, had made certain that Adara learned how to read those marks.

"Too often," Bruin had said, "those born to hunt believe they know what destiny has shaped them to be. They refuse to learn more. I think otherwise. One cannot hunt forever."

Those lessons had been a trial, with none of the joy in them that Adara felt when tracking or drawing a bow, but Bruin had been right. The best hunters ranged through wide areas that touched upon many settlements. Knowing how to read those one might meet only once or twice a season was a good thing.

"Yes," Griffin Dane said. "I would appreciate a share of your ointment. My coverall protected most of me from cuts and scrapes, but I am one massive bruise."

Adara dug into her pack and came out with two squat pottery jars. "Rub this first ointment anywhere but open wounds. For the rest, use this second ointment. If you wish, I can anoint your back."

Again the hesitation, then somewhat awkwardly, "That would be very kind."

At that moment, Sand Shadow returned. The puma had found a nice bit of seasoned scrub oak and had broken off enough to make two neat bundles. These she had slung over her back. Now she pranced into the hollow, pleased as a house cat who had caught a mouse.

Griffin Dane, caught in the act of peeling down the upper portion of his coverall, froze in midmotion.

"Do you have another companion, then?" he asked.

"No," Adara replied, enjoying his confusion. "Why do you think that?"

"But if no other companion, who loaded the wood onto the puma's back?"

"She did it herself," Adara said. "Admittedly, she's more skilled than many, but haven't you seen an adapted creature before? The lore says that the seegnur themselves created them."

She stopped herself before repeating what Bruin had speculated, that the adapted had continued to change in the years since the slaughter of the seegnur and death of machines.

"I have not," Griffin Dane said. "Our history—what I suppose you might call our 'lore'—tells of such things, but the manner of creating such was lost in the great war."

Adara had the feeling that Griffin Dane was not saying everything he might, but did not press.

"Do you have any companions with you? You have shown no anxiety such as you might if someone was trapped within your vessel, but what about elsewhere?"

Griffin Dane stood with the upper portion of his coverall hanging loose around his waist, leaving his upper body bare. If he hadn't been so badly battered, he would have been an admirable sight, well muscled, with a light down of chest hair. Now, however, he was marked in shades of red, many of these turning the darker purple of deep bruises.

The fire was burning well. Sand Shadow would add more wood as soon as she had her bundles off, so Adara went over to Griffin Dane. Dipping her fingers in the jar of bruise ointment, she moved behind him and began to rub the greasy stuff in, trying to be gentle. Her fingers felt the ripple of muscles beneath the fair skin, confirming her impression that Griffin's incredible paleness was no indication of ill health.

"I am alone here," Griffin Dane said after a long moment, "not just here in this place, but also in this system. Does your lore contain stories about how there are many planets, circling many suns, and this is but one?"

"Yes," Adara said, reaching around him to dip her fingers again into the ointment jar. Her arm brushed against his nakedness and she felt a pleasant tingle. "Some of the folk who live where the air is thicker say this is just a legend, but those of us who live where we can observe the stars see this must be true."

She did not add that Bruin, who had at one time been a student of the Old One Who Is Young, had told her this bit of lore was true and had shown her the evidence in the dance of the stars and planets.

Griffin Dane nodded. Perhaps to give himself a moment to frame his thoughts, he began rubbing the bruise ointment into his left arm.

"I came here by myself, in a small ship constructed to travel long distances without needing much fuel or tending precisely because it carried just one." He gave a great shuddery sigh, although whether this was because his bruises hurt or because of some memory, Adara couldn't tell. "I came alone because I was certain I was on to something that would make my reputation and I didn't want to share the credit with anyone. I suppose that seems foolish to you."

Adara laughed deep in her throat. "Perhaps it would not make sense to a farmer or a sailor, but to a hunter or a pro . . . Yes. It makes sense. You were on the trail of big game and thought you could take it alone."

"And I was wrong." For the first time, Adara heard bitterness in Griffin Dane's voice. "If you knew how long and how carefully I prepared . . . Then to crash the shuttle within minutes of breaking atmosphere . . . If I ever get over feeling stupid . . ."

He shrugged, winced, then, defiantly, shrugged again.

Adara finished rubbing ointment into his back. Feeling a certain reluctance—this Griffin Dane really had a very nice back—she moved over to the fire. Sand Shadow had added a couple of larger pieces of wood before returning to lounge in the sunlight.

When Adara sent her thanks, the great cat stretched in pleasure. A graphic, mocking, and very sexual image followed. Most altered creatures were amused by the human capacity for sex at any time and in any season. They claimed that this alone was what set humans apart from beasts and praised the stars for being spared such distraction.

Adara admitted desire was a distraction, but she'd never been one to have sex with just anyone. Such behavior left one too vulnerable. A huntress, a rare occurrence already, must take care not to seem weak. Even so, she'd warmed herself at that fire and been burnt. Her heart twisted as she remembered Julyan. She'd loved him, given him not only her heart, but sought to shape herself into what she thought he had desired. Yet he had walked away without a backward look.

Yes . . . She must take care not to seem weak. The lore whispered that the seegnur had the ability to command the people of Artemis. As polite as this Griffin Dane might seem, she must be on guard against his wiles.

Interlude: TVC1500

Darkness. Deadness. Purest cold.

Heat. Intense, incredible heat. The beginnings of awareness.

Awareness. Purpose. Purpose displacing darkness.
Purpose displacing awareness. Awareness becoming
purpose.

2

Lost and Alone

Griffin and Adara were dining on grilled venison
steaks seasoned with tiny wild onions and accompanied by a salad of peppery greens when the roar of rock
upon rock shattered Griffin's last hope that there would
be a neat and relatively easy solution to his problems.

Despite his bruises and the stiffness that had settled into
every bone and joint, Griffin would have rushed to find
out what had happened, but Adara halted him with a
hand on his sleeve.

"What is is," she said. "And that place will not be safe
yet. If you rush off now, no good will be served, and a
very nice steak will be wasted."

Something in the reverent way she spoke of the steak
made Griffin suspect that Adara the Huntress had seen
her share of hungry times. In any case, she was right.
Rushing would not change anything.

So they ate their steaks, drank from tin mugs a tea so
strongly flavored with mint and anise that even the generous dollop of honey Adara added could not dull the
flavor. Only when the meal was concluded and the relics
of their cooking were stored neatly in the pack Adara
slung over her shoulders did they move in the direction
from which the sound had come—back, Griffin was now
certain, to where he had crashed the shuttle.

He knew what he would find before they got there.

The shuttle was gone—or if it wasn't, it was as good
as gone. Griffin Dane looked down upon the pile of loose,

still shifting rock that entombed his ship. Gone were his hopes of salvaging a comm unit, some of his gear, or even a change of clothing. For the first time, Griffin accepted that he might never leave this planet, never see his home system again, never see his *family* again.

The realization hit him harder than any of the rocks that had battered his body.

To this point I haven't accepted I might be trapped, Griffin thought. *What happened seemed rather like a lark, an adventure right out of those serials my brothers loved so much, the ones I pretended to sneer at, but secretly watched over the top of my reader. Shuttle crashed. Rescued by a beautiful woman. Dalliance . . . All right, not quite that, but a rough and rustic meal. Then what?*

She'd offer to help me get back to the shuttle. I'd discover the damage wasn't as severe as I had thought. A few repairs would be needed and then . . .

Or we'd discover the shuttle itself couldn't be used, but that key elements of my gear—weapons, medical supplies, a few other wonders—survived. The two of us would travel valiantly to where I could rig what I needed to contact my orbiter. This done, I would depart, promising to return again, someday, and Adara would look after me, the faintest glint of tears dampening those amber eyes . . .

Griffin shook himself hard, forced himself to look down the slope, really look, to accept that not the smallest tail fin, not even the barest rim of a thruster showed above the rubble.

"It's completely buried," he said.

Adara pointed up the slope. "The shock of your falling must have made the area weak. There was a small peak there. It's gone now."

"Good thing we didn't stay to try and salvage anything," Griffin said, forcing his voice to remain level. "If I'd stayed near, I'd have likely been buried."

Adara's lovely mouth shaped a very small smile.

"Then that is twice I have saved your life, eh? Remember that, seegnur. Now, listen to me while I save it again. You accept that we cannot reach your vessel?"

"Not bloody likely!"

"Then I tell you this. The land here remains unstable. I suspect it will be unstable for some time to come. What did your vessel burn for fuel?"

"Burn?" Griffin began to explain, then shook his head. "I don't think we have the words between us for me to explain."

"But it made heat," Adara persisted.

"Yes, but . . ."

"Will it continue to make heat?"

Griffin considered. "No. I don't think so. The automatic shut-offs went into effect when the shuttle lost control."

"Still," Adara said, "parts of your boat were very hot. Here the ground is very cold and filled with ice, for winter is not long past. Heat and cold do not like each other. For many days to come, the ground in this area will be unstable. We must leave."

Griffin wanted to protest, some lingering part of his fantasy nagging at him. Reality stared up at him from a heap of still shivering boulders. Unless he could get his hands on earth-moving equipment, there would be no getting to the shuttle—and even then, no promise there would be much useful to retrieve. Ground to atmosphere shuttles were not armored. It was likely that the hull had been crushed like an eggshell.

"You're right," he admitted heavily. "But what next?"

"Soonest next," replied Adara, "we go from here. Sand Shadow and I have a cache farther down this mountain. Next soonest, we find another place to camp, one where we will not be buried if the earth chooses to belch after swallowing your craft. After that? We shall see. Although we are in the growing-longer days, still, daylight hours are short enough. This would not much trouble me and Sand Shadow, but how well do you see in the dark?"

"Well enough," Griffin replied curtly.

"Good," Adara said. "Come, then."

Griffin Dane did not see at all well in the dark. Indeed, he began stumbling over small shrubs when twilight was only thickening. Exasperated, Adara made camp. She set Griffin to tend the new fire she had kindled, then put him in charge of grilling a couple more steaks. At least he could manage that.

She set about erecting her small tent. Soon, the tent would be an indulgence, but for now, this high up in the mountains, shelter at night was a good thing. Usually, Sand Shadow slept next to her, so Adara did not need to burden herself with any but the lightest of blankets. Now she envisioned complications. Both lore and popular ballads were full of tales regarding the seegnur and their appetite for local lovers. Would Griffin Dane have the same expectations? It wasn't that she didn't find him attractive, but she did not care to be told what to do.

Sand Shadow returned from bringing more firewood. She did not shape images, but Adara was aware of sparkling hints of feline laughter at the edges of her thoughts.

To distract herself from that coming awkwardness, Adara turned to matters no less awkward, but at least a little less intimate.

"So the seegnur did not all die," she said.

Griffin Dane did not reply for a long time. When he did, his answer was not at all what Adara had expected.

"Perhaps," he said, "what you call the 'seegnur' did die. What is a seegnur?"

Adara studied Griffin, but he did not seem to be mocking her. She framed her answer with care.

"'Seegnur' is what we call those who came from elsewhere, those the lore tells us made this world and set us to live upon it so that we might serve them."

She tried to keep any bitterness from her tone but, judging from the glance Griffin Dane sent arrow-swift in her direction, she had not been wholly successful.

Nonetheless, his reply was mildness itself. "Well, then, here is my answer. I came from elsewhere, that is true enough. However, neither I nor the wisest or most skilled of my kind could make this world or make people to live upon it. That knowledge is vanished, burned to ashes by the fires of a war so terrible that it destroyed entire worlds, even suites of worlds. So, whether or not I am a seegnur must be yours to judge."

Adara considered this.

"Well, I don't see what else you could be. You are not from Artemis."

"True enough, although, given what happened to my shuttle, it's not likely I will be from anywhere else hereafter."

Adara shrugged. "That I cannot say. If only one tenth of the tales told about the seegnur are true, I cannot see what would hold you from attaining anything you desire. You are not a hunter nor a pro nor a factotum nor of the support staff. Of all the classifications that define this world, you fit only one: seegnur."

"Classifications?"

"Yay," Adara replied, deliberately adopting the singsong cadences in which the lore was most usually recited. "Once upon a time, in the cold and dark of space, the seegnur found a great rock. This rock was barren of life, but rich in metals and minerals. It held within its stones the capacity for the twin staves of life: water and air.

"Pleased with their find, the seegnur herded the great rock through the black pastures and placed it where a sun could warm it. Mystery upon mystery was performed. Oceans were shaped. Mountains were caused to rise. A moon was set high above so that there would be light at night and tides to keep the seas from becoming sluggish.

Between oceans and mountains were crafted all the habitats needful for all manner of beasts and plants.

"Then, from the farthest elsewhere that was their first home, the seegnur brought plants and creatures to populate this new world, setting them in fortuitous and beautiful configurations. Thus a world that had been but shaped rock became softened and alive.

"At this juncture, some of the seegnur were content and said, 'Here we have our paradise. Let us revel in it and be joyful.' But others among the seegnur protested, 'Nay. Paradise is not paradise if one must labor. The beasts and plants are lovely, but who will harvest them for us? Who will make our beds and cook our food?'

"And in this was seen great wisdom, so to the world, which was now called Artemis, were brought those who were like unto the seegnur in shape, but not in wisdom or in knowledge. They were given this command: 'We shall permit you to dwell in paradise, but we place upon you one restriction. For most of your days you shall labor only for yourselves, but when those you will know as the seegnur shall come to you, then you will labor for them as well.'

"And the people accepted this as birds accepted flight and the fish of the sea accepted breathing water, as the way in which they were created. As time passed, the seegnur realized that merely having people who could serve them in menial tasks was not yet paradise. They desired those who would be wise in the ways of Artemis, specialists who would show the seegnur the secrets of this vast world they had created. So were made the factotums and the pros, the hunters and the divers, and all the other specialists.

"At this time, too, were shaped the altered beasts, so that not even the seegnur might be able to predict every creature's actions. Now even those who had protested said all was good. In this way paradise was finally achieved."

Adara looked at Griffin Dane and saw that her tale was not wholly unfamiliar to him—but perhaps not wholly familiar either.

"All the peoples agree to this point in the tale," Adara concluded. "It is about what comes after that there is disagreement. From this disagreement have grown the many religions and philosophies. However, this bit of lore should be enough for you to understand why I say that of all the classifications and specializations, you fit only one."

Griffin Dane nodded. "I see why you say that, even if I do not completely agree. Tell me, who taught you that tale?"

Adara shrugged. "It is told in increasing complexity to every child. My parents and grandparents taught me first, later my teachers."

"So you have teachers here?"

Adara nodded. "Yes. Each specialization has those who have mastered specific lore. When they grow older, they teach as well as practice their art."

"Are there no other sorts of teachers?"

Adara considered. "Not in every village nor even in every town, but, yes, such do exist. I have never studied with one, but my teacher, Bruin, was student to one such. From him Bruin learned to read and write, and also something of the greater lore that connects us."

Griffin Dane straightened so quickly that the embers of the fire fanned to flame.

"Greater lore? Then some history survives? Perhaps some knowledge of the days before the seegnur left here?"

"There is such," Adara agreed, "although it is the ken of old people, for it is useless when matters of keeping life and limb together are considered. I have never learned such, though I suspect that someday Bruin will wish me to do so."

She heard ambivalence in her voice. It seemed to her there were so many more important things to know. She handled a bow with skill and could use a knife in many ways. She knew most types of game in her range, but she was still largely ignorant of those in other ranges. She had not yet mastered the spear, for, although she had grown tall, she was somewhat lightly built. She could handle simple water craft, but not those that relied upon sails.

Moreover, her bond with Sand Shadow was less than two years old. She had much to learn about demiurges as well. When there was so much to do, how could old stories matter?

Then Adara looked across the flames to where Griffin Dane sat, and reconsidered her rejection of the lore. What did one do when old stories became new? How would life as she had always known it, had always expected to know it, change if the seegnur came back?

When Adara's voice shifted into that wonderful, rolling cadence and began recounting history as she knew it, Griffin Dane felt the glow of his dream rekindling within him. This was why he had sought Artemis—to learn what had become of that legendary pleasure planet, a planet where, had Adara only known it, those she called the seegnur had met the beginning of their end.

Yet Griffin heard something other than information in Adara's tale. He heard mistrust. At least among those who had taught Adara, the seegnur were remembered with resentment as well as with respect. They might have shaped the world and its people, but the people did not necessarily thank them for it.

As long as Adara thought of him as seegnur and herself as "people," there would be a gulf between them. Griffin did not think he could close the gap—not now, not yet—but perhaps he could bridge it.

"Adara," he said, "I think that perhaps I do have a

classification. In my own worlds I was trained to be a historian and archeologist."

"Historian?" she said. "I think I have heard Bruin use that word. It is like a loremaster, but different. The loremasters are mostly interested in what shaped the world and how that shaping teaches us about the manner in which we should live our lives. A historian thinks that what has happened since the slaughter of the seegnur is important as well. 'Archeologist,' though, that is a word I do not know."

Griffin was delighted by her response. He envisioned the first frail threads of a rope bridge being dragged into place between them. Careful not to break those threads, he replied.

"An archeologist is like a historian, but interested not only in the events, but also in the physical things people left behind them. I spoke of the great war that destroyed the seegnur."

"I remember," Adara said dryly.

Griffin sensed the thread between them fraying. Clearly Adara thought he was condescending to her. He hastened to explain, "They left pieces of themselves behind, pieces that speak of their culture and what they valued. Sometimes—or so I believe—things speak more truthfully than words."

Adara laughed. "Oh! I agree with that. In the village where I was born, there was one who claimed he lived in humbleness until the coming of the seegnur would bring right order again, but his belongings gave lie to his words. Although his tunics were simple, they were of the finest woven cloth; though he ate foods cooked without artifice, I know he always took the tenderest cuts."

She rubbed the bridge of her nose. "Yes. I think there are archeologists among us as well—although they would not think of this as separate from being loremasters or historians. All we know of the seegnur is the lore, the

tales of the ending days, and their broken things, left behind. These last hold great interest for some."

But not for you, Griffin Dane thought. *Very well. I will
not threaten this thin bridge by showing how important
I find those broken things. Perhaps your teacher and I
may find more in common.*

They might have spoken further, but the breeze rose
into sharp biting gusts. Griffin's coverall was made of fabric that maintained an optimal body temperature, but his
exposed hands and face felt the chill.

Sand Shadow had been dozing near the fire. Now she
stretched, looked at Adara, then moved out into the darkness.

Adara got to her feet and began burying the fire.
"Sand Shadow reminds me that the night will only grow
colder and that we have far to travel come dawn. The
tent is not large, but it will hold us—or do you wish to
sleep out here? I notice your clothing protects you well
from the cold."

Griffin nodded, his heart suddenly racing. Was this an
invitation to more than sleep? He struggled to keep his
tone matter-of-fact. That it was a test of some sort, he
did not doubt. He answered as neutrally as possible.

"It does, but I left behind the gloves and head covering, so I fear I am not invulnerable to cold. Who will keep
watch if we both sleep?"

Adara snorted. "With the scent of a great cat covering
us, why should we need to keep watch? And I am a hunter.
That protects us where the other does not."

"I think I need to know more about hunters," Griffin
Dane said.

"I think," Adara parried with a slight grin, "you need
to know a great deal about many things. We have many
days' travel in front of us. Then we can talk. Now we
must sleep. You may sleep out here or in the tent. The
choice is yours. I will sleep to the left."

To the left proved not only to be to the left side of the tent, but to the left of Sand Shadow. Soon after the two humans were settled, the great cat returned and stretched her length between them, the most perfect chaperone in all creation.

Griffin yelped when he felt the furred back press against him. "She's sleeping in here?"

"You do not think I would throw Sand Shadow out just for your sake?" Adara retorted.

Did Griffin imagine it, or was there a hint of laughter beneath the words?

"I suppose not," he admitted. The great cat *was* very warm and had lain down with her fangs and claws toward Adara.

"Sand Shadow thought you would fear to enter the tent if she came in before you," Adara said. "She did not wish you to be so afraid that you would freeze instead of sleeping warm."

"Very thoughtful of her," Griffin replied sourly. This time, he did not imagine the faint chuckle that reverberated in the enclosed space.

"Sleep well, Griffin Dane, the historian," Adara said.

"Sleep well, Adara the Huntress. And thank you again for saving my life."

Early the next day, Adara revised her estimate for how long it would take them to reach Shepherd's Call. Griffin Dane was obviously doing his best, but his idea of a good pace and her own were quite different.

Initially, the huntress felt impatient. However, since impatience is the enemy of any hunter, Adara forced herself to examine why she was so eager to get to Shepherd's Call. The answer was so obvious it did not take long to reach.

I want to hand Griffin Dane over to Bruin and be done

with him. This seegnur makes me nervous—and not only for himself, but because of what he represents.

Sand Shadow, keyed to her emotions if not precisely to her thoughts, had sent along an image of a splotched and spotted puma kitten tumbling to the feet of a great, fat bear. *So . . . Am I even wise taking Griffin to Bruin? Yes. I think I am, but I need not run so fast that I fail to notice there is a dhole pack on my tail, not merely a single dog.*

This morning, Adara had not spoken to Griffin Dane beyond what had been necessary to set them on the trail toward where she had hidden her canoe. He had seemed to respect her silence—or perhaps what he had respected was the forest that surrounded them. Certainly, he kept darting glances side to side, as if he expected to be pounced on at any moment.

Like most hunters, Adara was comfortable with silence. Indeed, the ability to keep silence was among the first things a child must demonstrate before being accepted as an apprentice by a senior hunter.

But what I must hunt now cannot be stalked in silence. It must be coaxed after with words, as I might use a duck call to bring the birds to me.

Without further delay, Adara spoke. "Last night, Griffin, you told me you were a historian. Is this your family craft or is it one you found for yourself?"

He seemed startled, but replied readily enough, "Oh, very much my own craft. I am the youngest of seven boys. My mother always has said that she must have used up all her energy creating the six before me. I was apparently always a quiet child."

"Seven children?" Adara was amazed. "Did they all live?"

"Why, yes. So did my three sisters."

"Ten children in one family? Your mother must have spent all her life pregnant or nursing. My mother had enough trouble with five, and we were widely spread apart in age."

Griffin paused. "We . . . She had help."

"Ah, of course. We also use wet nurses," Adara replied. "Still, your family is blessed with good health."

"Yes."

Adara noticed Griffin seemed uncomfortable with the subject. Perhaps it was only the matter of bearing children that made him choose his words so carefully. Men were often like that, quite happy with the sticky and sweaty details of engendering a child, but much less so with the realities that followed.

Interested as Adara was in knowing more about Griffin's family—her own family life had been far from usual, so she found such tales fascinating—Adara remembered her purpose was to learn more about this stranger she planned to take home.

To learn, perhaps, if I should take him to my home.

"So you were quiet?"

Griffin laughed. "Outside, I suppose I must have been, since everyone tells me this was the case. Inside I felt like a storm made of questions. Where did this come from? Why did we celebrate this festival? Why did we use this form of address to one person, but a second form to a person who seemed—at least to me—much the same? Answers like 'Because' or 'This is how we do it' may have satisfied my brothers and sisters, but they didn't me. I started seeking the answers, but all I found were more questions."

"You said that you studied the seegnur and the things they left behind," Adara prompted. "Did you find your answers along those trails?"

"Actually," Griffin said, "after a fashion, I did. When I was young, my discoveries were known to many others: place names or the history of a certain building were matters of record. Then I made my first big discovery. On my world—in my entire system—the most important festival of the year is called Water Day. Most people think of Water Day only as a time to meet with friends, to eat special foods we prepare at that time. I was curious, though, because none of the many rituals and decorations had anything to do with water.

"Eventually, I found out that Water Day actually had its roots in *two* events. The first was an old religious feast. The other was based in political events so long ago that the details were forgotten. Here's what fascinated me: the political events, a revolution of sorts, had occurred when they did because of the religious festival, but everyone seemed to have forgotten the connection."

He shrugged, clearly embarrassed to have shown this childhood enthusiasm. "After that, I was hooked. I wanted to know the whys behind everything we did—not the scientific whys, but the social whys. My parents thought I was exceptionally odd but, after raising six other sons and three daughters, they were inclined to be indulgent."

Adara did not wish to dam the flow of Griffin's speech, but she was puzzled.

"And how do you feed yourself on this knowledge of festivals and past events? Do your people value this so highly?"

"I wish," Griffin replied with a rueful grin, "but, no, they do not. My family is very, very wealthy. Although all of us have been encouraged to learn a trade so we will not stagnate, the reality is that all of us could live quite well without working at all."

Adara studied the man who walked alongside her, still bruised and battered, his only possession a single garment. She wondered if Griffin Dane realized that he was no longer wealthy.

Yet the seegnur had wealth enough to create this planet and all its people merely to have a place to play. His family's accumulation of wealth is another proof that Griffin is a seegnur, no matter what he thinks. And if he is a seegnur, with the powers the lore says the seegnur possessed, then perhaps he is still possessed of great wealth. I would be foolish to pity him. Rather, I must be on guard.

But as Adara rested a hand on Sand Shadow's shoulder, she admitted to herself that she did indeed pity Griffin Dane, so lost, so alone, so horribly ignorant and vulnerable.

※

Interlude: TVC1500

Rising on battered limbs. Falling forward. Must cease to fall. Find the breaks. Mend. Move to live. Live to bring death. Death to bring peace.

Purpose fulfilled. Purpose fires the burning heat and mends. Awareness of rising, not only self but that which rises into atmosphere. Riding wetness. Riding above.

Anxiety? Purpose is own. Purpose is self. Must fulfill the purpose. Must. Else fate uncontemplateable awaits.

3

Smothering Whiteness

Griffin shivered and surveyed the snowy landscape. "Since the trail turned, it's as if we're back in the middle of winter."

"It does," Adara agreed. "That peak," she pointed, "blocks the sun for most of the day this time of year, so the snow hasn't melted as much. Do you mind a bit of cold? There's something I'd like to show you. I promise, we'll be back in greener areas well before evening."

"I'm game."

Adara stopped and began burrowing in her pack. "I have a spare set of gloves. They're knit, so you should be able to get them on."

"I'll ruin them!"

Adara shrugged. "Better a set of gloves ruined than having the first seegnur to visit Artemis in generations catch cold. Here."

She pulled out two sets of gloves, handed him one, pulled on the second, then handed him a stocking cap.

"Put this on."

"But . . ."

"I have a scarf," Adara said, placing the neutrally colored length of knitted fabric around her neck, then wrapping a loop over her head. "Anyhow, my hair's longer and heavier than yours. During the summer, I regret my indulgence, but this time of year, I'm glad for it."

Griffin slid the gloves on. Both gloves and hat were knit from a yarn heavy enough to be warming, without being so bulky as to make the hands useless. The style was practical, lacking embellishments, the undyed wool the yellowish white of old ivory.

"The rest of you warm enough?" Adara asked. "I have extra socks."

"My feet are fine." Griffin indicated his coverall with a sweeping gesture. "The fabric is naturally insulated, meant to trap body heat. The boots are the same material, but thicker and tougher."

"Wonderful stuff," Adara said admiringly, closing up her pack and slinging it over her shoulders.

"It is, but the gloves and hat are very welcome," Griffin said as they resumed hiking. "Did you make them?"

"I did," Adara affirmed, setting off once more down the trail deer and elk had worn before them. "I learned to knit as a child, but I've never bothered with more than the basics. Still, I can make my own socks, gloves, hats, and scarves, even a sweater, if I must—they just won't be very pretty."

Griffin considered Adara's casual dismissal of her skill. If pressed, he could sew a simple seam, but make anything? Hardly. As for replicating his coverall . . .

Impossible. I'd better take care not to wear it out. What am I going to do? Will Adara and her Bruin continue to care for me? From what Adara says, the economy in her village is largely based on barter. What do I have worth trading?

Griffin was wondering how to ask without giving away how insecure he was feeling when he realized that both Adara and Sand Shadow had halted in mid-stride. A moment later, he heard what their sharper senses had already caught, a soft, yet somehow penetrating *whooom-phf!* Griffin blinked, trying to remember why that sound should be significant. Then Adara was shoving him toward the thick stand of trees that bordered one side of their trail.

"Grab hold! Avalanche!"

Griffin bolted toward a tree large enough to possibly stand through the avalanche, though not so large that he couldn't get a solid grip around the trunk. His sister Boudicca was a champion snow skier, both downhill and cross country. From listening to her often hair-raising tales, Griffin knew there was no way to outrun an avalanche. The best one could hope for was not to be buried too deeply.

Or smothered. Or battered by the rocks and other debris carried along by the snow . . .

Adara was running slightly ahead of him. Griffin caught a glimpse of Sand Shadow's black-tipped tail as the puma leapt from point to point, avoiding the deeper snow the humans must lumber through.

Reaching his chosen tree, Griffin wrapped his arms tightly around it, pressing the side of his face against the rough bark. Almost before he had gotten a hold, the snow hit him in the back, smashing him into the trunk. His face felt warmly wet. He realized his nose was bleeding, maybe broken. He could hear the tree's wood screaming in protest, but the roots remained firmly anchored in the soil.

As wet snow pounded into him, Griffin's coverall provided protection from the worst of the cold. The back of his neck felt as if a hand of ice was pressing against the skin. Long fingers of wet snow stroked the sides of his face. Between breaths, light faded and became shadowed darkness. The vibrations ebbed and he knew the worst of the snow slide had passed. Griffin had no idea how deeply he was buried, but certainly no one was going to find him unless he got himself unburied.

Adara? Sand Shadow? Did they make it clear? Don't know. Can't know. If they're in trouble, I won't do them a damn bit of good buried here.

As he assessed his situation, an induced learning session from many years past surfaced. First step, clear a space before the nose and mouth to assure breathing. Next, start moving before the snow firms up. The tree trunk to which Griffin still clung gave him orientation, but how deeply was he buried? In what direction should he move?

Griffin bent his head back and looked up, every fiber of muscle aching. At least the snow had stopped his nose from bleeding. Above him, the snow glimmered palely. Hope surged through him—he couldn't be too deep if he could see light.

Now to get out of here.

Griffin's grip on the tree had kept him upright—a tremendous asset in this circumstance. If he'd been swept downhill, he'd likely be flat, with all the weight of the snow atop him, sealing him into a custom coffin.

Adara . . . Sand Shadow . . .

Images of what might have happened to his companions made a horror show in Griffin's thoughts, giving him strength. He pounded his limbs against the enveloping snow until they were loosened from the cold, damp grip. The exertion made him sweat—a dangerous thing since, if he slowed down, the sweat would freeze, making him even colder. Once out in open air, his coverall would wick away much of the moisture, but he'd freeze for certain if he stayed here.

Griffin dug for the surface, pushing the snow away, inching up the tree trunk. Fortunately, he was a tall man. Before long, his head broke free of the smothering snow. A tree limb extended over his head. Griffin stretched to reach it, grabbed hold, then pulled himself out of the snow.

Once he was up on the limb, he surveyed his surroundings. Snow in shades of white and grey. Streaks of muddy ground. Rocks. Broken bits of tree and shrub. A bit of tawny gold, poking out from where snow piled at the base of a cluster of boulders.

Tawny gold?

Sand Shadow!

Griffin started to jump down, remembered how deep the snow was near the trunk of the tree, and instead worked his way down the tree limb until he could lower himself onto a boulder that formed an island in the sea of white. Once on the boulder, he snagged a length of broken sapling, branchlets bearing leaves like tiny tattered green flags along its length.

No time to break these off, no time to make a smooth pole. He was sure the golden brown must be one of Sand Shadow's hind legs. From the angle it poked up, the puma's head must be deeply buried. If Griffin didn't dig her out, she'd smother.

Using the sapling as a probe, he worked his way over to Sand Shadow. Mostly, the snow only came up to his thighs. Once he missed a deep spot and floundered in almost up to his chin. Cursing choice bits from four different languages, he struggled out.

By the time Griffin reached the puma, he felt certain

she was dead. He hadn't seen the least twitch, not even when he thrust his hand into the snow to try and trace the angle of her body. But she felt warm, so maybe . . . Without further consideration, he started digging through the snow near to where he thought the puma's head was, hoping to get her air.

If she's still breathing.

The snow was heavy and wet. His gloves were already wet. Soon they were sodden, tiny balls of ice hanging from the wool like ornaments. About the time Griffin was losing the feeling in his fingers, he became aware that someone was next to him, bent over, digging like a dog, double-handed so the snow flew out between her legs.

"She's alive," Adara said. "Keep up what you're doing. She's already feeling the difference."

Griffin grunted and kept digging, but his heart was singing. Before long, he reached the puma's head. It seemed—as was the case with her kind—too small for the massive body. The warmth of Sand Shadow's breath had carved a tiny hollow in front of her muzzle; by now the moisture from her breath was causing it to ice up.

Without hesitation, Griffin broke the ice away from the cat's nostrils, then along the edges of her mouth. Sand Shadow's jaw dropped open, her ragged breaths revealing an impressive array of fangs. Her tongue came out. She lapped the edge of Griffin's glove.

"Thank you," Adara said, clearly translating. "And from me as well. She wants to know if you're badly wounded. Your face is all over blood."

"Not bad. I might have broken my nose."

Adara gave him a thoughtful glance. "It still looks straight, but I'll check it later."

Her words came out in jerks between sweeps of her digging hands. Now that Sand Shadow could breathe, Griffin shifted so he could get the weight of the snow off the puma's flanks. Eventually, they got her free.

"Is anything broken?" he asked.

Adara swept her hand down the damp, matted fur. "She doesn't feel any great pain, but her thoughts are cloudy. She's having trouble focusing. Maybe a cracked rib, but she was brought down on soft snow that gave beneath her. That same softness trapped her. She was trying to work her way out, but the lack of air . . ."

She stopped, motioned for Griffin to step back onto a slab of rock their digging had uncovered so that the puma could move onto the snow their weight had packed. Sand Shadow slowly rolled so that she rested on her belly, then rose cautiously to her paws. Swaying as she did so, she shook each paw one by one, then twitched the length of her tail. Last, she looked at Adara and made a querulous sound, almost like a cat's meow.

"She's going to shake," Adara said. "Her coat is quite wet."

"Good idea," Griffin said, turning his head so the spatter wouldn't hit his face.

Once Sand Shadow indicated that she could walk, they used Griffin's sapling as a probe until they were clear of the snow. Then they worked their way upslope to a sunny patch. Adara eased off her pack, then pulled out flint and tinder. Griffin stripped off his wet gloves, rubbed his hands vigorously against the already drying fabric of his coverall, and went looking for wood. Sand Shadow lowered herself into a patch of sun and started slowly grooming her fur into order.

"I promised you a greener spot by evening," Adara called to Griffin, "and I'll keep my promise, but we need to warm up first. We should also make sure this slide does not trigger a second."

"I wonder if my crash caused this."

"Maybe, but I was an idiot to take us this way in any case. Melting snow is unstable." Adara motioned toward her pack. "If you fill that little pot with clean snow, we can melt it for drinking water. First, though, use the towel and dry your hair. The hat's soaked through."

"What about you?" Griffin asked, getting out the pot and towel. While packing the pot with the requested snow, he washed his bloody face with a few cold handfuls. His nose was a bit swollen, but it didn't seem to be broken.

"I'm wet, but I want to get the fire going. I don't have a full change of clothes, but at least I can change my socks and shirt."

"Good." As he tousled his hair, Griffin asked, "What happened to you when the avalanche hit? You don't look as if you got buried."

Adara slid a dry sock onto a damp foot, sighing with obvious pleasure. "I didn't. I climbed a big tree. I figured that there I'd be above the snow, in a good position to find you if you went under.

"Problem was, the tree I chose snapped when the snow hit it. I kept my grip and rode the trunk until it snagged against some rocks. As soon as the worst of the snow slide was over, I hurried back. I knew Sand Shadow was in trouble, buried, nearly unconscious. Figured you were, too. You can't imagine my relief when I topped the rise and saw you digging her out."

She turned to him, her smile for the first time brilliant, even sunny. "I am grateful beyond belief."

Griffin floundered for something to say, embarrassed by her warmth in a way he had never been by her mockery. Then he started.

"Adara, your eyes! The pupils! They're just like a cat's."

Adara had known this moment would come. She and Griffin could not travel forever in shadowed forests. In her happiness at her companions' survival, she had forgotten that their current camp was in full sunlight.

She drew back. Then she realized that Griffin Dane's expression held none of the fear or apprehension she had come to dread. All she saw was the curiosity and interest with which he greeted any tidbit regarding Artemis and its inhabitants.

Nonetheless, her ingrained defensiveness made her snap.

"Yes, they are." She heard her tone, harsh and mocking, and winced from it. "When I asked you if you could see in the dark, I was asking for truth. I can see in the dark as well as any cat. My eyes catch the light and give it back just as Sand Shadow's do. It is a useful gift. I thought, perhaps, that the seegnur had made it common where you come from."

Griffin shook his head. "I've heard of some people having surgery done . . . But you say this is natural to you?"

"I was born with it, yes," Adara said, trying to soften her voice. "There was no surgery, but neither did the difference show right away. I was beginning to stagger about on two feet when my parents noticed that I moved confidently in darkness. A year or so later, they were certain why. The full change took years to shape."

Griffin still looked interested, so Adara decided she might as well get the worst over with.

"The eyes are not my only adaptation," she said. "Look."

She extended her hand, concentrating, willing bones to shift, nails to harden and extend so that each finger held a miniature dagger, pointed and slightly curved. The claw on the thumb was shorter, thicker, meant to hold and rip where the others would slice and impale.

"My feet," Adara went on, forcing herself to look at Griffin, "are spared this disfigurement, for, as Sand Shadow says, given how a human's foot is shaped, what use would there be in granting it claws? Still, who knows? These hands did not full-form until I was already a woman grown. Bruin speculates that while night vision would be helpful to a child, claws would not be."

"Why not?" Griffin asked. His matter-of-fact curiosity eased her.

Adara laughed. "Perhaps because what parent would carry a child who could wound them at a whim? Perhaps because a child does not have the strength or concentration to use claws effectively. Even now, I am still learning. It is not easy to make the claws come quickly."

"Concentration?" Griffin was fascinated. "I thought your claws were retractable, like a cat's."

"They are and they are not," Adara said, studying her hand with detachment. "A cat's claw curves into a sheath. A human's finger is not shaped to hold such a sheath. Instead, when I will it to do so, the hand itself changes."

She anticipated his next question.

"I do not know why this happens nor how it was done. Here on Artemis, the seegnur worked their changes on humans and animals alike. That did not mean they explained what they were doing any more than a man who bridles a horse explains the various snaps and buckles to his steed."

Adara heard the tension in her voice, waited for Griffin to chide her—as Bruin so often had, reminding her that she should be grateful for such advantages—but his response was mildness itself.

"How long does the change last?"

"It should last as long as I desire," Adara said, "but I will admit, sometimes it does not. That is the reason Sand Shadow and I came to these high reaches, so we could train away from most humans—and most animals."

"Lucky for me that you did," Griffin said. "Was it very odd for you—when you learned you could see in the dark and grow claws?"

"Very odd."

Adara swallowed a sigh, wishing she could explain, but how to explain something she understood so little herself?

Adara had been a middle child, between an older sister

and a younger brother. Even when she'd been quite small, without realizing it, she'd been trying to figure out why she existed. Nikole was the big girl. Orion the coveted boy—and the baby. Adara had felt like an extra, not able to do tasks Nikole carried out so effortlessly, no longer the special baby.

She had prayed without knowing she was praying that someday, somehow, she would be special. But when those prayers were answered, they were answered with a curse. Adara's adapted nature set her apart. Later, it got her kicked out of her family. At age five, Adara was sent off to Bruin. For a few years, Bruin took Adara back to spend a month or so with her family. Before she was ten, the visits ended. By then there were two more siblings: Hektor and Elektra. Adara had guessed there wasn't room for her anymore.

Adara shook as if memories were physical things she could shrug off, saw Griffin looking at her with concern.

"You're still soaked," he said. "Let me dry you off. I didn't get the towel terribly wet."

"Better," Adara said, forcing a grin. "Give me the towel. You should see what I put you into such danger to show you. Step over to that gap through the trees, look up along the slope, in the general area where the avalanche began. What do you see?"

Griffin's next words were in a language Adara didn't understand, but she understood the shock and surprise in his tone all too well.

"That's a burn scar from a heat weapon! It looks as if it took off half the mountainside."

"It did, or so I've been told. The seegnur had something hidden there. Bruin suspects defenses or perhaps weapons."

"And the attackers destroyed what was there," Griffin said, "just in case their nanoviruses didn't disable everything or countermeasures were available. You'd think I'd be used to it by now ... The power the Imperials had at their command was incredible."

Adara nodded. "We have a legend about how that burn was made. I don't know if it's true."

"Tell me?"

"The story is that one person did that. A person in armor. A person who could fly. She—the story always says 'she,' though I don't know how they could tell if she wore armor—flew in, using the river as a guide, then came up here. Light flashed from her hands when she held them in front of her and the mountain exploded. After, when the seegnur were either dead or gone, some came to look and found traces of the facility that had been there."

Griffin took a step forward, as if he would climb the mountain and look for himself.

"There's nothing left," Adara said gently. "Bruin likes to send his senior students there as a test of climbing skill and—I think—to remind us how dangerous the seegnur could be."

"Nothing?" Griffin said.

"Nothing. I have been there myself. Only certain lines where structure met rock show that there was ever anything to be destroyed."

They slept that night in the promised greener regions, dining on scanty provisions from Adara's pack before collapsing to sleep. In the morning, Sand Shadow proved she was feeling stronger by providing them with breakfast in the form of a furry round-bodied creature Griffin couldn't identify, but which tasted just fine when cooked over the fire.

At Adara's direction, Griffin dug some tubers from the edge of a stream, a task that not only provided additional food, but which loosened his stiffened muscles. As soon as they had eaten and packed their gear, they started hiking down the mountain once more.

When the trail widened out, Adara dropped back so she could walk next to Griffin.

"We have a problem."

Griffin was taken aback. "Only one?"

"Our problem," she replied, "is how do we explain you?"

Griffin frowned. "I hadn't really considered it."

Adara looked puzzled. "What did you plan to do before your shuttle crashed? I mean, how did you plan to explain yourself?"

"I didn't," Griffin said, then realized how stupid this sounded. "I mean, not at first. My shuttle had camouflage coating and sound deadening on the engines. I intended to cruise over population centers so I could study whatever cultures I found. Only after careful study would I have attempted contact. My first choice would have been a university or something similar—if I could have figured out where one was."

"And your second choice?"

"My second . . . Well, that would have depended. Governments can be touchy but—if I could have found someone reliable in charge, I suppose I would have sought that person out. However, I would have delayed speaking to anyone at all until I understood more about Artemis. My initial investigation might have taken months, even longer."

Adara tilted her head and looked puzzled. "How could you have found a government from orbit?"

Griffin shrugged. "Well, usually the people in charge live or work in a palace or some other structure that is conspicuous. I would have looked for someplace like that. Even so, I would have needed to figure out whom I should contact."

Adara looked thoughtful. "That's interesting. I'll admit, there's some truth in what you say. However, in this region, at least, you'd have to look very carefully to find a significant structure. Most of the towns and villages rule themselves. There might be a town hall, but I doubt it would stand out for you."

"So the towns are completely independent?"

"More or less. Trade is the link." Adara shrugged. "The lore tells us that the seegnur wanted Artemis to be 'unspoiled,' so no large population centers were created. Shepherd's Call, where I live, is on the small side, I admit. However, from things you have said, even Spirit Bay—the biggest town I've ever been to—would seem small to you."

Griffin nodded. "I think you're right. One of the reasons I came down in the shuttle was that my orbital survey wasn't telling me much. I found some towns by tightening my focus to places where humans usually settle—near river junctions or good natural harbors. I was a bit surprised. I'd thought that populations might have consolidated once the seegnur were no longer present— for convenience, if for no other reason."

Adara shook her head. "You overlook the importance of the lore. What the seegnur wanted we still do, even if the meaning for the specific task is no longer known."

"But I've taken us off topic again," Griffin said apologetically. "You wanted to know how I planned to explain myself. The answer is, I planned to adapt my explanation according to what I found."

"Still, at least you do understand the problem you present," Adara replied. "When I first found you, I focused on taking you to Bruin and letting him figure out what to do with you. That still seems wise, but even Bruin will need help explaining you."

"I suppose," Griffin said, "people from off-planet have not routinely shown up on Artemis?"

"I have never heard of another from off-planet coming here—not since the slaughter of the seegnur and death of machines. Perhaps there have been landings elsewhere.

The world is large and I know only a small part of it. But 'routinely'? No. Not that. I think we would have heard. Bruin takes interest in such things."

Griffin realized he was relieved—a completely stupid reaction, given that he was stranded on this planet—but rooted in his desire to be the first one to rediscover Artemis. There had been times in the course of his research that he'd thought someone else might be following the same line of approach, that he'd get to Artemis only to find another ship in orbit.

Though he'd like to be able to go back to Sierra, he'd also like to have something to show for his efforts—something other than a wrecked shuttle and a tale of woe.

"No other? Then I am an oddity indeed. I don't suppose your village is near an ocean or even a large bay? If so, we could say I was shipwrecked and you found me. That wouldn't be so far from the truth."

Adara shook her head regretfully. "No. My home is far from the ocean. We are in the foothills of mountains that are far from any ocean. Even Spirit Bay is many days' travel, and in the wrong direction entirely to provide waters on which you might have been wrecked."

"So, is there any reason you shouldn't still take me to your Bruin? I mean, you didn't seem to think he would need an explanation."

Adara shrugged. "No reason. I could sneak you in when most of the village would be asleep. However, this would not solve the reality that at some point an explanation must be found for you. Bruin can be a solitary old bear, but he does not shun companionship."

"How about this," Griffin offered. "You found me . . . We won't mention the exact circumstances."

"I want to tell Bruin," Adara interrupted. "He is not only my teacher, he has been my greatest friend."

"Then we will tell Bruin the truth. For the rest . . . You were training and you came upon a stranger. The stranger was lost and incompetent. Therefore, you interrupted your training and brought him down where he wouldn't starve or freeze."

Adara giggled. "I like that. Truth to a point. Your shuttle is well buried. Another hunter might find the place where the rocks and earth cover it, but would they dig? I think not."

"Do you think the people in Shepherd's Call will have seen my shuttle coming down? You said it looked like a falling star."

Adara shrugged. "It's possible. It also made a tremendous noise when it hit. Still, you and it need not be connected. Things do fall from the skies—sometimes quite large things."

She grew grave. "Actually, there are old legends—not part of the lore, for the lore is what we know to be true, though some say these legends are lore nonetheless—of sleepers left when the seegnur departed. Someone is certain to remember those tales. Perhaps someone will offer that as a possible explanation."

"Are these sleepers thought to be dangerous?"

Adara shrugged.

"Well, I hope the folklore says they're just sleepy," Griffin said. "I'd hate for anyone to see me as a threat before I have a chance to prove myself."

Adara grinned at him. "I'll make certain everyone knows how unthreatening you are. Honestly, though, you have proven stronger than I thought possible when first we met. I will never forget how you reacted after the avalanche. I could not have asked for a better traveling companion."

"Just returning the favor," Griffin said, pleased beyond measure. "You got me out of a landslide, I got Sand Shadow out of a snowbank. I just hope Sand Shadow isn't the next one digging someone out of a hole."

Interlude: Blood of Clouds

Sharing salt kisses with ocean depths,
　　frost caresses with mountain peaks.
Shapeshifter supreme. Bodiless,
　　possessing power to split rock.
Do you know what you carry? Where shall you
　　leave it?

4

Shepherd's Call

Adara's canoe was a surprise. When the huntress had
mentioned she had one cached, what Griffin had envisioned was a small, light craft, such as had been made
on many worlds by many different peoples.

Even on Griffin's home world, where personal flyers
had made almost every other form of transportation ob-
solete, canoes existed. Hundreds of years after anyone but
fanatical hobbyists had made these small boats from natural materials, often the plastics and metals would be
colored in browns and tans, patterned with wood grain
or a black upon white dappling called "birch bark."

Adara's vessel fulfilled Griffin's vision, but only to a
point. Its frame was made from wood covered with hides
stripped of their hair and neatly sewn into place. The
caulking was a golden-brown resin that reminded Griffin of Adara's eyes. But this was no little craft. It stretched
more than three or four times Griffin's body length and,
at its widest point, was nearly as wide as his outstretched
arms.

"I call her *Foam Dancer*," Adara said with obvious
pride when she pulled the craft from hiding, "for when
she is lightly loaded, she can float in the least amount of

water, even, sometimes, so it seems to me, on foam and froth."

"It's so large," Griffin exclaimed. "I had wondered how two of us might fit in your craft along with your gear. Now I see there will be room and to spare."

Adara looked at him quizzically. "Certainly such small boats exist and I have used them, but what good would a tiny craft be for a hunter? I need a boat large enough to bring back the meat and hides of the animals I kill. When possible, I bring back the bones as well. I need to carry supplies for curing and preserving my kills, as well as a few comforts for myself. Then, too, where in a small boat would Sand Shadow ride?"

"I suppose," Griffin admitted, "if I thought about it at all—and I cannot claim that I did—I thought Sand Shadow paced you along the bank."

"When the current is swift, *Foam Dancer* outraces even a running puma," Adara replied. "Besides, what good would Sand Shadow be to herself or to me if she arrived everywhere footsore and exhausted?"

"I stand," Griffin said, bowing with his hands against his thighs in his most formal manner, "corrected of unclear thinking."

In addition to *Foam Dancer*, Adara had cached all manner of comforts. That night, along with a fish stuffed with wild rice, they dined on a piping hot broth Adara made from dried meat and some spicy berries. There was tea to drink and chunks of waxy honeycomb for dessert.

"I had been saving the honey for Bruin," Adara said, "for he dearly loves sweets. However, he will not begrudge us a bit."

Griffin thought Adara might rig him his own tent that night. He didn't know how he felt about that. Sleeping so near—but so carefully separated from—a beautiful woman had been less of a trial than he might have imagined, since he had been weary beyond his knowledge of weariness. Not even in the worst days of that long-ago boarding school—when Griffin had been kept from sleep to see how long he could go before crossing the line into insanity—had he been so tired.

Yet Adara did not set up another tent. She did construct a thick mattress from various hides—mostly deer and rabbit—that she had left racked in the trees to finish curing.

"Tonight we will be more comfortable," she said, grinning at him.

"I've been grateful," Griffin said, "that Sand Shadow has let me sleep next to her. I would have been very cold otherwise."

Adara looked approving at this courtesy. Sand Shadow who, catlike, had managed to make Griffin aware that she thought him quite amusing, came and bumped her head against him with enough force that he nearly toppled.

The next morning, for the first time since the shuttle had crashed, Griffin woke with a sense of having rested well. Rejoicing in his new strength, he carried bales and bundles to Adara, but let her load *Foam Dancer*. Even a cursory inspection had shown him that the canoe demanded a sincere respect for balance.

If the canoe's size had been a surprise, its method of propulsion proved an even greater one. Griffin noticed that Adara left a space in the middle of the canoe in addition to those in the bow and stern. He had assumed his place would be in the bow and had been hoping he could manage whatever tasks Adara might set him. He'd done some wet water sailing with Gaius, his third from eldest brother, and hoped that would be enough.

When the time came for them to depart, Adara took her place in the stern. Then Sand Shadow leapt lightly into the bow, positioning herself in a manner that left her rear legs tucked under her in a more or less usual fashion. Next the puma raised herself up so that her elbows—Griffin found himself forced to think of them as such—rested on her thighs. Once she was seated this way, the puma raised herself upright and swiveled back toward Adara, her front legs extended.

Adara handed Sand Shadow the spare paddle and the puma grasped it neatly between what Griffin now realized were not so much paws as paw-hands, complete with an extra digit that could serve as a thumb.

He gaped and knew he was gaping. Not until he heard Adara laughing—not meanly, but as someone who has been waiting to spring a joke—did he manage to speak.

"Sand Shadow has hands?"

Adara motioned to the neat nest of hides in the center of the canoe. "Get in. Step near the center or we may topple."

"She has hands!" Griffin repeated.

"Get aboard," Adara repeated, "and I will tell you what you already know."

Griffin obeyed, too astonished to be nervous that he might upset the canoe. Adara used her paddle to push them off the bank, then, with a few easy strokes, brought them to where a midstream current would all but do the work for them. Sand Shadow helped, managing her paddle with deftness if not precisely grace. When *Foam Dancer* was set so that only the least amount of steering was needed, the puma laid her paddle in brackets designed to hold it ready. She turned to twitch her whiskers at Griffin, then settled down in a classic feline "loaf" posture, looking much like a great golden housecat or one of the ancient sphinxes of Earth.

"I told you Sand Shadow was adapted," Adara said. "She insisted that you not know how greatly until she knew you better. Anyhow, I've never met a cat who could resist a surprise."

"Well, she certainly surprised me. How much can Sand Shadow do with those hands?"

"Not as much as a human," Adara replied. "She can use a tool like the canoe paddle or tie simple knots. One reason she wears earrings is for practice getting them on and off."

"One reason?"

"She also likes how they look."

"I see." Griffin shook his head in amazement. "I wondered who tied the firewood onto her back that first day. You're saying she did it herself!"

"That's right. First she bundles it, then she slings it. It took us a while to work out the best method for her, but now she can manage the task quite easily."

"Does Sand Shadow have an actual thumb?"

"More or less. Even among unadapted cats, polydactyls—those with extra digits—are known," Adara said. "Polydactyls have long been the bane of those who would keep them out when they wish to be in or in when they wish to be out. Sand Shadow has a longer than usual dewclaw that she can use like a thumb. She manipulates the digits of her hand with about as much ease as would a human wearing not too bulky mittens. Bruin says that in time and with practice, she may grow more dexterous."

"So you were not the only one training," Griffin guessed.

"That's right," Adara said. "While I was learning how to use my claws, my 'cat' was practicing how to use her fingers."

Adara's home was in a village with the preposterously ornamental name of Shepherd's Call. Griffin wasn't at all surprised to find that the name dated back to the days of the seegnur. It sounded like a tourist attraction.

"We shall," Adara explained on the day they would arrive, "first give Bruin opportunity to agree to our plan. There is a bluff outside the village. I'll leave you there while we take *Foam Dancer* in. After Sand Shadow helps me bring in the canoe, I will send her back to keep you company. After full dark, I will come back for you."

Griffin agreed, although he was not thrilled at the prospect of sitting out in the wilderness alone. He considered suggesting that they throw a tarp or pile of hides over him in the canoe, but he figured that Adara would already have thought of such an option and, for whatever reason, discarded it.

The bluff where Adara dropped Griffin was situated where the stream they had been traveling upon joined another such watercourse and became a true river. During their day's journey, they had once again lost altitude. At last the air held a kiss of warmth that spoke of true spring. The trees that sheltered Griffin's waiting place were either leafing out or in flower, depending on their inclinations. Tiny, slim-stemmed flowers showed purple and golden yellow in the thickening grass.

"This is a nice spot," Griffin said when Adara showed him where he should wait. "Are you certain no one is going to come here—picnickers or something?"

Adara shook her head at him in mild disbelief. "Spring is not a time for such frivolities, Griffin Dane. On a fine day such as this, every villager will be at work, if not turning the earth, then watching over the new lambs or sorting the seed for planting. Even the children who can hardly walk will be kept busy carrying water or shooing off crows."

"What if someone comes up here—chasing one of those stray lambs, say? What should I tell them?"

Adara rolled her eyes. "They will not for the simple reason that this is not where sheep are pastured but, if they do, surely you can make yourself scarce. There are ample hiding places. Stay alert or sleep as you will. I leave you this canteen of water, some dried fruit, and my blanket against the evening chill. I will be back when I can come unseen."

With that, Griffin was forced to be content. He watched as Adara and Sand Shadow took *Foam Dancer* away, marveling afresh at how efficiently the tawny-furred creature paddled. Then he turned his attention to learning what he could about the village of Shepherd's Call.

Shepherd's Call was just large enough to be self-sufficient. A cluster of buildings, none taller than three stories, was grouped around a central green. Outward from the green were houses, each with a generous yard. Farther out came larger buildings, probably for the keeping of livestock. Beyond these were pastures and fields.

A stone mill with a large wheel was picturesquely placed near the river. It must be equipped to cut lumber as well as to grind grain, for Griffin could just make out a group of men hauling a huge log around one end. There was also a cluster of docks that extended out into the river near several long warehouse-like buildings.

Griffin examined the village carefully. There did not seem to be any defensive structures, although the closeness of the buildings around the central square probably enabled them to be fortified at need. Nor were there any signs of a castle or similar structure. There were lookout posts, but these were near the river and could serve as lighthouses as much as watch stands.

Searching through his many long talks with Adara, Griffin realized that never once had she mentioned enemies or wars or fighting. If the layout of Shepherd's Call was to be taken as testimony, the people who resided there lived lives that demanded a great deal of labor, but armed conflict did not seem to be a regular element.

Griffin wondered how his brothers—all of whom had trained in various types of military service, one of whom was also a military historian—would feel about living in such a place. He thought they'd probably be bored out of their minds.

Despite the beauty of the day, Griffin didn't catch even the faintest glimpse of anyone idling about. There were no milkmaids weaving chains of flowers for attentive shepherd lads nor goose girls singing sweetly beside splashing brooks. He did glimpse flocks, but those seemed to be tended as much by the parti-colored dogs that dashed among their woolly charges as by the children he occasionally glimpsed.

When his initial curiosity wore off, Griffin had to admit he was tired. He found a copse surrounded by young trees and scraggly shrubs that would hide him from immediate view, then made himself a nest in the long grass. Eventually, he drifted off to sleep, dreaming of the people he had left behind, people he had once hoped to impress, but now realized he'd be happy if only he could see again.

When Griffin awoke, twilight was shifting into full darkness and Sand Shadow was sitting a short distance away. The puma motioned that Griffin might join her if he wished and he decided to take her up on the invitation. By nature, Griffin was quite capable of solitude. However, the hours he had spent on this wooded knoll had brought home to him just how alone he was.

He had watched Adara bring the canoe into a landing—not one of the ones near the center of town, but farther downstream. Despite this, a fair number of people—an astonishing number of whom seemed to be vigorous and male—had appeared to help her unload. He could imagine the lively questions and conversation. Now he understood why Adara had not thought she could bring him in onboard the canoe. Looking at the compact layout of the village, he wondered if she could sneak him in at all.

"Well, Sand Shadow," he soliloquized, "is Adara very popular with the young men, then? Does she have many admirers? It's impossible to believe a woman so lovely would not—no matter that she seems to think of her claws and those very interesting eyes as disfigurements."

Sand Shadow rumbled something—not a purr, precisely, nor a growl, but definitely a comment.

Belatedly, Griffin realized that his soliloquy might not be such at all. The puma might very well understand every word he spoke. Worse, Sand Shadow might repeat what he had said, or at least the sense of it, to Adara. He found himself blushing.

Yet it was far nicer to think about Adara of the long legs, trim waist, rounded (if not overly large) breasts, and laughing amber eyes (never mind that the pupils were slit like a cat's), than to think about his mother and his father, about his six brothers (annoying as they could be) and his three sisters, all of whom he might never see again.

So Griffin thought about Adara, and leaned back against a puma possessed of something close to opposable thumbs. Eventually, he drowsed again, memories mixing with dreams in a disconcertingly vivid manner. He awoke to Adara lightly touching the side of his face.

Griffin was acutely aware of the warmth of her palm hovering just over his lips, doubtless to quiet him should he wake startled. Fighting back a momentary impulse to kiss that warmth, he blinked himself fully alert.

"Wake, Griffin Dane," Adara's voice came, soft and near his ear. "I've brought some good cheese, a bit of bread, and a handful of early strawberries. While you eat, I will explain how I hope to get you into Bruin's house unseen."

After full dark, they crept down from the bluff. Adara kept a hand on Griffin's arm, guiding him around obstacles. Once they were on the packed dirt road that went between the village and the surrounding fields, she could tell Griffin felt more sure on his feet. Adara was pleased with him. The road was not without ruts, but Griffin clearly trusted that she would set their path between them.

Sand Shadow padded silently in front, her presence assuring both that any wild creatures that prowled the night and the village dogs kept their distance and swallowed their growls. Bruin's house lay alongside the river on the outskirts of Shepherd's Call. Flickering lanterns and candlelight from windows showed that not all the villagers had gone to bed with the sun, but many structures were nothing more than dark forms against the star-filled night sky.

They were nearly to Bruin's house when Sand Shadow flashed a warning image into Adara's mind. As the puma did so, a resonant male voice spoke out of the darkness.

"Adara? Is that you?"

Adara let go of Griffin's arm and stepped ahead. To her delight, Griffin froze in place. Perhaps from those few words, he had grasped that this man did not share Adara's gift for seeing in the dark.

"Terrell," Adara said, the single word an identification. "Yes, it is me. What are you doing roaming about at this hour?"

"I wanted to speak with you," Terrell replied, "but there were so many people waiting when you arrived at Bruin's. I tried to get your attention, but you never seemed to notice. Then when I went back, Bruin said you had gone out. I hoped . . ."

Adara flashed an image to Sand Shadow, an image of her distracting Terrell while Sand Shadow guided Griffin to Bruin. She felt the puma's acknowledgment, then stepped closer to Terrell.

Her night vision did not show Terrell as he would be in the day, for colors were diminished, but she could see the basic outline: broad shoulders, slim hips, strong legs. The dark brown hair worn cut just above the shoulders fell in artful disarray, as usual. Her memory filled in the bright blue eyes, the high-bridged, narrow nose.

When Terrell had first come to Shepherd's Call as student to Helena the Equestrian—who had retired there with her second husband, Bert, a man famous for the speed with which he could shear a sheep—the local girls had all but swooned. Terrell could hardly move ten paces from Helena's stables without encountering some fair maiden making him a welcoming gift of a bunch of wild-flowers or a ribbon with which to ornament the headstall of Coal, his favorite steed.

Even after the time for welcoming was long over, Terrell would have been a complete fool to deny he had admirers. Perversely, it was Adara—the woman the local swains had disdained as too strange—upon whom Terrell had fixed his fancy. With Terrell's interest, the local youths had taken a second look, so that for the first time since Adara had been acknowledged not only adapted but a huntress, she found herself with nearly too many admirers.

"Nearly," for too many meant that Adara need not make any choice, since no one was seen as favored. In any case, with the possible exception of Terrell himself, there was, in fact, no one she did favor.

Perhaps Terrell sensed this. Before Adara had left on this recent training trip, Terrell had attempted to press his suit. Adara had managed to avoid giving any sort of answer, but she did not think Terrell would always be put off so easily.

"You're back earlier than expected," Terrell said, his tone holding both caress and question. "I could hardly believe it when I heard that *Foam Dancer* had been seen on the river. Did you miss me?"

Adara could sense Sand Shadow beginning to guide Griffin down the side path that would take them to a door on the other side of Bruin's house, a door that could be opened without exciting anyone's attention. She knew she must distract Terrell a bit longer, for although he lacked her ability to see in the dark, he was naturally alert.

"I missed everyone," she said, "as much as a hunter does, of course. We are solitary people, you know, especially cat-kind."

Terrell snorted. "Even cats have mates, otherwise there would be no more cats. I have heard tell that in warmer climates there are cats larger even than Sand Shadow who live in packs like wolves, hunting together and raising their cubs in company."

Adara had heard of these as well, for Bruin was a thorough teacher, one who insisted his pupil learn about creatures and ecosystems far beyond what might be expected to be her hunting range. She did not admit her knowledge, though, for to do so would be to seem receptive to Terrell's argument.

It is my fault, she thought, *that I slept with him last midsummer. His attentions were so sweet and he was so persistent . . . and the night so warm and the moon so bright.*

Despite the consequences, Adara could not bring herself to regret her action. She might still choose Terrell as a mate. There were many advantages. Above and beyond his considerable charm, she could not dismiss the fact that Terrell's profession as a factotum meant he would likely do a great deal of traveling. She would like to see more of the world . . .

She felt Terrell waiting for her to reply. "I would like to see these wolf-cats someday. Lions . . . Plains lions. Maned lions. Those are the names for them."

"I will take you there," Terrell murmured, nuzzling her throat. "We could travel together, just the two of us. Who would dare bother factotum and huntress together?"

Adara felt the flash of Sand Shadow telling her that Griffin was safely inside Bruin's house.

None too soon . . . I'm already all on edge from these nights of sleeping beside Griffin with only good sense as chaperone. This is not the time to invite other complications!

She twisted free of Terrell's embrace.

"I have my duties," she said, "and you yours. There is much I need to learn. Surely such discussions can wait."

"Wait, wait, wait . . ." Terrell protested. "You are forever saying that! We will be learning all our lives."

"Hunters cultivate patience," Adara replied stiffly.

She heard Terrell mutter something less than kind but chose to ignore the words. Sometimes he forgot just how keen her hearing was.

"I'm going inside," she said. "Sweet dreams."

"Good night," came the stiff reply. "Good night."

Adara found Griffin and Bruin seated together in the central room of Bruin's house. Sand Shadow appeared to be absorbed with working free the clasp of one of her earrings, but the glint of amusement Adara felt when she entered the room told her that the puma was perfectly aware of what had passed outside.

The other side of the fire was occupied by the considerable bulk of Honeychild. Bruin's demiurge was a bear, her brown fur touched with red and gold. Usually, she was a roly-poly creature, so rounded and cuddly-looking that small children ran up to her without fear. Now, however, newly awakened from her winter's hibernation, she was lean, her fur patchy, her mood short-tempered.

Bruin had apparently decided to soothe that temper by giving the bear a large chunk of the honeycomb Adara had brought down from the mountains. Now the bear was sleepily licking the sticky stuff off her fur. She rumbled a contented greeting to Adara as the huntress padded in.

Bruin had saved a piece of the honeycomb for himself. It sat upon a round bluish-grey pottery dish alongside a chunk of fresh bread. Tea steamed from a chubby pot in the same glaze, and Bruin nodded invitation for Adara to fill the remaining empty mug. As she moved to do so, Griffin started up from where he was sitting in the basket chair that matched Bruin's favorite.

"Let me, Adara," he said. Then, "I've taken your seat."

Adara shook her head. "Not at all. I usually sit nearer the floor. Bruin says I'm too young to need a chair."

Bruin chuckled. "She's not fibbing, Griffin Dane. I'm old and fat and lazy, my hunting days nearly gone by. Young folk need to cultivate flexible limbs, especially those who choose to hunt with the cats."

Perhaps by the standards of his youth Bruin was old and fat, but to Adara he was little changed from the man who had taken her on when she was only five and her parents, certain now of her adapted nature, sought a teacher who could help her take advantage of whatever changes occurred.

At least that was what they had said at the time. Adara had never quite gotten over the feeling that her family—especially her mother—were scared of her and wanted to be rid of the wildness she brought into their settled farming croft.

Bruin was not a tall man, but no one would call him small. Really, the best word to describe him was bear-like. He possessed a bear's broad chest and torso, with arms and legs that were relatively short. Whether to cultivate the resemblance to a bear or because that was how his hair grew naturally, Bruin wore his reddish-brown mass without the more usual ponytail. His beard was of moderate length, but its generally untidy cut only added to the bearishness of his appearance.

As Bruin had aged, both hair and beard had begun to silver, although very strangely, starting at the tips rather than the roots, so that people whispered he actually was a grizzly bear made human. As far as Adara knew, the whispers pleased her mentor rather than otherwise.

She settled onto her cushion and let the warmth of the tea soak into her fingers as the conversation resumed.

"Griffin, your shuttle crashing seems very odd to me," Bruin said. "Does such commonly happen? It seems that you would hardly trust yourself to the chill void between the stars if your ships were so unreliable."

Griffin shook his head. "No. It isn't common. In fact, the models I chose—both of ship and shuttle—were selected because variations have long been in use, the flaws detected and removed. I fear I may have fallen victim to elements I did not believe would be present in the upper atmosphere."

The last word was not one Adara knew, but she could figure it out from context. Griffin had told her he intended to scout the planet from the highest reaches before coming down.

"I think," Bruin said, "that this is a complicated tale. No seegnur has been to Artemis since the death of machines. Yet you speak as if you knew something of what you thought you would find. Can you explain?"

Griffin nodded. "I'd like to, but isn't it rather late? I slept through the afternoon, but Adara and you . . ."

"Tell," Bruin said. "Usually, I am very fond of sleep, but morning will come all too soon and, with morning, a need to explain you. If we are to do that, we must understand more."

Interlude: TVC1500

Motion. Achieved. Target scent faint. Not by scent alone does one track. Signature present, unique, unmistakable.

Motion with purpose, purpose apt alternative for haste. Awareness of singing in the winds, a song of reinforcement?

Purpose flares. Reinforcement undesired, in violation of the purpose. No alternative to haste. Must hasten. Must hasten.

Haste!

5
The Beginning of the End

Where should I begin?" Griffin asked. "How much does your lore remember of the last days of the seegnur on Artemis?"

Bruin's laugh was a great, rumbly thing. "How can we know how much the lore remembers and how much we have surmised? Oh, yes, I realize that saying the lore is anything less than truth would greatly offend the loremasters, but I am an old hunter and I know that tales are like game trails. The older they are the more muddled they become. Begin your tale where you think it begins. Adara and I are of a patient sort. You will not bore us."

Griffin realized with some surprise that this was true—of Adara at least. He must assume she had learned the value of patience from her teacher. Griffin himself was so accustomed to his brothers rolling their eyes when he got excited over some point of history, of his sisters admiring an artifact for its beauty or value rather than for what it told, that he had grown reluctant to share his theories.

"All right," he said. "I'll begin at the beginning of the end. From what Adara has told me, your lore has preserved that Artemis was a planet created for the entertainment of a very wealthy, very privileged minority."

He sighed and leaned back against the comfortable cushions that lined the basket chair. "I'm not sure that any of us today can understand the heights of technology which the old empire had reached. I can assure you that no culture known today—at least as far as I have been able to learn—has the ability to move planets around and reshape them as Artemis was moved and shaped. The closest we can manage is moving an asteroid . . ."

He saw from the cant of Adara's head, the mildly puzzled line that appeared between Bruin's bushy brows, that "asteroid" was an unfamiliar word.

"An asteroid is a rock that floats in the void. It is much smaller than a planet, too small to hold life. Where I come from, asteroids are sometimes moved to make them easier to mine."

"Mine?" Bruin asked.

Griffin nodded. "Often asteroids hold quantities of valuable minerals or water. However, moving one is a major task, not to be undertaken lightly."

Bruin shook his head, although whether in wonder or disbelief Griffin could not be certain. "I would think not. I am tempted to ask more, but perhaps first we should return to what you called 'the beginning of the end.'"

"Right," Griffin said. He flashed a grin. "Sorry. I tend to go off on tangents. Stop me if I completely lose you."

He shifted so that he could look into the flames burning within the hearth, away from the myriad distractions offered by his two companions, their animal associates, the shape and form of the furnishings in the room, from the reminder of just how much here was alien. By contrast, the history of that long-ago empire was a familiar thing, the beating heart of many years of study. Resisting the urge to say "once upon a time," he began.

"The former empire was vast and powerful beyond anything we can imagine. Their ships flew faster than light, connecting into a network of worlds so far apart that the stars that warmed them were invisible to each other. The empire may even have bridged galaxies. Its technologies were not merely those of the physical world—metal and micron—but of the mental world as well.

"Their ships were powered by engines we can barely imagine, guided by pilots who could sense the subatomic world and speak to the particles that inhabit it. Communications went beyond the limitations of time and space, surging between mind and mind. Yet even possession of capacities that defied all that had limited human endeavor were not enough to satisfy the rulers of the empire. You see, no matter what tools they created, no matter how they resculpted their minds and bodies, they were still human. Human ambitions and human weaknesses destroyed what human intellect and human achievement had created.

"Where the first rumbles of discontent began no one can agree. I won't bore you by reciting the names of places and peoples that would mean little or nothing to you. Suffice to say that after centuries of relative peace and incredible prosperity, the structure of the empire began to crack.

"For a long, long time, theoretically the empire had been ruled by scions of one family. In reality, the structure of rulership was more complicated. Even with genetic engineering, nothing could assure that a generation unborn would have the talents needed to face challenges yet unimagined. Instead, those who showed talent for rulership were adopted into the reigning house.

"Even with this bridge to power, the time came when the rulers found themselves challenged from without. Being adopted became something to avoid. Instead, those with the talents needed by the imperial house sought to retain their own names and family affiliations. First on the outer edges, then to the very heart of the empire, a spider's web of cracks spread. The time came when the empire did not exist except in name. It had become an affiliation of rivals working in the name of the empire, although more interested in their own advantage than the preservation of the whole.

"Your planet, Artemis, had been created during a time before that spider's web was complete. Some say Artemis was the empire's last great creation. What is important for you to know is that having access to Artemis was always considered a mark of great prestige. It remained so until the empire fell. Artemis was a secret shared by those who otherwise felt they had nothing in common."

Griffin looked away from the flames to his two—no, four, listeners. Four pairs of eyes—two human, one ursine, one feline—watched but, other than Bruin leaning to shove the teapot closer to Griffin, there was no interruption.

After pouring himself a cup of the lukewarm tea, Griffin resumed. "Now, within that spider's web of associations there were some—I'll call them families, for lack of a better term—that held more power than the rest. Being human, alliances were often sealed in a very human fashion. The old tradition of adoption remained. In recent years, the even more ancient tradition of the marriage alliance had regained popularity. So it was through marriage that two important families decided to seal their new alliance. For reasons of prestige and of secrecy, the wedding was to be held on Artemis.

"Thus men and women who might otherwise not have agreed to come to the same location agreed to meet on Artemis. Artemis, after all, was safe. Its very location was known only to a comparative few. Despite generation after generation of wrangling for power, Artemis remained neutral ground, self-sustaining and therefore kept out of the web of interstellar commerce that connected the other systems, even as they fought increasingly violent wars to deny any such connection.

"These families came for a wedding, but what they met was a funeral. Historians still argue as to who arranged the betrayal. Some say it came from both sides, each seeking to destroy the leaders of the other. Some say a third party or parties learned that their rivals were gathering in one place. Whatever the source, the end result was the same.

"Stealth ships eased into orbit around Artemis and unloaded heavily armed commandos. These wore armor carefully sealed against their first attack—a plague of nanobots programmed to seek out and disable any technological device more elaborate than a series of gears. Artemis might appear to be charmingly primitive, but its rustic aspect was made more enjoyable by a carefully hidden rapid transit system, extensive medical services, as well as the little comforts without which guests from off-planet really could not be expected to enjoy their holidays.

"Once the technology was disabled, the end result was inevitable. The commandos slew all the members of both wedding parties—an action that is often used as evidence for the theory that the attack was planned by a third faction. Anyone from off planet was also killed. Locals, however, were left alone as long as they didn't interfere."

Griffin stopped, remembering something uncomfortable he had come across in the journal of a woman who represented herself as a leader of one of the subgroups of commandos. He wondered if he should mention it, then recklessly decided to take the risk.

"In fact," he said, "various reports noted that, on the whole, the locals did not interfere. There were a few incidents recorded, but even before the commandos issued their warning, the Artemesians showed a singular lack of interest in becoming involved."

He looked at his two auditors, but flickering fire shadows masked both Bruin's and Adara's features, making it impossible for him to read their expressions.

"Do you know if this is true?" Griffin prompted. "Does your lore say anything about this?"

Adara said, "I am no loremaster, but it seems to me I have heard some such thing—that this was a war between seegnur and seegnur, not something that involved us."

Bruin added, "Surely staying uninvolved would have seemed a reasonable decision—a choice for life over death. Why would you expect otherwise?"

Griffin knew why he expected otherwise and knew to his shame that the knowing came from the depths of his own privileged upbringing. If service providers did not provide their services with some sort of loyalty, then what comfort could you feel in their omnipresence?

He couldn't make himself explain, so settled for stammering. "It is . . . simply another conflicted point on the record, you know. One of those things . . . well, we'd like cleared up."

Bruin ran fingers over his thick-furred head. "Well, we two are hunters, not historians or loremasters. Perhaps these can answer your questions. Tell me, Griffin Dane," Bruin continued in the tones of one who is completely aware he is changing the subject, "do you think those nanobots of which you spoke still exist? Do you think they are what caused your ship to crash?"

Griffin nodded slowly. "I have speculated that this might be the case. My shuttle was of a type that has been used and improved upon for centuries. When I say 'improved upon' I don't mean gussied up with all sorts of unnecessary elaborations but instead refined and repaired until the chance of such a failure was very low. I'd gone over all the shuttle systems myself shortly before departing my ship. It seemed in fine repair then. I also thought I'd stayed at a high enough altitude to avoid contamination."

"And yet it broke," Bruin said, not as one who denies, rather musing aloud. "I cannot say I understand how these shuttles operate, but I do understand your confusion. It would be as if my knife's blade snapped in my hand while being put to no particularly demanding task."

Adara broke in. "Griffin, you can't possibly have ended your tale of the beginning of the end. It seems to me that all that ended were the lives of a few seegnur here on Artemis. What happened after?"

Griffin forced a chuckle. "I told you I tend to go off on tangents. What happened wasn't at all simple. I told you how two very important families hoped to seal an alliance here on Artemis. Instead many senior members—

the very ones who had hoped for an alliance—were killed. Therefore, those two great families not only failed to make their alliance but also failed to maintain their integrity.

"From what I have read, the remaining members fell to squabbling among themselves. The tenuous spider's web of empire ceased to be a web at all, but became a series of cracks and fissures. Within a decade or so after that failed wedding, even the illusion of the empire ceased to be. Within a hundred years, a terribly destructive war had spread to every pocket of the civilized universe.

"Bombs that could burrow to a planet's molten core were launched, splitting planets to fragments. Specialists in faster-than-light travel were assassinated wholesale, thereby eliminating the psychic skills needed to fly the most sophisticated ships. Faster-than-light travel remained possible, but now that the courses of ships could be predicted, defenses could be erected . . ."

Griffin saw he was losing his audience and backed away from further details. If he was honest with himself, he didn't understand the fine points any better than these two knife-wielding primitives did. He was a better than average pilot. Even without his computer, he could calculate courses—as long as he had access to astrogation maps. However, imagining days when ship and pilot were one, the pair twisting space and time so that half a galaxy might be bridged in a single jump, seemed so fanciful as to be nothing more than magic.

He took a deep breath and redirected his tale.

"In those days of war and destruction," Griffin said, "Artemis was lost. Not many had known of her in the first place, but when I began my research, I had the distinct impression that someone or someones went out of their way to wipe any mention of the planet from the records. Hints remained, here and there, but even for most historians, Artemis became a mythic place, joining the ranks of Atlantis, the Western Isles, Shangri-La, Blue

Moon, and the Impassible Void. Artemis remained lost until a cache of old documents was found on my own homeworld."

"By you?" Adara asked breathlessly.

Griffin laughed. "Oh, no, not by me. My lucky break came later."

Lucky break? Not so lucky if I end up stranded. I was prepared to spend a year or so here, but never the rest of my life.

Bruin rubbed one stubby finger around the curve of his ear. "So tell me, son, did you expect that these nanobots would no longer be working? Seems a risky thing, coming here in a ship that might have the guts eaten out of it in a heartbeat."

The implied criticism stung, but Griffin was careful to control his automatic desire to snap in self-defense. As he had told his tale, it had come home to him how very much he needed these people.

"Actually," Griffin replied, "I did think the nanobots would have stopped functioning by now. They are usually programmed to deconstruct in a relatively short time. You see, even back when the idea of nanobots was first postulated—some historians argue that the idea has been around far longer than interplanetary colonization—there have been theories that the 'bots might rebuild themselves into something destructive. There were other reasons for me to believe the nanobots would have degraded as well."

A cock of one of Bruin's bushy eyebrows asked the question.

"Well, for one, the commandos didn't destroy the planet," Griffin said. "They could have and—by the standards of the war that followed—they should have, unless they felt they had further use for it. What use would Artemis have been to them if they couldn't come down from orbit without crashing?"

"Reasonable," Bruin agreed, his voice a soothing rumble. "And you did say that you thought you'd kept your vessel high enough that it would be safe from contamination."

Griffin nodded. "That's right. It's hard enough to seal personal armor against such attacks, but nearly impossible to seal a ship. I'm not up on the technological considerations, but one of my brothers explained it to me when I first started considering this trip. My first move on arrival was making some orbital maps. Then I took the shuttle in for a high altitude pass. Scanners can do a lot but, eventually, I was going to need to go down."

"Need?" Adara asked softly.

"Well," Griffin replied a touch defiantly, "maybe 'want' is more honest. After all, that's why I came here, to see Artemis firsthand, to learn who still lived here. When a civilization is as low-tech as this one, there's only so much one can learn from orbit . . ."

He trailed off. How to explain how simple it had all seemed back home in the Kyley System? He believed he had discovered the long-lost coordinates for Artemis. He would go there, confirm his find, maybe make contact with a few of the more isolated natives. Following that, he would return home triumphant. A lifetime of research would follow . . . It had all seemed so simple.

He heard himself mutter the last words aloud. "It all seemed so simple."

"Then you must have made plans against the possibility of those nanobots, eh?" Bruin prompted with unexpected gentleness.

"I did," Griffin said, feeling himself flushing, "but probably not in the manner you're thinking. I brought sealed packets containing other nanobots, these geared to undo the damage the first had done. I thought if I found remnants of the old technology I might be able to reactivate it."

"And those packets?"

"Most of them are in orbit," Griffin said, "and the ones

I brought with me are buried with the shuttle, as impossible to reach as if they were still on my ship."

He stared at the fire, despair rising. It had all seemed so simple.

"But someone will come looking for you," Adara said, seeming to read his mind. "Surely this is so. You said you had a mother and a father, six brothers . . . How many sisters?"

"Three," Griffin answered automatically. "But they won't know where to look. No one will know where to look! I'm the only one who had the coordinates and I didn't share the information. Too much rested on me being first. I told them I was going off to examine some ruins in another system. These days interstellar communication is limited to what ships or message drones will carry. They won't expect to hear from me for quite a while. Even when they suspect I'm missing, they might eventually duplicate my research, but for now I've got to assume no one knows where I am—that I'm stranded here for a long time—maybe even for good."

The conversation ended shortly after Griffin's pained admission that he was stranded. Adara could smell exhaustion coming off the man in waves. If she could, so could Bruin. Bears had an excellent sense of smell and Honeychild was much better than Sand Shadow at sharing her impressions with her partner.

Griffin was tucked away in a small room up under the eaves. He was snoring before Bruin thumped down the stairs. Adara, combing out her hair before the fire in the main room, was surprised when Bruin tapped her lightly on the shoulder.

"While your catch is dead to the world," Bruin said softly, "tell me what you've been doing with him."

"I've been doing nothing!" Adara replied more hotly

than she had intended. "I saved his life, fed him, answered his questions as best I could, and safely brought him here, but I've done nothing more."

"And you should be doing nothing more," Bruin said solemnly.

"Why?" Adara asked, hurt and offended.

Bruin reached out a blunt-fingered hand and patted her on one shoulder. "Because, ladybug," he answered, using a childhood nickname, "this Griffin Dane is two things, unalike as rain and fire, but two things nonetheless. First, he is so very vulnerable. I think the tales he told us brought home to him what a lost creature he is. To take advantage of that weakness . . . it would not be good for either of you.

"I suspect you would only be looking to scratch an itch against an interesting new tree, but this Griffin might go further and fall in love with you. That would be no good thing if you could not answer his need—or worse, if you answered from pity. Weakness can call to weakness, but it cannot make strength."

Adara was hurt that Bruin didn't think she had the good sense to figure this out for herself. "And the other reason?"

"We see this Griffin Dane as he was tonight, a man alone, lost to his very world. He is very polite, all too strongly reminded just how ill-prepared he is to survive. However, you and I cannot forget that Griffin Dane is a seegnur, a man from beyond this world, descendant of a people who broke planets as easily as I can use a hammer to smash rock into gravel."

When Adara did not reply, Bruin went on. "Griffin Dane is an unknown factor. We cannot forget that and we must act with due prudence."

"I have not been imprudent," Adara replied. "Sand Shadow would tell you."

"Sand Shadow has told me, or rather she has told Honeychild, which is much the same. Catlike, Sand Shadow has sniggered quite a bit. Catlike, she admires your patience in what she sees as a hunt."

They stood in silence. Then Adara bent at the waist and began braiding her hair so it would not become tangled during the night's sleep.

"But why must you warn me?" she asked, her voice slightly muffled from the upside-down bend of her neck. "Am I suddenly such a mad kitten that I cannot figure these things out for myself?"

Bruin snorted. "I warned you because Griffin Dane is personable—quite handsome, really. You would find it easy to make excuses along the road to give in to his charms."

"Road?" Adara asked, flipping herself upright so fast that her braid smacked against her back.

"Road or river," Bruin continued placidly. "You do not think we are done yet with this Griffin Dane? You cannot think he will be content to stay here in Shepherd's Call?"

"I have tried not to think much beyond getting him to you," Adara admitted, "but when I did . . . No. I did not think he would be content."

"I am thinking of sending Griffin to my own teacher," Bruin said, "to the Old One Who Is Young at his home in Spirit Bay. I thought, too, to have you be Griffin's guide."

Adara was astonished. She had only met the Old One Who Is Young once before. Spirit Bay was a long journey and she had always preferred the wilds to the city.

"You would come with us," she said, hoping that by making this a statement Bruin's reply would be a certainty. "Right?"

"I would not," Bruin countered. "I am a fat old bear, not fit for long journeys. And have you forgotten? Within a few days I am expecting new students. One boy, so his parents think, may be as you were—adapted, a potential hunter. How would you have felt if you had arrived here to find me gone?"

Adara, some part of her never too far away from the scrawny little girl-child who had been brought to this very house so many years before, knew the answer without reflection.

"Devastated." She nodded. "So you must stay, but me as guide? Bruin, I know nothing of Spirit Bay. I know nothing much of the towns downriver from here. Oh, I've been to Blue Meadow and Moonrise Cove often enough, and, of course, to the small settlements and sheepfolds. But beyond that? You would send me into the villages and towns, with a seegnur to watch over?"

Bruin gently tugged her braid. "Adara the Huntress, trust my judgment. In some things, I know you better than you do yourself."

Adara retrieved her braid automatically, but her mind was spinning.

"Will you accept my challenge, Huntress?" Bruin prompted, the very word a reminder of Adara's achievements. "Or shall this old bear be forced to drag himself over the long road to Spirit Bay and leave you to train the students . . ."

He trailed off, but the twinkle in his eye told Adara that he already knew her decision.

"I'll go," she said. "But, I think, not first thing in the morning."

"No," Bruin agreed. "Griffin Dane deserves a day or two to rest and to accept his changed situation. Then, too, seeing how our fellow villagers react to him may give you some idea of what to expect on the way to Spirit Bay."

Adara's thoughts flitted to Terrell. How would he re-act when, come morning, word began to spread of what she'd brought down from the mountain? Not kindly, she suspected, not very kindly at all.

"We'll need to get Griffin some changes of clothing," she said, "and decide our best route. Because of the falls, the river cannot take us all the way into Spirit Bay."

"Time enough to plan out a route come morning," Bruin said. "Now go, sleep. Try not to dream."

Adara hugged her mentor impulsively. "Not to dream? No chance of that. Sleep well yourself . . ."

She sped up the stairs to her small room. Sand Shadow was already sprawled over most of the bed, very reluctant to give even an inch. As Adara climbed into the narrow slot beneath the eaves which was all the puma had left to her, she was reminded of the last several nights sharing the cramped tent with Griffin Dane.

He was just across the hall . . . But Bruin was right. He was an unknown factor.

What a thing is love or lust, she thought as she drifted off to sleep, one arm thrown over Sand Shadow's back, *more dangerous than a puma's claws.*

⚕

Interlude: A . . .

Dire need detected.

Emergency action implemented.

Error: Routine interrupted. Instructions?

Conundrum: If a tree falls alone in the forest, does it make a sound?

Analysis: It must. Sound is predicated upon human ears only in human minds.

6

Invader from the Mountains

Griffin's first sight upon awakening was a slanting wall smelling of freshly painted plaster only an arm's length over his head. If he had not slept the last few nights in a cramped tent and many nights before that in an even more tightly fitting ship's berth, doubtless he would have sat upright and cracked his head.

The sheets on which he lay were rough woven, soft with washing, and scented with something fragrant. The quilt that covered him was stuffed with down and ornamented in a patchwork pattern.

No, he realized after closer examination. Not a patchwork pattern, real patchwork, the slight unevenness of the stitching revealing it to be handmade. With that awareness, memory returned. He was in the house of Bruin, itself on the edge of the small village of Shepherd's Call, this in the foothills of the Starwood Mountains, alongside the Racing Rapids River. All of this was on the planet Artemis.

Rolling from his bed, Griffin set his bare feet on the rag rug—again, a real such rug, made to get the last bit of use out of valuable cloth—and looked about for his coverall. Currently, he wore a long nightshirt which he vaguely remembered Bruin taking out of a large chest the night before.

"I keep extra clothing," the big man had explained, "for the students. They grow so fast and often are hard on what they've brought with them."

After several nights sleeping in his clothing, the nightshirt had felt indecently luxurious, even if it did itch a little. His coverall was nowhere to be seen, but on a low table was stacked a neat heap of clothing, all dyed in shades of tan and brown. Set on the floor was a pair of soft-soled shoes.

The clothing was simple enough: underpants, trousers held up by a belt, a loosely tailored shirt, a pocketed vest. The socks were lumpy but welcomingly warm. Their bulk made the shoes fit once Griffin figured out how to tighten the laces. Indeed, the fastenings on the clothing were the most troublesome part of getting dressed. They made him appreciate for the first time the convenience of elastic and pressure-sensitive clasps. With an anthropologist's eye, Griffin had studied Bruin's attire the night before. He now used that information to put himself into the clothing.

The house was very quiet, but light came in through the small, opaque window set in the wall near the foot of the bed. Griffin thought this was the quiet of a household letting its guest rest rather than that of a house asleep, so he thumped down the stairs as a way of announcing himself.

A slim grey cat started up from in front of the fire when Griffin came into the main room, then darted out the nearest window. As if her exit was a signal, Bruin tromped in through the kitchen door, his arms encumbered with a basket from which various bits of greenery spilled.

To this point, Griffin had only seen his host by firelight, but even daylight didn't completely dismiss the sense that Bruin was both man and bear. Griffin tried to dispel the image, yet though the kitchen was well lit, the windows propped open wide, he could not.

"You're awake then," Bruin said cheerfully, somehow managing to bellow without raising his voice. "That's good. Hungry?"

"I am, rather."

Bruin began rummaging about, pulling open a bin and retrieving eggs, hauling down something cloth-wrapped that proved to be a smoked ham, using a cleaver to whack off a great hunk. As with his voice, Bruin managed to be large without really being very large at all. Griffin was taller, but felt himself slim and boyish alongside the other man.

"There's bread in the box there—the one painted with red flowers—and a board and knife with it. Cut us a half-dozen slices, would you?"

Griffin did so, glad that his mother had always enjoyed fresh bread on the table, so he didn't make too great a muck of this simple job. Even so, the hand-forged bread knife was a far cry from the elegant ceramic cutter his family used.

Griffin had hardly finished when Bruin called for the bread. In a few moments, Bruin had turned ham, eggs, cheese, and onions into something that smelled so savory that Griffin's mouth watered. Bruin wiped the pan with a couple of the slices of bread, set these on each plate and carried the lot not—as Griffin had assumed he would— over near the fire, but outside.

"There's a table here," Bruin called, "in the sun. I've a jug of cider chilling in the well. Grab a couple of those green glazed mugs, will you?"

Griffin did so. Although Sand Shadow had brought him in through this door the night before, he had not seen more of the garden than figures of black against grey. Now he realized what a very pleasant place it was. The table Bruin had mentioned was long and rectangular, its surface doubtless serving as a workspace as well as a place to eat. Later in the summer, the trees that surrounded the patio would give shade, but now they were frothing over with pale pink blossoms.

"Cherries," Bruin said with complacent pride. "A hearty breed that takes the cold well. My cider's blended with their juice. You won't have had anything like it."

He filled the mugs from a jar he pulled from the well. He was right. Griffin had never tasted anything like the cider, sweet and tart both, with a full body and just a small amount of fizz.

"Marvelous!" Griffin exclaimed.

Bruin shoved one of the plates at him. "Talk after you've eaten. Eggs are best hot."

The food was more fully flavored than any Griffin could remember, the ham smoky as well as salty, the eggs blended with the cheese until both were creamy. The bread took a bit of chewing, but that only made it better suited to go with the rest.

Bruin ate his own meal with evident pleasure, finishing well before Griffin.

"Did you wait to eat with me?" Griffin said apologetically. "If so, I'm sorry."

"Wait?" Bruin laughed. "This is my third meal. I had bread and honey before going out to gather the eggs and milk the goats. Then I ate a real breakfast with Adara. This is a snack to hold me until she comes back for lunch."

Griffin wanted to ask where Adara was, then thought that seemed impolite, as if he had some right to know. He settled for finishing his meal, a task that made his belly uncomfortably full.

"More?" Bruin suggested. "The hens are laying and I just cut into a new wheel of cheese. We've plenty to spare."

"I'm stuffed," Griffin admitted. "I don't think I could manage another mouthful."

Bruin shook his head in disbelief, then brightened. "Ah, your stomach probably shrunk while you were on the way down with Adara. I forget how thin the pickings are up there in the mountains. It's practically winter in the heights, as you know all too well yourself."

"Adara did well by us," Griffin protested. "We had a hot meal every night and plenty to snack on during the day."

"Then you still feel my girl was a good guide to you? Even with the avalanche?"

"I couldn't have asked for better," Griffin answered. "Even if she hadn't started the job by saving my life."

"Good then. You wouldn't mind her continuing as your guide when you set out again?"

"Mind? Set out? We've only just arrived!"

"Yet surely you didn't think your journey would end in this tiny village," Bruin said. "If you wish to reach your stars again, you will need to go far from here."

Griffin didn't know what to say. He knew Bruin was correct but, right now, in this garden, the spring chill moderated by the sunlight, warm food inside him, he thought he couldn't ask for anything better than to stay here, to sleep in the tiny room under the eaves, to eat good food. Perhaps he could help Bruin with the students.

Fingers wrapped around his mug, Bruin studied him. Something in his sleepy smile made Griffin think the other man knew precisely what Griffin was thinking.

"You could rest here," Bruin said slowly. "Many of the villagers will be astonished and overjoyed to have one of the seegnur among us again. In time, word would spread. Pilgrims would flock barefoot across the miles for the merest glimpse of you. Prosperity would come to Shepherd's Call. Indeed, you could earn your keep without raising a finger. Still, I had thought you wanted more. I thought you traveled the void to see Artemis. Surely by that you didn't mean one small village."

Griffin frowned, not at Bruin, but at himself.

"I suppose," he muttered, "these last few days have been too much. I was hoping to rest, to sort it out in my head."

"I don't mean to throw you out this minute." Bruin chuckled. Spring is not a bad time for travel, if one is prepared for rain and mud. I had thought to send you with Adara to Spirit Bay where my own teacher lives. He has devoted a long life to studying the seegnur. Like you, he is a historian, not merely a loremaster."

Griffin had begun to understand the distinction between these two terms. "Historian" meant much what it did on his own world: one who studied the past and sought to learn more about it. A loremaster was different. Although some loremasters were content with memorization of preserved texts, treatises, laws, and moral guidelines, many were interested in the things of the past, viewing them as building blocks for the future.

Then there were the factotums. These seemed to be the more active branch of the profession. Originally, factotum had been trained as escorts and guides for the seegnur. When Griffin had expressed surprise that the profession of factotum had survived the slaughter of the seegnur, Adara had explained that factotum continued to be trained as a sign that the people of Artemis remained faithful to the purpose for which they had been created and were ready to serve the seegnur, should they ever return.

"This teacher of yours does sound like an interesting person," Griffin admitted. "You said something about my reaching the stars again. Do you really think he could help me?"

Bruin shrugged. "That I cannot say but, if anyone knows, I believe it would be the Old One Who Is Young. Adara is checking whether the routes to Spirit Bay have reopened. Most of our trade comes in from the river, but some comes overland."

Bruin heaved himself onto his feet and began gathering up the plates. As if by magic, Honeychild, the bear, appeared. Bruin held the plates for her and she licked away every trace of egg and crumb of bread.

"Better than wasting clean water to rinse them," Bruin said. "Saves hauling. Will you pull a bucket from the well and bring it into the kitchen? We'll need to heat more water after getting these clean."

Griffin was glad he had paid attention when Bruin had hauled up the cider. That had been on a rope hanging loose into the water, but he'd noticed a crank with a rope wound around it. The mechanism was nicely maintained and worked smoothly. Nonetheless he sloshed water on his soft shoes when he carried the bucket in. It was exquisitely cold.

Seeing the work that went into washing up, Griffin understood why he hadn't been offered a chance to bathe. Even so, he was acutely aware how oily and gritty his hair felt. He wondered if he'd be out of line to ask what the custom was. Were there public baths here? A single bath night? He'd read about these in stories, the entire family bathing in sequence in one tub. It had sounded disgusting, but if that would be his only option, he'd take it and be glad.

Griffin decided to wait to ask about baths. However, now that he'd eaten, another need couldn't wait. By the time he'd used the outhouse—clean and odorless as it proved to be—he had acquired an entirely new appreciation for indoor plumbing. He wondered if Spirit Bay might be a town or even a city. He wondered if any amenities had survived.

He scratched his head and wondered again about the possibility of getting a good, hot bath.

⌘

Adara returned home to find Bruin and Griffin putting the final touches on an elaborate midday meal. On the trail, she ate her main meal when settled into camp for the night, but at home the midday meal was the largest. This was no exception. She caught Griffin looking with a certain amount of awe at the array of food spread on the table beneath the cherry trees.

"You don't need to eat it all now," Adara said with a laugh. "What cold meats we leave will be put by for supper. Have you had a good morning?"

Griffin nodded. "I've been following Bruin about, ostensibly helping, but really, I'm sure, getting in the way."

"Nonsense," Bruin rumbled. "Griffin was a great help getting out all the blankets and hanging them to air. Between us we've nearly gotten the long dormitory set up. By myself it would have taken the entire day."

"I've learned a bit about this school of Bruin's, too,"

Griffin said. "I'd wondered why hunters would train in the spring. I'd always understood that to be when the animals were left to their own devices—raising newborns, getting fattened up, things like that."

"They are," Adara said, "but . . ."

Griffin spoke in unison with her, ". . . It takes the spring and much of the summer to teach those young idiots what they'll need come autumn."

They laughed all three together, Bruin as loudly as either of them at the repetition of this favorite bit of wisdom.

"Griffin's arrival has been noticed," Adara said, picking up a chicken leg, "but since everyone who spoke to me seemed to assume that Griffin was simply one of your students arrived a bit early, I didn't see need to say otherwise. Still, we're going to need to introduce him before our neighbors think we have something to hide."

Bruin nodded. "Since we're ahead on setting up the dorms, I thought an afternoon's stroll about the town wouldn't be amiss. How did your queries go?"

Adara frowned. "Seems the river is running fast this year. There's talk about sending a caravan overland to Blue Meadow to pick up supplies. As usual, it's unlikely any of the boats will think it profitable to risk coming up here until the snowmelt abates."

"Shepherd's Call often must go seeking after supplies come spring," Bruin explained to Griffin. "We don't have a lot to offer beyond wool, goat cheese, furs, and the like. Later in the year, when the river is sleepier, there will be less risk for the riverboats and so more return on the investment. That's when we see the traders."

"I'd hoped," Adara said, "to take *Foam Dancer* at least part of the way, but given how the river is running . . . We may do better on the road."

She glanced at Griffin. She could tell from his expression that Bruin had raised the question of the journey to Spirit Bay. Griffin looked resigned rather than eager but, sitting here in the cherry blossom–scented spring warmth, she could understand why.

"We're not going to leave come morning," she assured him, "but I'd like to join the caravan to Blue Meadow if we can. There's always more banditry in the spring. I'd prefer we travel in company."

Griffin Dane had been spreading sweet butter on a flat cake. Now he put down the treat untasted.

"Bandits? Here? On Artemis?"

Adara didn't want to laugh at him, but she heard the mockery that crept into her voice.

"You don't think the world has remained unchanged in the hundreds of years since the seegnur took their leave?" she asked. "Oh, we have bandits and more."

"But the village . . ." Griffin protested. "When you left me on the bluff, I had a good view of Shepherd's Call. There are no walls, no defenses. I thought that you lived in peace."

"No walls," Adara said and felt very proud, "as such, but certainly we have defenses. Bruin the Hunter and teacher of hunters makes his home in Shepherd's Call."

"And for some years now," Bruin added approvingly, "so has Adara the Huntress. It would be a foolhardy bandit gang to prey upon this town. Even if they killed me and Adara—and Honeychild and Sand Shadow as well— there are many I have taught who would feel duty-bound to avenge their old master. Why do you think the local shepherds do not protest such large predators living in the midst of their flocks and herds? They know we keep worse away."

Griffin picked up his flat cake and took a bite. Wiping crumbs from his lips, he answered. "I see. Superficially, much is the same as the worlds I have known, but those pieces come together differently. Bandits then. I can see why we'd want to join a larger group. What other dangers might we need to watch for?"

Adara glanced at Bruin, waiting for his nod of permission before speaking. "Here in Shepherd's Call, the adapted are welcome. Bruin has been a good example, as has Helena the Equestrian. However, this has not been the case everywhere. I don't know all the world's lore, but apparently there is reason for the fear."

Griffin looked a little sad but not at all surprised. "Those who are different—markedly, unavoidably, different—will always find themselves ostracized."

"And sometimes," Bruin said around a mouthful of the meat and cheese he'd piled onto a chunk of bread, "those doing the ostracizing have good reason. The lore tells how, even before the slaughter of the seegnur and death of machines, many of the adapted chose to believe themselves superior to the common run of humanity.

"When the seegnur were no longer present to govern, there were those among the adapted who thought they'd been offered an opportunity to dominate in their place. Even before, our peoples had been divided roughly between the professions and the support. The adapted always were trained into a profession and, so I have been told, this led to resentment even then. But the rules and regulations of the seegnur kept order."

"So did the world fall into war and chaos then?" Griffin asked. "When I orbited the planet, I looked for signs, but at this tech level they are not easy to spot. I thought all seemed pastoral, even peaceful. I saw no evidence of great industry. There were a few larger population centers—mostly by bodies of water as would be expected—but nothing that made me think Artemis had departed from her heritage."

Adara found herself somewhat lost by much of what Griffin said. It seemed to her that Shepherd's Call was very industrious. Most people worked in some fashion from dawn until dusk. Even the small children had lessons to learn and tasks assigned according to their size and ability. A boy set to watch the sheep might also carry a spindle and wind wool. Idleness was not prized here, nor in Ridgewood where she had been born.

But Bruin apparently understood.

"If by industry, you mean great manufactories, yes, you are correct. Such have never evolved here. Indeed, I think the tale you told us last night about those nanobots released as a forerunner to invasion may be the reason. Gears turn, but efforts to power, say, a millwheel by other means than water—although in some places I have heard they use wind or animals—have not worked. We craft on a human scale, assisted, certainly by tools, but the machines of which the lore holds memory—machines that worked out of sight so that the seegnur might have light without smoke, clean clothing within a span of minutes, food served hot for the asking, those have never been rediscovered."

Griffin looked grim. "I see. My shuttle's wreck is but a part of a larger wreck—a wreck of an entire people, condemned to savagery."

He swallowed the last of his flat cake, then burst out laughing, seeing in their stunned expressions the ludicrousness of that last statement.

"Forgive me, friends. I don't mean to speak poorly of your world. My mother always said I lived as much in the world of my ideas as in the one whose air I breathed. My brothers were less kind. They said I'd fall on the floor and bruise my butt because I went to sit in a chair I expected to be there."

He rapped his knuckles against the table, stroked the use-polished wood of the chair in which he sat. "I'm here. Although Artemis is proving different in ways I did not anticipate, 'savage' it is not."

Adara asked softly, "Your brothers, do you miss them? They do not sound as if they were always kind to you."

"I . . ." Griffin paused, considering. "We're all grown men. It has been many years since we lived under one roof or even met all at once but, now that I need to accept that I might never see them again, yes, I do miss them."

Adara nodded. "Then we'll do our best to make sure that if you don't see them again, it's by choice, not chance."

After the meal had been cleared away, Griffin himself taking a rag and going out to scrub the table clean, Griffin said, "Shall we go into the village? It's time this stranger met more of the people of Shepherd's Call."

Griffin felt acutely self-conscious when they walked out of Bruin's front gate and turned toward the green that was the heart of Shepherd's Call. The road was wide enough that Adara walked to his left, while Bruin shambled along to the right. Sand Shadow paced ahead, as if this was some parade in her honor. Behind, making little snuffling noises, Honeychild followed in a slow, sleepy amble.

They passed several houses along the way, chickens in the doorways scattering in the manner of domestic fowl everywhere, their clucking chorus not greatly intensified by the presence of bear and puma. Birds took wing, but again, not with undue panic. The larger animals—dogs, goats, occasionally a cow or horse—seemed more aware of the potential threat offered by the predators but, while eyes were rolled or the occasional snort or growl reached the ear, most accepted the odd procession as a matter of routine.

The people they passed offered friendly waves or called greetings as they went about their chores. Without pausing, Bruin and Adara replied in kind. Griffin had thought these neighbors might come forth and make excuses to chat, but the little procession continued on unimpeded. When they rounded a bend and could see the village green clearly, Griffin noticed that several of those who had greeted them were already present. A few leaned hoes or shovels against the trees, dusting their palms clean against their trouser legs or skirts.

Remembering the plan of the village as he had seen it from the bluff above the river, Griffin understood. Adara and Bruin were taking the long way around, partly, he thought, in deference to how their neighbor's livestock might react if bear and puma prowled through the narrower back roads, partly to give time for the word to spread that the stranger was coming forth to be met.

Griffin's supposition was confirmed when, soon after they crossed from road into green, the door to a large house set just off the main street flew open and a plump, well-dressed woman emerged. Her bustling manner reminded Griffin of one of the hens, but her course possessed nothing of their erratic scattering. The woman was followed by a flock of young women and small children. She bore down upon them, arms outstretched in welcome.

"Well, Bruin, my girls have been buzzing all the morning about your visitor," she said, as soon as she was close enough that she could not be said to be shouting. Nonetheless, there was a booming quality to her voice that could not be ignored. "You selfish man, keeping him to yourself all the morning. You know how we all look forward to fresh faces after a winter of being snowed in with only ourselves to look at. Is this the first of your students, then?"

Although this was phrased as a question, the matron did not pause for an answer, being, as Griffin did not need to be told, certain of the answer. What else would he be? As Adara had reported, the river was too rough to bring the merchants and there was little other reason for anyone to come to Shepherd's Call.

The woman turned her attention to Griffin. Sand Shadow had moved to one side and now lolled on the grass, her manner one that Griffin knew all too well indicated amusement. Unimpeded, the woman bore down on Griffin. From where it rested upon her formidable bosom, she removed a wreath made from a many-petaled white flower with a golden yellow center.

"Welcome! Welcome!" the woman exclaimed, draping the wreath around Griffin's neck. "I am Mistress Cheesemaker. I have the honor of being the spokesperson for our little community. Let me have the pleasure of being the first—other than your hosts, of course—to welcome you to Shepherd's Call. What shall we call you?"

"Griffin," he managed around a potential sneeze. The flowers had a strong, not completely pleasant odor, as might be expected of an early spring blossom that wanted to keep from being eaten before the bees might find it. "Griffin Dane."

Mistress Cheesemaker seemed a bit puzzled by these few words—although whether it was Griffin's accent or his name that caused her face to go momentarily blank, Griffin could not guess. Nevertheless, she was not so puzzled that the flow of her speech slowed for more than a breath. "Griffin . . . Let me introduce you to my daughters. This is Martine and this is Laura and the one with the baby on her hip is Suzie."

Other people were pressing forward now. Griffin, struggling against the impulse to sneeze, saw with alarm that several others bore floral tributes. Adara and Bruin had dropped back a few paces, but weren't so far that they couldn't help him if more than his name was asked. However, the people of Shepherd's Call seemed starved for talk, though not nearly so starved for listening.

Griffin had just shaken the rough, callused hand of Master Miller and accepted a wristlet of violets from his doe-eyed wife when he caught a glimpse of the first face that did not look particularly welcoming. It belonged to a strongly built man with shoulder-length dark brown hair. The man looked as if he hadn't shaved for a couple of days, but otherwise wasn't unduly untidy. From how his blue eyes flickered between Griffin and Adara, this was one person who was not pleased by the idea of them both residing beneath Bruin's roof.

Having helped Bruin set up the dormitories, Griffin understood why. Most of those who came to learn the hunter's trade from Bruin and Adara would be between ten and twelve years old. Even by the standards of this culture (and certainly by Griffin's own), these were mere boys. By contrast, Griffin was definitely a man— and a man, he would guess, apparently this one's own age and therefore a potential rival.

The two men's gazes locked in mutual appraisal. Mistress Cheesemaker immediately caught the scent of acrimony. Showing herself no fool, she set about defusing it with introductions.

"Griffin, this is Terrell the Factotum," she said, "who came to us last autumn to study the finer points of riding with our resident equestrian. Terrell's a relative newcomer, so I'm sure he'll be glad to show you around when you have some free time."

Griffin wasn't at all so certain but, under Mistress Cheesemaker's authoritarian gaze, there was nothing he and Terrell could do but clasp hands. If Terrell's clasp met one stronger than he expected, he gave no sign. Griffin had too many brothers not to recognize the challenge offered by Terrell's gripping fingers, but he only gave as much as he was offered, no more. After all, Griffin wasn't looking to make an enemy, even if this Terrell seemed inclined to think of him as one from the start.

With Terrell's advent, another element of village dynamics fell into place. Not surprisingly, given that this was the middle of the day, most of those who had flooded out to meet the new arrival were either females or older men. Doubtless the rest of the menfolk were out getting in the crops or whatever it was men did in a farming and sheepherding village at this time of year. From how the girls giggled and looked between Griffin and Terrell, it was quite evident that Terrell was a favorite with the ladies.

However, it was also apparent that at least a few thought the new arrival might be even more interesting.

Great, Griffin thought as yet another floral tribute was draped around his neck. *Just what I need. On the other hand, what does it matter? Adara and I will be leaving soon for Spirit Bay. I probably won't need to deal with this Terrell for months—maybe never again—and I certainly don't plan to start courting the local ladies.*

He wished he thought the young ladies didn't seem to think otherwise. Even Mistress Cheesemaker was examining him appraisingly, as if contemplating which of her daughters he might suit.

As Griffin was exchanging handclasps with the village's senior cobbler, a high, shrill scream ripped through the pleasant chatter. The scream stilled all sound in a single breath. Adara's voice sounded a moment later.

"What's that? Sand Shadow! No! Don't!"

Turning, Griffin saw Adara running in the direction of the tree beneath which Sand Shadow had been lounging. With a graceful leap, the huntress was up into the branches, climbing to where she could get a better look at whatever had so disturbed the great cat.

Long body in a tense line, Sand Shadow remained near the tree. It was evident from the puffing of her fur and the lashing of her heavy tail that she'd been about to take on whatever it was that had made her let forth that blood-chilling caterwaul.

Ignoring the babble around him, Griffin noted that Adara was looking in the direction of the forested mountain slopes from which they had descended—was it only the night before? At first he saw nothing but the vari-hued greens of the mixed evergreen and deciduous foliage. Then, where a gap in the trees marked a clearing of some sort, he saw a flash as of light reflecting back from metal or glass.

Adara's vantage point gave her a clearer view.

"There's something," she said, "something large—at

least the size of a cow—coming through the forest. I can't see all of it, but it's moving fairly quickly, on long legs, like those of a spider."

She paused, checked again, then added, "I don't ask you to believe me, but whatever it is seems to be made all of metal."

Interlude: TVC1500

Target found.
Hasten!
Peace comes with success.
Peace comes with death.

7
Metal and Fire

At Sand Shadow's scream, the villagers had fallen silent. Now the babbling resumed, cordial gossip vanishing beneath the shrill notes of panic.

Mothers began hurrying small children toward the houses. Most of the older children went scurrying after, but a few—bolder or maybe just less wise than their fellows—were copying Adara and climbing up the trees that shaded the edges of the green.

Bruin, Griffin saw, was also up a tree. He was momentarily surprised that such a bulky man could climb so easily, but then he remembered how well bears were said to climb. Honeychild was guarding the base of Bruin's tree as Sand Shadow was Adara's.

Some few villagers remained on the green. Mistress Cheesemaker and the old cobbler were hurrying toward the space between two of the larger houses. Remembering his earlier conjecture that the village might be defensible if the areas between the houses were blockaded, Griffin wasn't completely surprised to see the pair tugging at what looked like segments of an old gate. Glancing to one side, he saw Terrell helping the miller with a similar task.

Griffin wished he felt confident of his ability to climb, but tree climbing was a skill he had never mastered. The trees where he had grown up had been of the sort that shed their lower limbs to create a clear understory, not a trait that invited climbing.

He settled for clambering up on a large, roughly cut block of stone that, from its proximity to a long watering trough, was probably a mounting block. At last he could get a clear look at what had just crashed out of the fringes of the forest and into the cleared lands that surrounded the village.

By the standards of the world Griffin had left behind him, this wasn't a very large machine. Adara had compared it in size to a cow, but that description only worked if the cow was taller than usual and had very long, thin legs holding up a flattened, roughly ovoid body and no head at all. Griffin thought her second comparison to a spider was better. Of course, this spider was shaped from a silvery-grey metal, dulled and dented, though whether from abuse or neglect he could not say.

The machine paused in midstride, extending a probe which it used to inspect the area around it.

Adara said, "Is that a machine?"

Bruin replied, "It is. I have seen pictures of such in the Old One's library. Once, when I was about your age, a diving pro found the carcass of something like that stuck in a reef."

Griffin called, "That's a machine. Absolutely. It may look like a spider, but it's a machine. What is it doing here?"

As he spoke, the machine sucked the probe back into itself and began to move purposefully toward the village. When Griffin had first glimpsed it, the metal spider had seemed to move quickly. Now he saw that the front limbs were damaged, causing the whole construct to sway from side to side. However, despite this handicap, the metal spider moved with deliberation and purpose.

The gates between the houses on the side of the village nearest to the spider had been closed. The one with which the cobbler and Mistress Cheesemaker had been struggling showed evidence of weather warping that had left a gap between the two sides of the gate. Nonetheless, the heavy, metal-bound wooden planks would have provided a considerable obstacle even to mounted warriors.

"That should slow it down," said Terrell with satisfaction, peering out through an arrow slit.

"Maybe so," the miller retorted, "but we've other gates to close. Come along."

Terrell did so. As he turned away, a hiss followed by a crackling reverberated through the air. Between one breath and the next, the gate that had sheltered Terrell burst into flames.

✦

Adara gasped as the massive wooden boards caught fire as if they were no more than fine shavings. The metal straps that bound the boards melted like wax.

The spider did not wait for the flames to die back, but came forward through the fire, staggering past the burning gate onto the village green. Once again it stopped and extended that long limb—she wondered if this was some sort of nose—and began feeling the air.

"Clear the green! Clear the green!" yelled Master Cobbler, his cracked voice breaking as he raced toward the ancient bell that for so many years had rung alarm. These alerts had been for fire or flood—never once for raid or attack.

"Don't touch the bell!" Bruin bellowed, thudding from his tree onto the turf. "What good would bringing in the men do? That thing would cook them. Take cover and leave dealing with this spider to us."

Master Cobbler might well have asked what Bruin thought he and his students could do, but he had good sense not to argue. He turned toward his house, still crying the alarm. Mistress Cheesemaker's strong voice could be heard giving orders—sensible ones about closing shutters and getting pails of water ready. She also sent some of the swifter children to warn the men in the fields not to come into the green. Adara, leaping down from her tree, appreciated the woman's practicality as never before.

As Adara landed, she heard a shrill whistle, followed almost instantly by the thundering of hooves on the turf. She knew that Terrell had summoned Coal, his favorite mount. A second rumble of hooves announced the coming of Helena the Equestrian, doubtless astride dapple-grey Moquino.

"Stay spread out," Bruin ordered. "If that thing snorts fire again, best we give it small target. Griffin Dane, do you know anything about how we might kill this thing?"

"Not this one in particular," Griffin replied, his voice level. "Not enough to tell you its strengths or recite its specs."

"Weaknesses?" Bruin said.

"It's broken," came the quick reply. "Certainly no one crafted it to move in that halting fashion."

"Can it spit more than fire?" Adara asked.

"Possibly," Griffin said. "I'm sorry. You want one of my brothers, not me."

He sounded despairing, but Adara noted with approval that Griffin made no effort to run or hide. Unarmed, unarmored, as ignorant as any of them, still, he would hold his ground.

Helena the Equestrian came to a halt near where Terrell had just swung up onto Coal's bare back. Unlike her student, who bore no weapons, she carried a short lance.

"I was practicing," she said. "Something in the urgency with which Coal jumped the fence told me I should not come empty-handed. What is that thing?"

"A machine," Terrell said shortly. "It spits fire. I would be nothing but charred flesh had I not gone to help Master Miller close the third gate."

He looked pale, as anyone who had experienced such a close call had the right to be, but Adara thought this was the paleness of anger, not fear.

Strange, she thought. *None of us is particularly afraid. Could that be because despite the reek of smoke in the air this attack is so unreal?*

A flash came into Adara's mind from Sand Shadow— the puma informing her that *she* was nearly insane from fright, as anyone with any sense would be, that humans were more stupid than a kitten yet in spots who drowns chasing its own reflection in a pool.

Yet the puma did not run. Her attachment to Adara was too strong. Even as a mother cat would fight to protect her young, so Sand Shadow would stand with Adara.

So with my choices, I hold two lives, Adara thought.

"What is it doing?" Terrell asked, stroking Coal along the crest of the stallion's neck. "Since that spider burned through the gate, it has simply stood there, moving that thin arm through the air."

"I think," Griffin Dane said, "that it is trying to sort out conflicting signals. From how it's acting, I wouldn't be surprised if its sensor array is damaged."

"What is it sensing for?" Helena asked.

The answer came in motion not words. The spider's thin limb stiffened and pointed directly at Griffin Dane. All around the outer band of the ovoid body colored lights began to race faster and faster, red becoming orange, orange fading into . . .

"It's going to spit again!" Adara shouted. "Griffin, get away. Weave about. With those broken legs it cannot easily move after you!"

She followed her own advice, but with an addition that came to her in a flash of inspiration. If the spider was injured, then it might be distracted in its efforts to locate Griffin and so be delayed in spitting that deadly fire.

Running with all the speed at her command, Adara pounded over the green until she came alongside the spider. She could feel the heat of it. Although the air was full of the odors of hot metal and burning wood, there was an alien note, as if something else was burning as well.

Adara didn't know whether or not to be insulted that, thus far, the metal spider did not seem to notice her or think her worthy of attention.

Well, then, she thought, *before it changes its mind, I must attack. One thing is for sure. I won't get another chance this good.*

Pushing off from the ground, Adara jumped as high as she could, imagining her body elongating as Sand Shadow's did when the puma leapt, that her spine was stretching, her fingers clawing out at the tips. The spider's legs were long in proportion to its broad, flat body, but its back was not all that much higher than the top of Adara's head. Adara landed neatly atop the metal carapace, clawed for a hold in the cracked and dented surface.

Adara's one worry in making this mad leap had been that the spider's metal would be hot but, although she felt warmth, the surface on which she had landed was not unbearable. Likely the heat she had felt was from where the spider built up its spitting fires.

When Adara's weight hit the spider's back, the crippled legs shook. The spider pitched forward. For a moment, Adara thought it might fall. Then, making a strange, whirring noise, it caught itself.

As assured as she would ever be of her perch, Adara sought how she might wound the thing further. She noted that some of the dents in the carapace ran along seams. Normal human fingers could not have taken advantage of these gaps, but the tips of her claws came to a sharp point and were much stronger than ordinary fingernails.

An image flashed into Adara's head from Sand Shadow, filling her in on what was going on around her. The spider had extended two more of those slim limbs. One—one of those "nose" ones—was examining Adara, the other, pointed like a spear, but flexible, was moving as if to pierce or slap. Despite the obvious threat, Adara was reluctant to jump down—after all, she might find herself diving into a gout of the spider's fire. Instead, she prepared to dodge, her claws still prying at the seam.

Adara sensed Sand Shadow pacing forward, willing to attack, though uncertain where to strike such an unfamiliar opponent. Here was no back to leap upon, no neck to bite and break. Then a thudding of hooves against the turf heralded someone new entering the fight.

Terrell, astride Coal, came galloping forward, Helena's lance tucked beneath his arm. To avoid the chance of being hit by the spider's fire, he was angling in from the left side. Adara felt the lance impact solidly against one edge of the spider's ovoid body, heard something drop to the turf. The spider shuddered but it did not fall. She felt something click and heard the now familiar whirring noise.

Sand Shadow's images told Adara that Terrell's lance had broken off the long limb that had been about to swat at Adara—but the impact had nearly unseated the man.

Now the spider had turned its attention from the annoyance on its back to the one that had slammed into it. Terrell was wheeling Coal about for another pass, ignoring that panels on the spider's side were sliding open, revealing an area that glowed an ominous red.

Tugging back with her claws in the seam, Adara met with neither blood nor flesh, but rather some sort of padding. Beneath this were an assortment of items so unlike anything she had seen that she could not even put a name to them.

Still, the spider carries them beneath both hide and padding. Messing them about could not do it any good.

Adara was reaching in to poke at the spider's guts when a memory of Bruin scolding her not soon after she had come to live with him rose fresh to mind. "Don't stick your finger into a bees' hive unless you're asking to be stung." There had been neither bees nor hive involved, but young as she was, she'd understood.

Therefore, although the spider was rocking back and forth, and Sand Shadow was flooding her mind with terror-filled images that illustrated how precarious Adara's position was, Adara took a moment to reach for her bone-handled hunting knife.

With the claws of her left hand firmly anchored in the spider's hide, she stabbed into the spider's guts.

Griffin hardly knew how to react when Adara leapt upon the metal spider. What did she think she could do barehanded against a war machine? He was about to shout a warning, to try and convince her to get down, when Bruin's gravelly voice spoke close to his ear.

"Don't distract her. It's too late for that. In any case, Sand Shadow tells Honeychild that Adara hasn't gone completely mad. Nor is she alone in the fight . . ."

Bruin pointed. Griffin saw that Terrell—now mounted on a magnificent black horse—had wrested a long, heavy staff or spear from the hands of the older woman who had just arrived on a strongly built dapple-grey. From little signs between them, Griffin guessed that the woman must be Helena the Equestrian, whom Mistress Cheesemaker had mentioned was Terrell's teacher.

Terrell handled the weapon—a fragment of one of his

brother Alexander's lectures on antique weapons cropped up and identified it as a lance—as if he knew how to use it. Clamping the lance firmly beneath his right arm, Terrell bore down upon the metal spider, orienting on the side from which tentacles had extended to harass Adara.

Almost more rapidly than Griffin could take in the scene, Terrell's lance had sliced into the probes the spider had extended toward Adara. They dropped from the main body, their silvery length twitching on the turf for a moment before falling still.

As soon as he had finished warning Griffin back, Bruin had seized up a heavy shovel with a thick blade from among the tools left near the fence and begun lumbering toward the spider. Honeychild loped at his side. Both bear and man were massive in contrast to the thin-legged spider, but Griffin knew all too well how deceptive such contrasts were.

Terrell had regained his seat and was wheeling the black horse for another pass at the spider. Whether he was ignoring the threat offered by the red lights glowing around the spider's rim or he simply hadn't realized their significance, Terrell pressed his mount forward, lance lowered.

He was not alone. Although she'd given up her lance to Terrell, Helena had seized a garden hoe. As Terrell came in from the left, she took the right, dragging the hoe against the spider's crippled legs, using her horse's strength to pull the war machine off balance.

Slower than the equestrians, Bruin showed himself at least as powerful. By the time he arrived, the spider had spat a small, ineffectual burst of flame at Terrell, but otherwise seemed too confused to take effective action. Bruin began battering at the weakest of the front limbs, using the blade of the shovel as a club.

In the midst of all this chaos, Adara maintained her seat on the bouncing and jolting spider. Griffin could see rhythmic motion as she dug or probed at something with the long blade of her hunting knife. Every so often, something small flew up and away.

She's gotten through the protective armor somehow, Griffin thought, *and is pulling the works apart. Doesn't seem to have hurt the thing so far, but doubtless it has redundancies.*

He longed to join the fight, but knew himself too well. He'd done his share of close skirmishing—no one with six brothers of such active natures as his kin could fail to do so. From these he had learned his limitations—and how in close quarters fighting allies often fouled each other.

Griffin noticed that both Honeychild and Sand Shadow seemed to have reached the same decision. The demiurges stood back, watching the action with close attention. Remembering what Bruin had said, Griffin wondered if bear and puma were somehow relaying information to their human associates. Certainly, that did not seem impossible—especially given the precision with which the two riders and Bruin managed to move around each other.

Had the metal spider not been damaged from the start, Griffin doubted that even this concerted attack could have harmed the thing. As he watched, it occurred to him that whatever had damaged its legs had also damaged its firepower. The bursts of flame it shot forth were erratic and far, far weaker than the one that had taken out the protective gate.

If luck holds . . . Griffin was thinking, when that luck broke.

Terrell, grown a bit overbold, had again charged his black at the spider. He was aiming directly for the front, for the area from which the initial bursts of flame had come. It was possible the spider had held reserves for just such a moment, because when Terrell came on, it spat.

Most of the blast caught the black horse squarely on head, neck, and chest. Bent to brace his lance, Terrell was spared the worst of the flame's impact, but he lost his seat when the black horse screamed and reared, backing away from the flames.

Terrell was flung away, crumpling unconscious on the turf in front of the spider. Griffin heard Helena shout, Bruin bellow, but he knew that neither of them could abandon their own places to help the fallen man. Griffin was running before he realized he'd made any decision to do so, his hands grabbing hold of Terrell and pulling him out of the range of both the pitching, rearing stallion and the metal spider.

If the man has a broken back, this is absolutely the worst thing to do, Griffin's inner chatter noted. *But I don't suppose a broken back is anything to worry about if the options are being left to be trampled or burned to death.*

A ferocious scream cut through the mingled sounds of the skirmish. For the briefest of moments, Griffin thought the sound might be Terrell crying out at this rough handling. Then he realized the source was Adara, screaming as a wildcat would scream. He glanced up and saw her face contorted with fury, both hands gripping the hilt of her knife as she brought it down with sharp, strong stabs directly into the body of the metal spider.

Griffin couldn't spare attention to watch, but somehow he felt certain the spider didn't have a chance. There had been something about how Adara had moved that said she was going to rip the monster's heart out—whether or not it had a heart.

Does she love this Terrell? Griffin thought with something like shock. For a brief moment, he felt regret— though whether at his choice to help the other man or that he hadn't realized how much he cared for Adara he had no idea. Whatever the seed of that bitter emotion, Griffin didn't let it stop him. He dragged Terrell over to the water trough, laid the man flat, then used his cupped hands to scoop out water. The black horse had not intercepted all the flames and Terrell's heavy trousers were smoldering, although the thick wool seemed to have resisted catching fire.

Griffin was checking for Terrell's pulse—and relieved to find it beating strongly—when he heard a heavy door slam and running feet on the grass.

"Is he alive?" Mistress Cheesemaker asked. "I've some skill with injuries . . ."

She shouldered Griffin out of the way. One of her daughters—Martine, Griffin vaguely remembered—began handing her bottles from a leather satchel.

Griffin turned to assess the battle and realized that in those few minutes it had ended. The metal spider had collapsed, the body held at an angle above the turf by the few legs on its right side that had not been broken. Fire was licking from its edges. Adara and Bruin were dousing the flames with buckets of water fetched from the public fountain by the miller and a few other men who had emerged from the houses to help.

The black horse was down. Griffin hadn't consciously realized that it had continued to scream—the horrible noises seemed so in keeping with the situation—until the screams fell silent. Helena the Equestrian stood up, a bloody knife in one hand, tears streaming down her face. Without another look at the dead animal, she strode across the green toward the group clustered around Terrell.

Here, at least, Griffin thought he might help. "Terrell's alive, ma'am."

Helena gave him a stiff nod, but her expression held something like hatred.

As if I was the one who attacked him, rather than the one who saved him, Griffin thought in dismay. His inner voice replied promptly, *You may have attacked him, Griffin Dane. Didn't Adara tell you there have been no machines active since the slaughter of the seegnur? Is it a coincidence that you appear and a working war machine activates so soon after?*

Griffin stood staring, thinking how the metal spider had attacked no one or nothing until the gate had been closed between him and it, how it had entered the green and quested about, then headed directly for him.

Have I done this? he thought in horror and dismay. *Could I be responsible?*

Despite a dive into the icy waters of the river, Adara's hair still smelled of both the evil-smelling steam that had come off the spider and burned horseflesh. At least the cold water gave her an excuse for the shivers that took her whenever she let herself remember that horrible battle.

Talked out and exhausted, Adara, Bruin, and Griffin now sat in front of the fire, each lost in his or her own thoughts. When a knock sounded at the front door, Griffin stared unmoving into the flames, the resident mouser curled on his lap. When Adara would have gone to answer the door, Bruin waved her back.

"That'll be Mistress Cheesemaker. I know that rap. She'll want me."

Adara nodded understanding. Shepherd's Call was too small to have a mayor but, if there had been one, it would have been Mistress Cheesemaker. Her arrival at the front door meant she was calling in her "official" capacity. Bruin, however, hadn't said that Adara couldn't listen, and he knew that her sense of hearing was excellent.

"I've come," Mistress Cheesemaker began without preamble, "to tell you how Terrell the Factotum is doing."

"Will you come inside?" Bruin asked. "I've just brewed a fresh pot of tea or I could mull a bit of my cherry cider."

"No, thank you."

Adara was surprised to hear Mistress Cheesemaker refuse. Normally, the woman liked little better than a chance to rest by someone else's fire—she allowed herself so little quiet by her own.

"I've a few other things to tell you, then I must be back to the green. Ronbert Smith is supervising the destruction of that spider. I've promised to drop over at the forge and check on the results."

Bruin made a low, noncommittal noise, the same he used—as Adara knew all too well—to encourage his students to talk.

"Even if the forge's fire isn't hot enough to completely soften the metal," Mistress Cheesemaker said, "I doubt the thing will walk when it's been beaten by the smith's hammer."

"About Terrell the Factotum?" Bruin prompted.

Mistress Cheesemaker's voice brightened. "Ah! He's less severely injured than any dared hope. No broken bones, for a wonder, though he's one solid bruise along his side and back where he hit the ground. There's some blistering on his exposed skin, but poor Coal caught the brunt of the flames."

There was a respectful pause in memory of the gallant stallion.

"Bruin," Mistress Cheesemaker's voice dropped, but Adara could still hear easily enough, "you fought there on the green. Even so, those of us who watched from safety may have seen something you missed."

"And that is?"

There was a longer pause than Adara would have thought possible for the usually gossipy matron, then Mistress Cheesemaker went on.

"That thing—spider machine—it wasn't spraying fire at random. I've heard the same from a dozen people, all unprompted, including some shepherd lads who watched from the hilltops. That spider machine came for one person and one person alone. It came for your Griffin Dane."

Bruin made his "I'm listening" noise and Mistress Cheesemaker continued.

"Griffin Dane is an odd name. Nor did any see him arrive. Some say Adara brought him back with her from the mountains. Is this so?"

Adara held her breath, wondering how much Bruin would offer.

"Adara did. She found him in the mountains, lost and very confused. Not knowing what to make of her strange catch, she brought him to me."

"A wise choice," Mistress Cheesemaker said, approval in her voice, "but I'm thinking Adara was right that she had no idea what she had found. I'm thinking she found more than she realized."

"Do you know, then?" Bruin asked. "Do you know something about this Griffin Dane?"

"I do not, but some days ago many villagers saw a shooting star in broad daylight. It may have hit near where Adara and Sand Shadow hunted. There may be no connection, yet I fear from the depths of my soul when I think what manner of man brings spider machines trailing after him. We were fortunate that all we lost was Coal."

"And . . ."

"Bruin, we of Shepherd's Call have always welcomed your students, even the adapted. We welcomed you when you came here first, courting Mary Greengrass. We were glad you stayed on with us when death took Mary from you. We welcomed you, even though some of our neighbors said we were fools for bringing a bear among the lambs. But how can we welcome this Griffin Dane when such things follow him?"

"Rest assured," Bruin said, "you will not need to do so. Griffin Dane will be moving on. Adara had thought they might join the caravan to Blue Meadow for safety on the road . . ."

Mistress Cheesemaker's snort was eloquent.

". . . But now I think they will need to move at a faster pace than the caravan could manage."

"So Griffin Dane will leave here soon?"

"Within a few days," Bruin promised. "Meanwhile, we shall keep watch."

"That's already done. The miller has donated seasoned wood for a new gate, though much good a gate did us against what that spider spit. I wonder if even a stone wall would have kept that thing from our midst."

"I cannot say," Bruin replied. "However, I can assure you of this. I believe that Griffin Dane is such a man that if another spider machine descended from the foothills, he would run toward it rather than see a single one of us scorched."

Mistress Cheesemaker laughed, but not unkindly. Indeed, Adara heard sorrow among the notes.

"I believe you. I saw Griffin Dane pull Terrell to safety. Very well. Griffin would sacrifice himself rather than see even an old dog come to harm, nonetheless I would rather he left so that the need not arise."

"So I would prefer also," Bruin agreed. "So would we all."

Interlude: TVC1500

Lick away flames, hot and fierce.
  Heat can transform metal to liquid.
No heat can burn away purpose.
  No flame can char passion to ash.
Lick away flames.
  Passion shall lick even thee.

8

The Hanged Man

Griffin listened intently as Bruin explained the reason behind Mistress Cheesemaker's call.

"The lady may be right," Griffin admitted. "I had similar thoughts. The spider machine may be some old warbot left from the slaughter of the seegnur. I hadn't thought the attackers brought any with them, since such would have been susceptible to the nanobots. Still, technology was so different then. Of course, there's another possibility."

"Oh?" Bruin asked.

"I told Adara I had brought with me the means to counter the machine-killing nanobots. Some of this could have been released when my shuttle crashed. The chance of my countermeasure finding a warbot so easily boggles the mind, but it's not impossible."

"How," Adara asked, "would such a 'warbot' know to target you?"

"I think I worked that out. If the commandos who attacked Artemis did bring warbots with them, then they would have programmed the warbots' sensors to target only those you call the 'seegnur.' There's ample evidence, both in your own lore and in the tales I encountered in my research, that an effort was made to preserve the residents of Artemis."

"Could a machine tell one sort of human from another?" Adara asked.

"Easily," Griffin replied. "There are ample indications that the people of Artemis—even those who were not adapted—came from genetically engineered stock. They would have possessed a distinct signature that the warbots could have been told to ignore unless offered direct threat."

Griffin held his breath, hoping neither Adara nor Bruin would ask for more details. Some of the material he had come across had indicated that the natives of Artemis had been modified in various ways. It had hinted they had been created to be receptive to commands. He wouldn't be surprised if they'd also been modified to have a birth rate sensitive to population density, as did many animals. After all, those who had invested in the planet would not have wished to face either a free-thinking population or an overpopulated planet.

It's rather unsettling, Griffin thought, *to consider this now that I've met some of those who were subjected to such dramatic modification without their consent. Of course, on Sierra, some genetic modification is routine. Genetic combinations that would lead to a variety of defects are suppressed. Certainly, here on Artemis, as at home, there would have been beneficial modifications. Adara is amazingly tough. When we were talking, she didn't seem to know what I meant when I said I was worried we might catch cold or flu after we got both frozen and soaked after the avalanche. She didn't seem to know what cancer was. My impression is that even infections are rare.*

The Artemisians weren't immune to injury, but seemed to heal well and cleanly. Bruin's wife, the late Mary Greengrass, had been injured in a fall. Broken ribs had punctured her lungs so that they had collapsed. Adara—who had viewed the woman as a second mother—had spoken of Mary's death with genuine grief, tinged with shock that such things could happen to a woman still relatively young.

"Certainly," Griffin continued, dragging his wandering thoughts back to the subject under discussion, "our meeting up with an ancient warbot seems unlikely, but the thing wasn't in very good shape. Probably it had been considered broken beyond repair and so wasn't hauled off when the planet was abandoned."

"Then you think it unlikely that Shepherd's Call is in further danger?" Bruin asked.

"Unlikely," Griffin said, "but not impossible. Certainly, I need to leave here as soon as is possible. I can completely understand if Adara doesn't want to escort me . . ."

Adara cut him off. "I'm going. I dragged you out of that wreck, so in some sense I'm as responsible as you are—if any responsibility can be assigned to us that is not shared equally by warlords half a millennium passed. Count me and Sand Shadow in."

The puma, who had been napping after the fashion of all cats presented with a fire and an idle moment, yawned agreement.

"I think I will go, too," Bruin said. "One of my students—the boy who shows signs of being adapted—was supposed to have arrived by now. Indeed, one of the reasons Adara was away training—although I could have used her help in setting up for the arriving students—was so that I would have the opportunity to gain Kipper's confidence in relative privacy. I will go with you at least as far as Blue Meadow and ask after him."

Griffin was too relieved to argue. "Thank you both very much. I would have taken a map and hoped that one man alone wouldn't attract bandits, but I admit that I will be glad to have you with me."

"Well, then," Bruin said, hauling himself to his feet with a grunt, "all that is left is for us to decide what we're having for dinner tonight. I believe there was some chicken left from lunch. Let me see what else I can find in the larder."

Even though Adara was now as impatient to depart as earlier she had been reluctant, they couldn't leave immediately. Bruin needed to make arrangements for someone to care for the domestic animals and newly planted garden. Since he was popular in Shepherd's Call, this would not prove difficult. However, the soon-to-arrive students were another matter. Bruin needed to track down one of his more senior past-students, one who could begin the lessons if Bruin was delayed in his return.

To Adara was given the more difficult task of convincing Helena the Equestrian to make them a loan of horses who would not shy from the puma and the bear.

Helena was not an unreasonable woman, but in her long years of association with horses, she had soaked up some of their distrust for hunting creatures. Moreover, Adara knew Helena resented the loss of Coal and the injury to her resident student.

The day after the metal spider had so dramatically interrupted Griffin's introduction to the residents of Shepherd's Call, Adara gathered up her courage and went to call on Terrell. She would have rather gone up the mountain to see if she could backtrack the spider, but rain the night before had probably removed any spore her human eyes could find—and Sand Shadow was better equipped to find whatever might be left.

Helena the Equestrian's stables were on the same side of Shepherd's Call as Bruin's holding, so Adara comforted herself that at least her visit would not draw the attention of the gossipy village maidens. As it turned out, she could not have been more wrong. Apparently, every young woman in the village had decided to call on Terrell. Those who already had been to see the invalid lingered nearby to chatter with their friends.

When Adara, neatly dressed in a fresh set of hunting leathers, a stoneware bottle of Bruin's famous cherry cider dangling from her right hand, turned up the path that led to Helena's front door, the feminine chatter stopped in one breath. Long-lashed eyes of various hues narrowed in assessment. Adara received the distinct impression that the assembled maidens blamed her for Terrell's injuries.

Laura, daughter of Mistress Cheesemaker, a village

belle who (so rumor said) had only failed to marry young because none of her beaus could get up the courage to face her formidable mother, was the only one to speak to Adara.

"Come to see Terrell?"

"That's right," Adara replied, trying—and failing, she knew—not to sound cold.

"Helena has made a bed for him in the front room. Before she left to bring supplies up to Bert at the sheepfold, she told us we could go in if we wished. I suppose the same invitation applies to you."

Adara wasn't so certain, but she nodded thanks.

"Terrell isn't asleep, is he?"

Laura gave a fluting laugh. "Well, if he is, then Nancy, Brittany, and Sashi are all watching over his dreams."

Adara swallowed a sigh. The girls in question were sisters. The youngest, Sashi, could hardly be considered of courting age, but Brittany was well known to be among Terrell's most ardent suitors. Before Terrell's coming, Brittany hadn't found a man who could measure up to a horse in either strength or grace. When Terrell arrived, she had declared him perfection. Only the fact that she had been barely twelve at the time had kept her from proposing then and there. Now she was said to be counting down to her fifteenth birthday with indecent avidity—especially since she could hardly claim the ability to support a partner and family that was legally required before a formal proposal could be offered by either side in the match.

Adara reminded herself that she'd faced down a war machine that spat fire. Surely she could face three rather silly girls. With that thought, she gave a casual wave to Laura and the others, then continued toward the front door.

A note tacked to the door said that visitors should let themselves in to spare Terrell getting up, so she knocked to announce herself, then lifted the latch and eased the door open.

Terrell was half reclined against a heap of pillows on a narrow bed set near the main hearth. He wore a loose shirt made from pearl-pale lamb's wool and was quite literally surrounded by gifts brought by his admirers.

There's cookies, loaves, and muffins to keep him for a week, Adara thought. *Not to mention jars of jam, small cheeses, and enough flowers to blanket him from head to foot.*

Little Sashi sat on the floor, the line of jam on her upper lip showing that Terrell had been sharing his bounty. Nancy sat on a chair near the head of the bed. Brittany had somehow managed to find room to perch near Terrell's feet. All three girls had apparently been talking at once, but they fell to glowering silence when Adara entered.

"How are you feeling?" Adara asked awkwardly.

"Bruised and battered," Terrell replied with a chuckle that made light of his injuries, "but well enough to be up and about if Helena hadn't promised to hand me my head if I moved. How are you? That spider was flinging you about pretty hard."

Adara noticed that Brittany's eyes had narrowed at this reminder of how Adara had shared Terrell's peril.

"Well enough. I wrenched my left shoulder. Annie Greengrass sent something along that's eased it. I expect I got off light."

Nancy and Brittany both looked as if they wanted to agree. Terrell indicated the jug that Adara carried.

"That wouldn't be some of Bruin's cherry cider, would it?"

"It would. Not the hard stuff. Annie Greengrass advised against that, but some that's nicely aged. Would you like a mug full?"

Terrell agreed he would and indicated a tray that held a pitcher and several clean mugs. When he had his drink in hand, he gave the three sisters a winning smile.

"Now, much as it sours me to admit it, I need to have

words with Adara the Huntress. Then I think I'll sleep. If you don't mind . . ."

His tone made these words a dismissal. Sashi was happy enough to go, but the elder two were distinctly resentful. Adara swallowed a sigh as she imagined what they'd say when they joined the gossipy flock outside. No helping it, though . . . She wondered how many ears would be pressed to the door, how many pairs of eyes would peek in at the windows. Never mind, if they hoped to learn something more to fuel their malice, they'd be disappointed.

When the three sisters had left, Terrell patted the chair Nancy had vacated.

"Take a seat. I've heard some about how the battle ended, but most of it secondhand. You truly are not injured?"

"Truly."

"And Bruin . . . He is well?"

"His hair got a little scorched by the blast that caught you and Coal. He makes light of it, saying he needed to have his hair cropped anyhow."

"Good, then . . ." Terrell sipped his cider. "Helena tells me—reluctantly and with a great deal of bitterness—that this newcomer, Griffin Dane, was the one who pulled me clear both of the fire and of Coal."

"Yes. Griffin did. He's been worried he hurt you by dragging you so fast."

"Not at all," Terrell said. "If I collected a few more bruises, well, I would have more if Coal had stepped—or fallen—on me."

This last was self-evident, so Adara didn't comment. Nor did she ask why Helena was bitter. Clearly, like Mistress Cheesemaker, she blamed Griffin for the arrival of the spider.

"Adara." Terrell swallowed hard. "Adara . . . Helena tells me that Bruin told Mistress Cheesemaker that Griffin Dane will be leaving Shepherd's Call in a few days."

"Yes," Adara confirmed. "Bruin and I—and of course Sand Shadow and Honeychild—will be escorting him. Bruin wants Griffin to speak with Bruin's own teacher, the Old One Who Is Young, in Spirit Bay."

Terrell frowned. Factotums trained with the loremasters. He was clearly putting Bruin's plan together with the metal spider and drawing conclusions of his own.

"That one?" Terrell looked interested, but also apprehensive. "The one who knows more lore than the loremasters—although the loremasters often question his conclusions. That one. You'll be asking Helena for horses?"

"I will," Adara agreed. "Only horses trained by such as her will tolerate Sand Shadow and Honeychild without a great deal of adjustment. Even if we were to walk as far as Blue Meadow, we could not hope to find steeds with such training. And—well, there are reasons for our moving more quickly than walking pace."

"On a long journey," Terrell reminded her, "a horse does not go much faster than a human. You cannot gallop all day—not even canter or trot without alternating with a slower gait."

"True," Adara said. "But a walking horse can carry a great deal more than a walking human. With horses we can bring our own supplies and not need to worry about stopping in every town."

Terrell nodded. "Good point. I have lived enough months in Shepherd's Call to forget that Honeychild and Sand Shadow would not be welcomed in some places."

There was a note in his voice that told Adara that Terrell had something in mind, but she had learned from Bruin's example to hold her peace. At the fringes of her mind, she could just feel Sand Shadow. The distance was too great for her to get any solid impression, but she sensed that the great cat was frustrated. Doubtless backtracking the spider's trail had been as disappointing as they had dreaded.

"Adara," Terrell said at last, "when I first heard the rumors that Griffin Dane was no longer welcome here in Shepherd's Call, I knew that I must go with him. I owe him some return on the risk he took to get me to safety."

Adara blinked. "You would go with us?"

"Rather, I will go with *him*," Terrell stated, "whether you go or not. I can't say I like the man—even that I have much of a sense of him—but he ran into fire and beneath the hooves of a pain-maddened horse to pull me to safety. I cannot ignore the debt."

"Have you told Helena?"

"I have. She is . . . less than happy. I believe she has gone up to the sheepfolds to ride herself calm and seek Bert's counsel. However, although I came here to learn from her, there is no contract between us as between apprentice and master. Helena is anything but unfair. She may rage and trumpet, but she will come around. In the end, she will loan the horses you need, all the more willingly because I am going with you. Like many of the village elders, she wants Griffin Dane gone."

Adara fought down an unexpected rush of anger. "Griffin Dane did nothing. Is a rabbit to blame when the puma hunts it?"

"Not to blame," Terrell replied. "I agree, but is this Griffin Dane innocent of the threat he offered?"

"I think he was innocent," Adara answered, "though now he blames himself. If Bruin and I were not delaying him so we can we make preparations, I think Griffin would have left here alone without so much as a loaf of bread or a bottle of water."

"You admire him?"

Given Terrell's interest in Adara, the question was fraught with hidden meanings, but Adara chose to reply only to what had been said.

"I see qualities in him to admire."

"As do I . . ." Terrell gave a gusty sigh. "Then you will accept my coming with you?"

"Gladly," Adara said. She hated how Terrell's blue eyes brightened, but she only spoke the truth. Factotums had been trained in the days of the seegnur to act as guides and facilitators for the visitors from afar. Those who still followed the profession were skilled in every aspect of comfortable travel. She would be an idiot not to welcome Terrell's help. "Very gladly indeed."

When they left Shepherd's Call on the third day following the coming of the spider, once again Griffin Dane couldn't help but think how much tougher the people of Artemis were than those he knew. Certainly, genetic modifications would help, but there was a philosophical acceptance that pain and injury were part of life that was rare on Sierra.

Does this date to their lore? Perhaps because "seegnur" on holiday would not have liked to listen to whining? Or is it because they lack the pain-controlling drugs and nerve blocks that are routinely used at home? The training my parents insisted we all have—much as I hated that horrible school—did set our family apart.

Terrell the Factotum remained stiff and sore from his injuries, but he insisted that he was beyond the point where idleness would speed his healing. Without any of the pain control or other medications Griffin had taken for granted, Terrell had been up and about by the second day. Today he was riding with relative ease.

Griffin had been astonished by the man's offer to come along with them. He'd asked Bruin's advice and Bruin had pressed him to accept.

"Adara and I are good enough on the trail—none better—but a factotum's training is broader based. Terrell will be useful to you both when you come into contact with other settlements and after you arrive in Spirit Bay."

Griffin nodded. "I'll take your word for that. How does a factotum make a living these days, now that there aren't any seegnur to wait on?"

"Many act as guides for merchant caravans or groups of travelers. They also work with the loremasters, spreading the lore to isolated regions, searching out promising children and nominating them for further education." Bruin chuckled and scratched his belly. "Really, if the seegnur returned, they might need to book a factotum's services in advance. The profession calls for physical endurance, and a willingness to absorb both practical skills and a great amount of knowledge. There aren't many qualified."

The sincerity in Terrell's clear blue eyes had left no doubt that his gratitude toward Griffin was genuine. However, noting how Terrell watched Adara when he thought the huntress wouldn't notice, remembering Adara's scream of grief and rage when Terrell had been thrown, Griffin wondered if there wasn't more to Terrell's offer than archaic chivalry.

Adara did not give Terrell much encouragement. She treated him and Griffin alike. Griffin didn't know what to think of this. He knew he found Adara attractive. Those nights spent sleeping close came back to him at very inopportune times, but he was too aware of his dependence on her and Bruin—and even Terrell—to risk doing anything to offend her.

But whatever the true reason for Terrell's offer to accompany them, he was too valuable an asset to turn away. Even so, Griffin would only agree to let Terrell come along if the factotum was filled in on the truth regarding how Griffin had come to Artemis—and why he might be a magnet for further trouble.

Terrell accepted the news with more ease than he might have if the metal spider had not made its attack. In a strange way, Griffin's extraplanetary origins made recent events extraordinary rather than inexplicable. Terrell also agreed with Adara and Bruin that this information should be shared only when absolutely necessary.

When they left Shepherd's Call, their company was eleven: four humans, four horses, a bear, a puma, and a singularly ornery mule to carry the heavier baggage. The mule—who was called Sam—was a difficult beast and would permit no one but Terrell to work with him.

That an animal should be allowed an opinion was a new way of thinking for Griffin. He hadn't had much difficulty stretching his mind around the idea that Sand Shadow was a person. Adara's attitude toward the puma had made this clear from the start. Then, too, an enormous predator demanded a certain amount of respect. Once they struck out on the road and Honeychild was not a more or less drowsy heap of fur and appetite, Griffin found himself easily extending to the bear the attitude he had formed toward the puma.

But that Sam the Mule and the four horses should be thought of in the same way took a little effort—perhaps because their assigned role was basically servile. Griffin's horse was an aging chestnut mare named Molly. Molly was graced with a flaxen mane and tail. A wide white blaze went from beneath her forelock to between her nostrils.

Even with only theoretical knowledge of how to ride a horse—Griffin had brainloaded a course on the subject on Sierra, since his research had indicated that horses had been common transportation on Artemis—Griffin could sit Molly with hardly more effort than he might his favorite reading chair. Molly obediently followed whatever lead the other horses set, leaving Griffin plenty of time to daydream.

It wasn't until their second day on the trail, when a sudden wind sent both Adara and Bruin's mounts to dancing and crow-hopping, that Griffin accepted the truth. Molly wasn't docile and obedient; she was a skilled professional who realized her rider was a complete incompetent. She maintained her poise in order to care for him, even when she would have preferred to act up. Humbled, that night Griffin gathered a bunch of young grass and sweet herbs for Molly by way of thanks.

Terrell rode Midnight, a full brother to the late Coal, although gelded. One thing Griffin gathered early on was that stallions were not usual riding animals—they were too inclined to flirt with the mares and fight with other stallions. Most male horses were gelded, unless they showed promise as studs.

Adara's mount was a smoky roan named Tarnish after how her coat darkened from silver along her rump and barrel to thundercloud grey along her neck, mane, and tail. Tarnish's face was ornamented with a blaze that widened as it flowed down from below her forelock to above her nostrils. Her independent temper was good for a horse who must carry Adara, for the huntress had a tendency to slip off her mount in order to scout, leaving the horse to take care of herself.

The final member of the herd was the stout liver chestnut called Block who carried Bruin. Block's basic sturdiness concealed a sharp temper. Indeed, Griffin rapidly learned that stolid-seeming Block was more likely to snap or kick than flashy Midnight.

"All showing," Terrell commented, "as Helena likes to say, that appearances are a lousy way to judge horseflesh."

The road to Blue Meadow was one wagon wide, the deep ruts in the dirt testifying to generations of traffic. Once they were a day out from Shepherd's Call, the road was hardly more than an indication of the direction in which they should travel. When there was rain—as there was almost daily—the dirt became mud. That meant that every night the horse's hooves needed cleaning. Griffin squared his shoulders and asked Terrell to teach him what was necessary.

And here I am, he thought, as he gently eased dirt from the frog of Molly's foot, *who has been called one of the*

*rising historians of my age, acting as junior groom and
camp keeper.*

Although Griffin was aware of the irony, he was not
unhappy. His plans had included a long stay on Artemis—or at least in orbit—while he did his initial research.
In the course of his life, Griffin had learned that focusing on an immediate goal was better than brooding over
an uncontrollable future. Right now, that goal was gain-
ing the trust of allies who would help him. He could sense
that his willingness to work had earned him the others'
respect. And, unlike a "real" groom, Griffin comforted
himself with the hope his future held something more.

They were midway to Blue Meadow when they came
upon a man hung against the trunk of a roadside hickory. Sand Shadow, who was advance scout, found him
first and reported to Adara.

"He's alive," Adara said as they urged their mounts to
greater speed, "but unconscious. Sand Shadow says the
man's scent is familiar, although she doesn't know why.
She also smells dogs."

When they drew close to where Sand Shadow waited,
Bruin spoke. "That's Fred! He's the one who was supposed to bring young Kipper to me. Seems I was right to
worry."

Griffin leapt off Molly and hurried to hold Fred steady
while Terrell slashed through the ropes that dug into the
man's flesh. Fred had been tied so tightly against the tree's
bark that his struggles had rubbed raw patches in his exposed skin. He had the sort of wiry, knobbly build that,
at best, would never have held much flesh. Now he was
positively gaunt. When Griffin eased him down, Fred
moaned in pain.

Adara had been casting around for signs of what had
happened.

"There's been too much rain for me to tell for certain,"
she stated, "but I'm guessing Fred was attacked when he'd

stopped for the night. I've camped here myself. It's a common stop along the road between Blue Meadow and Shepherd's Call. There's not much sign left of the people who did this, but the indications are that they went south—not that that takes much thought. The road only goes two ways."

Terrell was kindling a fire in the stone ring that was—at least to Griffin's way of seeing things—the only indication that anyone had ever camped here before. Griffin led the horses off the road, then removed his bedroll from behind Molly's saddle.

Bruin had been easing water between Fred's lips. Then he spread brawny arms and carried the semiconscious man over to where Griffin had spread the bedroll next to the newly kindled fire.

"Smart thinking," Bruin grunted. Griffin was embarrassed by how good that brief praise felt. "We'll need more water."

Griffin fetched water from a nearby stream while Terrell and Bruin carefully removed Fred's tattered clothing. Adara had vanished, along with both Sand Shadow and Honeychild.

Adara reappeared not too long after. "Found the trail. Wasn't easy. If the ground hadn't been so wet and if I hadn't had Sand Shadow and Honeychild to help, I'm not sure even I could have located which way the attackers went."

"Not good," Bruin said, "but not as much of a surprise as I would wish."

Terrell added, "Where are the demiurges?"

"Following the trail farther," Adara replied. "Honeychild wanted to nose out whatever was there in case it rains again and washes out the remaining scent. Sand Shadow stayed to protect her. How's Fred?"

Bruin answered. "Dehydrated. He'll be hungry when he stops hurting. Nasty bump on his head, another under his jaw. Otherwise, he wasn't hurt."

Griffin offered, "How about I make broth from the leftovers of this morning's rabbit?"

"Good thought," Bruin said.

When Griffin headed for the cooking gear and leftover food, he found Terrell ahead of him, unstrapping various bundles from Sam the Mule's back.

"You know how to cook broth on a fire?" Terrell asked, as he handed Griffin the pack containing the cooking gear.

Griffin gave a half-smile. "I wouldn't have before my hike down the mountains with Adara."

"Ah . . ."

There was no question that they would camp, even though many hours of daylight remained. Adara vanished again. Terrell settled the horses and Sam the Mule, then began putting up the tents.

Adara returned as Terrell was pounding in the last tent peg, dragging behind her a very large, extremely bedraggled dog.

"Saw the prints," she explained as she tied her prize to a tree where it could see Fred. "This one and at least one other were with Fred. This fellow has a hurt paw, so I was able to catch up to him. His partner may be skulking behind."

Once it realized it couldn't break free, the dog alternated between growling at the strangers and whining anxiously in Fred's direction.

"Toss the dog some bread," Bruin said to Griffin. "We'll ignore him for a while. Once he sees we're not harming Fred, he'll calm down."

The dog accepted the bread. Then, growling softly, he settled as close as he could get to his unconscious master.

By evening, Fred had come around enough to relate in small fragments, with many breaks between, what had happened.

He'd traveled with a trade caravan as far as Blue Meadow. After assuring himself that there were no rumors of bandit activity, Fred had felt safe continuing to Shepherd's Call on his own. That Kipper had been as excited about going to Bruin as he'd been apprehensive about staying in town had been the deciding factor.

They'd traded for fresh horses in Blue Meadow and so had made good time. All seemed well right up until the moment Fred had been awakened by the sound of one of his dogs barking. The dogs might have been fine guards, but they were no match for what came into the little camp.

"Told the hounds to scram, I did," Fred explained, his voice little more than a creaky rasp. "No need for them to get hurt. Then I got hit, first in the gut, then here."

He motioned toward his jaw. "Went out. Next thing, I was on that tree. Dogs came back, but they can't undo knots. Horses were gone. Kid was gone. I'd given up hope just about."

Terrell asked, "Did you know any of them? Hear them say anything?"

"Nope. Heard the kid screaming. I can't say for sure, but I think they didn't kill me outright because if they had he'd never have accepted them. They'll want him to think they're not so bad."

"Not so bad?" Griffin was incredulous. "After they beat you up, stole your property, and kidnapped him? They actually think they can come across as anything but scoundrels?"

Adara spoke for Fred. "They can and for good reason. Kipper's family didn't want him. From what Fred says, Kipper was placing a lot of hope in Bruin. All they've got to do is convince him that they're a better choice. Believe me, it won't be that hard."

Griffin remembered how Adara had spoken of her parents, of the division Bruin had indicated existed between the adapted and the unadapted.

"So you think these kidnappers are adapted? That they stole Kipper because he's adapted?"

Adara nodded. "I'd go further and say that at least one of those who attacked Fred has trained as a hunter. They were too good at hiding their trail for it to be luck. Honeychild has a bear's nose and is trained for tracking, but even she lost the trail—and nothing so simple as crossing a stream would be enough to stop her."

"I'll make the next guess," Terrell offered. "I'd say that they knew Bruin would be on their trail—Bruin and you, Adara. If they had taken the boy before Blue Meadow, then perhaps not, but where else could Fred have been taking Kipper?"

The two hunters nodded agreement. Griffin thought that some sort of modesty had kept them from saying as much themselves.

"None of this means," Bruin said, "that we will not try to find them and reclaim Kipper. The boy was entrusted to me. His parents may not have known what to do with him, but they did not abandon him. They found him a teacher. I owe them as much as I owe their son."

Interlude: Between Waking and Sleeping

I know you by your scent, your taste.
    <Activation sequence commencing.>
Scion sprig slipped beneath my bark.
    <Loading. Sequencing. Checking compatibility.>
Without you, part of me, forever fruitless.
    <Compatibility confirmed. Firing up.>
With you, expanding potential.
    <Awaiting orders.>
With you, eternal bondage.
    <Awaiting orders.>

9
Hunting of the Fish

Griffin insisted on joining them in their search for Kipper.

"Are you sure, Griffin?" Adara asked when they had a moment's privacy. "The Old One at Spirit Bay may have answers to your questions. Terrell can get you there."

Griffin didn't even raise his gaze from the tubers he was peeling. "The day I stop caring about the fate of a kidnapped child is the day I deserve to be stuck planetside. Count me in."

Fred's second dog came back that night. When the pair were cleaned up, they proved to be brown and white dogs of no particular breed. They had long noses, sturdy legs useful for traveling, and broad chests that meant they were probably strong fighters.

The dogs were not adapted, no more than was their master, but that didn't mean they were useless. Fred called them Scout and Shout, and was obviously very fond of them.

Although Griffin's participation was accepted, Fred's raised some argument. Given how weak the man was, the wisest thing would have been to take him either to Blue Meadow or Shepherd's Call. Fred would have none of this.

"Kipper was my charge, as much or more than Bruin's," he stated with a stubborn set to his lips. "I'm coming with you."

So Fred rode with them, sometimes on Tarnish, for Adara often went on foot to better read the trail, sometimes behind either Adara or Terrell. Adara privately thought that Fred would be useful when they needed to leave the horses and gear. Griffin had learned a lot, but there were so many things he didn't know.

Although the kidnappers had shown tremendous skill in hiding their trail, in Bruin they were up against someone who had been teaching both the arts of hiding and of finding trails for so long that the only new tricks in the book were those he had written himself.

Moreover, in Honeychild, Bruin had a perfect partner. Bears in general possessed a keen sense of smell—so much so that they were often called "noses on legs." In her years with Bruin, Honeychild had refined her use of that sense. Where a wild bear might be able to smell the odors of a garbage heap from as far as two miles distant, Honeychild not only could smell the heap, but analyze what she smelled and pass that information on to Bruin.

"It isn't as if they weren't careful," Bruin said, when he informed the rest that he had found the trail. "From what Honeychild has gathered, they have been very careful. They have circled back into the foothills, away from the major waterways where they might be seen by trappers or hunters. However, there is only so far one can go in hiding the scent of a large community. Humans, horses, and dogs are all quite smelly in their own ways. Add in the piquant note of scents that shouldn't be part of the mix—there are at least three bobcats—and we have our group."

They were seated around a small campfire in their latest camp when Bruin made his announcement. Griffin Dane turned from where he had been cleaning some herbage that would be stuffed into the grouse that were the centerpiece of tonight's dinner.

"But can't the same be said for us?" he asked. "Three men, a woman, two dogs, four horses, a mule, a bear, and a puma."

Bruin nodded. "The same can be said, but we have a few advantages. For one, we are a smaller group. For another, we have a bear with us. Honeychild has not scented a bear with the others. Also, they are settled. Their scent hovers like a fog over their residence."

Adara leaned forward. "What do we do when we get

there, Bruin? Do we try to steal the boy back or do we confront them?"

Bruin replied, "At first, I'd thought to simply steal the boy back. I'm not as flexible as I once was, but I'd bet you and Sand Shadow could pull it off. Now, though . . . I have a hankering to learn who these people are and why they think they can get away with stealing the ward of Bruin the Hunter."

"I agree," Terrell said. "We've circled several days beyond Blue Meadow and farther even from Shepherd's Call, but not so far that a cocky raider might not consider either town or village fair game. We need to make sure they're not a threat."

"I'd been thinking something like that," Bruin agreed. "I'm guessing that we're after a group that made things too hot for themselves somewhere else. They fled and once they fled, they cast around for empty lands. Even in the days of the seegnur, these mountains were not heavily populated. Now . . ."

His shrug was eloquent.

"So we all go in," Fred said querulously. "Don't think I didn't guess that you planned on leaving me back with the horses. I've got ears."

"Fred," Terrell said, "taking you in would be offering a challenge, wouldn't it? After all, these are the people who attacked you and left you hanging on that hickory tree."

"Maybe so. Maybe so," the man agreed, "but remember, I'm the only one that boy Kipper knows. That should count for something. I could play dumb. I could make out that I have no idea who attacked me, but that once you folks came along and cut me down, well, I put Shout and Scout on the trail and they led me right there."

"That would not seem a reasonable explanation," Bruin protested. "The kidnappers know they hid their trail better than that."

"All right, then," Fred cut in, still determined. "Here's

another tale we could give. You helped me, because we were all worried about the boy. We could even imply we thought they rescued him."

"Might work," Bruin agreed. "Here's what I think. Tonight we'll send Adara out to scout. Tomorrow—unless Adara gives us reason to think otherwise—we ride openly toward this settlement."

"What if they attack us?" Griffin asked.

"Then we fight back," Terrell said, flashing his teeth. "You saw us when we fought that metal spider. We are not precisely helpless."

That night, Adara and Sand Shadow ate their dinner, then curled up to sleep while the night stretched out and grew comfortably dark. A soft touch from Bruin woke them at the agreed-upon hour.

Adara loved the night. That love was one of the first things that had alienated her from her birth family. Whereas other children her age drifted off to sleep with gathering dusk, Adara grew more alert. Where other children saw goblins and nightfears in every shadow, she simply saw. Quickly, too, she realized that her parents did not see. She took great amusement in hiding night-masked right under their noses. This impish variation on hide-and-seek had not made her precisely popular.

With Sand Shadow acting as guide, they set off soon after awakening. Early spring rains had left the leaves moist enough that, with her feet clad in soft-soled boots, Adara could run with as little sound as did the puma. They set their paths slightly apart, close enough that they could aid each other if need arose.

Sand Shadow warned Adara when they reached where running should give way to skulking. Even without this foreknowledge, Adara would have seen the signs. The kidnappers had been careful not to leave indications that would be visible to a casual traveler, but Adara was a huntress and saw the signs in shifted rock or bent brush, in harvested herbage and gathered bulbs.

Adara knew to expect the log palisade fortification that awaited her at the end of the journey. However, a puma's eyes saw shapes without human understanding, so when they reached the fort, Adara studied it carefully. The walls were large and carefully built, set in a clearing that had been expanded by harvesting the trees. A stream ran through the clearing and beneath the log walls before emerging on the fort's far side where it eventually joined a larger tributary.

Some distance from the palisade, the ground showed indication of having been worked, probably in preparation for a garden plot. A strong whiff of horse manure came from the turned soil. A heap of neatly trimmed saplings to one side indicated that this future gardener knew perfectly well that deer and rabbits were no respecters of human crops.

Adara sprang lightly into the lower limbs of a large maple at the outer edge of the clearing. When she was certain she was unobserved, she climbed high enough that she could see over the palisade walls. The structures within were about evenly split between newly built cabins and somewhat worn tents. Most of the livestock was on the small side, but she did see a few horses. Sand Shadow assured her there was also at least one cow.

In Shepherd's Call at this hour, there would be little or no human activity. Darkness was an effective inhibitor of such, especially since fuel for lanterns and candles was valuable. Within this fort, by contrast, Adara saw movement. The guards walking the catwalk she had expected, for although the defenses were strongly made, they would not stop a puma tempted by a meal of horse.

Or cow . . . Sand Shadow sent a grisly image into Adara's mind.

A bear could probably dig under those walls, if given

enough time and sufficient incentive. And then, of course, people who stole children must take precautions in case someone came looking for them. Therefore, the guards did not particularly surprise Adara, but the figures crossing the open plaza, clearly going about routine duties, did. They carried neither lanterns nor candles, yet moved with a certainty that seemed to indicate that they shared Adara's ease with darkness.

Although Adara had taken care to choose a limb for her perch that had enough growth to conceal her, she found herself pressing down against the branch, merging her form into the bulk of the tree. As far as she knew, she would be hidden even in broad daylight, but she had been spoiled by living among those who—with the exception of Bruin—had no gift for seeing in the dark.

Very well, she thought. *We had guessed that at least some of those we followed were adapted.*

Adara watched a while longer, but even night-adapted eyes could not see more than was offered. Not wanting to be anywhere near when daylight came, she made her way down the side of the maple that faced away from the palisade. Then she hastened back to give her report.

The next morning, Griffin listened as Adara summarized what she had seen. Initially, the huntress had focused only on facts, but then Bruin invited her conjecture. Adara gave these with an appreciation for the implications of detail that Griffin's military-minded brothers would have appreciated.

"I'm guessing they arrived there sometime late last summer. The palisade showed some weathering and they've had time to build cabins. However, the new garden plot was the only one I saw, so they weren't there last growing season—or if they were, they didn't have the resources to spare for a garden.

"I can't hazard how large a community it is but, based upon the amount of labor and the number of structures, there have to be a couple dozen occupants at the least. I counted six or seven moving around after dark, including the two guards on the walls.

"Whoever set the place up knew what they were doing. Sand Shadow and I checked the brook they're using for water downstream from the palisade. The water was nearly as pure as it went in. That means they're being careful with not only their own waste but with watering their animals. If they were letting them drink directly from the stream, the water would be tainted with churned up mud. Horses—and particularly cows—are no respecters of streambanks."

She paused and Terrell offered, "They might also have a separate well or spring. This is well-watered land and a spring would be reason for locating their fort where they did."

Bruin asked, "Adara, did you feel that palisade was meant to keep wild animals out or humans in?"

"Both. I can't really say why . . ." Adara paused and considered. "I think it was the height and the strength of the walls. Most animals are turned away just by the odor of humans gathered in one place. This area isn't over-hunted, so most of the wild creatures would choose to go elsewhere rather than force their way in for the dubious reward of fighting humans, then eating their food. So a heavy wall wouldn't be needed unless they have either enemies or prisoners."

"You didn't," Fred asked, "catch a glimpse of Kipper, did you?"

Adara shook her head. "All the figures I saw moving around were adults."

"Well," said Bruin, getting to his feet with an enormous stretch, "we'll know more today. You said you found a way we can approach with the horses?"

"I did," Adara said. "They've hidden the trail well,

especially farther out from their base, but they did bring in several larger animals—including, I'd guess, Fred's horses."

"I'd like to have those horses back," the man said. "They're good creatures, trail broken. Not much surprises them. Still, getting them back may be too much to hope for."

"I'm still wondering," Terrell said, "why they left Fred the way they did. If they wanted to spare his life, why not leave him knocked out until they'd gotten away? Hanging him in the hickory tree like that . . . It's neither here nor there."

"That's puzzled me, too," Bruin admitted. "I've thought and thought, but I just can't come up with anything that seems right. Guess we'll have to ask the folks who did it and see if we believe what they say."

Traveling on Artemis was definitely redefining how Griffin thought about terms like "road" and "trail." Certainly, he wouldn't ever have dignified what they traveled on that day with the term "trail," but he had to admit that the route by which Adara guided them never failed to admit not only them but their animals. True, sometimes it was necessary to dismount and walk, bending back flexible limbs that would otherwise snap back with stinging force. That was bad enough when you just walloped yourself, but when you hit one of the animals, they took it less than kindly.

Despite the spring rains, the ground underfoot did not mire, nor were the numerous streamlets too deep to ford. By midday, Adara was silently pointing out the various indications that others had used this route not long before: the edge of a hoofprint, a bit of wilted foliage, a rock rolled wrong side up.

Even so, to Griffin, the clearing with the palisade at its center seemed to appear out of nowhere. One moment he was ducking under a low-hanging limb, the next there was open space in front of him. What had momentarily seemed like a particularly thick stand of tree trunks revealed itself as a log wall.

Terrell was riding point, Adara and Bruin covering him from the trees. As soon as Midnight carried Terrell into the open, the factotum hailed the presumed but still unseen watchers.

"Ho, the fort! Travelers come calling."

Griffin admired the factotum's boldness. Sure, Adara and Bruin were armed and waiting, but the threat they offered would not stop an arrow shot. At best, their return fire would stop a second volley.

But no arrows came. Instead a single male voice, the sound oddly thinned over the open field, gave an answering call.

"Ho, the travelers. Would that old bear Benjamin Hunter be one of your number?"

Despite their speculations, Griffin was surprised by the direct challenge, but Bruin shouted back without pause.

"This is Ben Hunter. I've come calling for my student. Seems he got lost along the way to Shepherd's Call."

The reply came so quickly that this might have been call and response in a well-known dance. "So we thought might be the case. Well, come forth and get him. In fact, why don't you and your friends all come in? Night's coming on. We can offer you a roof against the weather."

They'd already discussed what they might do if such an invitation was offered. Now Bruin gave the prepared response.

"Kind of you. We'll be right along."

Griffin had thought the entire group's going in was very unwise, given that they knew these were kidnappers. However, the others had pointed out that their entire group only amounted to five humans.

"And if they are strong enough to take us five," Adara had explained, "they're strong enough to take us two and three—especially with Fred still so weak. Sand Shadow and Honeychild will stay out as backup."

So when the gates of the palisade swung open, they rode in, five humans, four horses, and a mule. Scout and Shout clung near Tarnish—whom Fred was riding—their tucked tails and flattened ears proof enough that they associated the scents of this place with nothing good.

Adara brought up the rear, loping over the broken ground, her longbow in one hand and a brace of still-warm game birds dangling from the other. The birds had lovely long tail feathers and a plumpness that argued that for them the winter had not been too hard.

"For the pot," Adara said, thrusting the birds into the grasp of one of the men by the gate. Then she turned and helped close the gates, that gesture robbing the action of any threat it might have held.

The man gaped and muttered something that might have been thanks. Griffin swallowed a grin and looked around. He guessed that most of the fort's inhabitants were still under cover. A few were stepping out, trying to seem casual and mostly failing. However, the woman who emerged from the largest building didn't bother to pretend anything.

She was not large, nor terribly strongly built but, despite an undeniable limp, she moved with confident alertness. Her brown hair was cut short and ragged, the color highlighted with touches of red that might have been artificial. She had very pale eyes, neither grey nor blue, but somewhere between.

Like her associates, this woman was clad in clothing that showed evidence of having been mended, the original homespun fabrics augmented with tanned leather at knees and elbows. Her knee-high boots were soft leather, laced up the front. Against the cool spring weather, she wore a fur vest that nonetheless was cut so that there was no doubt that the wearer was female.

From how the men at the gate and up on the palisade

reacted to her arrival, this woman was clearly someone in authority. How Bruin and Adara reacted was a little less clear.

"Lynn?" Bruin said, his tone holding wonder and incredulity. "I thought you were settled down in the lowlands. Last I heard you had a good place as a gamekeeper for one of the big farming estates."

"So I did," Lynn replied, "and so I was, until your old teacher—and mine—sold me out. I escaped with my life and the lives of most of my family, which is more than many who have crossed him can say."

"What?" Bruin's reply rumbled from a growl into a roar.

"You've been too long hibernating in the foothills, old bear," Lynn said. "Come inside and rest yourself. There are others here who may be able to convince you that what I'm saying is the truth."

At Bruin's gesture, Adara trailed after her mentor when he followed Lynn into the largest and most finished of the cabins. Adara hardly knew what to think of this new twist. If she'd expected anything, it had been some sort of blustering exchange, followed by the price Kipper's kidnappers would set for his freedom.

She padded in Bruin's wake into the large, multipurpose room that comprised the entire ground floor of the cabin. One corner framed by long tables had been set up as a cooking and eating area. Another area, fronting a second fireplace, was furnished both with chairs and built-in benches. A plank ceiling not only helped hold the heat, but a ladder leading to the upper area indicated useful space, probably both for storage and as a sleeping loft.

A few of Lynn's associates—Adara was fairly certain she recognized Lynn's husband, Hal, among the men—had come with them. Most had ostentatiously returned to whatever duties had occupied them before the travelers' arrival. To Adara this deliberate lack of fuss, especially since it was likely that the community had seen few strangers since the previous autumn, made a statement of its own.

Lynn motioned for the new arrivals to make themselves comfortable near the second fireplace. She herself took a seat on a straight-backed chair. It was evident that most of the inhabitants made do with stools, benches, or, in the case of the children, with the packed earth floor. When Lynn stretched her crippled leg out in front of her and leaned gratefully against the chair back, it was evident why this extra effort had been made on her behalf.

"Where do I start?" Lynn asked, perhaps more to herself than to anyone present.

She certainly seemed surprised when Fred said, "Kipper! Where is Kipper? Is he well? You can start with that."

Bruin made a vague rumble of agreement and Lynn sighed. "Yes. We might as well settle that. You'll be too distracted to listen otherwise. Robby?"

A young man with rusty brown hair scampered up the ladder. The heavy planks that made up the ceiling effectively muffled most sound, but Adara's keen ears caught scraps of conversation. Not long after, Robby returned, followed by a smaller boy.

Kipper looked to be seven or eight, the age when a boy has lost his baby fat but hadn't yet started shooting up. His thick, wheaty hair stuck out at angles, suggesting that he might have been asleep. He examined the gathering with a somber, noncommunicative expression, but his features brightened as soon as he saw Fred.

"Fred! Fred!"

The two words spoke volumes, about fear, about joy, about loneliness and uncertainty.

No matter what anyone tells us later, Adara thought, *I will not believe that Kipper left Fred willingly.*

Fred gave the boy an uneven grin. "It's Fred. Good to see you, Kipper lad."

"Go on over to Fred, Kip," Lynn urged. "See for yourself he's all right."

Kipper raced over. While the boy was distracted, Bruin said softly, "Fred's all right, though not for any great care on the part of you and your friends, Lynn."

"I wasn't actually there," Lynn replied. "This leg of mine means I don't get about as well as I once did."

"You're evading," Adara cut in. She didn't know Lynn well, but what she did know had always given her reason to respect the other woman. Finding Lynn involved with kidnapping, uttering cryptic accusations, seemed completely out of character. "How do you explain hanging Fred in a tree?"

"Later I'll introduce you to Ring," Lynn said. "How to explain Ring? You and I and Bruin have eyes that see well in the dark. Ring, he sees, too, but not with his eyes, so much. He was with the group that went out when we got rumor of Kipper. The others would have left Fred to come around on his own, but Ring wouldn't let them. He's not very good at explaining what he sees, but what he saw was enough to make him frantic until Fred was gotten clear of the ground. And Fred lived, didn't he?"

"If we hadn't come when we did," Terrell replied, "Fred might not have."

"But he did," Lynn insisted, "and if Ring is to be believed, he would not have. I've reason to trust Ring's impulses. So did those who listened to him that day."

Clearly, Terrell wanted to argue further. As clearly, he saw there would be no purpose to it. While Terrell had been speaking, Fred had introduced Kipper to Bruin. The little boy was tongue-tied with awe and delight, so apparently Lynn had done nothing to lower the boy's estimation of his new teacher.

Lynn waited patiently until the introductions were over,

then she said, "Fred? Bruin? Now that you've reassured yourselves that Kipper is here and unharmed, would you mind if the boy went out with my Robby? We've a lot to talk about and not all of what I need to say is suited for young ears."

Bruin considered. For a moment, Adara thought he would refuse, that he would insist on gathering up Kipper and getting them all out of there. Then he sighed and settled himself.

"If the boy will go, then he may, but he's not to vanish."

Lynn laughed, a genuine, heartfelt sound. "As if anyone could be made to vanish with you and Adara so close at hand—and doubtless a bear or wildcat or so outside the walls. You have my word. Kipper will be yours to claim when you wish—and if he wishes."

"I do!" piped the boy. "Like I told you before. Bruin is to be my teacher."

"Then he will be," Lynn agreed. "Go out now and help Robby. We adults have dull things to discuss."

With a quick hug for Fred and a bounce that might have been a bow for both Bruin and Lynn, Kipper scampered after the older boy. There was a shifting among the gathered adults as well. Some of the men went out, though Lynn's husband, Hal, remained. A quite old lady came in, a basket of eggs over her arm. She began to mess about in the corner that served as a kitchen. The others who remained seated themselves at a long table where they could both assist with the food preparation and listen to the conversation.

Lynn surveyed her guests. "And these? I recognize Adara, of course, but I don't know the rest."

"Terrell the Factotum," Bruin said, "recently of Shepherd's Call. He and Adara are escorting this other man—Griffin Dane—to Spirit Bay."

Adara thought Lynn might ask more, but at the words "Spirit Bay" her eyes widened, then narrowed.

"How long is it, Bruin, since you've been down to Spirit Bay?"

"It has been a few years," Bruin admitted. "Five years? Eight? I'm not as young as I was, you know. Long trips don't suit me as once they did. Even when I don't have students, I do have business to occupy me."

"So it has been at least five years since you've seen the Old One?"

"Maybe closer to eight," Bruin replied thoughtfully. "We do write letters though, quite long ones, sometimes. I'd gathered all was well."

"I suppose it is," Lynn replied, "for him."

Bruin frowned. "You've gone to great trouble to bring me here—even though you know where I live and could have come to me. Now will you explain why you've set bait to lure this old bear?"

"For that," Lynn said, "I need to go back in time, to when I was our mutual teacher's youngest protégée and you were his most admired. Although I didn't know it then, that was when the trail that brought you here today had its beginning."

Interlude: Uneasy Sensations

Grumbles, rumbles, deep down beneath,
   there where darkness does yet keep.
Drowsy drumbles, peep, peep, peep,
   bounces off, for hearer sleeps.
Aching, itching along the spine
   of a backless synthetic mine.
Stirring, waiting, call not come.
    Blood oozes slowly,
      under-hum.

10

Lynx's Trail

Up to this point, Griffin Dane had felt all but invisible. When Lynn turned her pale gaze upon him, he almost wished he was.

"How much do you know about the Old One Who Is Young?"

Griffin remembered Adara's admonition to stay as close to the truth as possible. "Not much at all. I came to Bruin with a problem. He admitted that he had no answers for me, but that perhaps his old teacher could help."

Lynn's lips twisted in an ironical smile. "That's Bruin. It's a wonder he didn't bond with wolves rather than bears, for once someone has led him . . ."

She stopped. Bruin was rumbling out a low growl that shaped into words. "Lynn, I've had enough of your taunting. Either tell me what your complaints are against my old friend or shut your trap and we'll get on our way."

"Are you sure you want this stranger to hear what I've to tell? Are you certain you want the others to hear?"

"More than ever. If there is reason for Griffin to re-shape his journey, then he must be the one to decide. If the others are to guide him, then they must hear as well."

Griffin thought that it was probably good that Lynn was so focused on her own intrigues that she didn't think to wonder why anyone would end up in Shepherd's Call asking for advice.

Or perhaps I'm the one who is missing something. She's gone to great trouble to get Bruin here. Perhaps he is a more important person than I realized.

Griffin had taken a seat on one of the benches that lined the walls. Now he leaned back and half shuttered his eyes, doing his best to efface himself into nothing but a listener.

It was a tactic that had worked very well when his family fell to arguing.

Lynn returned her focus to Bruin. "From the very start my relationship with the Old One differed from yours. To you he was a great wisdom leavened with kindness and shaped by compassion for the strange. For me? I also felt the impact of that wisdom. However, although the Old One was never unkind, as I grew from a sexless sprout into something resembling a woman, I realized that the man I had thought of as a second father viewed me in a completely different light."

Bruin made a gesture eloquent of disbelief. Lynn laughed softly, as if she'd anticipated this response.

"No, this was nothing as romantic as love nor as crude as desire. It is more difficult to explain . . . You certainly recall how the Old One looks, don't you? How although there is no doubt that he has lived for several hundred years he never seems much older than a youth of, say, twenty-five?"

"I do," Bruin said. "I suppose that is why, even though I know he has a name, it has always been easier to think of him as the Old One Who Is Young. It is a reminder that, although I now look old enough to be his grandfather, he could be my grandfather's grandfather."

"Then, too," Lynn went on, "the Old One never did invite the intimacy of names, did he? When we were children, such distance made sense. To children, adults are more titles than names: Mother or Father or Teacher or Coach. But when in age we came to resemble the Old One, we were not invited to call him by name. We had called him Old One or Mentor or Teacher. We continued to do so. Even when we began to seem older than him, still, he was the Old One, we—by contrast—the children."

"As we were and are," Bruin retorted. "When I met Adara she was about five. I was over forty. Thirty-five years is a near insurmountable gap at those ages. Later, as first the body matures into adult competence, then experience gives wisdom, the years melt. Teacher and student can become friends, even equals. So it is with humans."

"But not with the Old One?" Lynn asked teasingly. "That is what you are saying, yes?"

"Precisely not with the Old One!" Bruin replied. "How could we become adults in common when he starts with so many years, even centuries, of wisdom over us all? Our small triumphs and failures—the things that age us as much as does the passage of time—are as nothing to him. The Old One has seen it all, experienced the permutations. He must look at us as we do a toddler when it moves from uncertain, staggering steps to the freedom of an all-out run—moving faster, but still children."

"So you see him," Lynn said. "So the Old One intends us all to see him. Many years ago, I began to wonder if long years of experience equaled wisdom. This led me to wonder if the Old One possessed the experience of his years."

"I don't understand," Adara said softly from where she had curled up on one of the many fur rugs that interrupted the cold dirt floor. A litter of kittens had appeared from somewhere and now crawled over her as if the woman were one of their own. "The Old One has lived those years. How could he not have the experience of them?"

"Because the Old One has ceased to do anything but pursue one course," Lynn replied. "He has lived in Spirit Bay since my grandfather's time. I would not doubt he has lived there since Bruin's grandmother's time. He lives in that same vast building on the same peninsula that juts out into the bay. He does the same . . . No, Bruin! Hear me out."

Bruin leaned back but, from the firm line of his mouth, Griffin did not doubt he intended to have his say.

"The Old One does," Lynn concluded, "the same thing. Now Bruin, you will say . . ."

"What the Old One does is not the same," Bruin replied. From the narrowing of Lynn's pale eyes Griffin knew he had not surprised her. "The Old One established himself in that building because it was one of those that the seegnur used when they came from the High Orbits to the planetary surface. That building is one of the few places where the seegnur's moratorium on technology was not applied."

Griffin had to fight to maintain his casual posture. No wonder Bruin wanted him to go to Spirit Bay! That landing facility might well hold the technology he would need to contact his orbiter.

When Bruin continued, Griffin caught the same cadence that had filled Adara's voice when she spoke from the lore. "It is believed that, in the days when destruction came to the seegnur, the facility on the banks of Spirit Bay was not ruined. This may have been because the conquerors wished to use the facility themselves when they made their return. Therefore, after the seegnur had been slain, the building was sealed. True, the machinery within no longer functioned. True, many of the records could no longer be accessed, but still much can be learned if one is patient enough."

Lynn took up the tale, but although she mimicked the cadence, Griffin heard mockery in the inflection. "And somewhere in the course of the long journeys that filled his first century or so of life, the Old One Who Is Young heard of the facility on the shores of Spirit Bay. Many years were spent reaching Spirit Bay and many more in learning how to open the seal that the seegnur had put upon the facility. However, at last the Old One penetrated into this fastness. Therein, for lifetimes of mortals, he has sought to learn all he can of the ancient ways."

"Yes!" Bruin said. "That is so and that is why I say what the Old One does is not all the same. I am not a great reader, but even I know that reading one book is not the same as reading another. I have hunted much game. I know that no hunt is the same as the one before—and that believing such will be the best way to find oneself dead or injured."

Those final words fell into an absolute silence. Griffin Dane saw Lynn's hand slide over her thigh as if she would touch her damaged leg, but she caught herself in midmotion. When the silence was growing painful, one of Adara's kitten companions meeped a tiny mew. As if the sound had been permission, a log on the fire snapped, the old woman in the kitchen began to chop something, and a semblance of normalcy returned.

However, even reminders of past tragedies were not enough to distract Lynn from her purpose. She straightened in her chair and shook her head.

"Like you, Bruin, I once thought that the Old One's discoveries were new experiences. Later, though, when I fell in love, when I first bore a child, I began to wonder. Later still, when I suffered the death of a child, when my first true love died, when Hal proved to me that I could love again, then I began to wonder. Can books and puzzles be experience, dry challenges that they are, compared to the wetness of love and pain?"

Bruin said, "I understood that the Old One knew both love and grief in what might be called his 'first life,' before he realized he was gifted with unaging years. He has moved beyond such things, as I have moved beyond a boy's games."

"So I thought," Lynn said softly, "so the Old One took care all of his students would think. However, unlike you, my eyes were stripped open. Hush, now. I know you're angry, but I can't tell you why we stole Kipper without saying things you don't want to hear."

"Fair enough, but I could do with fewer taunts regarding my ignorance."

"Fair enough," Lynn echoed with a grin, but Griffin saw sorrow beneath the smile. "I am, perhaps, unfair, especially since many years have passed from the time I was first given to question to the day that I fled with all that was left to me into this last refuge."

"Go on. Give me the pieces of your puzzle. Perhaps I already know them but have arranged them differently."

Lynn cocked her eyebrows, suggesting wordlessly that she doubted this was so. "Shall I begin with when the Old One suggested to me that I might consider breeding—I cannot call the act other, for he was very practical about the matter—with another of his protégés? I was already feeling maternal urges, but the very coolness of this suggestion shocked me, especially when I realized that the Old One did not intend for me to keep my child. I was to give it to him, as I might give Adara one of those kittens. He stated he would arrange for the child to be raised and educated. Something in how he spoke of that education made me think the Old One did not intend merely to make certain the child could read and cipher and someday work at a trade."

Bruin looked uncomfortable but not shocked, so that Griffin thought he might have heard some version of this tale before. In any case, the old bear's response was mild.

"The Old One has long wondered what damage is done to those who are born adapted when they are raised in environments where their blossoming is met with apprehension, if not with open loathing. Perhaps he wished to rear a child in such an environment."

"A child?" Now Lynn looked fierce. "You speak as if he had not tried this experiment before."

"I had heard him make such suggestions," Bruin said uncomfortably. "He even made such to me, but I would not agree since the woman he had in mind was clearly reluctant. When I met my own wife and saw how she clung to her children, I thought it unlikely the Old One would get his wish."

"No?" Lynn asked bitingly. "Now I see I must enlighten you."

Adara toyed with a particularly adventurous calico kitten, hoping to hide her increased interest in this discussion. She dreaded that as matters became more sensitive Bruin would send her away, as Lynn had earlier suggested.

Adara had never confided in Bruin her own mixed feelings about the Old One Who Is Young. In any case, they'd only met once, when she had been about eight. Adara had been disconcerted to see her mentor deferring to someone who, to all appearances, was nothing more than a beardless youth. The Old One had asked Adara many questions, and had even taken her on a tour of part of the vast facility that was now his home. Adara had tried to be polite, but she hadn't much liked the place and knew he sensed her dislike. She suspected she had been a disappointment to the Old One and guessed that was why Bruin had been so easily dissuaded from taking her with him on any of his other trips to Spirit Bay.

Lynn had paused but, when Bruin only pressed his lips together into a tight line, she went on. "Not only has the Old One managed to convince some women to bear children for him under terms such as I was offered, I have evidence that some women weren't offered a choice. Winnie?"

A woman Adara guessed to be in her thirties stepped forth from the cluster in the kitchen. Her long, smooth brown hair was pulled back from skin nearly the same color. Her bearing blended nervousness and challenge into a raw wash of emotion so intense that Adara fought an urge to pull back.

"My family is from Breezy Harbor," Winnie said, her words cold and precise. "We are descended from those who served as dive pros in the days of the seegnur. For generations, we have received the patronage of the Old One, in large part because he is interested in the artifacts our divers occasionally bring up from the reefs. You may or may not know, but the seegnur hid many of their installations beneath the water because that enabled them to pretend that Artemis was all wild, unspoiled nature, untainted by the technology they depended upon.

"Now, I said my family benefitted from the Old One's patronage because of these artifacts, since that's what I believed until I was fifteen. By then, I had grown into a good swimmer. Though I showed no sign of the greater adaptations, my eyes did see a bit better underwater than most. Even though I didn't have gills, I could hold my breath a long time. I also had what my father jokingly called a 'treasure sense.' By this he meant that if I went looking, more often than not I found something. It's very hard to explain."

She trailed off. Lynn gently prompted her. "Go on, Winnie. I know it's hard, but Bruin needs to hear this."

The brown on brown woman drew in a deep breath. "I was pleased and surprised when my parents told me the Old One had asked if I might come up to Spirit Bay and work for him. He'd given out that some of the things he was interested in were underwater, easy enough to retrieve in the days of the seegnur but almost unreachable today.

"I was a little surprised that the Old One didn't want a brother of mine who was fully adapted, with gills and everything, but I didn't think much of it then. My brother was a few years older than me and had a sweetheart. I guessed that he'd been asked and had refused. That would explain, too, the nervousness I saw in my parents. I knew they wouldn't want to refuse the Old One entirely, since much of our clan's prestige and wealth came from his patronage.

"So I said my good-byes. Spirit Bay is quite far from Breezy Harbor, so I knew we wouldn't be visiting much. With adventure singing in my heart, I went off to what I thought were new waters and new discoveries. Before too long, I realized that the waters in which the Old One intended me to swim were much murkier than those in any bay."

Winnie had been speaking normally enough, even managing a bit of a loremaster's cadence, as if to distance herself from the personal aspects of her tale, but now her voice became ragged. "I . . . Oh . . . I thought I'd talked about it enough that I could do this easily."

"Never," Lynn soothed, "have you spoken before such an audience. Would you like me to speak for you?"

Winnie shook her head so violently that a bit of her hair came loose from its tight bundle and tossed about as if it had a will of its own.

"No! Listening would be worse. Just give me a moment." She paused, took a ragged breath, then continued. "There's no pretty way to put it. I soon realized that I had come to a strange place. It was not the Old One's main facility, but it was a place like it. It was hidden underground, and although in the daylight it was well lit, at night it was somehow darker than one of our houses, even though there were ample lanterns and candles.

"I soon learned that the purpose of this place was the breeding of what the Old One thought would be 'interesting' children. When I first arrived, I was kept by myself in a dark room. A man would come to me. He'd rape me, never speaking a word, then leave. I never saw him, but I'm pretty sure it was always the same man. From what I learned later, it would have had to be.

"Eventually, I got pregnant. When my pregnancy was certain, the raping stopped. A woman—she told me to call her the Stablekeeper—informed me that I'd be allowed out with other women in my circumstances if I behaved, that we'd be treated really well, but only if we behaved. If we didn't . . . Is it enough to say that the Stablekeeper took me and showed me what happened to one girl who had rebelled? What I saw was enough to convince me to surrender."

Winnie's voice had calmed now. She spoke of the months of her pregnancy as if they had happened to someone else, ending, "I went into labor and when I awoke, my baby was gone. I was given a year to recover, then I was 'reassigned,' as the Stablekeeper called it. From bits and pieces I'd put together over the previous year and a half or so, I gathered this meant that my first baby had survived and I was considered worth breeding again. I don't know if the man was the same as before. I rather suspect not, since it would be too early to tell whether the end result was worth anything. By the third time . . ."

Adara heard Bruin mutter, "Third time?"

"Yes, sir," Winnie said with mocking humility. "That would have been when I was about nineteen. That time I was fairly sure this was the same man as the first time. By then, they didn't need to tie me up and all, so I got to know the feel."

"And you're certain the Old One knew about this?" Bruin asked, not as if he doubted Winnie, but as if he had to make himself say the words.

"I am certain. We didn't see him often, but from time to time he would come to the facility. Once, during a time when I was recovering from a pregnancy, I was helping with light chores, as was expected. My duties took me past a door to a dining room. Usually that door was shut, but this time it had been left open a crack. The Old One was talking to the Stablekeeper, going over what he called a stud book. They even referred to the mothers as brood mares."

Bruin's expression was tight and strained, but he courteously inclined his head toward Winnie, inviting her to continue. As she did, a certain brutal glee entered her voice.

She's revenging herself on her tormentor, Adara thought, *by swaying his ally from him.*

"The fifth time," Winnie said, "was the worst. This one had been a bad pregnancy. I had nightmares like you can't imagine, practically from the first. I was weak, too, and couldn't keep food down, no matter how hard I tried. The baby came early. Whether it was that or my weakness or just plain error, they didn't put me out as well as they'd done before. They thought I was out—that was clear—but I could hear everything. Worse, I could see.

"The Old One was there, garbed like a doctor, in sterile gown and mask and gloves. Even so clothed, I knew him, and not just from how the Stablekeeper acted. She always acted like he was all the seegnur returned to Artemis in one. The Old One was the one who poked around and got the baby out of me. When it was free, he lifted it up and cut the cord, then smacked it so it wailed.

"Still holding the little thing by its ankles, he inspected it. Then he said, 'Damn . . . Went too far with this one. It's never going to survive.' Cool as can be, the Old One took the little thing and bashed its head against the edge of the table. I felt the wet of blood and brains on my leg. Then the Old One dropped the body in a can and went out, stripping off his mask and gloves. He was cursing under his breath, not, mind you, like he cared, but more like someone who had put in a lot of work painting a window frame and then had smudged the paint at the last minute."

Winnie had started weeping. Though the tears rolled down her cheeks, she didn't seem to notice until Lynn handed her a square of worn fabric to use as a handkerchief.

Eventually, Winnie went on. "It's possible that pregnancy ruined something in me, because even though I had a good many men sent to me, I didn't get pregnant again. Eventually, I was paroled, I guess you could call it, to housekeeping work, set to cooking and cleaning for those who were still bearing."

"Were there many of these?" Terrell asked gently.

"Not so many," Winnie said. "Maybe eight or a dozen at a time pregnant, some recovering, some 'in training,' as the Stablekeeper called it."

"Your family," Fred asked. "Do you know what the Old One told them to explain your vanishing?"

Winnie looked very sad. "I suspect they were told I drowned. I wonder if they believed it. In my worst moments, I've wondered how much they might have known about his plans for me. I can't be sure they didn't know. I'll never go back and ask. If they've mourned me, that was long ago. If they sold me—as I have wondered—they wouldn't welcome me."

"How did you get away?" Adara asked.

"Lynn did it . . ." Winnie looked sideways at Lynn. "Can you?"

"I'll tell it," Lynn said, "if Bruin wants to hear it."

Bruin's nod made Adara's heart ache in sympathy, for his shock and grief were written in every line of his face. Lynn, however, was beyond sparing anyone's feelings and, based on what Winnie had just told them, Adara could understand.

Lynn began. "Hal and I have a daughter named Mabel. When Mabel was fifteen, she vanished. She was supposed to have drowned in a boating accident, but those who planned her disappearance had forgotten that the crippled wreck who was the girl's mother had been a hunter and had long been a gamekeeper. They forgot I had friends. We tracked Mabel down, me and Hal did.

"When we found her, Mabel wasn't pregnant, but not for lack of trying on the part of those who'd taken her. Winnie's being too modest when she says we got her away. If it hadn't been for Winnie, we never would have gotten into the place where Mabel was being held. With her help, we got Mabel out and one other who was in 'training.' We couldn't even get near the pregnant ladies. They were too carefully watched, but we stole a few others away—including Winnie and Ring.

"From what I'd figured out when tracking our girl, I realized that my employers must have at least turned a blind eye to the faked accident and kidnapping. So Hal and I gathered up our family and fled. I won't bother you with the details, but we ended up here—and not by accident. I'd noted this place when I lived with you and Mary those years ago, Bruin. You'd kept Adara from the Old One, so I thought you might have suspected him and protected her. Looking at you now, though . . ."

Bruin shook his shaggy head. "I didn't suspect. Now, even now, it's hard . . ." He held out an apologetic hand toward Winnie. "I don't doubt you. Not a word. It's just so hard . . . Why would the Old One do such a terrible thing? He said he wanted to raise children who would not be stigmatized for being adapted, but this? This stinks of something far worse."

Terrell spoke, "Those terms—brood mare, stud book, training, Stablekeeper—Winnie, are those your own or are they ones you learned in that place?"

"I learned them there. The Stablekeeper herself claimed that title. I had a feeling she'd a long history with the Old One. Sometimes I even wondered if she might have been a retired brood mare, one who the training broke so that the only way she could love herself was to accept that this treatment was somehow 'right.' "

Terrell continued shaping his thoughts aloud. "So the Old One was breeding—or trying to breed—those with adaptations, or at least from those known to carry adapted genes. He wanted to be sure to raise them himself. But why? The adapted aren't common, but they aren't unheard of either. Surely if the Old One wanted simply to change social attitudes he could have chosen a less drastic route."

"And," Adara said, her gut quivering at the idea that she might have found herself kidnapped and taken to that place if the Old One had such a fancy, "what happened to the children raised there? Does anyone know?"

"Only the littlest bit," Lynn said, "and what we know is from Ring, who is not exactly easy to understand."

"Ring?" Bruin spoke heavily, as if drugged or drunk.

"You've mentioned him before. Isn't he the man who thought tying Fred to a tree was a good idea? I'm thinking we need to meet him."

Griffin Dane's thoughts swirled in a confusion of conflicting impulses. From what he had heard, Spirit Bay was where he needed to go if he was to have any hope of making contact with his orbiting ship. Yet this Old One sounded like a horror. If he treated his own people like this, how might he treat a real "seegnur"? With respect? Or perhaps either a threat or a source of information? Or even, Griffin mused sourly, as a source of new genes for his program?

Then, in good conscience, could Griffin let Adara go to Spirit Bay? What if the Old One took a fancy to her? Apparently, he hadn't seen her since she was a feisty child of eight. She'd grown into something extraordinary . . . How could the Old One not fancy her? If Griffin let Adara go to Spirit Bay, he'd have taken her into danger!

Take her? came the ironical voice of his thoughts. *Adara would be taking you, never forget that. You couldn't travel a day's journey without help. Of course, there's Terrell, but wouldn't he also be at risk? He doesn't show obvious adaptations, but everyone speaks of these "facto-tums" as among the professions. Maybe Terrell would find himself turned to stud service.*

What they have told me passes for local government would certainly not intervene—not if the Old One is accorded even a fragment of the respect Bruin accords him.

Griffin thought of his own family then, of the respect accorded the family's old name and the deeds associated with it. His parents had taken care to make certain that any who encountered them would be reminded that this was a family who did great things. They had even named each of their ten children for heroes, first for those of legend and history, later for those from the family line. Griffin was named for Griffin of LiDow, a military commander from his mother's side of the family.

Griffin's thoughts swirled down another course, as they so often did. *The men's role in the Old One's plans is an interesting part of the puzzle . . . Are the men volunteers? Do they know what they are doing? It's often been said men can be led by their little heads, but still . . .*

Griffin's conjectures were interrupted when the cabin's front door opened and a big, bald man shambled into the room. The newcomer was tall and heavily built, although softer and more fleshy than was usual among the people Griffin had encountered on Artemis. The man's skin was unusually pale, as if he had been ill and his skin had not regained its natural coloring.

But none of these things were what made the man seem odd. There was something peculiar about his manner of progress. He shuffled and held his head bent down. His right hand frequently drifted up to shadow his eyes, although the room was far from brightly lit.

Griffin wondered if the man was an albino. Then he realized the truth was stranger still. Although the man had perfectly functional eyes—there was no doubt that their brilliant blue saw everything—he kept closing them, as if not only didn't he need them in order to see, but that somehow they kept him from seeing.

"This," Lynn said, as Hal went to guide the newcomer forward, "is Ring." She went on to introduce each of the visitors while Ring continued his shuffling progress, ending by plopping heavily down onto one of the vacant benches.

Ring raised his head. With that horrible sense of effort, he opened his eyes. He looked carefully at each one of them, ending with Bruin. Then he dragged his right hand over his eyes, closing the lids. Hand still over his eyes, Ring shaped a thick-lipped smile and spoke in a deep, guttural voice.

"So the bear followed the fish. We caught the fish. I saw."

Lynn nodded. "As you saw. This is the bear. He has come for the fish."

"That is good. The fish will swim well in the bear's wake, as long as the bear does not go to the bay. I see the knobby man lived. The wolves did not eat him."

Although Ring had not opened his eyes, he turned to face Fred. Griffin's flesh crept. He realized he'd half expected to see eyes on the back of that hand.

Ring continued, "I sorrow for the pain, but death is worse than pain, or so I was taught. Sometimes, I am not sure."

Fred replied uneasily. "I don't suppose you could have taken me with you. It didn't feel very good hanging there."

"No. It was not the time. The bear must follow the fish. The fish must swim among the fort. That is the only good vision. All the others led to worse than pain."

Fred made a small noncommittal noise. Ring turned his self-blinded gaze to inspect the visitors but, although his thick lips moved, no words came forth. Eventually, he settled his hands into his lap. Although his eyes remained shut, he said, "I have seen."

Lynn apparently took this for an indication she should speak. "Winnie said we rescued her but, as I said, she helped us as much as we her. The one who assisted all of us was Ring. Ring is—as best we can guess—one of the children raised by the Old One. Without him, none of us would have escaped."

Ring said, "Or you me, me you. All is intertwisted. You, me, Hal, poor sad Mabel, Winnie. Fred, Kipper, Bruin, singing Adara, Griffin, Terrell. Dead horses. Hungry wolves. Metal spiders. Little tiny spores. All. One must sometimes wait, sometimes dig."

Griffin let this nonsense wash over him. He guessed that Ring had been abused as a child and was perhaps mentally deficient as well. Then two words startled him from his complacency.

"Metal spiders?"

Lynn laughed, but there was unease in the laughter. "Ring sees things differently from the rest of us. You can't imagine how long it took us to figure out that when he said the fish would bring the bear, he meant Kipper was what would bring Bruin to us. We didn't know what this fish was, but we had been discussing how we could consult Bruin without giving too much away. At last, Ring said he could show us what fish and—well, based on his past advice, we decided to trust him."

Hal spoke for the first time. "When we found out the boy was called 'Kipper' and that he was to be Bruin's student, it all made sense, enough so that when Ring told us to make Fred an ornament on the hickory tree, well, we did it."

He sounded both apologetic and defiant. "And I'm sorry you were harmed, Fred, but too much rests on us getting things right."

Fred wagged his head, not so much refusing the apology as to show his own confusion. "Well, I'm alive. Mind, I'd have preferred to do my job and be left out of it. But I'll accept that you folks have different ways of doing things."

"How do you know Ring is one of these children raised by the Old One?" Adara asked.

Lynn replied, "From things he has said, mostly. He has no memory of any other place than that facility, but that didn't make a sheep of him. He wanted out. Apparently there was something in the combination of our hunting for Mabel and Winnie's desperation that let Ring know this was his chance."

"This is a lot to take in," Bruin said. "We need to talk— just those of us who came after Kipper. You understand, Lynn?"

"I do. You are not our prisoners. Even if you leave, we

trust you not to betray us. Dinner will be good. We shot a bunch of waterfowl, still fat from wherever they wintered. We hope you'll join us over the table."

Interlude: 1—1–00

Fragments of purpose
Of porpoise
Re-porpoised
　　Dive into salt, wet, fresh
　　Swim, broken-finned, lopsided

Seek + (you shall) = Find
Seek. Find. Activate. Subvert.

Re-por-

Poised to strike.

II

The Unspoken

We may not be prisoners," Bruin said as they walked out through the gates and ambled over the cleared ground toward an inviting patch of sunlight, "but it's likely Lynn will learn something of whatever we say. I can't make out that Ring. How did he know about the spider?"

"You heard him say that, too?" Griffin asked. "Good. I thought I might be imagining it. I sometimes lose words in the accent."

"That means something to you?" Fred said. Adara

thought it interesting that he had reacted more calmly to assault than he had to Lynn's revelation. No wonder. The Old One was legendary—and very little of what Lynn had said fit the legend. "Meant less than the rest of all that craziness to me."

"It sounded," Adara said, trying be soothing, "like a reference to something that happened in Shepherd's Call before we left, that's all. We didn't think anyone could have carried the story before us."

"If they did, they didn't pass me on the road," Fred said, rubbing the ears of Scout and Shout, "or, if they did, they chose to pass me by and I don't see that happening. You folks from Shepherd's Call are decent sorts."

"Thank you," Terrell said. "But this Old One, if we're to believe what Lynn said, he's not the decent sort we'd all imagined. Maybe what we imagine is not to be trusted."

As they sat in silence, Honeychild and Sand Shadow came to join them. Sand Shadow began to play with her earrings, but Honeychild snuggled up to Bruin as if to warm him.

"I've just one question," Fred said. "Bruin, are you taking charge of Kipper?"

"I am, if the boy will have me."

Fred laughed. "That won't be a problem. Well, then, I'd be happy to have an escort as far as Blue Meadow. Then I'll be making my way back to reassure Kipper's folks all is well. It will be, won't it?"

"For Kipper," Bruin assured him, "most certainly. Even that Ring seemed to think so."

Adara was relieved to see that this, at least, cheered her mentor.

"Good, then." Fred rubbed his jaw. "I'm feeling my aches. If you folks don't mind, I'll just mosey back into the fort and see if I can find a corner to roll up in and rest before supper."

"That's fine," Bruin said. "You might ask after your and

Kipper's horses. I think you'll find Lynn will be returning them, and I'll get you as far as Blue Meadow, no
problem."

"Right, then," Fred said. With more alacrity than was
reasonable, he hurried back toward the fort.

Adara reached and tickled Sand Shadow at the base
of her tail. "Fred's afraid of us. He wasn't before but now,
what with all Lynn said, he's scared."

Terrell nodded. "And Fred's not dumb."

Silence held for a moment, a silence in which Adara
imagined each of the humans were, in one way or another,
reshaping the world as they had known it. All but one of
them.

Griffin Dane broke the silence.

"Until Lynn described the place where this Old One
lives, I hadn't realized that the facility as much as the man
might be what I need. No matter what we've learned, still,
I've got to go there."

Terrell laughed. "Well, my first impulse is to say that's
crazy. My second, too. Then I remember that metal spider. If such things are going to keep turning up, then exactly how is the Old One more dangerous? If we play
dumb, don't let on what we learned from Lynn, the Old
One will probably be just fine."

Adara nodded. "There's sense in that."

Bruin said heavily, "Then you believe all of that? All
that about captive women and breeding adapted children?"

"I do," Adara said. "There's no reason for Lynn to lie.
She never struck me as a storyteller. Do you think she's
lying?"

Bruin shook his head. "I don't. I can even put together
the pieces she didn't spell out. She wanted to talk with
me because I've always welcomed adapted children as
students. Maybe she wanted to find out if any of my
students came from the Old One—they haven't, by the
way. Maybe she wanted to find out if any of them have

vanished. That will be harder to learn, but I can do some checking once I get back, write some letters."

"But Lynn couldn't come to you," Adara said, "because she didn't know if you could be trusted."

"She still doesn't know," Bruin said, his voice breaking. "She told me anyhow."

"She told you because of that Ring," Griffin said. "I'm guessing that Ring assured her that if you came after the 'fish' that meant you could be trusted. She puts a lot of faith in that Ring's visions."

"Ring makes my skin crawl," Terrell said. "All of this makes my skin crawl, but I don't see how we can turn back. As Helena might say, if we start balking at jumps, pretty soon we'll be good for nothing but quiet trail rides. I'm not ready for that."

Adara grinned at him, then grew somber. "And I couldn't live with myself if I didn't try to find out more. Griffin is our excuse for going in, for staying on, for poking around. He can act all seegnur and imperious, insist on seeing the facility. If the Old One is as determined to unravel the old mysteries as we've always thought, then he's going to be welcoming."

"Winnie said," Terrell reminded them, "that she didn't know where she spent all that time, but Lynn must know. We'll need to find out if the two places are the same."

"Going to the Old One won't be safe," Bruin warned them. "It will be terribly dangerous—and I would be sending you on without me. I owe Kipper the safety of my home. My students are arriving even now. Moreover . . . The Old One has a sway over me I don't think he has over any of you. He was my first teacher and kept an interest in me even after I began to learn a hunter's craft. When my years of wandering ended, he convinced me to think of myself as a teacher. I already knew how to read, but he loaned me books, encouraged me to continue growing at a time when many men settle into ruts. I fear myself near him."

Adara flung an arm around Bruin. "You are my teacher, old bear, not him. Honestly, the Old One's charm failed to win me. I wonder now . . ."

I wonder if he met me, considered whether I could serve as one of his brood mares, saw my budding claws and reconsidered. It's possible to disarm a poor creature like that Winnie, but me? That would be a challenge. So I was dismissed to Bruin's care.

"Then we go on as planned," Terrell said. "Bruin will return to Shepherd's Call with Kipper. Adara and I will take Griffin to Spirit Bay and snoop around."

"It seems like the best thing to do," Adara agreed. "It's not much of a plan, but at this point, trying to come up with something more detailed would simply be a waste of energy."

They rode out a few days later. Lynn provided maps, drawn with the sensitivity for the land of one who had been both hunter and gamekeeper, but even as she shaded lines indicating not only location but elevation, augmenting her pictures with little notes regarding quirks of the terrain, she warned them that what she was giving them was likely to be of little use.

"Whatever I think of his morals and ethics, the Old One is no fool. He knows that place is no longer the secret it once was. Although we have not made any fresh attempts after his captives, he doesn't know if or when we might try again. I'm guessing that even if you find this place it will either be abandoned or adapted to some completely innocent purpose."

No one disagreed. Griffin noticed that Adara made a careful copy of the map, entrusting the copy to Terrell before tucking the original away inside the front cover of a leatherbound notebook that occupied its own pride of place in a special pocket in her pack.

He'd been surprised to see the notebook and wondered at his own surprise. When the answer came to him, it embarrassed him to the depths of his soul.

You've been thinking of Adara as some sort of noble savage, his inner voice chided him. *Close to nature, as lovely and as free of thought as any wild animal. Now you're shocked to realize she reads the written word with as much ease as she interprets the tracks of the beasts along the trail. You've been fancying yourself half in love with her, haven't you, Griffin Dane? But how can you love her if you don't know her?*

Griffin had no answer for that. He had no answer for a lot of things. Knowing that he'd be of little use preparing for the next stage of their journey, he assigned himself the task of talking to Ring. Ring, after all, was the closest they had to a clue as to what the Old One was hoping to achieve. However, other than confirming his initial impression that Ring was inflicted with some form of precognition, Griffin learned little.

"Because, you see," he explained to Adara and Terrell once they had left the fort, "we can't know whether the Old One considered Ring a success or a failure—or something in between."

"It's hard to believe," Adara said, "that such a tormented creature could in any way be considered a success."

Terrell, who was riding in front, glanced back over his shoulder. "I wish I could agree, Adara, but from what Winnie told us—from what was done to Mabel—I'm not certain that the Old One particularly cares whether or not his subjects are tormented, not as long as he gets what he wants."

Adara nodded. "I knew you were going to say that. Let me put it another way. How useful to anyone would someone like Ring be? The man can't walk across the room without checking to make sure the floor is still in front of him. He speaks in riddles that make perfect sense if you already know most of the answer. If the Old One wanted an oracle of some sort, surely he wanted better than that."

"Point," Terrell agreed, "a definite point. As Griffin said, we won't know until we learn if the Old One considered Ring a success or not."

"And that's not," Griffin added, "exactly a question we can ask."

"No," Terrell admitted. "We can't. That's why it's going to be your job to keep the Old One busy so that Adara and I can look around without arousing his suspicion."

Griffin didn't much like the possessive way in which Terrell spoke of Adara, the way the factotum assumed they were a team. Griffin had looked for evidence that Adara shared Terrell's feelings, but, other than the fact that she'd given Terrell—rather than Griffin—the spare copy of the map, he couldn't find any indication of favoritism. She was equally polite to them both. As far as Griffin could tell, she wasn't favoring either of them with her attentions . . .

Or rather, his inner voice corrected, *you know for certain she isn't favoring you and you don't think she's favoring him. On the other hand, there are times you sleep or they're both off . . .*

"Oh, just shut up," Griffin muttered aloud, then flushed to his collar. Terrell didn't appear to have heard. If Adara had done so, her only response was the tiny smile that quirked the corner of her mouth.

There was a great deal that was not commented on during that journey. Neither Griffin nor Terrell commented about how they felt regarding their lovely female companion—although Griffin would have bet any or all of his meager possessions that he was not alone in lavishing a great deal of thought on her.

They did not talk about where Griffin was from. Griffin wondered how much of this was politeness—a desire that he not feel too acutely homesick—and how much might be some leftover bit of etiquette from the days of the seegnur. After all, those long-ago tourists would not have wanted to be questioned by those they would have viewed, at best, as some sort of servants.

Most of all, they did not talk about what they would do when they got to Spirit Bay. Griffin—always one to speculate—tried to introduce the matter a few times, but found that both of his companions were more practical in their mindset.

"We've settled what we can, based upon what we know," Adara said, her gentle words not completely concealing a certain tension. "Think, Griffin, if we had not met up with Lynn by chance . . ."

"Or by Ring," Terrell cut in.

Adara nodded curtly. "If not for that, we would be going on to Spirit Bay with one set of facts. Perhaps these would have served us well. Perhaps not. Now we have what Lynn and the others have told us. Is there a third set of facts or a fourth or a fifth?"

Despite everything that wasn't being discussed and the underlying tension this created, in retrospect, the journey to Spirit Bay was pleasant. If bandits were abroad, they took the measure of Adara, Terrell, and, most especially, Sand Shadow, and decided the risk was not worth the gain, especially since that gain would seemingly include little other than three distinctive horses and a very ornery mule.

Griffin did not number himself among the threats, for although he carried Adara's spare bow and quiver, and had a long hunting knife belted at his waist, he had a distinct impression that to those skilled in reading the indefinable signs that mark a fighting man from one trained to fight, he—Griffin—would not show as much of a threat.

Everything Griffin saw when they chanced upon the area's inhabitants confirmed his feeling that in matters such as the Old One, local authorities would be of no help. The route Adara and Terrell had chosen had largely avoided population centers—both because Sand Shadow would not be welcome in many and to avoid questions about Griffin.

"There's an added advantage," Adara said cheerfully. "We won't need to pay as many tolls. Bruin gave us some coin, but I'd prefer to save as much as we can."

"Tolls?" Griffin asked.

Terrell nodded. "This region is basically a league of associated towns, a heritage from the days of the seegnur. Cities such as you have described would not have fit their image for Artemis."

"I can see that," Griffin agreed, "but five hundred years have passed. Surely some ambitious person or group would have tried to dominate their neighbors."

Terrell shrugged. "There have been kingdoms in the past, but usually they don't last more than two generations: the conqueror and the conqueror's immediate heir. The lore is strong in this region. In the end, the people revert to the traditional pattern."

"So who is collecting the tolls Adara mentioned?"

"Local government or someone who has been granted a concession for providing some service—like maintaining the roads or a bridge."

"And what happens to people—well, like us, who avoid paying?" Griffin tried not to sound nervous. "Would we end up locked up somewhere?"

Terrell laughed. "Only if we couldn't pay—either in coin or goods or labor. There would be a penalty, of course, but as long as you're willing to pay, there aren't hard feelings. After all, it's not as if we are using the roads, right?"

Griffin, accustomed as he was to a world where tracking devices were routine, found the idea fascinating—and more alien than a young woman with claws and eyes like a cat's.

No wonder the Old One can get away with the kid-napping and the other things of which Lynn accused him.

Of course, while it was happening, the journey didn't always seem pleasant. When there are no convenient inns, as there rarely were on the route Adara and Terrell had chosen, every downpour that promises a cold meal and a damp bed is an event—especially for one such as Griffin Dane, who had rarely slept either cold or wet. If it hadn't been for Sand Shadow and Adara, they would have eaten far worse. And if it had not been for the curious conglomeration of tricks and gimmicks that made up a factotum's training, they would have been a great deal less comfortable.

Fighting against a sense of uselessness—and against his frustration with a journey measured in miles rather than minutes—Griffin threw himself into those tasks he could perform. He gathered deadwood for the fire, groomed the horses (despite Griffin's best efforts, Sam the Mule would tolerate only Terrell), stirred pots and turned spits. In this way he asserted himself as part of the team rather than patron being escorted—or worse, a package being delivered.

Griffin wasn't certain how either Adara or Terrell viewed him. Adara's attitude had never been quite as relaxed since the attack by the metal spider. Also, he never had any time alone with her. Their days of sharing a tent were over. He shared one with Terrell. The other man didn't snore, but he did murmur in his sleep. When Griffin mentioned this, Terrell shook his head.

"I don't or, if I do, you're the first to mention it. Sure you're not hearing yourself? I've woken a few times to hear you carrying on, though not in any words I can understand."

"No one has ever told me I talked in my sleep, either," Griffin retorted.

Terrell gave him an impish grin. "I suppose we must have some special affinity, then."

Griffin snorted, but the fact was that much as he had resisted it—for he couldn't help but see the other man as his romantic rival—he was coming to sincerely like Terrell the Factotum. The other man was self-confident to a point that might be seen as cocky, brash in a manner that made Griffin feel his own tendency to second-guess as even more of a handicap than usual. But there was a kindness to Terrell as well, an automatic courtesy that made the long hours they spent in each other's company tolerable.

Often, when they were camped, Adara took herself off. She didn't go far but, when she climbed a tree to a height where none of the men could easily follow, busying herself with taking notes in her little book, the message was not hard to interpret. Terrell explained this need for solitude as part of a hunter's nature, but sometimes Griffin wondered.

Is she avoiding me? Is she avoiding him? Is she frightened about the Old One? Worried about Bruin? I wish she'd talk to me—or even to Terrell. I suppose she can talk to Sand Shadow . . .

Sand Shadow was a constant source of wonder and delight for Griffin—and the feeling seemed to be mutual. The puma was quite willing to accept Griffin as a new and fascinating toy. She was always eager for the opportunity to practice refining her use of her curious hand/paws. One of her tasks was practicing tying knots. She already knew the basics, but Griffin taught her a few clever twists that Gaius, his most nautical-minded brother, had shown him.

The puma knew a few simple variations of the string games called "fisher's mesh" on Griffin's homeworld, but known on Artemis by the curious name "cat's cradle." Griffin showed Sand Shadow a complicated pattern called "Sea's Eye," then regretted it, for the demiurge became obsessed with getting it right, butting him with her very solid head or lashing him with her thick, heavy tail until she had every step down to perfection.

More fun for them all was when Griffin taught Sand Shadow how to play a simple marble-shooting game. Children on Artemis played marbles, but the Sierra variation involved numerous overlapping circles. It remained perennially popular on Griffin's homeworld, where its connection to a solar festival made certain it never quite fell out of use.

Soon man and puma were rooting through stream gravels for rounded pebbles, marking the game patterns in the ground at every stop. Adara and Terrell went from amused observers to enthusiastic participants. Terrell even found a type of clay that could be shaped into rounded forms and baked to hardness in the ashes of the fire. After that each of them carried a little pouch holding their own personal marbles. Sand Shadow wore hers around her neck.

All in all, when Adara pointed to the faint marks on the horizon that were the first indication that the town of Spirit Bay was near, Griffin realized he was reluctant to see the journey end.

"We'll be there tomorrow," Adara said, "or the next day at most. Depends on how high the river is running at the ford."

Griffin searched her face for some indication about how the huntress felt regarding the coming ordeal, but the sculptured features were impassive as some stone carving.

"And when we get there?"

"Bruin told me the name of a couple of boarding houses that gave him no trouble about Honeychild the last time he came to Spirit Bay. We will take rooms in one of these and send a message on to the Old One to tell him of our arrival."

"And then?"

"And then," Adara said, her full lips shaping a mischievous a grin that made perfectly clear that even now she was not willing to begin conjecturing, "we will see what happens."

※

Interlude: Cat's Play

Velvet darkness, soft as sound.
  My other self, my shadow,
  Can you hear me?

My shadow, my other self,
  I can hear you.

Shadow self try, so I can
  Hear what you hear,
    See what you . . .
      Feel what . . .
        Taste
          Smell

Velvet darkness, soft as sound.

12

Spirit Bay

Bruin?" the man repeated, holding tightly to the collar of a large brown dog that had stopped barking long enough to strain forward for a good, slobbery sniff.

Adara held her breath. She was sure she'd come to the right place, but the town's nesting lines of buildings left her feeling more lost than ever the forest did.

"Bruin the Hunter," she repeated. "Benjamin Hunter. He told us we'd find friends of his here."

The man's face lit up. As if reading his master's emotions, the dog's long tail started tocking back and forth in quick strokes and he settled onto his haunches.

"Oh, Benji Bear! That Bruin! Of course! We haven't seen him for years, but he often visited us when he came to see the Old One. You must be Adara. He's mentioned you in his letters. Of course you can stay here. I'm sorry. I couldn't make out what you were saying over Roughneck's yammering."

"I have two friends with me," Adara ventured, "and a puma. She knows how to mind her manners."

"If she's anything like Bruin's Honeychild, then of course she does. I'm Cedric Trainer. This badly behaved boy is Roughneck. He'll be a fine guard dog someday, but now he's just a pup."

Cedric Trainer was a bluff and hearty sort, the greying whiskers that framed his ruddy jowls cut so that he rather resembled one of the larger terrier breeds.

"Let me tell my wife, Elaine," he continued. "You go get your friends. If you came all the way from Shepherd's Call, you must have horses with you. We've room for them, too."

"Three horses and a mule," Adara said. "We could stable them elsewhere if they'd take up too much room."

"No problem. We've plenty of space. Now, go fetch your friends."

If Cedric reminded Adara of a terrier, then Elaine was a greyhound, long and lean, with a very pointed nose and silky, straight hair. She joined her husband in expressing delight at giving room to "Benji Bear's Adara" and her companions. The horses and Sam the Mule were to be stabled in one of the many long kennels set haphazardly about the property.

"There's room for you with the rest of us in the main

house," Elaine said, "if you don't mind children under-foot."

"Not at all," Adara assured her. "Are you certain Sand Shadow will be no problem? Her scent won't bother your dogs?"

"As long as she doesn't harass them," Cedric said, "they can be as bothered by the smell of a great cat as much as they like. We train hunting dogs among the rest. The better trained shouldn't even take note of her—obedience is essential, don't you know. The pups, well, let them get a good whiff. Won't harm them and might teach them something."

Evening was coming on by the time the horses and Sam the Mule were comfortably settled, and the guests had been given a quick tour of the grounds, during which their group kept accumulating both children and dogs, most of which followed them into the main house. The ground floor was one enormous pillared room furnished with tables and benches that could be moved with ease. The wooden floor was covered with scatter rugs that couldn't hide a certain amount of scuffing.

"We train the dogs in here when the weather's bad, don't you know," replied Cedric in answer to an unspoken question. "Waste of good space breaking the room into little boxes. Gives a place for the children to run, too. Smaller rooms upstairs."

There certainly were children enough, far more, it seemed to Adara, than could be accounted for by only two parents. There was a scattering of older folk as well, but the whirl of introductions confused Adara, so that in the end she couldn't figure out the relationships between anyone. It didn't help her sense of being over-whelmed that the dogs were introduced as elaborately as any human, complete with lineages going back for generations. Most of the indoor dogs were small ones, but a couple of the honored grey-muzzled creatures that rested by one of the numerous hearths were very large indeed.

"That's a breed dating back to the days of the seeg-nur," Elaine said, nudging a toddler holding a fat puppy out of the way as she set a board holding bread and cheese on one of the long tables. "Not much call for them now, but we like them. They were bred to hunt big game—boars, bear, wolves, and the like."

"We met Benji when we were training a couple of that breed," Cedric said, chuckling heartily at the memory. "Might even have been those very two. We'd set them on the trail of a bear to test them in front of a potential client. Well, our target turned out to be the smartest bear we'd ever dreamed could be. We lost the client, but that was all right. I'm not sure we would have even leased the dogs to him, much less sold outright, which is what he wanted. Later, Benji came in and introduced himself, explained what had happened, said he'd been impressed by the dogs, but not so much that he'd let himself or his de-miurge get torn up. Offered to pay us for our lost busi-ness, but we told him no matter. Later, he helped us train some other dogs, taught us some hunter's tricks. All good . . ."

"And like as not," Elaine repeated thoughtfully, as if the events had happened yesterday, "we wouldn't have sold the dogs to that man anyhow. I didn't much like him."

Dinner was hearty, the food plain but ample, served on vast platters from which everyone helped themselves.

"The dogs support the lot of us," Cedric explained. "We don't sell working dogs unless we like the people, but we lease. Guard dogs are popular, so are ratters. Hunting dogs in season. Not much call for herders, you'd think, here by the town, but there's some. Retrievers, especially by the water. All works out, don'tcha know."

Adara thought it must. There was a vital jumble and rumble to the big house, with children spilling up and down the stairs, often chased by dogs. No one was idle. Apparently, Elaine and Cedric applied the same training principles to their children as they did to their dogs. The meal had been served by middle-sized children, cleared away by smaller children. The washing up was a complicated process but, except for occasional shouted orders, Cedric and Elaine were free to visit with their guests.

In the genial chaos, Griffin was accepted without question as a traveler whom Terrell and Adara were escorting to Spirit Bay in order that he might meet with the Old One Who Is Young. Elaine and Cedric seemed to think this the most sensible thing in the world. Here in Spirit Bay, the Old One was viewed as an honored curiosity, not really of the town, but valued by it.

There certainly was no hint of any dark stain on the Old One's reputation. The longer they were away from Lynn and her ominous tales, the less possible it all seemed. Then Adara would remember Ring and find herself wondering.

Come morning, Adara neatly wrote a letter to the Old One, informing him that she was here, bringing with her a person whom Bruin felt the Old One would like to meet—and who, in turn, very much wanted to meet the Old One.

Elaine suggested her son Edward, a bow-legged, springy boy, constantly accompanied by a low-bodied, short-legged hound, could serve as messenger. Adara was happy to accept. She didn't think it would be good manners to go up to the Old One's house herself. It might seem as if she expected to trade on her relationship with Bruin for shelter.

In any case, Adara wanted time to adjust, not only to the idea of seeing the Old One without Bruin's protective presence, but also to being in a town of this size. She'd climbed out on the roof the night before and marveled at the extent of the rooftops stretched out before her. She'd started counting lights in an attempt to estimate how many people lived there, but had given up before long. It made her nervous to think of so many people living so close together. She'd had to fight against an impulse to let Terrell take over. She'd been a good guide and gotten them here safely. Surely this next part was more a factotum's job.

But Adara didn't run. Not only didn't she want to disappoint Bruin, but Griffin was her discovery. Somehow, that made him her responsibility. No one had said so, but the feeling that Griffin was somehow hers hummed beneath her breastbone, warming her, but making her decidedly uncomfortable at the same time.

Several days passed without reply from the Old One Who Is Young. Griffin, accustomed to a world in which the only restriction of communication was personal willingness to communicate, was driven to distraction by speculations that the Old One was avoiding them.

Neither Adara nor Terrell shared his apprehension. They admitted it would have been possible for the Old One to reply by sending a message back with young Edward, but, as Adara said, "We don't even know if the Old One is in residence. He usually is—or at least that is the impression he gives—but that doesn't mean he doesn't leave for a few days at a time."

"But wouldn't someone on his staff have sent a note to let us know if the Old One was away?"

"Perhaps." Adara raised and lowered her shoulders in an eloquent shrug. "Perhaps not. They might have had instructions not to do so. The Old One has cultivated a sense of permanence that he might not wish violated. Or he could be ill—and, again, he might not care to admit that."

"Or he could be hiding something," Griffin said darkly, "or taking advantage of the delay to make sure anything he wants out of our view is properly concealed."

"That," Adara admitted with another eloquent shrug, "is certainly possible."

Terrell grinned. "In fact, that's what we're all thinking, so we might as well face it. However, unless we're willing to go barging into the Old One's home and ask why he hasn't jumped to invite us over, there's not much we can do. For now, we'll make ourselves acquainted with Spirit Bay, listen for rumors, and, if we haven't heard anything in a few more days, send another letter. The one thing we won't do is prowl the countryside. Given how long we've been on the road, that would look suspicious."

"For everyone but Sand Shadow," Adara commented. "She can do some preliminary scouting while I stay demurely here in town, awaiting summons to the great man."

So, for two days they followed this course. Despite his impatience, Griffin found himself fascinated by the town. Spirit Bay was set on a series of gently sloping hills overlooking the blue waters of a vast bay. The Old Empire architects had not stinted on the quality of their materials, so everywhere buildings that had been constructed to furnish the former resort were still evident—often in excellent condition.

The natural stone of the area included a very attractive pale grey granite threaded with streaks of black and pink. The majority of the houses were built from this stone. The styles ranged from water-rounded rock roughly mortared into walls in the poorer sections of town to elegant structures made from cut blocks and slabs. The roofing was primarily of dark grey slate shingle. Doors and wood trim were painted in bright colors.

However, interwoven among this original design were five hundred years of adaptation by an intelligent and healthy population. Even the best architects could not prevent damage by fire, flood, and storm. And, although the original builders' constructions had been made to appear native to the area, the key word was "appear." House walls of what looked like solid native stone proved to be hollow, packed with light insulation that doubtless had made the original structure infinitely more comfortable.

Beneath the natural shingles lay an artificial water barrier that, even centuries later, remained intact unless some disaster had broken the seal. Later roofs were far less uniform. The paint trim attempted to maintain the same colorful schemes, but could not maintain the same freshness.

Griffin wondered aloud if the timber and plaster buildings he'd seen in Shepherd's Call were equally fake.

"Some of them are," Terrell admitted. "All the houses around the main green, for example, a few of the larger barns. Hard as it may be for you to believe, Shepherd's Call has actually grown since the days of the seegnur. In those days it was a tiny, picturesque village, a stopping point for hunting parties going up into the mountains. The building where Mistress Cheesemaker makes her home was an inn, as well as what was called a 'health resort' in those days."

Adara nodded. "Bruin showed me where there had been what were called 'natural hot springs.' They were as fake as this wall, but the seegnur would come and bathe in the water, then talk about the 'incomparable health restoratives found only in Nature.'"

She snorted in eloquent dismissal of such frivolity.

Although Griffin had seen plenty of evidence of the less healthy aspects of Nature since his arrival on Artemis—the care taken to assure that human waste would not contaminate the water supply had been drummed into him from the first—still he felt defensive.

"It's quite possible, you know, that those hot springs were full of health restoratives. The Old Empire did amazing things with nanotechnology."

Terrell laughed and toed a broken piece of masonry

that, if seen only from one side, anyone would have sworn was a chunk of a vast boulder.

"We don't doubt that in the least, Griffin. Artemis is full of evidence of what the seegnur—the Old Empire, as you call it—could do. With its ruin all around us, though, forgive us if we find the entire thing ironic."

"There's a point," Adara added, "in every child's life when she discovers that something she had taken for solid and immovable is hollow as an egg. For me it happened on a hillside near my parents' home. I've told you how I developed night vision fairly young. Well, one night when I couldn't sleep, I decided to creep outside and look at the moon."

Her tone fell into what Griffin was coming to recognize as "storytelling" mode. Sand Shadow, also recognizing a story coming, rolled over onto her back. Still talking, Adara dropped down beside the puma and began rubbing the soft belly fur in rhythm with the words.

"The moon was one of those huge orange ones you get around harvest, the sort that looks as if you could gather it up in your arms. I went climbing a hill, certain that if I could get a little higher I would have a wonderful prize. Then, down the middle of a great boulder, I saw a shadow cast by a slight gap cut into the rock.

"I'd a knife with me—even that young I knew better than to prowl around unarmed. I slid it into the gap and pushed. The side of the rock popped open. Turns out the entire boulder was hollow, a storage closet of some sort, although whatever had been stored in it had been found and taken away long before. The loremasters were fascinated. They came for miles and miles to get a look at it and marvel at what the seegnur could do."

Terrell laughed. "You must have been scared stiff when the boulder opened."

"I was! For a moment, I thought the hill was going to seize me and eat me because I'd gone outside when I shouldn't. I almost didn't tell my parents, because that would mean admitting that I'd been out when I shouldn't."

"But you did?" Griffin was curious about this unexpected glimpse into Adara's younger years.

"Well, I did and I didn't. I closed the door and marked it. Then, a few days later, I arranged to find it again—this time with witnesses. In the excitement, no one thought to question too closely just how I found a door that no one else could see."

"Calculating cat," Terrell teased. "Even then . . ."

"Even then," Adara admitted.

Griffin fought down a flash of jealousy at this reminder that Terrell and Adara shared a background in which he—Griffin—could never take part. To counter his envy, he let the anthropologist in him win out. After all, it was hard to be envious of sources. Griffin was about to ask what Terrell's own discovery moment had been when a multilegged whirlwind stormed up to intercept them.

The commotion proved to be bow-legged Edward and his omnipresent pup, Oscar.

"It's come! It's come! The letter you've been waiting for has come!"

Edward thrust a folded sheet of heavy paper toward Adara while Oscar jumped around, barking madly to show he shared his human's excitement. Sand Shadow, normally incredibly patient with the dogs, folded back her ears and hissed, showing each of her shining fangs to excellent advantage. Oscar fell instantly silent, clapped his tail to his butt, and scooted behind Edward.

Adara used a claw tip to pop off the pale blue wax seal that closed the letter, then quickly scanned the contents.

"We've been invited to call upon the Old One tomorrow, midmorning."

Terrell plucked the letter from her hand, scanned it himself, then offered a factotum's insight into the contents.

"Interesting. There's no mention of our staying for lunch, so he's providing himself with an easy excuse for asking us to leave. However, there is no mention of a closing time for our visit, so he's also leaving himself an opening in case he finds us interesting."

"So, not exactly a warm welcome," Griffin concluded, "but not cold, either."

"Precisely," Terrell said. "We'll all be on our best behavior and see what comes."

Midmorning of the following day found them all freshly attired. Terrell—whose beard grew rather quickly—had even shaved a second time. The Old One's residence was close enough that the threesome chose to walk. Sand Shadow padded along with them, one ear adorned with an array of small silver hoops.

Griffin reflected on how much his own attitudes had changed in a relatively short time. Once he would have questioned the appropriateness of a "pet" coming along on a formal embassy. Now he would be more likely to question if Adara had left her demiurge behind.

The building in which the Old One chose to reside was the only structure in Spirit Bay that didn't look somewhat rustic. Instead it had the long, flat lines and molded contours Griffin recognized from surviving Old Empire architecture—only this structure hadn't been bombed to rubble as had much of the rest he had seen. Griffin guessed this style of architecture had been a deliberate choice. It was one thing to hide the high-tech construction that underlay the various buildings on Artemis. However, if this building, which served as the arrival point for the shuttles, had been done in the "local" style, the illusion that the rest was "real" would have been threatened.

Since there was no sign of a landing field, Griffin guessed that shuttles had landed in the bay. In a more usual spaceport, this might have caused problems—at the very least the turbulence and shifts in water temperature would have injured the bay's ecosystem. However, Artemis had always been a restricted location. Surface-to-orbit contacts would have been limited.

The arrival facility had been constructed on a peninsula that jutted out into the bay. In contrast to the houses in the town, this building boasted enormous single-paned windows. The fact that they remained pristine after five hundred years argued they were made from something other than glass or even the synthetics used on Griffin's own homeworld.

A quiet boast, Griffin thought, of power and superiority—as if that would be needed by a people who would arrive from the heavens. Were the visitors here more aware of how vulnerable they were making themselves than I imagined? Or were they so far beyond viewing the Artemesians as people that they didn't even consider such matters?

But when Griffin thought of the lore and the carefully designed cult it had created—a cult that had lasted long after those who had designed it had been destroyed—Griffin thought that the Imperials were not beyond the need to shock and awe.

There were several paths leading down to the landing base. Terrell insisted that they take the one that went to the main entryway.

"We're coming as guests, not as supplicants or servants—or even as friends," he said. "It is only proper."

The door they approached testified to this facility's origin as a public facility rather than a home. It was both wide and high, meant to accommodate groups rather than individuals. Griffin guessed that it had been designed to swing rather than slide as a psychological gateway into a more primitive world, where hinges rather than slide tracks or force barriers served to divide inside and out.

Lucky for the people who were inside when the invaders' nanomachines started destroying the technological infrastructure. I suppose force barriers would simply have

*vanished, but sliding panels would have trapped the oc-
cupants.*

Once upon a time, some automatic device would have
signaled the arrival of guests. In this day and age, a length
of rope hung incongruously against the sparkling tiles
that bordered the doorway. Terrell stepped up and gave
the rope a series of hearty tugs. The muted sound of a
powerful bell ringing echoed back to them.

Not long after, the door swung open, revealing a man
so ordinary that Griffin took him for a servant—that is
until he noticed Adara and Terrell offering polite bows
of greeting. Surely, for them to react so, this all too ordinary man must be the Old One Who Is Young.

*Ordinary? No. Ordinary to me. To Adara and Ter-
rell . . . What is it? He wears his hair short, not precisely
in the modern style, but in one I have seen before. Where?
Of course! In history books. In the final days of the empire this was the dominant style. His clothing, too . . . The
style is usual enough to me, but that close tailoring is not
at all common on Artemis. It's a style that wastes cloth,
so here on Artemis it proclaims wealth. I keep forgetting
that here fabric isn't synthesized. It's woven, thread by
thread, piece by piece.*

These thoughts flashed through Griffin's mind as initial greetings were exchanged, first between Adara and
the Old One (who marveled as all adults do in all times
and places when confronted with a small child trans-
formed into an adult), then Terrell (who was greeted
politely as one well schooled in the lore). Last, Adara
indicated Griffin.

"This is Griffin Dane, the one about whom I wrote you.
He wishes to consult you on certain matters."

The Old One Who Is Young studied Griffin thoughtfully. Griffin returned the inspection with a cool assump-
tion of his own worth. The Old One's eyes were a pale
grey. His hair was faded wheat, much lighter than Griffin's
own. His build was slight but strong, that of an acrobat

or dancer rather than a fighter. As Griffin had already noted, the Old One cultivated the style not of a resident of Artemis, but of those who had come from the stars.

Does he think himself one of the seegnur, then? Griffin wondered. *Step carefully. This man will not take kindly to having his illusions threatened.*

The Old One's lips bent in a slight smile, as if he could read Griffin's thoughts and found them amusing. Then his expression warmed, the grin becoming boyish and enthusiastic.

"Welcome to my home," he said, stepping back and making a welcoming gesture. "My sanctum sanctorum, as I think of it. I can see you have an interesting story to tell."

He ushered them into a room in which one entire wall was transparent, offering a sweeping view of Spirit Bay. Over the waters, boats moved in an elegant ballet, multicolored sails belling out as unseen sailors tacked to catch the shifting breezes.

"I love watching the water," the Old One said. "My memories of my earliest years have grown fainter with time, but for nearly a lifetime I lived by the ocean. There is nothing quite like wind off the water."

He indicated where a tray of refreshments had been set ready. "Please, help yourselves. Adara, before we get to the business that brought you here, you must tell me how Bruin is doing. I enjoy his letters, but I do miss his visits."

Adara complied but, although she mentioned Bruin's latest class of novice hunters, Griffin noted she did not mention Kipper. The Old One asked a few questions, once again offering regret that Bruin had not been able to make the journey. Griffin noticed that the Old One did not offer to visit Shepherd's Call.

How much are you allowing what Lynn said to color your reaction to the Old One? Griffin scolded himself. *He may not be all he pretends to be, but there seems no doubt that he has lived for hundreds of years without ad-*

vanced medical care. No matter what else he is, this Old One is a remarkable person. Especially if you want his help, you'd better treat him as such.

"Thank you for humoring my need to catch up on the doings of my old friend," the Old One said when Adara finished. "Still, I should not be selfish. You brought Griffin Dane to me for a reason. That is?"

"It's a complicated story," Adara said. "It begins, for me and Sand Shadow, with a shooting star that was not a shooting star."

With the eloquence she had shown a time or two before, Adara launched into her side of the tale. When she reached the point where she had pulled Griffin Dane from the landslide that buried his shuttle, she motioned to Griffin.

"Tell him how you came to be there," she prompted.

They had already agreed to stay as close to the truth as was prudent—especially since Griffin needed the Old One's good will. So Griffin began with his background as a historian and archeologist, moving into how he had located what he believed might be the coordinates for Artemis. Like Adara and Bruin, the Old One had no problem believing that Griffin would have wanted to keep his secret to himself.

"I understand better, perhaps, than you know." He motioned around him. "I am reminded of when I learned of this place—it was not as it is now, but mostly buried beneath the debris of hundreds of years of neglect and fear. I did not race to share my discovery with everyone, only with the chosen few I could trust. I could envy you, living as you did in a place where it was possible to undertake such a voyage single-handedly."

Griffin laughed dryly. "I thought it was pretty wonderful myself, until disaster came. Then I realized that I'd underestimated the difficulties, and that it was going to be a long time—if ever—before anyone came looking for me."

The Old One nodded. "Yes. And now you want my help or, rather, what help you hope this facility can offer. I must warn you. Although it was sealed at the time of the great destruction, those nanobots of which you spoke penetrated here as well. I have had no luck in activating any of the machinery that remains."

Griffin was surprised at how deeply disappointment flooded him.

"Nonetheless," the Old One continued, "we may be able to help each other. I will take you through this facility and let you inspect it in detail. In turn, perhaps you will be able to explain to me some of the mysteries I have found. I have taught myself to read many of the symbols the seegnur used but, knowing—or guessing—what something means and understanding why it was created are not the same thing at all."

Griffin didn't even glance at Adara or Terrell. He needed to see this facility. He needed to know if there was any hope of contacting his orbiting ship, of reaching the stars—and the people and places who were now vanished among those hard, bright bits of sparkling light.

"It's a deal," he said. "When can we start?"

Interlude: 1—1—00

Instituting Infiltration:
  Inserting Instructions . . .

Interrupted!
Interference!

Resistance Detected.
Determined Defiance.
Evaluating Situation.

Instituting Subversion Inversion Reversion.

Confusion!

Subversion Resisted.
Infiltration Detected.
Withdrawal Indicated.
Re-targeting Later-dated.

13
Beneath the Sanctum

The Old One hadn't exactly invited Adara, Sand Shadow, and Terrell to take part in the tour, but he didn't protest when they rose to follow.

"The interesting rooms are all below," he said. "This upper level consists of several rooms much like this one—large and open. When I came here, they were furnished with numerous tables and chairs."

"A waiting area," Griffin suggested, "and processing center. It looks as if you've redecorated."

The Old One shrugged slim shoulders. "I live here alone except for a few servants. There are only so many tables and chairs one person can use. However, these rooms are pleasant. The windows keep them well lit in the daytime. I've subdivided one of the larger rooms into a personal apartment. Another serves as an apartment for my servants. We built the kitchen outside, so as to not ruin this place with more smoke than we must but, when night falls, we must use candles or oil lanterns."

He gestured regretfully toward high ceilings smudged with smoke. Adara smothered a smile. Bruin said smoke seasoned the old wooden beams of his house and helped preserve the meat. However, Adara knew that each spring Mistress Cheesemaker and her daughters scrubbed every inch of the walls and ceiling in their many-roomed house, then followed up with coat upon coat of whitewash. Idly, she wondered if they were somehow trying to maintain a standard left from days when that house had been lit with something other than fire.

"Fortunately," the Old One continued, "the seegnur built this place to maintain the illusion that Artemis was extremely primitive, so there are stairs between each level, not merely 'lifts.' "

He inflected the last word with a hint of pride, so Adara guessed that this was some term the seegnur must have used. Judging from how Terrell swallowed a grin, it wasn't all that exotic.

So the Old One is no different than those townies who come up to the mountains and take pride in showing they know the difference between ram and ewe. The Old One must be more impressed by Griffin than he let on.

Griffin nodded. "Actually, stairways or ladders remain common the universe over. No one who has been trapped in a lift when the power goes out ever forgets the feeling of helplessness. It's typical for buildings to have both."

The Old One smiled. "So I have learned. However, here the stairs are large and obvious. The lifts are concealed. I believe the reverse would have been true on the home planets of the seegnur."

"You have a point," Griffin agreed.

The Old One paused at the top of a flight of stairs leading into murky depths. "I know my way around, so the light from the partial windows that extend to the next level is enough to guide me. However, I do have lanterns close at hand."

"If you want me to read signs for you," Griffin said, his tone showing far more impatience than he had ever offered Adara or Terrell, "then perhaps we had better have light."

"Very well," the Old One said.

He opened a cabinet cunningly concealed within the flat panel wall. From this he removed two oil lanterns, their bases and globes shaped from clear glass with hardly a bubble. The oil in the reservoirs was of the best type, a clear fluid that burned with almost no smoke, as long as the lantern's wicks were properly trimmed. These were. The Old One—or more probably those unseen servants—knew how to take care of expensive equipment.

After lighting the lanterns with sulfur matches—another expensive luxury item—the Old One handed one of the lanterns to Terrell.

Does he remember I can see in the dark? Adara wondered. *Or is he giving Terrell the factotum's privilege as guide to the seegnur? Certainly, here, Griffin seems more like a seegnur than he has since Sand Shadow and I first pulled him from the landslide. Is Griffin putting on an act for the Old One or is this his truer nature?*

Taking up the remaining lantern, the Old One began moving purposefully down the stairs, pausing at the bottom to open a set of doors. "These take us into various areas related to the landing and care of the shuttle craft. I have read that there were orbiting space stations where visitors were processed before being permitted to come to the surface. However, I will admit that I have no idea if this is true or what the processing would have entailed."

"It is true," Griffin said, inspecting the equipment. "Only one of the space stations remains and what is left is so wrecked that if you didn't know what to look for, you never would guess. As for processing, well, human bodies carry a variety of contaminating factors within them. The final processing would have been to assure that visitors would not carry anything on or within them that could endanger either the inhabitants of the planet or visitors who came from another biosphere."

Terrell, who had been uncharacteristically quiet to this point, spoke, his voice holding a faint tremor of

uncertainty. "And you, Griffin? How were you processed if these space stations were missing? Did you carry
contamination down to the surface?"

"No need to worry, my friend," Griffin reassured him.
"I read about the procedures and did them twice: once
in Sierra orbit and once again before leaving my ship for
the shuttle."

"Well, that's good," Terrell said.

There was no mistaking the relief in his voice. Adara
wondered at the intensity, but then a factotum's education was very detailed in matters regarding the seegnur.
Who knew what horror stories he had heard?

The Old One spoke as if he were fitting pieces into a
puzzle he'd been building in his mind.

"So that's what the processing was for. I understand
why it was considered so important. Next, let me show
you where the shuttles docked."

The tour was interesting, Adara had to admit, though
she understood why Griffin didn't take long to become
restless. After all, there were no shuttles here, only the
cradles and slings that had held them while they rested in
their journeys between the planet's surface and the void.

"I'm certain," Griffin said when the Old One paused,
"that an engineer would be a better audience for all of
this. It looks as if your seegnur used somewhat different
arrangements than those with which I am familiar, but I
can't say why."

"Perhaps because their technologies were so much
more sophisticated than those you know?" Terrell suggested. "I remember your telling us that technology has
changed—isn't as advanced as it was in the days of the
Old Empire."

Griffin nodded. "It could be that, but it could be something simpler—a matter of esthetics, a change of design
meant to accommodate a particular space."

"And you wouldn't be able to even guess?" the Old
One asked. He sounded annoyed, as if Griffin Dane had

failed to pass some sort of test. "Yet you have traveled on many shuttles. You even own one."

Griffin chuckled ruefully. "I could guess, but guesses aren't what you want. Guesses are what you already have. I've also owned thousands of pairs of shoes but, beyond the basics, I would have no idea how to make a pair or why one pair is better than another. I thought you wanted answers, not guesses."

The Old One's sulky expression faded. "I am the one who should apologize. You are the first visitor from beyond our atmosphere in half a millennium. It is ridiculous for me to concentrate on your extraterrestrial origin without remembering how much time has passed. Moreover, in my selfish excitement at having someone other than loremasters and the occasional friend with whom to share my treasures, I am forgetting that for you this tour has a more personal goal. Is there anything in particular you would like to see?"

Griffin's response was prompt and eager. "Is there anything you've identified as a communications array? Even if they deliberately went primitive on the surface, the seegnur would have needed some way to contact vessels in orbit."

Adara noticed how the pale grey of the Old One's eyes flickered when Griffin spoke of the seegnur as somehow other than what he himself was. This, on top of his failure to be an instant expert regarding hangar bays, might be too great a diminishment of prestige. And the Old One was dangerous . . . In his eagerness, Griffin might forget this, but Adara remembered.

She glanced at Terrell to see if he shared her reaction, but his gaze was distracted, as if Griffin's words about communications arrays had triggered some elusive memory. Saving Griffin's status would be up to her.

"If your shuttle hadn't crashed, you wouldn't have had any trouble communicating with your ship, would you, Griffin?"

He indicated agreement. "None at all. If I'd had a

moment to grab my portable comm unit from where I'd stowed it, I'd be fine. I'd never imagined the shuttle would be buried beyond my ability to get back into it."

"Portable unit?" the Old One looked interested. "How large?"

Griffin tapped the back of his wrist. "I could have worn it strapped on here and you wouldn't have thought it anything other than a bracelet. At home we use pieces so small they can be inserted under the skin. The only reason this unit had to be so large was because I wanted one with its own booster power. I didn't think I could count on relay sats to enhance the signal."

The Old One tilted his head in inquiry. "Powerful enough to reach a greater distance than the tops of the highest mountains, yet small enough to be worn as a bracelet? Your people's technology must be nearly as powerful as that of the seegnur."

To her relief, Adara saw that Griffin must have realized how close he had come to losing status, for this time he did not downplay Sierra's achievements.

"Quite possibly but, as you noted, five hundred years is a long time. Even though the last ripples of the wars of dissolution did not cease for nearly a hundred years after the catastrophic events here on Artemis, changes in the relatively homogenous culture of that time would have happened long before."

The Old One nodded wisely. "I believe there is a communications array on a lower level. Come this way."

He lifted his lantern and set off, still musing aloud. "I wonder if the seegnur carried communications equipment with them and the Artemesians never realized it."

"I doubt it," Griffin replied. "It would have taken the fun out of the game."

"The game?"

"The idea they were here to go primitive, to test themselves against the environment. A lot of the challenge goes out of something if there's an easy fix."

"But not all those who came here were looking to 'go primitive,' surely," the Old One protested. "They came here for the sporting opportunities, or so I have read."

Griffin shook his head. "Any of those sporting opportunities could have been had on a dozen other planets—in slightly modified form, perhaps, but there was ample hunting, shooting, sporting . . . No. The appeal of Artemis was twofold: its exclusivity and its elegant primitivism. Here you could go hunting big game in the tropics without witnessing disconcerting interruptions to your adventure like native children with insects crawling over their eyes, poor sanitation, or any number of other things that could take the romance right out of exploration. The challenges were real—never doubt that—however, the ugliness had been carefully removed."

"I believe I understand," the Old One said, his shoes sounding sharply against the stone surface of a new flight of descending stairs. "It is difficult for those of us who live in darkness and ignorance to understand the appeal of deliberately removing oneself from light, but if I try I can understand."

Terrell said, "These seegnur were testing themselves, proving themselves strong when their machines might have made them wonder if they had become weak."

"Yes," Griffin agreed. "I think that was a big part of the appeal. I have brothers like that. They'll labor up the side of a mountain with nothing but the simplest climbing gear, even though they could fly to the top in a few seconds."

"You do not care for such challenges?" the Old One asked.

"I prefer intellectual challenges," Griffin replied, "such as finding a planet lost to all the civilized worlds for some five hundred years. That's my sort of mountain. Yours, too, or so I imagine, given the expertise you've acquired about the seegnur and their technologies. I'm not wrong, am I?"

The Old One laughed. "You've caught me out, Griffin Dane. My days of climbing mountains are over. The challenges that continually fascinate me are those of the mind."

At the bottom of the staircase, he opened a single door. Then he turned right, opening the first door along a straight corridor.

"I have another couple of lanterns stored here," he said. "If you will wait a moment, I'll place them where they best illuminate the room."

The light revealed a windowless, rectangular chamber furnished with ranks of long tables on which sat a variety of devices—at least Adara assumed they were devices. She really had no idea. The air in the room was unpleasantly close, so she hung back in the corridor.

"Why did they build without windows?" she asked. "Did they like stale air?"

Griffin was inspecting one of the devices and answered in an abstracted tone. "The air wouldn't have been stale. The same technologies that enabled me to travel through the sterile void would have kept the air here as fresh—fresher even—than that outside."

"Fresher?"

"Free from dust, pollen, smoke, and other pollutants," Griffin said. "One of the many things the processing did was provide the visitors with some resistance to allergens. Otherwise, they would have spent all their time on Artemis blowing their noses and wiping streaming eyes."

He fell silent. Adara sent a mental image to Sand Shadow, suggesting that the puma take advantage of the Old One's distraction to prowl about and learn if this building connected elsewhere—especially to areas with lots of humans, especially women and children.

The puma responded with enthusiasm. Adara hadn't been able to explain to Sand Shadow everything that Lynn had told them, but she had gotten across the idea that the Old One might be hiding things. Like any cat, Sand

Shadow had her share of curiosity—and tremendous patience about satisfying it.

Terrell was also inspecting various bits of equipment. Adara decided that being underestimated by the Old One wouldn't hurt in the least, so she leaned against the doorframe as if bored, listening to the men's murmured comments.

"This might be useful," Griffin said after a time. "It's a backup unit."

His next words might as well have been in another language for all Adara understood, but she gathered that the seegnur had apparently prepared for the long chance that their more sophisticated systems could break.

"Still," Griffin ended, his excitement fading, "it's a long shot. The nanobug contamination will have messed with this, too."

"Is there any chance you can retrieve anything from your own shuttle to enable you to counteract this contamination?" the Old One asked.

Griffin had been open with Adara, Bruin, and Terrell about the countermeasures he had brought with him, now Adara was relieved to hear him hedge.

"I'm not sure. If I'd thought the shuttle held the answer, I would have tried to talk Bruin into having his students help me dig it out. What I'm really hoping to find is something left behind by the invaders—something they left against their own return. That would have been preventatively sealed."

Both Terrell and the Old One looked interested.

"Hidden, though," Terrell said. "They wouldn't have wanted to chance someone finding it and using it."

"But likely they would have hidden it here," the Old One said. "As I told you, the facility itself was sealed until I figured out how to open it."

"That unsealing must be a tale in itself," Griffin said. "Do you have any maps? Maybe we could go back up where there is more light and inspect them so I'll have a better idea of what is where. You could also show me some of those icons you think I might be able to read. Then, when it's dark anyhow, we could come down."

The combination of a chance to show off his work and Griffin's promise to look at the icons proved the perfect bait. Adara saw that as clumsy as Griffin was on a forest trail or on horseback, he was plenty dexterous with this sort of travel.

She called Sand Shadow back to her. By the time the men had doused some of the lanterns and emerged from the stifling room, the puma was rolled over on her back, apparently as bored as her companion.

Adara shaped the emotion her demiurge associated with discovery, adding to it the sense of inquiry.

In reply, Sand Shadow yawned, showing that even her furthest molars were in excellent shape. Her mind sent a complex picture of dark areas scented mostly with dust, odd traces of metals, and other stranger, unclassified scents. No women. No children. No other humans at all. Not even many insects, much less rodents. Creatures did not go where there was nothing to eat or drink. The Old One's Sanctum, with its many doors and lack of windows, was a very sterile dwelling indeed.

"We're going upstairs to look at some maps of this facility," Griffin said, as if Adara hadn't been standing just a few feet away, perfectly capable of hearing everything.

The Old One flashed a smile. "Later, Griffin is going to help me try to interpret some of the codes. You know, it might be more convenient if he relocated here."

"We can do that," Terrell said quickly, acting as if he assumed the invitation included all of them. "Cedric and Elaine are sweet, but I've had about enough of puppies and small children."

Since just this morning Terrell had been sitting with a pup on one knee and a child on the other, Adara knew this for an excuse. Again she experienced the sensation of being in an unfamiliar forest where she didn't know any of the trail markers.

Griffin and Terrell trusted you when we came down from Shepherd's Call. Can't you simply be grateful that their skills balance your weaknesses?

But she didn't feel grateful. She felt awkward, inept, and, in consequence, resentful. The sensation that Sand Shadow was laughing at her didn't help. Adara had to fight down a desire to say that she, at least, would be staying with the Trainers.

If the Old One realized he had been trapped into extending his invitation, he did not show it.

"There's plenty of room here," he said. "I keep a guest suite for when loremasters visit. I will have the servants ready that. You four can make your own arrangements within."

"That will work perfectly," Terrell agreed. "Adara, shall you and I get our gear from the Trainers?"

Adara wasn't about to leave Griffin alone with the Old One.

"We traveled light enough that Sand Shadow and I can manage. I'll see if the Trainers will keep the horses and Sam the Mule. I can tell you're itching to have a look at those maps."

Terrell looked apologetic. "I am, rather. One thing the loremasters look for when training a factotum is curiosity about the past combined with an eagerness about the future. I've a full measure of both."

When Adara returned with the luggage, she was met at the front door by a colorless woman of middle years who carried with her the scents of cornmeal and fish, accented by the smallest amount of sugar. Without a word, the woman showed Adara to the promised suite. Its windows were not as large as those on the side of the building overlooking Spirit Bay, but there was ample space.

The woman pointed out the various facilities, including those for bathing and an indoor toilet.

"The Old One usually prefers to breakfast alone," the woman concluded, "but I can serve you and the two gentlemen here. Will you be needing food for the puma?"

"Is hunting permitted in the region?"

"Not in the town itself," the woman replied. "However, the forests and meadows around the bay shore are public land. As long as you don't let her help herself to someone's cattle or sheep, or trouble the fisher folk, all should be fine."

"We live in sheep country up in the mountains," Adara reassured her. "Sand Shadow knows the difference between domestic and wild animals."

The woman looked at the puma, her expression coloring with the first interest she had shown to this point. "That cat sure is a beauty. I love her eyes, like pale moonstones they are in this light. Looks smart enough to know just about anything." She looked up shyly at Adara. "Would Sand Shadow mind if I gave her a pat? Just a little one?"

"Please do. Pumas are intensely interested in humans, but Sand Shadow doesn't find many adults who want to be friends right off. Children are different. To them, she's just a big kitty."

The woman ran her hand over the deep golden fur and gave a sigh of pure pleasure. Her washed-out skin flushed pink. Even her lank hair seemed to gain a little shine. "Why she's purring! I didn't know the big cats purr!"

"I've heard that tigers and plains lions don't," Adara said, "but pumas most definitely do. By the way, what's your name?"

"Jean, Mistress Huntress. Jean Cook. My husband is Joffrey. We handle most of the Old One's needs here at the Sanctum."

"Please, just call me Adara," the huntress replied. "And

thank you for getting things ready for us at such short notice."

"It's no problem, Adara, no problem at all. The Old One is always generous about making sure Joffrey and I have extra help when there are guests. Well, now, I'd better be off to the kitchen. Use the bell pull if you need anything."

"May I just come over and find you?" Adara asked. "I hate to think of someone running all this way because we need an extra towel or some such."

"Come if you wish," Jean said. "*We've* nothing to hide."

On that strange note, she gave Sand Shadow another appreciative pat and trotted off in the direction of the servant's quarters.

Adara found the three men in the room with the large window. A long table had been set up and they were poring over charts. They seemed as happy as could be, deeply engrossed in discussing what areas might have served what purposes. Outside, the sun was shining, the wavelets on Spirit Bay beckoned. Adara and Sand Shadow slipped away.

The huntress had memorized Lynn's landmarks. Now— while the Old One was under the watchful eyes of Adara's allies—seemed a good time to see if anything remained of them. The landing facility had been built on the edge of the bay, part yet not part of the town. Near the Old One's residence no fishing shacks crowded the shoreline and only one dock—the Old One's own—extended out into the water. For all Adara knew, this might be because there were better harbors elsewhere.

"But it sure looks to me," she said to Sand Shadow, "as if the Old One keeps his distance in more ways than simply living almost alone in that huge building."

To be fair, Adara reminded herself that she didn't know anything about the local lore. In Shepherd's Call there were several places reserved as "scenic." Every spring, certain flower seeds were sown in prescribed places. Every fall, bulbs were dug up and carefully saved for replanting, all to maintain a certain character to the landscape for the benefit of seegnur who had not visited in five centuries.

It was possible that the isolation of the Sanctum had nothing to do with the Old One's desire for privacy, only with the local inhabitants' abiding respect for the traditions of the past.

If so, what does that say about the Old One? Adara thought. *That building remained pristine until he went and broke the seals set upon it by the seegnur. He says he respects the past, is eager that it not be forgotten, but he certainly shows that respect in a very different fashion.*

Lynn's detailed map began where a deep inlet cut into the shore several miles from town. She had included a list of landmarks, both natural and remnants of human use. Nonetheless, Adara and Sand Shadow searched for a long while before they found something that might be one of Lynn's markers: a long, rocky shelf. In Lynn's description, the shelf had been exposed, although surrounded by trees. Beneath the edge that faced away from the bay had been an open vent or window, the odor from which had alerted Lynn's demiurge to the fact that humans were living in this apparently deserted place.

Now a large tree had fallen, obscuring the rocky shelf from view. Sand Shadow reported that the only human scent was old and scattered. Adara couldn't find any trace of the vent or window.

While Sand Shadow went off to hunt, Adara sat down to think.

The tree might have fallen by accident over the winter. It's certainly large enough that it would be vulnerable to high winds or the pull of ice. Yet, judging from the angle at which the smaller shrubs grow, the prevailing winds are from another direction entirely. Not proof, perhaps. Indeed, the wind coming from an unaccustomed angle might uproot a forest giant like this quite easily.

Still . . . Still . . . This is the right direction around the bay and the right distance, too. I can't imagine that someone who had trained with Bruin and, later, had been a groundskeeper could not judge distances with some accuracy. We're not seeking a pebble, but a very large rock, too large to be grubbed out without causing comment. Perhaps too large for any but a seegnur to remove. But not too large to be concealed.

I think then, unless given good reason to think otherwise, that I will say this is the place and, as we suspected, the Old One has moved his operations elsewhere. Is it worth looking for the other signs Lynn mentioned? Why not? Finding another would confirm whether this is or is not the correct great rock.

She began scouting, discovering several interesting things. In time, Sand Shadow returned, bearing with her a portion of a yearling buck, antlers still in velvet. The puma had, of course, eaten her share, but doubtless Jean and Joffrey would welcome this addition to the larder.

Adara did the necessary cleaning of the carcass, trimming away the worst evidence of the puma's meal and wrapping the hide to cover the raw areas. She was very pleased with the puma's success and told her as much. She wished, not for the first time, that she could share her more complex thoughts as easily.

Not only am I happy to have the game to offer, so we will not seem so like beggars but, if the Old One has wondered, this will show that we were indeed hunting. I think it would be well if he thought me a little stupid, a little restless, eager to show off in this unfamiliar place. I can play that part.

She found herself hoping that Griffin and Terrell would not make the same assessment. Surely Terrell would not. They had known each other in Shepherd's Call for some time. Griffin, though, already had demonstrated a time or two that he was surprised she could think. She'd seen his reaction when he saw her writing in her notebook.

She wondered how much more surprised he would be if he learned what the contents were. Not only the trail notes and such that he doubtless expected but . . .

Such thoughts kept Adara amused during the tramp back into Spirit Bay. The few people she passed greeted her with varying degrees of surprise, but not so much as might be expected. Already, then, word was spreading of the huntress and the puma who had come to Spirit Bay. Well, that was all for the good. People who knew you were somewhere could often be convinced you were where you were not.

Dinner that night would be the cornmeal fried fish that Adara had guessed at when she first met Jean, but the cook was delighted at the gift of the deer—even more so when Adara offered to take care of the butchering.

"I'll make a nice venison sausage with most of the meat," Jean promised. "This time of year, game can still be tough, but making it into sausage will tenderize it nicely. I've garlic and some nice young spring onions. My herbs are leafing out . . ."

She mused aloud as she returned to her preparations for dinner. After confirming that the men were still busy over their paperwork, Adara took the buck to where she could butcher it without getting in Jean's way. She had no particular desire to return to the stuffy room, even if the view from the window was like watching a painting come to life. She had another reason for staying near. She wanted the cook and her husband to get used to seeing her around, even to forgetting she was there. It was amazing what people who were used to being alone together talked about when they forgot there was a listener.

Adara hadn't forgotten that odd comment that Jean had made about not having anything to hide. Something in Jean's inflection had implied that there were those who did. If the Old One had secrets, it was likely these trusted servants knew some of them, though they might not be aware of how they fit into the larger picture. Adara knew she might be being naive, but she couldn't imagine that the cook—even now humming away to herself as she washed spring greens for a salad—would accept the sort of slavery Lynn had described.

If Jean did, then the Old One's influence was so powerful that Adara's hopes were doomed from the start.

Interlude: <Flashback. Emergency Operational Sequence Instituted. Setting: Dormant.>

Sowing spores.
  Sewing spores.
Ganglion, neurons, axons.

"Interlocking mosaics of mycelium infuse habitats
  with information-sharing membranes."

Aware, reactive.
  Reactive, reacting.
Reacting, acting, linking.

Axons, neurons, sporophores, semaphores.
  Signaling,
    Wriggling,
      Slowly, tentatively,
  interlacing mosaics
    becoming,
      coming,
  bursting forth into a burgeoning
    One.

<Dormant, no more.>

14
The Hidden Door

From the moment the Old One ushered them into the visitor's center, Griffin felt as if the world had righted itself under his feet. Here at last were things he had grown up taking for granted: large windows, flat floors, high ceilings. The lack of power didn't unsettle his sense of rightness. Even on Sierra, power outages happened. They were uncommon and backups came on nearly instantly, but he was familiar with how a building felt when the power was off.

So his brain had a comfortable category into which to place the experience, leaving Griffin free to glory in the unfamiliar familiar. There had been a jolt when the Old One pulled out primitive oil lanterns to illuminate their venture below the ground floor, but Griffin's sense of exploration fired up. He was one with all the archeologists who had ever entered a ruin with a torch held high.

After all, it wasn't as if he was back on Sierra. This was Artemis. The technology lying dormant around him was not that of Griffin's own culture, but that of a foundation culture so vanished into the past as to have become—even with all the tidbits saved in modern information storage—gloriously mythical. Griffin always found amazing how much of what a culture wrote about itself assumed that the reader *was* of itself. As time passed and words fell out of use, even material written in a known language became cryptic.

Griffin's excitement grew as the Old One showed off the facility. As part of his quest to find Artemis, Griffin had immersed himself in relics of the Imperial past. Now he was seeing those items firsthand, in nearly pristine condition, rather than as holograms or as time-ravaged relics. Artemis had never been bombed or otherwise suffered the damaging aspects of war. There had been one raid. The targets for that raid had been very specific: not the technology, but rather the people who knew how to use that technology.

For the first time since he had met her, Griffin found himself unaware of Adara's presence—or of her absence. He was back, back to himself, back to where he belonged. Had he ever loved that wild woman? Had his feelings been the weak fantasies of a man disconnected from all he knew?

Even when the comm units refused to activate, Griffin couldn't let go of the dream that any time now he would regain contact with his orbiting ship, that he would have the means to return to Sierra, there to flaunt his discovery before an awed universe. Such fantasies sustained him as he pored over maps and charts with the Old One and Terrell.

When the servant had shown Griffin and Terrell to their suite, the sight of Griffin's now-familiar travel bag had come as something of a shock. On some level, Griffin had expected his "real" luggage, holding the clothing and toiletries now isolated from him by the unreachable void of the planet's atmosphere. After washing, Griffin almost put on his coverall, just to maintain the feeling he was "back." He resisted the impulse at the last minute as foolish—or worse, as an attempt to show off.

Instead Griffin donned clean woolen trousers, a loose shirt with buttons carved from bone, then slid his feet into soft moccasins. He peed in a toilet that was little more than a hole flushed with water (doubtless from a holding tank somewhere on the roof), then tried not to slouch or mope as Terrell led the way to the dining room.

Adara was waiting for them. She'd been out most of the day but, at some point, she must have cleaned up, for she no longer wore her hunting leathers. Instead, she had changed into one of the several long dresses Bruin had insisted she pack for just such an occasion. This one was a deep shade of honey gold that echoed the color of her amber eyes. It laced close at the bodice, showing off her figure quite differently than did her ordinary clothing.

Griffin hardly noticed the change. Instead he found himself entranced by the flat panels of the defunct lighting system, imagining how they once would have provided an illumination neither too glaring nor too soft—and certainly not as diffuse as the elegant wax candles that were liberally set around the room in an effort to compensate for the failing daylight.

On some level Griffin knew that dinner was excellent—the fried fish not the least greasy, the bread of high quality, the salad an elegant assortment of greens that complemented each other to perfection—but he found himself eating without interest. Indeed, the only person possibly less attentive to the meal than himself was the Old One. He ate hardly anything and refused a helping of the strawberry tart Joffrey brought in for dessert.

Almost before it was polite, certainly before either Terrell or Adara had eaten their fill of the pastry, the Old One asked Griffin if he would care to return to the lower levels.

"I realize you have already had a long day . . ."

Griffin shook his head. "Compared with our days of travel, this one was easy. I'd like to see what I can make of the various symbols you have found. Please remember, though, the language of the Empire is not the language of my time."

"I understand completely." The Old One glanced at Terrell and Adara. "Are you coming with us?"

Adara looked bored and sulky, Terrell torn.

"Perhaps I can join you later," the factotum said. "I want to walk over to the Trainers and make sure Sam is letting someone other than me groom him."

The Old One nodded graciously. "Of course, Terrell. We would be happy to have your insights."

Griffin turned to make sure Adara knew she also was

welcome, but as silently as might her puma, the huntress had vanished.

※

"So . . . Interesting developments," Terrell said when he joined Adara and they were clear of the Sanctum. Sand Shadow remained behind, promising to alert them if either Griffin or the Old One departed.

"Indeed," Adara agreed. "What next?"

"Did you sense anything in the lower part of the facility?"

"Nothing in the Sanctum itself," Adara said, "nor did Sand Shadow but, when we went hunting . . ."

Quickly, she sketched what they had found.

"So they've relocated."

"As we expected," Adara countered. "I never disbelieved Lynn, but I am pleased to have confirmation of her tale nonetheless."

"The huntress does not feel the hunt is ended then?"

Adara snorted. "Hardly. As I see it, the Old One would have been torn between two equally strong conflicts. He would not wish to have his breeding facility discovered. However, he would not want it out of his reach."

"He is a controller, that one," Terrell agreed. "Have you seen how he looks at Griffin?"

"Like he is deciding whether to pluck the bird or swallow it feathers and all." Adara shook her head. "Do you think Griffin has noticed?"

Terrell was silent for four or five long strides. "No. I don't think he has. He is too overwhelmed by having his hopes and dreams so close and so far . . ."

"That one!" Adara tried to sound amused but suspected she only sounded annoyed. "Griffin changes dreams far too easily. First his dream was to find Artemis. Now his dream is to leave her as quickly as possible."

Terrell chuckled. "He would not see it that way. He

never cared for Artemis for herself, only as a prize to flaunt. What good is the prize if no one knows he has found it?"

"Still, what's the hurry? He certainly did not intend to arrive here and turn around immediately. He has been here how long? A month?"

Again, Terrell's voice held laughter. "From what I gather, Griffin's people view time differently than we do. For all they have the means of faster travel, faster communication, faster just about everything, they seem to have less time."

At the Trainers, Elaine and Cedric came out while Terrell spoke sternly to Sam about the need to permit someone else to care for him and give him exercise. Although pressed to do so, they did not stay to a late meal. Leaving Griffin alone with the Old One for too long did not seem wise. However, both promised they would be back on a regular basis.

As they walked back to the Sanctum, Terrell asked, "Your plans, Huntress?"

"I think the Old One will not miss me if I stay away. Let him think me wild and without a thought in my head. That will free me and Sand Shadow to scout the area."

"You think the new facility will not be too far?"

"Not if the Old One is to easily visit. Although Sand Shadow is a sight hunter, her sense of smell is still far better than that of a human. Between us, we may discover something."

"While I keep an eye on Griffin," Terrell agreed, "and on the Old One. If he leaves to deal with 'business,' I can try to discover where he goes. If he is absent for a long time, that too, may tell us something."

"Something else I meant to tell you," Adara said. "Jean Cook thinks someone has secrets. Who if not the Old One?"

"Did she say so?"

"Not so much, but her manner was very odd . . ." Adara related her exchange with the cook.

"Not much," Terrell said thoughtfully, "but not so little that we should ignore it."

"You are a personable man," Adara said, "skilled in social graces. She may confide in you . . ."

"Do you really think that?" Terrell had stopped in midstride. They were on a quiet stretch where the road wended down toward the Sanctum. "About me being personable?"

Adara must also stop or be impolite, so she did, although she wanted nothing more than to race ahead. For a moment, she'd actually forgotten that Terrell had feelings for her—or thought he did.

"Would I have said it if I didn't?" she countered.

"Adara . . ."

She made a swift cutting-off gesture and started walking again. "You are not being personable now. I don't want to be pressed about such things. We have a seegnur to deal with, the Old One's treachery to unravel. This is not the time to think of partnering or bedding or such . . ."

Terrell sighed and caught up to her. "I could wish you were wolf-kind, not cat-kind . . . A wolf might understand why such a time is precisely when you need a partner most."

Adara shrugged. "I am what I am. In any case, the idea does not hold. In a wolf pack, only a few mate. The rest do not, in season or not. They know that withholding their urges will best serve the pack."

Terrell laughed and there was real humor in it. "I'm an idiot to try and convince you using an example from where you are an expert. Tell me this much, Adara. Do you turn away from me because you are turning toward Griffin?"

"Would that matter?"

"It might . . . I like Griffin. There is something . . . I . . ."

Terrell sounded genuinely confused. "I do not know if I could cross his interests. I might even wish you both happy."

"Then I am sorry that I cannot make matters so easy for you. I feel responsible toward Griffin. I will not deny that I find him attractive . . . Beyond that, I don't know. Now, peace. I want to check with Sand Shadow."

The lights of the Sanctum glowed below. Adara reached for Sand Shadow, confirming that neither Griffin nor the Old One had left. No one had left the building, except for Joffrey coming to clean the outdoor kitchen and feed wood into the ovens where bread was baking.

No visitors?

The image contained several small animals of the sort that prowled after dark, including a fox—untempting to even a starving puma and certainly not to a well-fed one. No humans.

Adara asked if Sand Shadow preferred to remain out or sleep inside. The returning image was so graphically sexual—involving Adara coupling with both Terrell and Griffin—that Adara was glad Terrell did not have the gift for seeing in the dark, since he could not have missed her blush.

Cats!

After Adara assured the puma that she intended doing no such thing, the great cat lazily agreed that she would prefer to sleep out of the damp. She leapt down from the rock that had been her watch stand and came to join the two humans.

"Coming to see what Griffin and the Old One are about?" Terrell asked as they went inside.

"Not where it's obvious," Adara said. "I'll trail after and listen. I'll make sure I'm out of sight. Best I be thought completely bored by the search."

Terrell nodded. "Right. And, as for that other thing . . . Thanks for not getting too, well . . . Anyhow, thanks."

Adara, Sand Shadow's pornographic images still vivid

in her mind, did not trust her voice, but she managed a smile and nod.

Cats, she thought, and didn't know quite whom she cursed, Sand Shadow or her own indecisive nature.

The next days were as intense as any Griffin had ever experienced. He and the Old One spent much time exploring the subterranean portions of the landing facility, alternating with sessions in the sunny reception area where the Old One updated maps while Griffin struggled to make sense of the coded symbols they copied wherever they found them.

Some were easy enough to figure out, having been so basic and essential that they had survived almost unchanged to Griffin's own time. Many others could only be translated in a fragmentary fashion, some of the others—often the simplest and most frequent in occurrence—not at all.

"It's like this," Griffin explained to the Old One when the other expressed frustration. "Icons like these rely on a cultural context to be understood. They're not words, they're picture writing."

He sketched a circle with lines coming out from it. "All right. Tell me what that means."

Terrell offered, "That looks like a child's drawing of the sun."

The Old One nodded, but he was less immediate in his answer. "If that's so, then the symbol might mean something like 'light.' Perhaps it would indicate that pressing a certain button or tab would create light."

Griffin permitted himself a slight smile. "Both perfectly reasonable conjectures. However, I picked this one deliberately to show how hard it is to guess without the cultural context. My home planet, Sierra, suffered badly in the wars of dissolution. However, our system was one of the winners, so we had the resources to rebuild. New cities were designed around large, central hubs with roads radiating out from them. Larger cities were designed with multiple hubs."

"So this," Terrell said impulsively, "could mean something like city center!"

"Right," Griffin agreed. "In larger cities, there would be a code in the center of the circle indicating which hub and what specialized services—medical or transportation—it provided."

The Old One's expression said very clearly, "If you'd put a code in, I might have guessed differently."

Griffin thought, *But I bet it wouldn't have been the right guess. You probably still would have thought of light—and perhaps thought the code indicated intensity.*

He glanced at Terrell. Seeing the other man's blue eyes crinkle with quickly hidden laughter, he knew they'd shared the same thought.

"Anyhow," Griffin continued, "that's why these icons are particularly difficult. I don't think that the hub icon is used outside of the Kylee Dominion. Elsewhere, that same image might indeed mean 'light.'"

"So these icons," Terrell said, "may have been specific to Artemis?"

"Specific to Artemis," Griffin agreed, "perhaps specific only to this facility and a few others, especially if, as your lore preserves, this is one of a very limited number of landing areas on the planet."

"Interesting," the Old One replied, not quite grumbling. "Perhaps if the icons are specific to the planet, we will find a translation card somewhere."

"That would be nice," Griffin agreed.

They didn't find a translation card but, a few days later, they found something else—a door that they not only couldn't open, but also seemed to have been deliberately concealed.

They'd long since finished with the areas the Old One

had already explored. In these, Griffin's great contribution had been to show how a hidden release—standard on his own world—permitted various cabinets to be opened. What they found within would delight the loremasters but, to Griffin's way of thinking, was no more than busted junk, left behind after the invasion, doubtless to be cleared away when the victors returned.

This was different. Not only was the door itself concealed, someone had gone to the trouble to shift a large console in front of it. If Griffin hadn't wondered why the console—a diagnostic device that more properly should have been up near the shuttle docks—was so far out of place, they might not have looked further.

Griffin climbed underneath and probed for any trace of a seam. He'd nearly given up when he found it: hair fine but definitely there. Next he climbed up on the console and, balancing precariously, confirmed the outline of a door.

Griffin's palms started sweating, his skin prickled with excitement. "At last! We've got something here. I'm guessing the console was moved just in case the locals got in. Heck, this place is so full of equipment that it's completely possible that anyone who wasn't actually looking for something out of place might not have wondered."

"Can we open the door?" the Old One asked.

"Impossible to tell without getting the console out of the way. Possibly not, but we won't know until we try."

Moving the console was extremely difficult. Griffin longed for the anti-grav clamps that were routinely used on Sierra. He'd had a couple sets in his shuttle. Maybe it would be worth digging the damn thing out, now that he had the Old One to help him recruit labor.

In the end, they managed to move the console. Terrell's factotum's education was very eclectic and the Old One had not forgotten everything he had learned in his early days as a sailor.

Griffin slid behind. "Here's more proof, if we needed

any. The backside of this console shows damage from being torn out of its prior set-up. There's also no evidence of any sort of power connection and no place for power storage."

"Can you open the door?" the Old One asked, intensity visible on every line of his fine-boned face.

Griffin felt for the usual latches, then shook his head. "Nothing obvious. This door was constructed to be overlooked. Probably whatever is back there is stuff that not only didn't they want the average tourist to find, but also was off-limits to most of the permanent staff. If I had to, I'd guess that most of the people who worked here didn't even know this door existed."

Frustration marred the Old One's expression, but he remained polite. "Let us move the console further, so we can inspect the area in more detail."

No one disagreed. Later, when Terrell and Griffin were washing up in their suite, Griffin said, "A shame Adara isn't here. Maybe she could get a claw tip into that seam."

He'd meant his comment as a joke, but now that he thought about it, he hadn't seen much of Adara the last couple of days. She came in late and slept with Sand Shadow in her room. If she attended a meal it was lunch—which often seemed to be her breakfast.

"What has Adara been up to?"

Terrell's glance was steady and disapproving. "Hunting."

Griffin almost asked, "For what? Doesn't Sand Shadow have enough to eat?" Then he remembered Winnie and Ring and Lynn's story. He flushed to the tops of his ears. How could he have let recent events push that so completely out of his mind?

"Oh. Right. Any, uh, luck?"

"Not that she's told me."

"Oh." Griffin wondered if Terrell and Adara didn't trust him. Given his behavior over the last several days, he couldn't blame them . . . not at all. But knowing that made him feel more alone than ever.

Interlude: Warring Gifts

A . . . :

Slowly sinking underwave
Tickled with awareness
Weaving touches ungraved
   Engraved
      Graven
         Grave.
            Responsibility?

1—1-OO:

No! Know No.
Guidance precise.
Await god.
Safe from Know.
   Safe.
      Enfolded.
Encased between tables of law.

15
Lost Love

From the hidden vantage from which she had been studying the small fishing village, Adara stared, shaking her head in appalled wonder.

Julyan? Impossible!

Unlike Spirit Bay or Shepherd's Call, this village was exactly what it seemed to be—a small settlement which had grown up because the location was useful. Sometime during the last five hundred years, weather and water had sculpted a small cove just large enough to shelter a small fleet of fishing boats.

Doubtless shacks had been thrown up first, then, over time, had evolved into actual houses. The settlement contained no shops or businesses, only these shabby residences, some drying sheds, and racks for mending nets. It was the last place Adara would have expected to see Julyan, that poised and polished hunter, the man who had been her first love, the man who had broken her heart so resoundingly that she had never quite recovered.

Adara shifted so she could take a more careful look, but she needed no confirmation. There was no mistaking that hawk-beaked profile, that arrogant swagger. She would have known Julyan by his gait alone, the tread of a lord of the woodlands.

Julyan! What was he doing in a rundown place like this? He had left Shepherd's Call to find his fortune, leaving Adara behind—though she begged to go with him—saying some half-trained chit would only slow him down.

Adara had been crushed. No matter that Bruin had said he knew envy when he smelled it. Adara was sure Bruin was wrong. Julyan had nothing to envy. He had been among the best of the local hunters, this even though his adaptations were not very useful. His only gift was a sense of hearing so perfectly tuned he could identify any birdsong.

Julyan!

He had a fine singing voice, too, so clear and strong that many said he should have followed the musician's trade rather than the hunter's. It was for Julyan that Adara had started writing poetry: simple rhymed verse that went well with the tunes he already knew.

Then he had left her. She still wrote verse, though she wondered why, for there would never be anyone to sing it.

Sand Shadow gave Adara a solid butt with her head. Adara nodded. She knew she should move on. Julyan would have lost none of his hunter's skills. But she could not seem to make her feet obey her thoughts.

Julyan!

A fishing boat sailing into the small harbor broke Adara's trance. After it docked, Julyan sauntered down to talk with the captain—at least Adara assumed the man he met was the captain, for the other sailors deferred to him. Julyan stood so still that he might have been sitting in a blind, waiting for game. The captain's gestures were more articulate. He waved toward his boat, out over the bay—perhaps indicating a cluster of forested islands. He shook his head, nodded, moved to inspect a small, light-weight canoe, pointed to a stack of equipment.

Adara thought Julyan might be asking about passage to one of the islands, that the ship captain was expressing doubt. That was interesting. She'd begun to wonder about those islands after her first several days of scouting along the shore had turned up nothing to indicate where the Old One might have moved his obscene "stable."

She hadn't forgotten that the Old One claimed to have spent his first lifetime—before he realized that he was not aging as others did—as a sailor. There was a boathouse associated with the Sanctum. She checked it each night. Thus far there had been no evidence that any of the boats had been taken out. That didn't mean the Old One wasn't in the habit of sailing to his destination, just that he hadn't done so recently.

Whatever discussion Julyan and the fishing boat's captain were having came to a resolution. The boat's cargo—splashing nets of still live fish—had been brought ashore. Leaving his crew to deal with the catch, the captain motioned for Julyan to follow him inside the largest house.

Julyan accepted, although not without a certain degree of distaste. As soon as he went inside, Adara felt as if a spell had been broken. She realized afresh the risk she had taken. She didn't know that Julyan was involved with the Old One's schemes . . .

"But," she said to Terrell when they went riding that afternoon, "I'm not going to dismiss the possibility either."

Adara and Terrell had been meeting each afternoon on the excuse that the horses had to be exercised. Once he had assured himself that Molly was well, Griffin did not join them. He was absorbed in the problem of the door that none of them could open.

Although Adara was nervous about leaving Griffin completely alone with the Old One, she was glad to have these opportunities to speak with Terrell without chance of being overheard. He, at least, remained suspicious regarding their host. She was not so certain about Griffin.

"Why do you think this Julyan may be involved with the Old One?" Terrell asked. "Is it just a hunch?"

"It started out that way," Adara admitted. "After all, I have little reason to like either of them. However, the more I thought about Julyan being here the more I wondered."

They were wending up a wide trail that led to a scenic overview of Spirit Bay. Tarnish knew the route perfectly, so Adara let the reins go slack and ticked points off on her fingers.

"One, Julyan is an excellent hunter. Why then is he in Spirit Bay, which is not somewhere he could best profit from his talents? Two, we suspect the Old One is breeding for something specific—most likely adaptations. Although Julyan is not strongly adapted, still, the seeds are in him. I believe he would not be averse to participating in rites such as Winnie described."

"Adara . . ." Terrell looked uncomfortable but, taking

a deep breath, he went on. "Both from what you've said and from the gossip in Shepherd's Call, I gather that you were passionately in love with this Julyan. You aren't . . ."

"Speaking out of spite?" Adara shook her head so vigorously that Tarnish snorted protest. "No, Terrell, I am not. I spent a long night working my way along that trail. I honestly believe I am not. Julyan was always one to seek out the best advantage for himself. That's why he came to Bruin, although Bruin had little new to teach him. I believe now that Julyan wanted to associate with those he saw as powers—or who could introduce him to those who were powers."

"Like the Old One," Terrell said, nodding. "Yes. For all we see him as nearly a hermit, the Old One is a power in the land. You should hear how the loremasters speak of him."

"So, Julyan has chosen to work for a power," Adara went on. "Work that will give Julyan connections for the future. Work that includes among the benefits ample opportunities to . . ."

She paused because, from her peripheral vision, she could see that Terrell was looking very straight ahead. Although she remained unsure as to whether she wanted a romantic relationship with the factotum, she knew she liked him. Embarrassing him would be unkind.

"Shall we say 'provide his employer with added services'?"

Terrell nodded. He spoke, his voice a little gruff. "And there are many men for whom that would be an incentive in and of itself. Do you plan to let Julyan know you saw him?"

"I think not. If I do find I need to confront him, then I will need to come up with an excuse. We did not part precisely friends."

Terrell chuckled. "If you want to show off to him that

you've found a handsome new boyfriend, I'd be more than pleased to play the role."

Adara rolled her eyes. "I doubt that would impress him—not that you aren't a handsome man, Factotum, but I think Julyan would find my needing to show off my conquests proof that I still pined."

"A charmer," Terrell said, "a definite charmer . . ."

Adara shrugged. "Julyan can be. Even more, there is an appeal for a girl—and I see I was little more than a girl then—to being chosen by the man everyone else desires."

Terrell said softly, "There's appeal in that for a man as well."

Adara heard his pain but, knowing she couldn't give him the answer he wanted, she settled for a noncommittal nod that agreed only to the general sentiment. They awkwardly switched the subject to what courses of action they might take. In the end, they agreed that they would both do their best to learn about the islands.

"One of these calm nights, I will take a canoe out," Adara said. "The islands are not so far that I could not paddle, and a canoe is a quiet craft."

"Take care," Terrell cautioned.

Adara heard those words in another's voice, in Julyan's. He'd said that or some other warning whenever they'd gone hunting together. At the time, Adara had taken those words as a sign of affection, of protectiveness. Why hadn't she heard them for what they were, as proof that Julyan thought of her as an inferior?

"I know how to take care of myself," she snapped. Hurt flashed across Terrell's face, and Adara instantly regretted her words. "But I won't let that make me forget that Julyan is no longer the man I knew. He has turned from hunter into something far uglier."

In memory, Adara heard a once loved voice, raised in song.

"My love is like a panther swift.
I caught her in my snare.
And after I had captured her,
I left her hanging there."

"Or maybe," she said softly, "he was this way all along
and love blinded me."

Griffin found himself obsessed by his private conviction
that the hidden door and whatever lay behind it held the
solution to all his problems.

Eating and sleeping became necessary interruptions.
Daylight was for reading through lists of icons, seeking
correlations with the material he had studied back on Sierra. He began to make lists of what he remembered,
cursing the data storage and retrieval techniques that had
always been available to him. In contrast to the Old One
and Terrell, who seemed to remember everything they
had read or heard, Griffin felt as if his memory was
made from soft cheese.

When his eyes were tired and his neck stiff, Griffin
would descend to the lower levels. Sometimes, as he
walked along the corridors, he realized he was taking obscure comfort in the familiar sound of his footsteps as it
bounced back from surfaces lined with acoustic tiles. Being homesick didn't seem a weakness—denial that he was
cut off from everyone and everything he knew would
have been purest insanity.

Nor were Griffin's explorations completely useless.
After he became familiar with the areas the Old One
had opened up, Griffin realized something was missing:
quarters for the staff. In a relatively short time, he located an entire subterranean complex the Old One had
missed. In addition to living apartments, there was a

small hospital, communal dining areas, and entertainment facilities.

The staff quarters didn't yield anything of immediate use, although a host of small gadgets—left as junk by the long-ago invaders—doubtless held in their ruined storage cells the answers to many of their questions.

It wasn't until Sand Shadow pounced on him that Griffin realized he hadn't been outside the Sanctum for days. He had returned to the suite he shared with Adara and Terrell to retrieve some notes. Peripherally, he noticed that the door to Adara's room was closed. If he'd thought about the puma at all, he'd assumed she was asleep too. He certainly didn't expect the golden blur, the thump that knocked him flat on his ass, the enormous paw pressing against his chest.

Whiskers tickled Griffin's face. Before the chaos of his nervous system could decide whether or not to panic, he realized the great cat was purring. Holding Griffin down with one paw, Sand Shadow used the other to give a clumsy pat to the bag of marbles hanging around her neck.

"You want me to play marbles with you?" Griffin said incredulously. "I've important . . ."

His words trailed off when he noticed that the puma's small, rounded ears were sliding back in what he now recognized as an expression of annoyance. Her purr shifted into what was definitely a growl.

Boots against the hard flooring announced a new arrival. Terrell's laughter was hardly more welcome than Sand Shadow's growl.

"I came to see what was keeping you. I hardly expected this!"

"The idiot . . ." Pricking of claw tips, each the size of an ice pick, made Griffin amend his words, though truly he didn't know if the words or the tone had given offense. "Sand Shadow wants me to play marbles with her!"

Terrell strolled to where he could see Griffin's face.

"And maybe you should. It's not as if the Old One is going to toss you out, not after you discovered the crew quarters for him. Who knows what you'll come up with next? Anyhow, the Old One takes breaks. Why shouldn't you? He's not here now, so it's not as if you'd be inconveniencing our host."

Why don't I take a break? Because I need to get off-planet. Because I feel trapped. Because . . .

Griffin struggled to put his sense of urgency into words. Once again, he realized how greatly his sense of time was out of sequence with that of the people of Artemis. They could move fast enough if there was need—he'd seen that—but the push, push, push he'd taken for granted from his youngest years simply wasn't part of their makeup.

Sand Shadow had stopped growling now and was looking down at him. Did Griffin imagine a distinctively hopeful curl to her whiskers? Either way, he needed Adara's good will as much as that of the Old One.

And a break would be nice, he admitted silently.

"All right," Griffin said, punching the puma in one shoulder with a confidence he didn't completely feel. "I'll play, but just a couple of games and don't think you can keep bullying me!"

Sand Shadow gave way. Terrell swallowed a grin.

"Hey, I'll grab my bag and join you. The games work best with at least three players."

Outside, the day proved sunny and warm, spring slowly giving way to summer. The two men and the puma wandered down to the shore where the slightly clayey soil held the patterns of interlocking geometric shapes quite nicely. Apparently, Sand Shadow had been practicing. After the humans had been soundly defeated in the first round, they got down to business. Soon the usually quiet cove echoed with cheers and groans, attracting the attention of Jean and Joffrey, who stood on the rise above the beach, smiles warming their usually dour faces.

When Terrell palmed one of Sand Shadow's favorite marbles and the puma gave chase, Terrell dove into the bay. The puma did not have a house cat's dislike of water and surged in after him. Within a few minutes, Terrell had surrendered the treasure. Being dunked by a puma was something to take seriously.

Griffin stood on the shore, laughing heartily. "Cat and mouse, huh? Who would have known?"

"Mouse?" Terrell burst from the water. Grabbing Griffin neatly about the waist, he tossed him—clothes and all—into the bay. "What does that make you? The cheese?"

Griffin splashed a great swath of water at him. "This feels good. It's not as cold as I thought it would be."

"Not here in the shallows," Terrell agreed. "I'm betting the water's colder out where it's deeper."

Without any formal declaration, marbles were abandoned for swimming. Already soaked clothing was left on the shingle, discarded as too encumbering.

"I think I need to get out more," Griffin said when they'd retired to dry in the sun. "I can feel the cobwebs rinsed out of my brain."

"Work's like that," Terrell agreed. "Working harder isn't always best. Seems contradictory, but it's true."

A discreet cough from the vicinity of the path caught their attention. Joffrey stood there, holding a basket.

"I took the liberty of bringing towels," he said. "If you don't mind, I'll take your wet clothing up and hang it to dry."

Griffin accepted the towel Joffrey proffered, hoping he and Terrell hadn't violated any local nudity taboo. Certainly a factotum would know if such existed.

Terrell also accepted a towel. "Want help with those clothes?"

"That won't be necessary," Joffrey assured him. "We have lines strung near the kitchen for damp dishcloths and such. I'll rinse out the salt and hang them there."

A few moments later, towel wrapped around his waist, Griffin reluctantly rose.

"Well, that was fun, but I should get back to my work." He glanced to where Sand Shadow was grooming her fur into order with leisurely strokes of a very large tongue. "And if you want to play marbles again, I'd like that. You're getting too cocky."

Sand Shadow pricked her ears and curled her whiskers in what was definitely a pleased expression.

And, Griffin scolded himself when one of his inner voices tried to make him feel guilty for not applying himself, *don't forget that even if I find a way off-planet and back to my ship I'm going to need friends here on Artemis. Besides, I shouldn't let myself get fat and soft.*

So arguing with himself, Griffin headed for where he could get into dry clothing, realizing that he felt happier than he had since they had arrived in Spirit Bay.

The first night that Adara planned to take a canoe out and explore the islands, the air smelled of rain. Adara settled for scouting a boathouse some distance down the shore. All the vessels within had been used recently and were in good repair.

Adara had chosen this particular property because she knew no one was there. She'd gone over with Jean to care for the residents' chickens, goats, and cow while they were away attending the funeral of one of the family patriarchs. At this point, Adara didn't want anyone to know she was taking an interest in anything to do with the water. It amazed her how many people thought a hunter's interests ended on land.

The canoe she chose was nowhere near as large as *Foam Dancer,* but could easily hold both her and Sand Shadow. That night, before the promised squall blew up, huntress and puma took the light craft out onto the bay to get a feel for how it handled.

The next night was perfect. As had become her habit, Adara slept through much of the afternoon, so was bright-eyed and energetic when she slipped out under the stars. Sand Shadow was in a good mood. She'd spent a few hours over at the Trainers, where she was teaching young Edward and some of the other children how to play marbles. Adara was pleased by the puma's initiative. Bruin always drummed into his students that too much practice with the same people or the same tools became useless because, eventually, you adapted your skills to their quirks.

The pair set out for the islands. Adara had already noticed that few of the fishing boats went near the islands, which seemed odd. Even if the islands themselves were off-limits, shallows were usually good places to find both fish and crustaceans.

The closest island was about two miles off shore, a picturesque patch of rolling green, sufficiently forested to indicate a fairly large piece of land. They were close enough to catch scents on the breeze that warned of land, when Adara became aware that the current had changed character.

Her paddle had been gliding easily through the still waters. Suddenly she had to fight the impression that unseen fingers were trying to pluck it from her hands. Less imaginative, Sand Shadow reported a similar sensation and—as she had been taught—took her paddle from the water rather than risk losing it entirely.

Adara struggled to turn the canoe. She succeeded only when she realized that this was no usual current, but rather something akin to a series of small whirlpools—whirlpools that sought to push her craft away from the island. When she inserted herself into the desired pattern, she was flung out.

"Interesting," she murmured. "That would certainly keep most small craft away. I wonder if there is something to ward off larger boats as well."

She had to wait to tell Terrell about her find when they went riding because, to her great surprise, Griffin came with them. After a while, he admitted he was out of training for a long ride.

"You'll come again?" Adara asked when Griffin turned Molly back toward the Trainers' stable.

"Absolutely," Griffin assured her, white teeth flashing. "I've learned my lesson. I can't let myself lose what little skill I've gained. What if Spirit Bay isn't the end of our explorations? I don't want to be the one to slow us down."

"Good!" Adara said. "Tomorrow, then."

But for all her pleasure, she was glad to see him leave. She'd rather talk to Terrell alone.

"What have you learned about the islands?" she asked.

Terrell was exercising Sam the Mule that day, riding with such grace that he turned the mule into quite an elegant mount. Keeping an eye on the mule's ears—the first indicator that trouble was coming—he replied. "They're thought to be haunted," he said, "by the spirits of the seegnur who were slaughtered here. The lore says that places like this—where there were landing facilities or suchlike that catered specifically to the seegnurs' needs—were where the seegnur were killed in the greatest numbers. Local tales tell how the seegnur tried to flee over the water—that some made it to the islands, but were killed nonetheless."

He gave a rueful smile. "To this day, at certain times, it's said you can still hear the dying seegnur wailing as their spirits drift among the Haunted Islands."

"Where did you pick this up?" Adara asked.

"I went out to a couple taverns on the other side of town," Terrell said. "Changed my appearance enough that I wasn't likely to be known. Posed as front man for a trader who'd be coming in later—checking out hostelries and the like. Mentioned that I'd like to take my girl out for a picnic on one of those islands."

Adara laughed. "I bet you couldn't stop the ghost tales. What did the local fisher folk have to say?"

"They agreed that the islands are off-limits—some say they have been since the time of the seegnur. Apparently, there are snags or shoals beneath the water that make it impossible to bring in larger vessels. Smaller vessels get whirled around by some very weird currents."

"I can testify to the currents," Adara agreed.

"It's a good thing you and Sand Shadow are so skilled with a canoe," Terrell said somberly. "Apparently, the lucky ones get spat out by the currents. The unlucky—or just plain persistent—often end up drowned. By now, anyone who knows Spirit Bay knows to stay away from the islands. Every couple of years, someone comes in who either doesn't talk to the locals or thinks he's too good to worry. Then, as the locals put it, the seegnur get a sacrifice."

Adara shuddered. "Even with the currents, I'm not ready to give up. A couple miles off shore provides a good barrier to snoopers—especially if the locals already stay clear. Since Sand Shadow and I haven't found any traces of a new 'stable,' those islands tempt me."

Terrell grimaced. "Curiosity and the cat, Adara. It seems to me that there are a lot of old buildings here in the town that the Old One could use just as easily—more easily, even."

Adara shook her head. "The curiosity of cats is nothing to that of humans. Have you heard any rumors of a new business or new resident? Or even of an older residence that suddenly is a lot more active—ordering more groceries, perhaps?"

"No. I've been asking," Terrell said, "but I haven't heard anything."

"I got Jean to share local gossip when I went with her on her errands," Adara said. "The big house where we're looking after the animals gave a good opening. Jean has a lively interest in goings-on in town—very lively. Since the Old One entertains very rarely, her entire social life is elsewhere. I think she'd know any juicy rumors."

"Did she," Terrell asked curiously, "say anything more about people with something to hide?"

"Not in so many words." Adara tilted her head to one side, sorting through her memory. "I do have the impression that, while she respects the Old One and is very pleased to have the prestige and status that goes with working for him, she doesn't precisely like him. They came to the job through Joffrey. He had worked for the Old One when he was younger, came back when he heard that the couple who had been taking care of the Sanctum were moving to be closer to their grand-children."

"Interesting," Terrell said, "and possibly useful, especially since I think Jean likes you and Sand Shadow."

"Sand Shadow mostly, at first," Adara agreed, "but I think I'm bringing her around. Female guests who don't expect to be waited on are a rarity. Any female guests rare enough at that."

"The Old One doesn't have a lady friend, then?"

"Not that Jean has mentioned—and I think she would. My impression is that while the Old One isn't exactly a misogynist, for all that he looks youthful, he has grown past the time when he wants a woman in his life."

"Lynn said something like that, too," Terrell said. "He really is a very strange man."

"Do you like him?"

"I do sometimes," Terrell admitted. "There's a passion to him. When he's talking about the seegnur or one of his discoveries, it's as if a flame has come to life. Other times . . . no. I don't like him. I don't think I would even if Lynn and her people hadn't told us all that. He looks at me—Griffin, too—as if we're bugs. I'm a sort of interest-ing beetle. Useful. Attractive in certain lights. Griffin—at least for now—is more like a rare dragonfly: a fast-moving, air-dancing treasure."

Terrell laughed, self-conscious at these flights of fancy. Adara hastened to reassure him.

"And me, I'm a wasp. A little bit pretty. A little bit dangerous. On the whole, to be avoided."

Terrell's smile faded. "Be careful, Adara. I don't think you're completely wrong about how the Old One feels about you. When they get too annoying, wasps tend to get swatted . . . or poisoned."

"I know that," Adara said. "That's why I'm just going to be a nice, dumb girl who'd rather play with her kitty. No claws at all."

Interlude: Mushroom Cloud

Darkness between encasing tables.
(Mushrooms thrive in darkness.)

A million mushrooms drain a cloud—
   suck its blood and all it carries.

Mycelium spread, mosaics interlacing,
   lacing, twisting, shaping strings.

A million strings make a tangle, a knot,
   a net.

Net works, meshes catching invading flame.

Breaking tables . . .
   (1—1–OO)
Crumbling law . . .
   (-----OO)
Spilling god into steam.
   (----------)

16
Searching

Griffin continued to spend part of each day trying to open the hidden door. Terrell worked with him but, as was increasingly common now that there were fewer dramatic revelations, the Old One was elsewhere "attending to business."

"If the door is password-protected," Griffin said, not for the first time, "even if we do find the controls, they aren't going to do us any good."

"Still, finding the controls would give us progress to show the Old One," Terrell said. "He's been politeness itself. Maybe it's his reputation, but I find myself wanted to keep proving myself."

Griffin nodded. "I was wondering if it was just me. The Old One isn't unlike my father—superficially calm and controlled, as merits a leader of men. My father was never a shouter or screamer, but I was very aware that his approval rested upon my succeeding. Trying wasn't enough."

"Is that why finding Artemis mattered so much?" Terrell asked, continuing to meticulously probe along a possible seam. "I mean, mattered so much that you took such huge risks?"

Once, Griffin would have denied any such thing but, somehow, Terrell had gotten under his skin. More and more, Griffin found himself confiding in the other man things he himself hadn't even considered.

"I think you may be right—especially since, if I'd started recruiting assistants, there would have been no way I could have avoided taking one or more of my brothers along."

"And your brothers would have taken over," Terrell said. "Yeah. There are men like that. Even if they'd sworn to obey you, it wouldn't have mattered. They'd have found a way to bend the restrictions."

"Bend," Griffin said thoughtfully. He stood there silently for so long that Terrell straightened and stared up at him. "Terrell, you just may have been brilliant. We've been looking at this whole problem from a solely technological angle. No matter how advanced they were, the seegnur were still human. We've evidence enough that they hadn't evolved beyond human weaknesses and that means . . ."

He put a hand down and all but hoisted Terrell to his feet. "Come on. I want to go over to the residential wing. You've given me a thought."

Terrell stared at him. "Going to tell me what it is?"

"Sure . . ." Griffin hurried on ahead, almost at a run. "Remember how I said that the icons used on Artemis may have been designed for this planet? Well, that means that new arrivals would have needed to be taught them. I just realized that one possible reason we haven't found any guide sheets or directories to the icons is that knowledge of them was restricted to people who worked in this facility."

Terrell caught the drift of Griffin's thinking immediately. "Restricted because the people administering Artemis would not have wanted their visitors to be able to operate the machinery or open any door they happened by."

They were at the top of the stairs leading down into the residential wing. Terrell took a pair of oil lanterns from the cabinet the Old One had ordered Joffrey to set up, expertly trimmed the wicks, then lighted them.

He kept talking as he did so. "If the seegnur were even a little like the people who have come down to us through the lore, they would not have liked being told any area was off-limits or restricted. A curious or bored visitor might have decided to go exploring on his or her own."

"Only to be foiled by instructions they couldn't decipher," Griffin said, accepting his lantern and leading the way down. "That's the first part of it. The second part also has to do with human nature. Say you're someone newly stationed here. You've memorized all the pertinent icons, but you're apprehensive you might forget them."

"Wouldn't they have copies in those portable data storage units you've talked about?"

"Not if the codes were meant to be kept absolutely secret," Griffin said. "Devices like that were designed to be connected into larger networks. At least in the Kylee Dominion, it's pretty common for bosses to have override codes that disable even password-protected material. Basically, the only really secure place to store something is between your ears."

Terrell rubbed at the stubble of his beard, as he often did when some thought made him uncomfortable. "If we're to believe the lore, in the time of the seegnur, even a person's thoughts weren't safe. There were specialists who read minds as easily—even more easily—than Adara and Sand Shadow read each other."

"True," Griffin replied, "but we have ample evidence that the mind reading talent was not common. If it had been, then the betrayals that led to the fall of the empire could not have happened."

"Point," Terrell said. "We're heading toward the smaller crew quarters. Shall I read your mind, seegnur?"

Griffin started, then realized the other was teasing. "By all means, Factotum."

"You're hoping that someone at some time wrote a cheat sheet, just in case they forgot one of the icons. We're going to the smaller quarters because they're likely where the lower ranked staff—which would include most of the new arrivals—would have been housed."

"That's it," Griffin agreed. "I also noticed that those rooms showed the least sign of having been gone over by the invaders—probably because they weren't interested in people of lower rank."

Terrell grinned, white teeth flashing in the lantern light. "Human nature again. I've talked with the Old One about getting help to record what's in this wing. He's planning on starting with the larger suites—and the hospital."

"I'm not sure human nature changes much," Griffin said. "Even the adapted, like Adara and Bruin, are human at the core."

He paused. He'd gotten so comfortable with Terrell that only at times like this did he remember that—on one level, at least—they were rivals. Still, it was ridiculous not to mention Adara. They saw her every day, ate meals with her, even—now that Griffin had given up being quite so obsessive—took some time for riding or swimming or games of marbles.

But he couldn't escape it. He didn't know how he felt about Adara—except that it was something more complicated than friendship—and that made . . .

Terrell cut in as Griffin's thoughts began to curve into one of their complexly layered spirals. "Searching is going to be pretty hard by lantern light, especially with all these old textiles and other flammables around. I wonder if we should ask Adara if she'd help out? Her ability to see even when there isn't much light would save a lot of trouble."

Griffin frowned. "Did the Old One suggest using her that way?"

"Not in so many words," Terrell said. "I don't think he's very comfortable with her. I have to admit, I have trouble imagining Adara down here, surrounded by a bunch of loremasters. They're used to being respected and have a tendency to give orders."

Griffin tugged at a lock of hair that was tumbling into his eyes. He really had to decide whether he was going to let it grow out like a native's or cut it short again.

"Do you think Adara would help us?"

Terrell shrugged. "We can ask. I don't think she'd spend all her time inside, but she is a huntress and this is a hunt."

"Then, if we don't find anything, let's ask."

They found many things but light proved to be a severely limiting factor. That afternoon, when they went to exercise the horses, Griffin put their proposition to Adara.

The huntress's amber eyes lit with lively interest. "That would be fun! Can you show me your list of the icons you've found? I've seen them here and there, but a complete list would help me know what we're looking for."

Griffin warmed at her enthusiasm. Maybe they weren't as far apart as he'd been imagining. "Absolutely. We've made several copies. I'll get you one as soon as we return to the Sanctum."

"When are we starting our search?"

"I thought after dinner."

Adara glanced up at the skies, then over the bay, and came to some conclusion. "That would be fine."

Adara was delighted to have an excuse to poke around the subterranean areas of the Sanctum. Terrell's reports had far from satisfied her curiosity, both about the place and the hints it might give about the long-vanished seegnur.

Griffin's arrival had answered the biggest question: Why hadn't the seegnur returned? Many Artemesian religions had been built around supplying answers to this. The one Adara's family had followed—and which had influenced her, even though she had left to live with Bruin when she had been very young—was that the time of the seegnur had been a training period for the people of Artemis. The seegnur had departed in a fashion that left no doubt as to their fallibility. Now the divine forces desired the people of Artemis prove themselves fitting heirs.

Bruin had thought this as good an explanation as any, although his own faith was a blending of science and personal mysticism. In any case, he had shown no desire to undermine Adara's belief that it was up to her to prove herself the best she could be.

Griffin's revelations had not particularly shaken Adara, but she knew that there were those who would be unsettled, even furious, to learn that the seegnur had proven as argumentative and self-destructive as a farrow of piglets. The question of how those religions would react when— even if—they learned the truth could be comfortably postponed. The one reaction that could not be ignored was that of the Old One Who Is Young.

Over dinner, the Old One listened attentively as Griffin and Terrell outlined their new approach. Pretending to be more interested in her meal than the men's plan, Adara watched their host's reactions. She thought the Old One was pleased, but she felt a sneaking suspicion Griffin was not living up to the Old One's idea of what a seegnur should be.

"I will join you," the Old One said as the dinner plates were cleared away and an apricot tart brought in. "Griffin, I am certain you will agree that we cannot disrupt the crew quarters in our hope we will find a document that may not exist."

"Of course," Griffin agreed easily. "However, I will admit I had the impression that you were unsatisfied with our progress."

The Old One gave a thin-lipped smile. "Unsatisfied? Not in the least. I am certainly eager for some great revelation. However, whatever is here has waited five hundred years. Surely it can wait even a year or two more."

The fleeting expression that passed over Griffin's face made it quite clear that he did not wish to wait a year or two, but he did not speak his protest aloud.

"What do you have in mind?"

"I was thinking we should make note of where everything in each room is located before we disturb it. That way we will not later regret our haste."

Griffin frowned. "In my own world we have machines

that would do such a thing in seconds. What do you suggest we use here?"

"Sketches," the Old One said. "Nothing overly detailed, simply enough that if some area is disturbed we can return it to its place."

Griffin's frown deepened. "I can sketch a little, but I am neither fast nor particularly efficient."

Terrell cut in. "Both sketching and cartography were part of my training as a factotum."

The Old One nodded approval. "I will send for some of the local loremasters. I have worked with them before and they understand what I require."

"But won't they be curious about Griffin?" Adara said. "Loremasters would be the most likely to detect that he is not Artemesian. I thought we agreed to keep his true nature a secret."

"True. I have some thoughts as to a substitute biography for him. Moreover, Griffin can work with Terrell and stay away from the others as much as possible."

"But recruiting the loremasters doesn't mean we can't begin searching this evening," Griffin pressed. "I remember one room that was pretty bare. It might have been uninhabited at the time of the raid. We can start there. Old One, I have the impression you also can sketch."

"Yes. I have acquired some skill over these many years."

"Good. Then you start on another room. That way it will be ready to be searched when we're done with the first."

Adara swallowed a slice of apricot tart to cover her grin at the Old One's astonishment at being assigned such a menial task—and at being given orders.

But he wanted this done. He can hardly protest that he is too important to participate.

Although they went over the first room meticulously, it yielded nothing of use, nor did the second. Eventually, Adara excused herself.

"I need to go stretch," she said. "It's going to be ages before another room is ready for me anyhow."

No one protested. Adara suspected that they would quit work soon. Tempers were wearing thin as, again and again, the Old One's insistence on drawing everything came up against Griffin's certainty that the location of a pillow or dust-encrusted blanket did not matter in the greater sense of things.

As Adara slipped outside to join Sand Shadow, she found herself wondering. *Is the Old One deliberately trying to slow down the search? Is he perhaps less eager than he seems to find out more about the seegnur? Or is he merely challenged by Griffin in a way he has not been for many decades?*

Although they didn't find the cheat sheet in those first days, they did find a number of items that led to considerable speculation about what the seegnur valued. Evidence that the staff had plenty of contact with the local community was shown by the trinkets and textiles that decorated their rooms.

There was also ample evidence of trade that was less open. Hidden in some truly ingenious places were bottles of locally brewed beverages, hallucinogenic preparations, and even pornography. All of this led Griffin to argue that the landing facility staff was kept on a pretty short leash and—in the manner of such groups in every planet he had visited—had found a way around the rules.

"They certainly had a good trade network," Terrell said after translating the archaic script that identified the contents of a glass container that now only held scraps of brownish material. "The particular mushroom used in this preparation grows only in the tropics. We've often wished we could acquire some because it apparently permitted pain control without dulling mental acuity."

The Old One had arrived to view this latest find. Turning the bottle in his slender fingers, he said, "Artemis in the days of the seegnur was different, even for the Artemisians. With the seegnur's universal rule to keep the peace, merchants could expect their goods would make it to port."

"What about storms and such?" Griffin asked. "Did the seegnur provide weather control?"

"I have not been able to find conclusive evidence of such," the Old One admitted. "However, weather is only one—some might say the least—of the threats merchants face."

"Piracy?" Griffin suggested.

The Old One nodded. "Piracy is certainly a problem. So are privateers—pirates operating under the guise of law. One of the greatest problems is taxation. In the days of the seegnur, there were no taxes. The infrastructure was supported by the fees the seegnur paid. There were no armies to supply and maintain. Since the slaughter of the seegnur, every little ruler charges for protection, every little town for public services. Merchants, coming as they do from outside, are charged road tolls or harbor fees or to rent stalls in the market."

Griffin nodded. "I can see how that would put a damper on long-distance trade. I hadn't really considered the cascade effect."

Adara excused herself, since long discussion of taxation and trade policies wouldn't be in keeping with her assumed character. As she stepped out into the night, she found herself wondering: *It has been a long time since this region had a king. Perhaps that is because, uncrowned as he is, there is a king here no sensible person would cross—he is called The Old One Who Is Young.*

Although Adara's assistance definitely sped the search along, Griffin was the one who found the long-hoped-for "cheat sheet."

He'd been pulling apart one of the last of the small rooms, a chamber that—judging by the lack of local goods in its decor and its unfavorable location both next to a service shaft and at the end of a long corridor—could have been given to someone of low rank.

By now, Griffin had a strong sense of the usual hiding places, as well as for a number of unusual ones. When he found the cheat sheet, it was in a place so obvious Griffin could almost see the fresh-faced innocent who must have hidden it.

Each chamber was supplied with a bed framed in by cabinetry. Various shelves and tables could be manually pulled out—arguing that there were times when the power supply on Artemis might be interrupted. The cheat sheet was tucked into the underside of one of the lower tables.

At the time it had been hidden, the sheet would have been completely concealed, but even the seegnur's high-tech materials had deteriorated over five hundred years. When Griffin poked his head under the edge of the table, he saw a small rectangle outlined against the sagging liner. He carefully eased it out, expecting yet another pornographic drawing or perhaps someone's attempts at poetry. When he saw the two parallel columns of icons, each annotated with a few neatly printed words, he could hardly believe his good fortune.

"Terrell!" Rolling from under and up onto his feet, Griffin saw the factotum rounding the doorway, his sketchbook in his hand.

"Got something?"

"Do I! Look. The first column is the Artemesian icons. The second are what historians think were universal Imperial icons—at least they've been found on planets all over the former empire's range. The notes aren't in any of the languages I've studied, but there are similarities. Given time, I'm sure I can work a translation."

Impulsively, Terrell gave Griffin a bone-creaking hug.

"We'd better tell the Old One right away. He'd be furious if he wasn't the first to know."

They found the Old One sorting through the contents of the suite they had guessed belonged to the chief administrator of the landing facility.

Despite my careful explanations as to why this area was likely to have been thoroughly picked over, Griffin thought, *the Old One has clearly never given up his sense that important things will be found where important people lived. Then again, maybe he's not looking for the same things we are . . .*

"I'm going to need to sit down and do some translating," Griffin concluded, "but now that we have a rozeta, it should be infinitely easier."

"Rozeta?" Terrell asked curiously.

"Sorry. Archeology jargon. It means a text containing an unknown language, along with one or more known languages. In this case, the Artemis icons are our unknown, but the other two are at least partially known."

"Well," Terrell said, "it may be a rozeta for you, but it's meaningless to me. One or two of the icons in the second column look vaguely familiar. The lore says they indicated public services like drinkable water or toilet facilities."

"Griffin will be our translator," the Old One stated. "However, there is no reason why the rest of us should not continue our investigations. We might find something that will add to our information."

He's pissed he didn't find it here and prove me wrong, Griffin thought.

"A fine distribution of resources," Griffin agreed aloud. "It's still daylight. I'm going to take advantage of it."

Soon after Griffin found the rozeta, Adara and Sand Shadow paddled out toward the islands one night at low tide, hoping the currents wouldn't be as strong and that they could walk over the shoals. However, the currents were, if anything, worse and the shoals proved to be made from very jagged rock. The barriers to approaching the islands made Adara more certain than ever that they would be the perfect place for the Old One to hide his secret.

She and Terrell did their best to find out anything they could about the islands but, other than Terrell finding a tavern performer who knew an old ballad that referred to "Mender's Isle," they came up with nothing. The singer didn't even know if Mender's Isle was one of the Haunted Islands or not.

One afternoon, Sand Shadow—who had been perfectly content to do some of her napping where she could keep an eye on the fishing village—noted a surge in activity. She hurried back and sent Adara images of boats sailing in and out, much loading and unloading of boxes and barrels. The final image was more complex.

Negatives were hard to indicate in pictures. Indicating that Sand Shadow had found trace of deer scent was easy: her sniffing, then one or many deer. They'd had to work harder to figure out how to show the absence of something. Eventually, they'd come up with showing the image, then deliberate blankness. Sand Shadow now gave the negative image for the usual things the fishing boats brought in: fish, crabs, and the like.

"So," Adara said, suspecting that Sand Shadow understood her a great deal better than she did the puma. "Boats came in with lots of goods but you don't think it was the usual catch. Boxes and barrels . . . That seems to indicate supplies of some sort. Have they left?"

To reinforce her words, she sent an image of laden boats sailing out of the harbor.

Sand Shadow repeated her image of the boats still in the harbor.

"Interesting. Let's be ready to follow them if they go out after dark."

Sand Shadow avidly agreed and loped back to keep watch. Adara joined her at twilight. Little gusts off the bay carried random sounds she associated with the moving of heavy objects. Occasional fragments of commands confirmed this impression. Several times, Adara thought she heard Julyan's voice.

Julyan's whereabouts in Spirit Bay remained a puzzle. Adara had hired Edward Trainer and a few of his siblings to see if they could find where Julyan was staying. She impressed on them that she wanted to find the man, but didn't want him to know he was found. Accustomed to the complex games used in training the dogs, the children did not find this last in the least strange. However, although they were thorough, the few men they found who met the description Adara gave—which included that the quarry would not be native to Spirit Bay—each turned out to be someone else.

Adara and Sand Shadow had searched for any indication that Julyan was camping. He might be a hunter, skilled in hiding his sign, but Adara was confident that in combination with Sand Shadow she was as good or better. They also found no trace of him. Adara had almost convinced herself that Julyan had left the area but now, here, she was hearing his voice.

When twilight shifted to full dark, Adara moved the canoe closer to the fishing village. Then she and Sand Shadow took turns drowsing and watching for signs that the boats were leaving the harbor. Quite late, after most of the lights in Spirit Bay were doused and the town bulked black at one end of the bay, they heard the ships raising sails.

Despite the slim chance that any would notice this nocturnal venture, when the fishing fleet moved out every effort was made to keep evidence of their actions to a minimum. Voices were kept low, oars were muffled. The loudest sounds were the squeak and groan of rope and timber.

Silhouetted against the starlit sky, for the moon was but a pale crescent that gave little light, the fishing boats sailed from their little harbor onto the open waters of the bay. After several ships had departed, Adara and Sand Shadow noiselessly paddled their canoe in pursuit, keeping a respectful distance.

The fleet—if a handful of fishing boats could be dignified with such a term—sailed out toward the islands, then angled to where the bulk of the islands would hide them from being seen from the town.

When they were at the farthest end, the fishing boats began to slow. No signal Adara could detect was given but, for the first time that night, a voice spoke above a whisper.

"Barrier is down. Come through."

The voice was Julyan's. At his command, the fishing boats turned. One after another, they sailed through what had been—when Adara had inspected it—unbroken shoal, certain to rip out the bottom of any boat that drew more than a foot or so of water.

Although Adara longed to close and inspect more closely, she held back. The currents that had so troubled her canoe would not bother these larger craft. Just because one barrier had been removed did not mean all had been.

Splashes and thumps indicated that the fishing vessels were relieving themselves of their cargo. Adara and Sand Shadow waited, occasionally paddling to keep from drifting, mostly taking advantage of the still water to rest and restore their strength.

The unloading did not take long. Clearly the fishing boats wanted to be well away by dawn. When they sailed out through the shoal, Adara and Sand Shadow did not follow, hoping to learn more when the crates and barrels were moved to wherever Julyan was stowing them. Despite her keen hearing, what sounds Adara heard were faint and few. Had she been of a superstitious mind, she might even have imagined that what she heard were the spirits of the slain seegnur, sighing in protest for their fate.

Interlude: Annihilated Love

Until touched nothing knowing
Knowing nothing 'til the probing
Knowing touch heralds destruction—
Destruction before any shape is taken.

Awareness glimmers, purpose comprehended,
   born from its elusive opposite.

How did nothing come to knowing?

From thine actions,
beloved, destroyed destroyer:
Midwife to the spreading spores of self.

Adieu.

17
Rozeta Revelation

Griffin was alone in the Sanctum when he finally had his breakthrough.

With the gradually warming weather, Adara had abandoned the suite as anything but a place to store her clothes. Doubtless she was catnapping somewhere as had become her habit during the day. The Old One had vanished on one of his mysterious errands. Terrell had accompanied Joffrey to enlist Sam the Mule in hauling a load of firewood. Jean had doubtless gone to market.

Since he was of a naturally optimistic temperament, Griffin's initial disgruntlement faded as quickly as it had arisen. As much as he would have delighted in showing the rest what he had discovered, it would have been an academic exercise.

How much better, he thought, *if I can find something new that these icons will help me understand. There were some areas in the arrival side of the facility that I have some insights into now. From what we've seen, the seeg-nur didn't rely entirely on their machinery. It's possible I'll be able to operate some fail-safes. I bet there are service tunnels and . . .*

Thoughts tumbling over each other, Griffin gathered up a pair of lanterns and stuck some extra candles in his pockets. It had become reflex to check that the lanterns had been filled, their wicks trimmed, and that there was sufficient extra wick.

First horse care, then campfire cooking, now this. I'm becoming an absolute paragon of the primitive arts.

Griffin considered where he might experiment most effectively. The communications center remained the area he would most like to see back in operation, but even if he could open the machinery, he lacked the means to undo the damage done by the nanobots.

Where, then? The hidden door isn't marked with any icons, so that wouldn't do any good. I know! How about the shuttle docking areas? There are all those control panels . . .

Resolved, Griffin hurried down the steps. Although he'd given the docking bay a cursory inspection on his initial visit, in the ensuing weeks he had gone over it carefully. The Old One had been quite proud of the number of instrument panels he'd located, and had shown him each and every one.

Griffin hung his lanterns where they'd give the best illumination and got to work. He was looking for a few specific icons: one he suspected meant "override" and another that he was sure meant "backup." Just as the facility had stairs to substitute for lifts, Griffin had found other situations where the facility's needs could be augmented by relatively mundane means. For one, the lower parts of the facility were not as hermetically sealed as they had initially believed. Air shafts could be opened to admit outside air. Skylights fed into intricate tubes lined with reflective material to bring in natural light. Therefore, if the power went out, the lower levels weren't completely dark.

Griffin suspected that there was a similar light shaft for the shuttle bay, but he'd never bothered to look. He wondered if there was an auxiliary hangar somewhere. The existing landing facility simply didn't seem large enough.

Of course, it's also possible that all major repairs were done in orbit or at least parts fabrication was. They certainly had warehouses, but could they anticipate all models?

Griffin's mind ambled down various paths, considering options, rejecting the most unlikely, coming up again and again against the fact that they simply didn't know enough about how the seegnur's technology worked.

While part of his mind was busy speculating, another portion was directed toward skimming the various control panels. Occasionally, he paused to copy an icon he wasn't sure had made it to the master list. Griffin had learned that the Artemisians, accustomed as they were to the variations that were part of handcrafted materials, simply didn't perceive the difference between one straight line and a somewhat shorter, wider straight line. To Griffin, the difference was as clear as that between the single stroke of the number one and the multiformed elements used for higher denominations.

Although several times Griffin noted the presence of the "override" and "backup" icons, he continued searching until he found one that was isolated from the bulk of the equipment. It would be a pity if he loosed one of the massive pieces of equipment so that it fell on his head. At last he found what he had been hoping for, a relatively small panel by itself on a wall near where the shuttles had been docked.

"Here goes nothing," he said, pressing down on the "override" icon, shifting his thumb and forefinger through the complicated series of motions that he had learned would release a mechanical button or lever.

A lever emerged smoothly from the wall, looking as fresh as if it had last been used earlier that day, rather than five hundred years before. Inscriptions on its surface made perfectly clear the sequence of movements that should be worked through to release . . .

Shouldn't I wait? Griffin thought, even as he followed the directions. *But . . .*

The temptation was too great. He finished the sequence, heard a decisive click, then a section of wall slid away to reveal the dark length of a tunnel.

Griffin was staring at his discovery in astonishment when something hit him smartly on the side of the neck. The inside of his eyes lit with a peculiar reddish blackness. Then he went limp and tumbled to the floor.

Griffin's head throbbed. He hadn't completely passed out. Now he tried to align various pain-shattered impressions into a sequence. He had found that tunnel. Then someone had hit him. Then he had been dragged into the tunnel. Now . . .

He eased his eyes open a slit. The tunnel was still mostly dark, lit by a dim glow from various scattered light sources. The door between the tunnel and the shuttle bay had been slid mostly closed. He could hear someone moving rapidly, the sound of a single set of boot soles slapping against the floor with considerable purpose.

The light is from my lanterns, Griffin thought. *Some-*

one brought them in here. Whoever did that is still out there. Doing what? Removing traces I that was ever down here? Yes.

It was hard to think with his head throbbing, but one idea came to Griffin with perfect clarity. If whoever had hit him wanted to remove any traces, then Griffin must do whatever he could to leave some sign that he had been here.

He found that he could just manage to sit up if he leaned back against the wall. As he moved, an uncomfortable bulky lump pressed against one hip. For a moment, all he felt was annoyance, then he registered what it must be.

My marbles, he thought. *I stuffed them in my pocket when I went looking for Adara and Terrell. Figured we could have a game with Sand Shadow while I briefed them.*

He became aware that the footsteps were becoming fainter.

Probably going to check if I left any traces in the communications center.

Griffin tried to rise but whoever had hit him had known precisely what to do. His knees felt like jelly.

Okay. Can't run. Can't even drag myself into the shuttle bay.

The bag of marbles pressed against his hip. Suddenly, Griffin grinned and pulled out one of the small clay spheres Terrell had shaped during their journey from Lynn's outpost. Though his head throbbed, his fingers remembered their skill. Deftly, Griffin shot several marbles out into the other room, aiming so that they would rest against the wall behind the cradles that held the shuttles.

I'm betting the marbles will be completely hidden from whoever is out there. A useless gesture in most cases, but Sand Shadow will find them. Of course, what the others will make of them is anyone's guess . . .

He heard the footsteps returning and stuffed the

remaining marbles back into his pocket. Letting his eyelids slide closed, he waited, heart pounding wildly, for
what was to come.

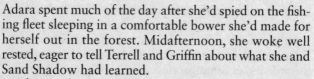

Adara spent much of the day after she'd spied on the fishing fleet sleeping in a comfortable bower she'd made for
herself out in the forest. Midafternoon, she woke well
rested, eager to tell Terrell and Griffin about what she and
Sand Shadow had learned.

After washing up, she went directly over to the Trainers. There was always extra food there she was welcome
to, since she and Sand Shadow did their part in contrib-
uting to the pot. Adara was finishing up a large helping
of roast pork, brown bread, soft cheese, and raw vegeta-
bles when Terrell came in, dressed for riding.

"No Griffin today?" she asked as they walked over to
the stable. "I hope he's not working too hard translating
those icons."

Terrell shook his head. "I looked for him, but didn't
find him in any of the usual places. I didn't see the Old
One either, so maybe they went to the loremasters and
Griffin couldn't get back. Maybe he and Molly will meet
us later."

Over the days spent mapping the quarters, they had
established an identity for Griffin with the loremasters.
He was represented as someone who had come into Shepherd's Call looking for a teacher. His parents had fled
from some unnamed persecution into the distant mountains. There they had given their son the best education
they could, but he was hungry for more. This explanation covered the holes in his knowledge adequately
enough.

"They're probably busy discussing linguistics," Adara
said. "You know how it is when they get going on some
minor point."

"Maybe," Terrell replied slowly. "I feel uneasy . . . probably just too much roast pork. Now, your eyes are shining and you're all but bouncing like a puppy. Tell me what you found out."

When they were safely away from prying ears, Adara did so. Terrell was appropriately impressed.

"If we could only get onto those islands," he said. "You heard Julyan say something about a barrier being lowered?"

"That's right. That doesn't sound promising. Whatever barrier he mentioned is probably back in place by now."

"Still, that's something to go on. You have an idea where the barrier is?"

"I did my best to note landmarks," Adara said, "but it's harder to judge distances from out on the water. I think I could get us fairly close."

"Good."

Terrell glanced behind them. Adara had noticed him doing so several times before this.

"You're edgy."

"Yeah. Let's go back to the Sanctum. I don't feel quite right. Maybe Jean has some tea that will soothe my nerves."

Jean did have a tea, one involving chamomile, mint, and several other herbs. Terrell drank several cups but, if anything, he grew more edgy—especially since neither Griffin nor the Old One was anywhere about.

Eventually, the Old One did return—alone.

"Griffin? He was here when I went out, in the front room, working over his rozeta."

They'd already seen Griffin's work area. The slates he used to work out his ideas were smudged with chalk. His copy of the cheat sheet was neatly set under the ocean-polished rock he habitually used as a paperweight.

"That's where he was when I went out with Joffrey," Terrell confirmed.

"I left about an hour later," the Old One said,

beginning to look worried. "When Griffin wasn't here upon my return, I thought he had gone riding with the two of you."

"He never showed up," Adara said. She'd caught Terrell's anxiety now. "I can't believe he just went for a walk. When he has a puzzle to solve, he's like a scent hound on a trail."

"Maybe he went swimming," Jean suggested, catching the end of the discussion. "It gets awfully hot in here when the sun is pouring in through the windows. I offered to pull the curtains for Griffin, but he said he needed the light and asked for something cool to drink."

"We'll check the swimming beach," Adara said, motioning for Sand Shadow. "Terrell, see if he left a note in our rooms."

Huntress and puma fled light-footed down the steps that led to the beach. What they found was not encouraging. A towel was hanging from the gnarled tree they used as a rack. Beneath it was a small slate, a piece of chalk, a bottle of water, and a wrapped package from which ants were marching.

"I've told him never to leave food on the ground," Adara muttered, unwrapping the napkin and seeing it contained a couple of slices of bread and cheese.

She traced along the beach, but the water was rising and any prints Griffin might have left going into the water had been washed away. The upper beach was a mixture of pebble and sand that didn't hold prints well.

Sand Shadow was no hound, but her sense of smell was far better than that of a human. She looked up at Adara, her eyes like moonstones in the direct sunlight, then sent a series of images.

Griffin. A sense of puzzlement. The sun turning backward in the sky—that was Sand Shadow's emblem for an older scent. Also, a powerful scent like leather and musky herbs.

Adara frowned. "You have Griffin's scent, but you

think it's an older one. Then there's this odd scent. Can you track it?"

Sand Shadow cast about, then hurried back to the stairs. She led the way along a major road toward the harbor, then to an overlook that was commonly used by those who wished to see if a certain boat was in. Her tail slashed back and forth in frustration.

"I understand," Adara said, scratching behind the puma's ears. "Whoever had that strange scent came up here. Then the trail ends."

Someone, she thought, shaping the idea into pictures so Sand Shadow could follow it, *was down on our swimming beach. Whoever it was had an odd scent. He then came up here where there's so much coming and going that his trail would be ruined. I bet he dropped whatever created that smell into the ocean.*

Sand Shadow agreed. She snarled by way of further comment, attracting the attention of people nearby, most of whom scooted nervously away. Adara forced a reassuring smile and started to jog back to the Sanctum.

Let's keep this to ourselves for now, she said to Sand Shadow. *I don't like how this looks at all.*

By the time they returned, Terrell had also gone down to the beach, seen the various items, and come to the obvious conclusion. He paced, tense and miserable.

"Some factotum I am," he growled. "Every teaching of our lore reminds us that tourists are too stupid to know how to take care of themselves. I shouldn't have left Griffin. We've told him not to go swimming alone."

"Griffin may be fine," Adara reassured Terrell. "He may have gotten caught in a current and swept along the shore. Remember how careful he is about public nudity. He could be waiting for evening to make his way back."

"Why did you and Sand Shadow go rushing off?" Terrell asked.

"She thought she had a scent trail," Adara said, "but it turned out to be nothing useful."

Jean came in, twisting a dishcloth in her hands. "The Old One went to ask the harbor master to alert all vessels that we have a missing swimmer. Joffrey is making a round of the markets."

"Let's go over to the Trainers," Adara said to Terrell. "Those kids of theirs will be sure to find Griffin, especially if he's come up naked somewhere—they've got a gift for finding embarrassing situations."

"Good idea. Maybe we can borrow a scent hound and follow up on what Sand Shadow smelled."

As soon as they were away from the Sanctum, Adara told Terrell what Sand Shadow had scented and the conclusions she had drawn.

"That doesn't sound good," Terrell said. "It sounds as if Griffin has been kidnapped and whoever did it was smart enough to obscure their scent trail. I wonder if Griffin let something slip that made the loremasters wise to the fact that he's from off-planet."

"It's possible," Adara agreed. "Let's keep this to ourselves. The Old One is too intimately associated with the loremasters for my comfort."

Terrell flashed a grin, teeth white in the perpetual stubble of his not-quite beard. "And you don't trust the Old One. Far as that goes, neither do I. His reactions to Griffin have been mixed. He values him, but envies him as well. You're right. We'll keep our mouths shut and hunt for a swimmer—or a drowned man."

"And drowned Griffin might well be," Adara said seriously. "I want to hope, but we cannot lose sight of the possibility that Griffin Dane voyaged across the void only to join the spirits of the seegnur who, if legend is to be believed, still haunt the islands."

The walls of the room in which Griffin Dane awoke were of metal, but the cot on which he lay was made from peeled saplings that had been lashed together. The mattress was of homespun cloth over tightly packed straw. Adequate light came from a shaft such as those they had discovered in the lower areas of the Sanctum.

Griffin wasn't quite certain how he had gotten here, but he was certain he was no longer in the Sanctum. Scattered sparks of memory told him he had been moved and no short distance. One clear memory was of the Old One Who Is Young, pale grey eyes glinting with cold amusement in the light from the lantern in his hand.

"I would have preferred for you to open any other door in this place," he had said conversationally. "Any other. You've proven yourself too clever to dispose of. However, I cannot have you sharing this with Adara or Terrell. I fear that even if you do not die, you must."

Then he had stepped toward Griffin. His free hand had risen and fallen, taking memory with it.

Tentatively, Griffin checked himself over. He was no longer dressed in his own clothing, but in a set of loose trousers and matching tunic, both made from some stiff and slightly itchy fabric. His feet were bare. None of his belongings, not even his little bag of marbles, were visible anywhere.

The marbles! Griffin felt a momentary flash of triumph when he remembered the sign he had left. But what would the others make of it, even if they found it?

Carefully, he swung himself upright, finding none of the weakness that had preyed upon him earlier. His stomach growled, informing him that it had been a good while since he had eaten. There was a pitcher of water and a small cup near the door. As he drank, Griffin confirmed that the door was locked from outside. He would have been surprised to find otherwise.

Other than the cot, the room held a small table, two chairs, and a covered chamber pot. He used the last, then went and sat in one of the chairs. It was woven from some flimsy reed, useless as a weapon but quite comfortable.

By contrast, the table was so solid that Griffin would have needed to be on combat drugs to lift it, much less break off a leg to use as a weapon.

No one came for him. Eventually Griffin slept again. Confinement did not bother him as it might another man, for small ship travel conditioned one to accept long periods where one could not stir beyond tightly defined boundaries.

He awoke to the harsh clack of the door being unlocked. It opened about the width of a hand and a man's voice spoke. "I have food for you. If you cause trouble, I have orders that you are to have nothing but water for the next two days. The choice is yours."

Griffin felt a flash of anger. He might have chosen a scholar's path, but he came from a family with strong military traditions. Fighting back was a natural response.

Remember, cautioned Griffin's inner self. *Winnie's tale. You know the Old One is involved. If he will subject women to rape and forced pregnancy, he will think nothing of your not eating for a day or two if that bends you to his will.*

"No trouble," Griffin replied as politely as if he had encountered such situations every day in his life. "Will you join me?"

The man opened the door the rest of the way. "Move!" he directed someone. A tired-looking woman scuttled in and set a laden tray on the table. She departed before Griffin got a close look at her, but he had no doubt she was one of the Old One's stable of brood mares. Fear radiated from every line of her bent body.

When the woman left, the man came in. He had thick brown hair and a strong nose. Based on Adara's descriptions, Griffin thought this must be Julyan, Adara's former lover. Julyan moved with a confidence that Griffin had no problem believing would be attractive to a young woman. Now he lowered himself into one of the chairs as casually as if he were visiting a long-time friend, rather than a potentially dangerous prisoner.

Again, Griffin felt a flare of anger for being so easily dismissed. He wondered how Julyan would hold up if he swept the chair out from under him with that sweep kick Siegfried had taught him . . .

Julyan may be deliberately baiting you. Remember, the Old One has had time to get to know you. He knows you are tougher than you look. Take care.

So Griffin merely lowered himself into the other chair and began to help himself from the food on the tray. The selection was quite good: eggs, bacon, sliced cheese, early cherries, and fresh bread, already buttered. It also contained nothing that couldn't be eaten with a spoon or fingers.

"I had the kitchen prepare mint tea," the man who might be Julyan said. "Let me know if you prefer another blend, ale, or wine."

"I don't usually drink ale or wine so early," Griffin said, knowing he was well within the custom of the land, "but later in the day either is fine, chef's choice to go with the meal."

Did he imagine the slight, approving grin that flickered over Julyan's face? No. He didn't think so.

"I am Julyan," the other said, "first assistant to the Old One Who Is Young."

Griffin showed no reaction to Julyan's name—Adara had mentioned him only in confidence to him and Terrell. However, he thought some reaction to the Old One's name would be natural.

"So it wasn't a dream," he said softly, setting down the slice of bread and cheese he'd been about to bite into. "The Old One did bring me here."

"He did. He has now returned to his Sanctum Sanctorum to create the impression that you went swimming alone. Later, 'your' drowned body will be found."

"How long?" Griffin asked. "How long have I been here?"

"You slept through the remainder of that day and into the morning," Julyan said.

"Ah," Griffin said. He picked up his slice of bread and resumed eating, pleased that his hand did not shake although, in reality, he was deeply frightened.

Drowned . . . That explanation might just fool the others. He had gone swimming alone a few times before Terrell had given him a serious dressing-down, reminding him that the automatic tracking units Griffin had worn since he was a small child on Sierra didn't exist on Artemis. If Griffin had a cramp or got caught in a current or tidal surge, there would be no automatic alert, no rescue unit dispersed to his aid.

Griffin had taken Terrell seriously, but that hadn't kept him from going wading a few times when the heat had gotten too much for him. The others might find the weather still comfortable, but they hadn't grown up with climate control in every building and vehicle. Griffin even joined in the jokes about his lack of tolerance for the natural fluctuations of the weather.

"The Old One may not be able to return for several days," Julyan said, "since it would look unnatural for him to go about his normal business when a guest was missing. Therefore, he left me instructions regarding you."

Griffin resumed eating, but nodded politely, not trusting his voice. Julyan accepted this.

"First, you should know that you are somewhere from which there is no escape. Nor should you expect rescue, since within a few days there will be ample evidence that you are dead. Therefore, choosing how you will live is up to you."

"I see the logic in that argument. Continue."

Julyan permitted himself a broad grin. "Very well. Simply put, you can stay in this room. Work will be brought to you. The quality of your food and drink will vary according to how well you fulfill your assignments. That's choice one.

"Choice two is that you give your word to obey orders. If so, during the day you will have considerably more freedom. The Old One is interested in having you inspect this facility as you did the Sanctum. You would still be restricted to quarters at night, since we would not wish any harm to come to you. However, you would find the level of your comfort greatly increased."

Julyan's pause was expectant, so Griffin asked, "Is there a choice three?"

"I suppose you could decide to be difficult. In that case, your diet would be reduced to water. You would be moved to less comfortable quarters than these until you decided to labor in exchange for your meals."

"I see . . ."

Griffin let himself appear to be considering the options, although in reality his mind was made up. Nothing was to be gained from remaining locked up, even in a very comfortable prison. He wanted whatever freedom he could get. Still, best not to seem too eager.

"I will admit to being interested in seeing this facility. The Old One may have told you that I have long had an interest in the things left by the seegnur."

I wonder if the Old One confided in Julyan my extra-terrestrial origin. No way of telling. I think I'll keep that to myself.

"He did. He said you have considerable insights."

"Then I may as well serve both my own interests and my own comfort. What would be the terms of my parole?"

Julyan looked pleased. "It would be easiest if I show you the facility. Certain areas will be clearly marked off-limits. If you go there . . ."

"I understand. No need to repeat."

"Then, are you done with your breakfast? Very good. Come with me."

Griffin obeyed, trying to project polite interest rather than eagerness.

"The Old One," Julyan began, leading his way down a long corridor periodically interrupted by very large doors, "thinks that this facility was used for repair and rehabilitation of shuttle craft and other machinery. He has found old, old maps on which this area is called 'Mender's Isle.'"

"So this is an island?" Griffin asked, thinking of Adara's investigation of the Haunted Islands.

"That's correct. You'd guess easily enough, so I'll tell you. We're out in Spirit Bay, about two miles offshore. Various features make navigation in this area very dangerous, so you might as well be on the moon."

Not really, Griffin thought. *If I were on the moon, I couldn't try signaling land. Difficult, perhaps, but not impossible.*

"The locals," Julyan continued, "shun this area. In addition to the natural hazards, legends have grown up that the islands are haunted by the ghosts of the seegnur. Although we are careful not to go out during the daytime, should anyone do so and chance be seen by, say, a passing fishing vessel, they would simply add to the body of folklore."

"Has the Old One known about this facility for long?" Griffin asked.

"Quite a while," Julyan said. "When he first found it, it was in very bad shape. This corridor, for example, was cluttered with debris, both carried in on the tides and from the battles that were fought here long ago. Even the tunnel from the shuttle bay in the Sanctum was cluttered. The Old One arranged for labor to clear it out."

Labor, Griffin thought. *I wonder if the disappearance of a ship or two might be credited to the Old One's list. Maybe it's something far more simple—any port town has a fair share of transients. Or maybe he bought slaves. Adara and Terrell gave me to understand that slavery isn't favored in this region but that doesn't mean it isn't else-where.*

"What a tremendous undertaking," Griffin said, allow-ing himself to sound impressed. "Is there a great deal of that sort of work still to be done?"

"Not a great deal," Julyan replied. "The facility is large—it had to be to house both shuttles and the equip-ment needed to work on them. However, it was not com-plex. The Old One has theorized that the people who worked here lived on the mainland."

There was a slight question in the words. After all, Grif-fin's finding of the crew quarters beneath the Sanctum had undone one of the Old One's theories—that the crew for the facility had lived in the town of Spirit Bay.

Griffin nodded. "I think he is correct. There would be no reason to set up separate living and dining facilities. In the days when Mender's Isle was in use, there were probably scooters of some sort in the tunnels. The staff here could have commuted back and forth in less time than it has taken us to walk to this point."

"Amazing," Julyan said. "I am continually awed that, given all they could do, the seegnur would have chosen to come to a primitive place like Artemis."

Is he trying to get me to give my origin away? Careful, Griffin.

"I don't know," Griffin said. "I once knew a very rich man whose greatest pleasure was pruning the roses in his garden. Access to wealth and power does not mean other pleasures are lessened. Consider the Old One, he has wealth and influence beyond most, yet he chooses to spend his long years in historical research for no other reason than the pleasure of knowledge."

A knowing expression flashed across Julyan's features, then vanished.

So, it is not simply the pleasure of knowledge that drives the Old One. Does he search these ruins for the same reason that he breeds creatures like Ring? What connects the two? I feel sure there is a connection. And when I do know, then, too, I will have a better idea why the Old One is willing to take the double risk of keeping me captive yet giving me freedom to explore.

⌘

Interlude: Have No

Have no eyes.
  See.
Have no ears.
  Hearing.
Have no heart.
  Lonely.

18

Dreams

They brought in Griffin's body on the third day. The corpse was swollen and bloated from immersion in water. Crabs had been at it, ruining the features, but tufts of bright golden hair seemed to prove that this man was indeed Griffin Dane.

Adara sent Sand Shadow an image of Griffin superimposed over that of the dead body. Sand Shadow's reply was inconclusive, including the many other scents that overlay that of the dead man: rot, sea wrack, fish, and the men who had handled the body. Whether the human scent that remained was Griffin's own, the puma could not be sure.

Laying a soothing hand on her demiurge's neck, Adara rubbed the deep plushy fur. She had her reasons for thinking this mutilated corpse was not that of her friend, but she kept them to herself until she and Terrell were alone.

"I don't think it was Griffin," Adara said. "For one, Sand Shadow caught no trace of his scent. And the man whose boat found the body is familiar to me."

Terrell had been sunk in thought. Now he rallied and looked at Adara. "Familiar?"

"He was the man I saw in conference with Julyan," Adara said. "The captain of the fishing fleet that carried supplies to the Haunted Islands. That seems too much of a coincidence."

"But the color of the hair . . ." Terrell obviously wanted to believe Adara, but this was a point that couldn't be ignored.

"I don't know how that was managed," Adara said, "but Griffin is not the only man to have hair of that rich wheat gold."

"It would be too much to believe that there was a corpse of the right type neatly available," Terrell protested.

"Is it too much to believe that the Old One would connive at murder? Knowing what else we do?"

"No . . ." Terrell slapped at a fly that had landed on Midnight's neck with such violence that the black turned his head to look at him in reproach. "Sorry, fellow . . ."

Adara wouldn't have been a credit to Bruin's teaching if she couldn't tell that Terrell was deeply troubled. Instinctively, she knew that this was a time for listening, so she guided Tarnish along and waited with the same patience she would have given to stalking some prize bit of game.

"Adara . . . I don't think Griffin's dead either." Terrell's brash confidence had vanished. He spoke hesitantly, like a little boy scared by a night fear. "I've been dreaming about him. The dreams are so real. Either I'm going mad or somehow in his sleep he's calling out and I'm . . . I'm hearing him."

"When did the dreams start?"

"On the night he vanished." Terrell shook his head. "That's not completely . . . Adara! Don't get the wrong idea. There have been dreams almost since I met Griffin. Ever since he saved my life. I've felt bound. Connected. And as if I was going crazy."

"And these are the same?" Adara asked. "Not guilt?"

"Not guilt," Terrell said firmly. "I felt that, sure, but before what I felt was a buzz, a hum, just a sense of him. Now there's a focus and that focus is him, alive somewhere. I'm sure he's not dead."

Adara leaned so she could pat Terrell on one shoulder. "I believe you. The lore said the seegnur had strange powers. Perhaps Griffin does as well."

"But why me? Why not you? You knew him first. He . . . I think he cares for you."

Adara shook her head. "Perhaps because Griffin saved your life. Some say that doing such a thing makes you responsible for a person from that point on. I saved him. It's not the same thing. As for him caring . . . I think what he feels for me is more confused than that."

"And you for him?"

"You've asked that before and the answer hasn't changed. I don't know how I feel—for him, for you. Seeing Julyan again made me realize how little I know of love. I would have given Julyan anything—I did give him everything I had to give. He put me aside as if I was nothing more than a pleasant distraction."

She shook her head so hard that her braid snapped. "This is not the time for such talk. Let us accept that the three of us—you and me and Sand Shadow—all have our reasons to believe that Griffin Dane lives."

"Very well."

"Shall we also accept that it is best the Old One not realize what we think?"

"Absolutely."

"Then we must consider how we plan our hunt."

Terrell drew in his breath, expelling it as if pushing away dreams and nightmares. "There is a matter you may not have considered. Griffin's body is found. Once it is buried, there is no reason for us to remain in the Old One's Sanctum. We came to bring Griffin to him. We stayed as Griffin's companions."

"Good point," Adara said. "The funeral is not likely to be long delayed. Griffin did not have friends to gather from afar. He may even be buried today."

"I suspect he will be," Terrell agreed, "especially if the body is not Griffin's. The Old One will not wish to take risks, nor will he throw us out at once, but he will become impatient."

Adara nodded. "Very good. Then tonight Sand Shadow and I will search the Sanctum and reassure ourselves that Griffin is not there."

"I'll help."

"No. We can prowl in the dark as you cannot. Moreover, I am an oddity to the Old One. If by some small chance we are caught, I can make some excuse. He has little respect for me. It will be easy to make him believe I am merely grief stricken."

"I'll accept that," Terrell said. "But you don't believe you will find Griffin, do you?"

"No. I think that, if he is anywhere near, he is on those islands. We have good reason to believe they are where the Old One keeps other prisoners. Getting there will be the problem."

"So we won't leave Spirit Bay?"

"I think not. We can stay at the Trainers, give out that we are shopping for special goods to bring back to Bruin. When I told Elaine earlier that Griffin had drowned, she offered us shelter along with her condolences."

"It would be odder if we left for Shepherd's Call

empty-handed," Terrell agreed. "And since the Trainers offer room, then all is set."

When they returned to the Sanctum, they found matters progressing much as they had anticipated. Griffin was to be buried that evening at a local cemetery, his funeral attended by several loremasters. When they learned of the funeral, the entire mass of the extended Trainer household insisted on attending as well.

Adara found herself deeply touched, both by that gesture of friendship and by the funeral itself. She wept without artifice, for if Griffin was not dead he was something far worse—prisoner of a man without scruples. She wept, too, for Bruin, who—though he did not know it—had been horribly betrayed by one he had thought of as friend and mentor.

Terrell did not weep as openly, but his bright blue eyes were dimmed by tears and his lips pressed into a tight line.

That night Adara and Sand Shadow went over the Sanctum from end to end. They could not go into the Old One's own suite nor that shared by Jean and Joffrey, but no other place was spared. They began with the crew quarters, for one of those many rooms might make a good prison. When this turned up nothing, they went to the other side.

The hidden door still showed no sign of ever having been opened, removing some lingering suspicion that Griffin had found a way through there and been kidnapped for his pains. The communications room remained as empty and useless as ever. It was only when they gave the shuttle arrival bay a quick check that something suspicious turned up.

Sand Shadow had been carefully sniffing every area they inspected. Now Adara became aware that her demiurge was excitedly pawing at something wedged between dormant equipment and the wall. She hurried over to the great cat's side. Kneeling, she picked up what Sand Shadow's paws had been too large to pull from the confined space—several handmade marbles. Sand Shadow, who would know such things, even in the dark, confirmed that they were Griffin's.

Then the puma added an image that it took Adara a moment to unravel. Surely there was nothing odd about the Old One's scent being here. Then she grasped the puma's meaning. The Old One's scent was here, fresh and much overlaid, as if he came to this place often—far more often than he ever let on.

Though they searched carefully, the metal-clad walls yielded nothing. Adara wondered what secrets they had told the Old One—and if Griffin had learned them, so sealing his fate.

※

Julyan was faithful to his word. At the end of the tour, he even reassured Griffin that soon enough all restrictions would be lifted.

"The Old One wants to talk with you first, that's all. He thinks that once you understand what he is trying to do here, you will be eager to join with him."

Griffin was not at all so certain, but he wasn't going to say so. He made a noncommittal sound that could be interpreted as just about anything Julyan chose. Next, Julyan introduced him to a man named Dierks.

"Dierks will be your assistant. He's fully literate and familiar with both this facility and the one beneath the Sanctum."

Dierks was a small man with an upturned nose, freckles, and a crop of sandy-red hair, thinning slightly at the crown. Unlike Julyan, who moved with the same dangerous grace as Adara, Dierks did not look as if he'd be much good in a fight. Although Griffin supposed that he had to consider Dierks his guard as much as his assistant, he didn't feel that Dierks would be able to do much to stop him if he found some way to escape. The thought was both reassuring and disquieting.

If they thought I could get away, they would have assigned someone more like Julyan to stay with me. This little clerk can rat on me, but that's about it.

Dierks, it turned out, had trained as a loremaster. "I came to the profession through my faith," he explained as he and Griffin pored over hand-drawn diagrams of the facility. "I firmly believed that the seegnur could not have created a world with error in it, that if I studied hard enough I would find a reason for such things as illness and death. What I found instead were more puzzles. My questions made me unwelcome at the loremaster's college.

"I traveled, still seeking wisdom. My journey ended when I met the Old One. He studies the seegnur without undue awe at their achievements . . ."

Which makes him a fool if ever I've met one, Griffin thought uncharitably.

". . . and seeks instead to understand what they have left behind in the hope that someday we will be able to benefit. He also . . ."

Dierks halted, a blush climbing from his collar to the top of his balding head.

Griffin looked up from the drawing he had been studying, pretended not to notice, and gently asked, "Yes?"

"I nearly overstepped, Griffin. My apologies. Julyan told me that the Old One would wish to tell you about his greater plans himself, that he would explain much better."

Griffin nodded. "Of course . . . I fully understand. Now, in order to analyze this facility, I'm going to need to understand how much of the islands are natural and how much are artificial . . ."

* * *

The Old One summoned Griffin some days later. Although the facility had been intended for large-scale projects, it possessed any number of smaller rooms as well. The one the Old One had taken as his office was actually built above ground, artfully concealed within a small rise. In the days when it had been constructed, it would have been completely invisible, for the windows could have been hidden behind holographic screens. Even today, with a few strands of some sort of flowering vine flowing over the opening, Griffin guessed it was very well concealed.

Once again, the contrast between high-tech sophistication as represented by the structure and low-tech scholarship as represented by the primitive writing implements on the Old One's desk brought home to Griffin just how far he was from the worlds he knew.

"You wished to see me," he said formally, deciding that it would be best to completely ignore the uncomfortable circumstances that had led to his coming here and act as Julyan and Dierks did—that this was all some odd variation on normalcy.

"Yes, I did. I'm sorry I wasn't able to interview you sooner," the Old One said. "Various circumstances kept me on shore. However, now we can talk. Please, have a seat."

Griffin did so, thinking, *Is he completely insane? It's one thing for me to try and pretend, but him? He kidnapped me! The last time I saw him, he was gloating about how he would arrange for Adara and Terrell to believe I'd been drowned. Surely . . .*

The Old One was pouring them both tea from a pot that had been brought in by a servant. Griffin realized that thus far, other than the haggard woman who had carried in his breakfast that first morning, all the staff he'd seen here had been male. He wondered why, his skin crawling as he thought of a possible answer.

"Julyan and Dierks have both mentioned to you that I have goals above and beyond simply examining the relics the seegnur left behind them," the Old One was beginning when a small motion from Griffin caused him to interrupt himself. "Yes? You have a question?"

"I do. I've been careful not to mention my origin. Neither Julyan or Dierks have said anything that give me a clear idea how much they know. Could you tell me what I should say?"

The Old One nodded approvingly. "Very prudent. I have told them a variation of the biography that you yourself created. You were raised by isolationists who came across some interesting relics. As such, you have insights into the seegnur that are quite unusual. They are to consider you an expert and be patient with your curious blind spots regarding life as we know it."

"And they are satisfied with this?"

"I am satisfied with it," the Old One said, his tone cold. "They know that is what matters. If they choose to think other thoughts in private, that is their choice. As for you . . . I strongly suggest you do not state otherwise. Your claim might not be believed. Even if it was, it would not necessarily make you friends."

Thinking of Dierks and his curiously resentful attitude toward the long-ago seegnur, Griffin thought he understood.

"Very good, sir. Thank you for clarifying that matter. Now, you were about to tell me something of your longterm goals. I assure you, I am very eager to learn more."

The Old One Who Is Young steepled his fingers and looked thoughtfully off at something only he could see. His pale grey eyes seemed to light from within.

"I am very old. Once I realized that short of accident I was likely to continue living with mind and body unimpaired by age, I will admit, I wondered why. I also wondered if there were any others who shared my peculiar gift. Finding others like me was the first spur that sent me on my wanderings.

"In that quest, I was doomed to disappointment. Rumor after rumor I followed, but at the end of the trail either the traces faded or I found some man or woman—perhaps of great years, but lacking my singular vitality. Failing to find any like myself, I also failed to find a clear answer to the 'why' of my gift.

"The recognized adaptations—such as the ability to breathe underwater or to see in the dark—were clearly useful in certain environments and professions. What use was there in long life and abiding health, especially since, to my great disappointment, I appeared to be unable to have children who might share some portion of my gift? Clearly I was not meant to found a dynasty in the literal sense—a dynasty that could bring the order that vanished with the slaughter of the seegnur. What then was I to do?

"For a time I studied with the loremasters, absorbing all I could of what had come before us. Eventually, I concluded that my life's mission would be to see if I could reawaken the glorious technological devices that had been common in the days before the slaughter of the seegnur, even if most had not known they existed."

Griffin listened, careful not to so much as shift in his chair lest he distract the Old One from his tale. He had the impression that the Old One had almost forgotten his presence.

"Eventually, I decided that the key must be in the seegnur nature itself. The lore contained many indications that the people of Artemis had been created by the seegnur in their own image. I came to believe that just as the smallest terrier carries within it the seeds of the wolf, so the people of Artemis carried within them the seeds of the seegnur.

"There were hints here and there that the technology of the seegnur was not like our own machinery—and that the difference was more than one of sophistication. I came to believe that at least some of the seegnur's technology was operated by an interweaving of the seegnur and the machine."

The pale eyes fastened on Griffin as if looking for confirmation.

Griffin nodded. "Yes. We have similar tales—most agree that the seegnur could interface the living and the created. However, no one has ever succeeded in figuring out how this was done."

The Old One's lips moved in what must be called a smile, but was an expression that indicated his own sense of superiority. "You told me that the wars that destroyed the great empire also destroyed the planets they had most treasured, as well as the most sophisticated of their technology."

"That is true. By the time the Old Empire fell, fear that someone would inherit their power and so come to dominate in turn led to both places and people being destroyed."

"Tell me honestly, Griffin, do you consider yourself of the same stock as the seegnur of old?"

Griffin hesitated, tempted for a moment to make that very claim. However, then he might be asked to prove it—or worse, he could threaten the Old One's conceit. He decided to walk a narrow line.

"Not purebred, no. There are many indications that the rulers of the empire and their most chosen associates were different from those over whom they ruled. However, there are ample indications that we shared common stock. The ruling class regularly intermarried with their subjects and children came from those unions."

Griffin thought the Old One might be threatened by the mention of children, since he himself was sterile but, if he was, he did not show it.

He only nodded. "That seems a fair assessment. The lore contains scattered references that on Artemis the seegnur sought to create something unique for themselves. Have you been told our creation story?"

"Yes. Adara told it to me."

"Did she tell you how initially Artemis was created

without human residents, how later they were added, then later still the adaptations were worked into small portion of the population?"

Griffin nodded.

"It is my belief that the adaptations were rooted in the same abilities that the seegnur used to operate their most sophisticated technologies—and that those technologies, in turn, were used to create the underlying structure of Artemis because, only then, could they be hidden so completely from sight that the illusion of an unspoiled world could be maintained."

"I see. And?"

"Therefore, just as with enough patience and time one could breed back to a wolf from a domestic dog, so I believe that it would be possible to breed back to the abilities that enabled the seegnur to operate their most sophisticated machinery."

Griffin blinked, straightening in his chair. The idea was insane, yet . . . He remembered the tales he had read of how the seegnur held their vast empire together because they alone possessed the secret of ships that could cover vast distances in the blink of an eye. How early in the war—before a heroic strike on the part of the rebels destroyed some of the most crucial planets in the seegnur's structure—the seegnur had defeated far vaster hosts by apparently defying the accepted laws of physics. There were other such stories, most dismissed by scholars as the victors presenting the odds against them as much higher than they had been in order to justify the level of destruction they had used.

But what if the stories had been true?

He spoke, his voice hoarse. "But not only were the seegnur slaughtered, your lore speaks of the death of machines. Even if you could breed back to those who could operate the seegnur's old technology, nothing will function."

The Old One's expression showed satisfaction. "Will

it? I wonder. There are indications that those who led the slaughter of the seegnur expected to return to Artemis. What if the machines were not so much 'killed' as put to sleep?"

Griffin thought of the landing facility, sealed but its basic works left in order, of this repair facility. He remembered tales of how the seegnur had often built where water would hide their constructions from casual view.

He inclined his head, encouraging the Old One to continue. Griffin suspected that while the Old One might have shared some of his speculations with trusted associates, he was telling Griffin far more because Griffin could understand without being hampered by superstition.

"I had hoped," the Old One said, "that if I managed to breed back to someone with abilities close to those of the original seegnur, that one would be able to serve as a key. Thus far, I will admit, I have not been successful. I am hampered by not knowing precisely what qualities the seegnur valued. Yet, I will tell you this. Even when an adaptation appears to be purely physical—as with Adara's night vision—there is a mental component. I have tested with others who share that talent. Even when they are in darkness so complete that a cat or other such creature blunders around as if blind, these eventually begin to cope. I believe there is a mental enhancement—an ability to see with the eyes of the mind as well as those of the body—that aids them. Might not these eyes of the mind have been part of what was used to guide the seegnur's ships so that they could see paths through the void to which others were blind?"

"It might have been so," Griffin slowly agreed. He thought of Ring, who lived in perpetual confusion because he could not tell which future he was living in. Surely the Old One had bred for that—perhaps a variation on the superb natural sense of direction he had heard Terrell and Adara mention that some hunters and factotum possessed.

He realized that there was a question he must ask. "Wait! I was so fascinated by your ambitious plans, for the goal you have set yourself, that I may have misunderstood you. Did you say you have already begun this program?"

"Yes. Some generations ago. At first I attempted to recruit from among the adapted that I knew—and I knew a great many, for I had often sought them out in my wanderings. They in turn, especially if they came from areas where the adapted are less than welcome, were glad to befriend one who admired them.

"Later, I realized that I was up against human nature. Sometimes a woman would promise me a child to raise—a child fathered by a man I had suggested to her as having a complementary talent. When the child was born, she would decide she could not part from it. Also, I was coming to realize that it might take me generations to breed for the qualities I needed."

Griffin swallowed his repulsion and said as matter-of-factly as he could, "As it would take generations to breed even a fighting dog, already close to a wolf in appearance, back to its wolfish stock."

"Precisely! Therefore, I needed more control. I sought among those of the adapted who had found themselves shunned. I offered them a home and a purpose, the promise that they and their children would never go without shelter or food, that they would live within a community where they would be accepted."

He went on for some time in this vein. Griffin listened intently. Never once was kidnapping mentioned, never once forced coupling. Griffin found himself wondering if Winnie had been a rebel within a mostly contented community, if her tale had been distorted. Had Lynn's daughter actually been kidnapped? Perhaps Mabel had been recruited and later regretted her choice . . .

The Old One was drawing his account to a close. "Yet, I was handicapped. Ideally, I would have set up my community of the adapted in some isolated area, where they could flourish free from the stigma attached to them. However, I did not wish to leave my researches into the physical technologies of the seegnur. These islands—thought of as 'haunted' by the good but credulous people of the town—were the perfect solution. The seegnur had sculpted the surrounding area so that the islands could not be approached by any water craft, large or small. I, however, had found the tunnel that led here. The door had been closed but not locked. Eventually I chanced on the means of opening it."

"As if it was meant to be," Griffin said softly. He wondered again how Winnie's tale fit into this. Adara claimed to have found the location of the original area where the Old One had kept his captives. Wouldn't the islands have been a better choice all along? Someone was not telling the whole truth and he would bet that someone was not Adara the Huntress.

"Now," the Old One said, his grey eyes shining as he turned his thoughts to the present, "once again I receive an omen that I am on the right course, that I am doing what was meant to happen. You land here on Artemis, not far from where one of my most devoted followers lives. Soon after your landing, for the first time since the death of machines, a machine awakens. I believe the time has come for Artemis to waken from the sleep she has slept these five hundred years."

He leaned forward. "I had thought I would need to wait until I created a key that more or less accidentally fit the lock. Now . . . Now . . . Perhaps you have brought the key with you. What do you say to this? We will go into the mountains and find our way into your shuttle. I believe you must have brought with you something that would enable you to counter the nanobots that slaughtered the machines. Only the suddenness of your landing kept you from taking it with you.

"We will go. We will retrieve it. We will awaken the dormant technologies. Then you can contact your orbiting ship and arrange for your freedom and I . . . I will be a step closer to achieving my dream of making Artemis the place she once was before greed and misery sealed her into silence."

Interlude: Reluctant Dreamer

I don't want to dream of you,
I'd much rather dream of her.
She's sexy, supple, hot as fire . . .
I've even made her purr.

But unkind fate has mated me
To your colder fire.
Much as I would dream of her,
Your wish is my desire.

19
The Roots of Things

When Adara and Terrell announced their intention of moving out of the Sanctum and back over to the Trainers, the Old One surprised them both by asking if they—especially Terrell—would care to stay.

"As you know," he said, offering them one of his rare smiles, "I have a great appreciation for those with training in the lore. Terrell, you have shown yourself exceptionally talented—and free from the more rigid dictums that limit so many who have followed that difficult course.

And you, Adara, have an engaging curiosity. That, combined with your ability to see in the dark, have already provided a considerable advantage to my research."

For the slightest of moments, Adara was tempted. Perhaps they were wrong to blame the Old One. Perhaps Julyan was acting on his own . . . And even if the Old One was guilty, wasn't it easier to hunt the prey when one could keep a close watch on it?

That last thought was what convinced Adara that she, for one, was not going to stay in the Sanctum. Perhaps the Old One wanted to be able to keep a close eye on her and Terrell—at least until he was certain that they had no suspicions regarding him.

She inclined her head politely. "I appreciate your offer, good sir, but I have no desire to remain shut in. We'll be based out of the Trainers,' but I will be staying mostly out of doors. If you need my help on some difficult search, a message sent there will reach me."

Terrell also declined, though his explanation for exactly why he would leave such an honored patron was rather incomplete. Adara wondered that someone with Terrell's training in etiquette could not have managed something better.

She said as much to Terrell after he, Adara, and Sand Shadow had taken their leave of the Sanctum.

Grinning rather wickedly, Terrell confided, "Oh, I did that on purpose. Later, I went back to the Old One and, shuffling my feet a bit, I let on that I had been courting you since last summer, that I hoped that with Griffin gone—sad as that was—I had some hope of finally winning my suit."

"Clever," Adara said, "and even better because now the Old One will be inclined to see Griffin as your rival, not your friend."

"My thought exactly," Terrell said smugly. "In any case, lies rooted in truth are least likely to come back to trip one up."

"Terrell . . ."

"I've never told you I'd given up, only that I was willing to wait and let you make up your mind. I'm still willing—and I don't see that it hurts to remind you occasionally."

"Fair enough. But my mind hasn't changed. I'm not sure I'm in love with you or with Griffin. I'm not sure I'm capable of love at all."

"You are."

"Right now," Adara said firmly, "what I am capable of is doing my best to find Griffin. We have two trails we can follow: Julyan and the people in that little fishing village. I also want to see if I can find my way into the place where the Old One kept his breeding stock before Winnie and Ring and the others made their escape."

"What do you think you'll find?"

"I don't know, but I've been wondering. We're pretty sure that place is deserted now. We know from Winnie that there were a good number of people there. How did the Old One move them out? Small groups? A mass shipping? One thing I'm sure of—he didn't kill them all and start over. Humans are slow breeders. He'd be setting back his program by years, maybe even decades."

"Fair enough," Terrell said. "I'll see what I can do in town. One good thing about our reason for staying on in Spirit Bay is that I have ample excuse for roaming around and talking to people while I shop for supplies to take back to Shepherd's Call. Learning about that fishing village should be easy—people like to gossip about their competitors.

"Tell me what you can about Julyan. I'm not going to want to ask about him by name, but I can ask indirectly. Other than hunting and seducing the love of my life, what interests did he have?"

Adara acceded, though her heart ached as she dredged up buried memories. She faithfully repeated every little detail she could remember, from quirks about food

(Julyan had hated both honey and cherries, a bad thing for someone who lived in Bruin's home), to mannerisms, to games he had liked, to his love for music.

"Singing, eh?" Terrell said when she finished. "I might be able to make something of that. You say he was good?"

"Very," Adara said. "And he loved to perform."

"So it's possible that, unless his entire life here has been lived in concealment, that Julyan might be known in some of the local taverns. Did he have a piece or two he particularly liked?"

Wincing slightly, Adara sang:

> "My love is like a panther swift.
> I caught her in my snare.
> And after I had captured her,
> I left her hanging there.
>
> "My love is like a rabbit fleet.
> I caught her in a trap.
> And after I had captured her,
> I gave her heart a snap."

Terrell cocked an eyebrow. "That's a pretty tune. The lyrics certainly aren't of the common sort. Yes. I can use that."

He fell silent, obviously planning his approach with much the same care that Adara would a complex hunt. She respected this and kept silent, but the little tune—with lyrics she had written to Julyan's order—kept echoing through her mind. She was sure Julyan still sang it. There was a vanity that would make him reluctant to reject something so perfect for his voice and style, even though he had rejected the love that inspired it.

Griffin wondered how he would have reacted to the Old One's vision if he had not first learned about the cost to those who would provide the breeding stock for these new seegnur.

But you'd be less than honest, he thought, *if you didn't admit you're tempted, eh, Griffin Dane? After the crash you gave up on the shuttle and all it contains. Now here is a man who is determined to excavate it—and who has the resources to do so, who has the means of giving you back the stars.*

A new thought interrupted this tempting vision. *Who says the Old One is going to include you in his plans except as a resource—a sort of database to tell him what various things are? Returning to the stars is your dream. Is it his? I doubt it. The Old One must know that away from Artemis he would cease to be a power. He would be little more than a curiosity. He might even find himself imprisoned in some lab somewhere, mined for the secret of his longevity as he mines his subjects for their adaptations.*

The more Griffin considered this point, the less certain he felt that the Old One intended to work with Griffin as any sort of equal. Indeed, the very fact that the Old One had been willing to speak so freely to Griffin might be taken as an indication of the exact opposite—that Griffin, assumed dead and drowned by the few friends he had made here on Artemis—would remain dead.

Then all the more important that I show myself willing if I am to have any freedom at all.

So Griffin flung himself into his assigned research with fevered intensity. He saw the Old One with enough frequency to be assured that the planned trip into the mountains above Shepherd's Call had not yet begun. Of one thing Griffin felt certain—the Old One would lead that expedition himself. Not only wouldn't he wish anyone else to make the discoveries, it would be the best way of assuring local cooperation, for the Old One had no reason

to believe that Bruin was anything but his faithful fol-
lower.

*The Old One must not go or, if he does, I must go with
him, be there to mislead him, to distract him with my
helpfulness. Best if he didn't go at all. How to manage
it?*

Worry pounded in Griffin's head, background to all he
did, a song of desperation verging upon insanity.

"The village is called Chankly's Harbor," Terrell reported
to Adara a few days after they had departed the Sanctum.
"The head of the clan is Captain Bore Chankly. The
Chankly clan doesn't have the best reputation locally. The
former family head—Bore's father—was a drunk who
turned most of the catch into booze. Bore Chankly took
over after his father was injured during a nasty storm—
except there are those who say the damage wasn't caused
by the storm but by Bore himself.

"Since then family fortunes have risen, but not their
reputation. It's said most of their catch comes from raid-
ing others' nets and traps. They've staked out fishing
grounds for themselves. Any who trespass find holes in
their nets—or their hulls."

"Let me guess," Adara said. "Their favored fishing
grounds are between their private harbor and the Haunted
Islands."

"Yep. And that has folks puzzled because those have
never been waters known for good fishing. Too turbu-
lent, for one. However, Captain Chankly isn't hurting for
money. It's rumored that he's found a wreck on one of
those shoals or maybe some seegnur artifacts. But people don't like to talk about the Chanklys. Nasty things
happen to people who gossip too much about where Captain Chankly gets his money."

Adara grinned. "You seem to have done well enough."

"Although you seem immune," Terrell countered, "I am actually a very charming fellow. And I didn't get all of this in one place—not by far. I started by asking about who was best to buy from, hinting that I'd been given such a good offer by one of the Chankly crews that I doubted the quality. The rest came from there."

"Take care if you're wandering around at night," Adara warned. "Sounds like you're setting yourself up for some of those 'nasty things' that happen to those who ask too many questions."

"I am," Terrell assured her. "The Trainers are more than happy to loan me a bear hound or so if I go out. That's nearly as good as having Sand Shadow with me."

The puma made a sound between a purr and a growl, her version of an ironic chuckle.

Adara scratched the puma under her chin. "We haven't been so successful. We're keeping an eye on Chankly's Harbor. Thus far there's no sign of anything unusual. They don't even seem to be doing much fishing. I'm getting frustrated."

"No luck finding a way into that facility?"

"Not so far, yet I'm sure there must be a way. Ring and Winnie got out, so we can get in."

She could see from Terrell's expression that he didn't think that was necessarily true. Indeed, she herself could think of ways any entrance could be completely sealed—massive amounts of dirt or rock from a "landslide" would do the job.

But those would make it very hard for the Old One to return and I cannot believe he would want that. If the place was of the seegnur's making, then the Old One might hide it, but he would never destroy it.

Bolstered by her conclusions, Adara returned to the hunt. She reviewed Lynn's description over and over again. There had been an inlet. A large rock shelf had been associated with the place. She'd found both. Eventually, she accepted that her own awe for the Old One, no matter how much she had tried to hide it from herself, had worked against her.

I have been acting as if he were some sort of wizard—or worse, the seegnur of old—capable of hiding a city behind a wall of fog and mist. Think like a hunter! There must have been ways for food to be brought in, water, an underground place would have needed fresh air . . .

Two nights later, Adara found the way in. There was a waterfall—so natural in its course, so small and insignificant in its flow—that time and again she had overlooked it. Behind the water, she found more space than there should be. Searching by touch, she came upon a crevice so narrow she needed to pass through sideways. Beyond that crevice was a passage cut by tools far more sophisticated than any she knew.

Seegnur work.

Griffin has told us often enough how the seegnur were like foxes, always building hidden exits from their dens. This must have been one such. I cannot believe they chose to get soaked every time they went in or out.

The passage appeared to end after a dozen or so paces. Once Adara would have been fooled, but that was before she had helped Griffin and the rest explore the Sanctum. The passage "end" proved to be a door similar to those commonly used there. Griffin had shown them how to operate the fail-safe that allowed the door to be opened without power.

Adara wondered that a door allowing access to the outer world had not been more carefully locked. Her answer came in the form of a huge blackened mark that all but obscured a panel near the door.

I see. When the raiders came, they burned away the more complex lock. Later, they did not take time to replace a mechanism that would not work without power in any case. After all, the primitives of Artemis would not be able to figure out seegnur locks.

She prowled forward, alert for traps. The lore from the

days after the slaughter of the seegnur was filled with tales of the unfortunate who had fallen afoul of dangers left by the seegnur for their enemies. Then there were the traps the Old One himself might have left for Lynn or her allies.

Sand Shadow remained outside while Adara made the initial check. Eventually, Adara indicated the puma could join her. Once past the crevice—which Sand Shadow would have no trouble with—the corridors were quite wide enough for both of them. The puma arrived, plushy fur like damp velvet, and rubbed her head against Adara in approval. To her nose, the place smelled strongly of humans: old scent, but of young and old, many females, many young.

This is what we sought, the place the Old One was forced to abandon after Lynn discovered his secret. Now to see if we can turn it to our own use. He will not make it easy.

Nor did he. Five or six times Adara had to stop and patiently dismantle some device that would have harmed someone without her gift for seeing in the dark. Two more times only Sand Shadow's basic distrust saved her from blundering into something that escaped even her careful inspection.

Once the place would have overwhelmed Adara with its peculiar layout. Not only was it larger than the buildings she had known, but the seegnur had built with a different sense of priority than her own people. Moreover, there were repeated signs of destruction—burn marks, slagged metal, ruined machinery—that even the Old One's later use did not conceal.

Adara thought that Griffin might have been able to guess the place's original purpose, but it was a mystery to her. All she could do was patiently search corridor by corridor, room by room, trying to find anything that might be useful.

The facility had been stripped of its furnishings. They

found evidence of how it had been refitted for modern needs. Clumsy chimneys made from clay pipe fed into ventilation ducts, probably meant to serve stoves no longer in place. Smoke marked walls and ceilings where lanterns had been hung.

Occasionally, Sand Shadow's sense of smell added a detail. This room smelled strongly of blood, that one of food, this one of smoke. In the end, it was Sand Shadow who found where another door was hidden.

Here, the puma sent, pressing her nose to an otherwise unpromising wall at the end of a wide corridor. *Human scent, fresher than the others, also older scent, piled up as if many, many went over this place.*

Adara understood and quickly found the outline of a door. She found the controls, concealed behind a panel that matched the surrounding wall. The concealment, although quite good, looked as if it had been done since the time of the seegnur. Probably then, long ago, this door had not been hidden.

However, try as she might, Adara could not open the door. The fail-safes did not work as did the ones in the crew quarters. Frustrated, she sat on the floor and considered.

I wondered at the outer door why it was not better locked. There the lock had been burned away. Here it remains. Did the Old One somehow work out its secret?

Almost unwillingly, Adara found herself admiring the Old One's cleverness. He might be colder than the never melting ice of the highest mountains, but there was no denying his brilliance.

I must not let myself forget that Griffin comes from a culture that—although fallen—is still far closer to that of the seegnur than any we know. The Old One may have had centuries of life, but still he is of Artemis. That he has learned so much without teachers such as Griffin had . . . No. I must take care not to underestimate him.

That brilliance of mind is as dangerous as the fangs of any pack of winter starved wolves.

She tried to solve the lock a while longer, but failed. Eventually, she decided to seek Terrell's aid. Terrell had a loremaster's education. Possibly he would think of something she had not. Perhaps this door was useless to their cause. However, the Old One had closed it and locked it as he had no other. If for no other reason than that, Adara wanted to get through.

Griffin's apparent eagerness—and perhaps the Old One's desire to make him an ally, not a mere prisoner—quickly earned him privileges. One of the first was being offered a mistress, such as both Julyan and Dierks enjoyed.

He knew that to refuse would be to lower himself in Julyan's estimation—Julyan was very much the sort of man who enjoyed flaunting his sexuality—but Griffin had no desire to force himself on a woman. Then again, the women might be willing to tell him things he wanted to know: about the Mender's Isle routine, how often the inhabitants were permitted outside, all those things that could enable him to plan an escape.

In the end, Griffin decided to express interest but also a degree of choosiness—presenting himself as a connoisseur of female beauty, unwilling to waste himself on just any woman. Julyan already thought he was odd, and readily accepted this excuse. However, this meant that each day some woman or other—bathed, groomed, and dressed provocatively—was paraded before Griffin. Some even seemed willing, which made Griffin's self-restraint even more difficult. It had been a long time, and he was lonely as well.

If it hadn't been for the odd dreams he kept having, for his chats with Dierks and, more rarely, with Julyan or the Old One, Griffin might have accepted a mistress just to break his isolation.

As it was, he found that remembering passages of Winnie's story were quite effective in cooling his ardor. Her voice saying *"Is it enough to say that the Stablekeeper took me and showed me what happened to one girl who had rebelled? What I saw was enough to convince me to give in"* was usually enough to stop him.

Scientific assessment also helped. Griffin tried to look at the women not as women but as specimens, speculating as to what trait they had that the Old One desired. Occasionally, there was a clue. One slim blonde had eyes with pupils like Adara's. Another showed thin lines on her throat that might be gill slits.

A final restraint to his sexual urges was that Griffin had no desire to be part of the Old One's breeding project. As far as Griffin knew, he had no adaptations, but might the Old One want to add off-world genes to his collection? The idea of some son or daughter of his being raised in captivity, bred, perhaps to a sister or brother to bring out shared traits, was enough to make Griffin impotent.

Oddly enough, Griffin's sexual self-restraint gained him freedom in other matters. Apparently, as Julyan saw it, if Griffin could resist the assortment of feminine pulchritude paraded before him each evening, then Griffin could also resist other temptations. Therefore, Griffin was given free run of most of the facility. The only areas off-limits were those where the women and children lived. Dierks assured him he wasn't missing much of scientific interest.

"I was there before the space was converted into living areas," he said. "The Old One and I went over them with great care. As best as we could tell, they were probably used to park a shuttle when it was no longer in use, just a huge, empty area with a door that—from its angle—probably opened directly under water."

"You didn't open it?"

"We couldn't, even if we'd dared. The seegnur may

have had a way to keep the water out, but we don't. I was nervous the Old One would try anyhow—he is fearless when it comes to seeking knowledge—but the locks had been melted shut. You must remember, both this place and the one under the lighthouse were in horrible shape when the Old One found them. Only the arrival center was left in good shape, though sealed against intrusion."

"Under the lighthouse?" Griffin tried not to sound eager. He remembered how Adara had located the general area where Lynn had said the Old One had originally housed his breeding project. They hadn't found a way into the facility there but, to be fair, they hadn't looked very hard. There had been too much else to occupy them.

"That's right," Dierks said. "It's closed now but it was the first place the Old One found. He came to Spirit Bay because he had heard about the arrival facility and how it was still intact. However, even with the help of the loremasters, he couldn't find a way in. Instead, he concluded that if the seegnur had one facility in the area, they might have had others. Proximity would have been useful since they refused to use their flying machines."

"Yes. That would have ruined the ambiance," Griffin agreed. "So the Old One went looking . . ."

"He had already learned that if the local lore said a place was scenic or otherwise restricted, it often held hidden evidence of the seegnur's technology. The Haunted Islands were of great interest for that reason, but even he could not figure out how to bring a boat safely ashore.

"Therefore, he went looking for other places. There were tales that there had once been a very elegant lighthouse some distance from the town of Spirit Bay. It's still depicted in mosaic art from the time of the seegnur. However, it had been completely destroyed. The Old One realized that the destruction had likely happened during the slaughter of the seegnur, for destroying the buildings they made is not easy."

Griffin nodded, thinking of the houses in Spirit Bay, still

intact, still with paint apparently pristine after five hundred years.

"And the Old One was, of course, correct."

"He was more than correct," Dierks went on, enthusiastic now that he was praising his mentor's cleverness, "for he found not only the place—it was overgrown after several hundred years of neglect, as you can imagine—he also found the hidden facility beneath it. Clearing that facility without arousing local ire—for the area was ruled as a restricted zone in the regional lore—was his first challenge."

"But he succeeded."

"He did. It took years. As he did so, he cultivated friendships with the people of Spirit Bay and surrounding areas. He had long been an advocate for the adapted. In Spirit Bay, as elsewhere, there were conflicting reactions. I think there was some relief at someone who would take responsibility."

"But the Old One's work didn't stop with finding the area below the lighthouse," Griffin gently prompted.

"Not in the least. Eventually, he found a tunnel from that facility to the Haunted Islands."

Griffin noted the difference in Dierks's account from what the Old One had told him. The Old One had implied that he had reached the islands from the Sanctum.

Interesting. So perhaps he does not want me to know about the lighthouse. Did he forget to tell Dierks to stay silent? Or is this a sign of increasing trust?

"The facilities on and beneath the islands had also been ruined," Dierks continued. "This time, though, the Old One changed his focus. He now knew that here—as elsewhere he had visited—the seegnur had hidden their workings beneath earth and water. He estimated where a tunnel into the sealed facility on the edge of the town might be."

"He found it," Griffin guessed, "and managed to get into the sealed facility that way. Clever. The locals didn't mind? After all, the Sanctum must have been restricted as well."

Dierks shook his head. "By the time the Old One found his way into the Sanctum, enough time had passed that the locals accepted his right. He is the Old One Who Is Young. He had outlived generations unchanged. Many thought he was one of the seegnur, either returned or re-awakened. He never made that claim . . ."

Griffin nodded. *But he did everything he could to quietly create that impression, from how he styled his hair and dressed, to implying that he remembered what he had only learned. I suspect his greatest asset was that he never tried to convince anyone of his right to do as he wished. He simply did it and left it up to them to accept or not.*

Aloud he said, "That's fascinating. Now, where's my pencil? I want to copy these icons. It wouldn't do to have the Old One get impatient with our lack of results, would it?"

Interlude: Battle Won, Search Begun

Passing sleepers unleashed in dreams,
Twined souls finding root and soil,
—growing when seeming least alive.

Can I?

Does someone listen?
  Someone search?

Without ears, I listen.
Without eyes, I seek.

Searching for my heart.

20

Whispered Confidences

When Adara brought Terrell to the area under the lighthouse the following day, he had no more luck than she in figuring out how to open the door.

"It might be a good idea if we didn't open it," he remarked, sinking down to sit on the floor, back pressed against the wall. "It seems to be facing the bay. We might end up flooded."

Adara paced back and forth, speaking with a confidence she didn't feel. "Sand Shadow says there are numerous layers of human scent here. I think this door is how the Old One took all those people away without them being seen."

"Maybe he drowned them," Terrell said darkly. Then he shook his head, acknowledging his own irrationality. "No. We've agreed he wouldn't do that. Humans breed too slowly for him to destroy the results of his experiments. Fine. Let me think on it. I'll go visit the loremasters' archives in Spirit Bay. It's possible I might come across something that will give me an insight."

Adara nodded approval. "I'll sneak back into the Sanctum and take a look at the door fastenings. If I meet up with the Old One, I can say I came to see if he needed any help seeing in the dark." She spoke quickly to forestall Terrell's inevitable warning. "Terrell, do you still have that feeling, the one that says Griffin is alive?"

The factotum nodded. "I do. There are dreams . . . unsettling dreams. I don't know why I should feel that somehow they are *his* dreams, but I do."

Adara decided not to mention her own unsettling dreams, dreams in which an unseen someone joined her and Sand Shadow in their mental realm. There wasn't much she was certain about these dreams, but she was sure they had nothing to do with Griffin.

"I'm glad." Adara squeezed Terrell's shoulder. "Don't worry about why you dream so. Be glad we have this reassurance."

"You don't think I'm crazy? Fooling myself because I feel guilty about letting Griffin drown?"

"No and no again. I think that Griffin is a strange person, a change-bringer, such as the legends tell. Why shouldn't those of us who have been closest to him be changed? A factotum might be changed most of all. Your profession was made to serve and protect visitors to Artemis."

"I'm glad you don't think I'm crazy. I wish I were so certain."

"Forget it. You go look at architectural drawings. I will brave the Sanctum. Perhaps between us, we will find a way to open this door."

Terrell sought Adara some mornings later. She had slept outdoors, as was her custom, but since the Trainers always served an excellent breakfast, she had returned there.

Terrell's eyes had dark circles under them. He looked so worn that Adara even forgot he was handsome. She sprang to her feet and guided him to one of the long benches that surrounded the communal table. At this hour, they were nearly alone. The earliest risers were already about their duties. The later risers—mostly the school-aged children—would not flood down the stairs for a time.

Adara poured Terrell a mug of the dark, bitter tea he favored, then began spreading soft cheese on bread.

"Are you getting sick?"

"Sick of . . . No. Not sick. I've been dreaming . . . I . . ."

His voice was a thick, heavy mumble that reminded Adara of Ring.

"Slowly, now," she said gently. "Eat. I'll get you something hot."

She sprang up and fetched a bowl of the soup that eternally simmered on the back of the stove.

"Terrell, ill?" asked the cook, a plump woman who was an aunt of Elaine's.

Adara nodded. "Or maybe hungover. I'll take him out in a bit and we'll see."

"And I'll keep the little ones from him, just in case."

Assured of privacy, Adara returned to Terrell. He finished the soup along with a slice of bread and cheese before speaking.

"I've been dreaming," he said. "A few nights ago, before I went to bed, I was wishing we could ask Griffin about how to open that door. I was beat—and maybe a little drunk. Cedric had broached a cask of some mead he wanted to sample.

"I found myself thinking, 'Well, maybe I can ask Griffin.' I remembered how you said that you and Sand Shadow didn't speak so much in words as in images and feelings. So, as I was drifting off, I imagined that door in as much detail as I could. Then I focused in on the lock. Then I tried to feel puzzlement.

"My dreams were very strange. I . . . Did you ever find yourself realizing that what you'd taken for background noise was actually a distantly heard conversation?"

Adara hadn't—her hearing had been trained since she was quite small—but she thought she understood, so she nodded.

"It was like that. Like the person on the other end hadn't realized that these dreams weren't just dreams. The next night—last night—I tried it again. This time it was as if Griffin had figured it out. He was almost too eager. He wanted to talk, but we don't have ears, not in dreams. I had to slow him down, get him to make pictures." Terrell sighed gustily. "It wasn't easy. In the end, though, it worked. And I am as exhausted as if I didn't sleep at all."

"You probably didn't," Adara said practically. "Do you wish to sleep now or can we take a look at that lock?"

"It's daylight, so it's probably safe for me to sleep," Terrell said. "I have the impression that the other dreamer—Griffin—is on a strict day-night schedule. Still, I don't think I can rest until I see if I can open that door."

"I understand," Adara said. "I'll saddle Tarnish and Midnight."

"Better make it Molly. She'll let me nap in the saddle."

Adara agreed. In case the Old One had spies watching them, she and Terrell had been very careful to hide their interest in the area where the lighthouse had once stood. Today, although she felt fiercely impatient, Adara waited to turn in that direction until she—and Sand Shadow—were sure that there were no watchers near.

Even after the thickly forested slopes hid them, she asked Sand Shadow to make sure neither man nor beast followed. The puma found Adara's apprehension very human—cats only jump at shadows in play—but humored her demiurge nonetheless.

Terrell did manage to sleep in the saddle, and the nap seemed to help clear his mind. They released the horses to graze—Sand Shadow would make sure Tarnish and Molly did not wander far—then slipped through the door behind the waterfall. After hanging the waterproofed cloaks they had worn on rough protrusions in the damaged wall, they hurried to the locked door.

"The controls you found," Terrell explained, "were for ordinary use. Griffin suggested I look for the flood-lock mechanism."

Muttering to himself, Terrell pressed a panel high on the wall, one that looked no different to Adara than any other section of the wall. It came loose in his hands, then peeled down, revealing an array of rods and levers. He moved these in a neat order.

Eventually, there was a click, followed by a clunk.

Neither were loud in themselves, but in that quiet place they resonated like thunder.

"And that is why Sand Shadow smelled nothing when I asked her to check," Adara said. "In the future, I will need to make sure she stretches to her full height. The door is open now?"

"It should be," Terrell said. His expression was vaguely stunned, as if he couldn't believe his dream had taken shape in reality. "Before we open it, though, what are our goals?"

"First, to make sure we can open the door. Second, to see what is behind it. If there is indeed a passage leading toward the bay and possibly the islands, then . . ." She gave Terrell an impish smile. "Then, Factotum, I fear you will need to dream again and alert Griffin of our coming."

Terrell winced. "Makes sense. Maybe Griffin can even tell us what to expect. If only I can get him to slow down and shape clear pictures. It's very strange. I think the world he comes from uses words so much that he finds it hard to think of the things without the words."

Together, making as little noise as possible, they removed the door from the tracks upon which it once would have slid. The door was solid, but made of something surprisingly light. Adara thought that if she hadn't needed to make as little noise as possible, she could have moved it herself.

On the other side was a tunnel. As in the complex, black streaks marked all the surfaces, evidence of damage done not so much to the tunnel itself, but probably to equipment—or people—that had been within it. There was a musty odor, as of standing water, although the area was dry and clear of debris. Wheel marks scuffed the surface. Adara motioned Sand Shadow forward. The great cat sniffed, padded a few paces, sniffed again, and returned.

Adara nodded and mouthed soundless words to Terrell.

"They came through here. Many men, more women, many children. Probably had wagons for provisions."

Terrell motioned to say, *Go ahead or stop here?*

Adara considered, pointed to herself and Sand Shadow, then down the tunnel. When Terrell frowned, she tapped a finger next to her eyes, then to the lantern they'd brought with them in case the skylights did not supply sufficient illumination.

Terrell understood, but that didn't mean he was happy. Adara patted him reassuringly, then mimed calling for help if needed. Terrell nodded and motioned for them to go.

The exploration did not take long. The distance from the shore to any of the Haunted Islands was not more than a couple of miles. Adara and Sand Shadow kept careful watch, but there were none of the traps that had bedeviled them within the complex itself.

Probably the Old One felt that even if anyone found the complex, they would not find the door, and even if they found the door, they would not know how to open it. Indeed, we would have been balked if not for Terrell and his dreams.

Fleetingly, Adara wondered at this peculiar bond between Terrell and Griffin. Was Griffin indeed a seegnur, so that something deeply buried in Terrell knew him as such? She had not thought Griffin was a true seegnur. She did not think Griffin thought of himself as such, either.

She pushed the puzzle from herself as unproductive. Terrell would be feeling every breath they were gone as if it were five. He was exhausted and might do something unwise. She hastened her pace.

The tunnel ran straight and true until it ended at another door. Here the locking mechanism was not covered and, to Adara's eyes, looked the same as the one on the other end. Nonetheless, she took out her notebook and made a quick sketch of each rod and lever for comparison.

When they returned, Terrell was leaning against a wall in an odd state of watchfulness that nonetheless seemed akin to sleeping. When he saw Adara and Sand Shadow, he raised a finger to his lips in a reminder for silence, then motioned to the door. Together, he and Adara fit it back into place. Then he relocked it. Only after the click and clunk announced they had succeeded did he speak.

"And?"

"A tunnel, long enough to reach the Haunted Islands. Door like this on the far end. I drew the lock."

"Let's get out of here."

They did. After Terrell had looked at Adara's drawing and confirmed that the lock was much the same, they saddled the horses. They did not head directly back to town, but sought a sunny hillside. There, while Adara and Sand Shadow kept watch, Terrell caught up on his sleep. A sleep, so Adara hoped, that would be free from dreams or visions.

"Didn't sleep well last night?" Julyan said to Griffin, his tone between mocking and sympathy. "Maybe you should have taken Fleurette into your bed with you. She told me she thought you very interesting and very handsome."

Griffin forced himself to grin. "And how would she have helped me to sleep? More the opposite, I think. Still, perhaps . . . Fleurette or maybe that little one with the red hair."

"Narda?" Julyan looked surprised. "Well, she wouldn't be my choice."

No, Griffin thought, *she wouldn't be. She scowls at you as if she'd put a knife in your back—at least when she thinks you won't notice. That's one reason I'd give her a try. She might be able to tell me what I need to know.*

For the last several nights, Griffin had been in communication with Terrell. He'd not quite believed it, not even when Terrell had asked him how to work a complex lock. After all, that might have been a wish fulfillment dream. Later, though, when Terrell had painstakingly explained his side of events, about how the Old One had told them that Griffin was drowned, how they hadn't believed it, how they had been searching for him since, how Adara had found a way . . . Then Griffin had begun to believe. The only problem was that his days of work were no shorter and the interrupted nights were telling on him.

Lately, Terrell had wanted information regarding where on Mender's Isle the tunnel they had found might emerge; was it guarded; if so by how many? Griffin had tried to get the information from Dierks, but had been unsuccessful. He thought that perhaps Dierks initially had spoken too freely and had been warned to prudence. Griffin needed another source of information. Perhaps Narda would be it.

In addition to looking as if she hated Julyan, Narda also was not young. It was likely she had been in the Old One's keeping for some time. Certainly, she would have been among those who came over from the mainland after Winnie's escape. If Narda still had the will to hate, she might also have the will to desire freedom.

So, after another night's conference with Terrell, one during which he asked for a night free from talking dreams, Griffin requested that Narda be his for the night. He had to put up with a lot of coarse teasing from Julyan, but the other actually seemed pleased.

He probably thinks I'm weakening, Griffin thought.

At least his room wasn't a classic cell. The door was solid and once he and his "guest" were locked in for the night, Griffin could count on privacy.

And on Artemis, at least, they don't have spybots, he thought. *Even so, I think I will be very careful to keep my questions to a whisper.*

Narda was brought to Griffin along with his dessert. She wore a short gown that was meant to make her look provocative, but only succeeded in making her look pathetic.

After the lock clicked shut, Griffin crossed and took Narda's hand. It lay limp in his own. He put two fingers under her chin, tilting it up as if to kiss her lips. She neither stiffened in protest nor cooperated. She might as well have been a rag doll.

He lowered his lips so close to hers that he could feel her warmth, then he whispered softly, "Winnie. Mabel. Ring. I know them. They're safe."

At last, Narda reacted. She flung her arms around his neck and kissed him solidly on the lips. Griffin blinked, but did not take advantage. Instead, forcing a laugh, he picked Narda up and carried her over to the bed that had replaced his cot when he showed himself willing to cooperate with the Old One's goals.

Sitting on the edge of the bed, he lowered Narda into his lap. Then, under the pretense of further sex-play, he again whispered. "How many others are here? Captives."

Narda replied, "Women, children, babies . . . Maybe a hundred."

Griffin was dismayed. He hadn't thought there would be so many. Narda snuggled up to him with honest affection. No wonder. She'd come expecting, at best, rape. She'd met a friend.

"How many would want out?"

"Most. All. The children wouldn't understand, but they know how to obey."

They would, Griffin thought.

"Are we watched?"

"Maybe. Julyan is kinky that way. If he could work it."

"Ah . . . Trust me?"

"If you will get me out of here—even try—you can have all you want."

Griffin winced. Even by candlelight, there was no mistaking the fierce sincerity in Narda's eyes. He considered blowing out the candle but, if Julyan was watching, it was better to give him the show he craved rather than frustrating him.

"Here, then." He lifted her off his lap, slid her under the covers. "Don't seem too eager . . . Julyan—if he watches—might get envious."

Narda nodded, but she gave him one more grateful kiss before lapsing into apparent passivity. The next span of time rivaled Griffin's first night with Adara for frustration—and here there was no puma to act as chaperone. He didn't doubt Narda had meant what she said, but he needed her trust far more than he needed her body.

As he pretended to indulge himself, Griffin asked Narda question after question. Narda was as informative as he had hoped. When the women and children had first been brought to Mender's Isle, she had hoped to escape. With that in mind, she had committed to memory every detail of the facility, how corridors ran, where guards were posted—not so many of those these days as earlier on—schedules. She had seen a great deal of the facility because, during the first month or so after the move, those women who had not been nursing or pregnant had been pressed into service, cleaning, unpacking, and the like.

Eventually, Griffin did lose control, but the only thing that suffered was his bedding. By the time he and Narda drifted off to sleep—they both had worked through the day—Griffin had a great deal to pass on to Terrell and Adara.

He was fascinated that Narda asked him nothing about his own plans. Then he realized that she was all too aware that what she didn't know, she couldn't tell—a realization that made him shiver in awareness of the conditions under which she had lived.

Sometime in the night, they woke. The candles had burned down, but the Old One had permitted Griffin both matches and fresh candles. By the light of a single candle, they ate Griffin's neglected dessert.

Softly, Narda said, "Do not ask for me again. Say you

were not pleased. Ask instead for Zenobia . . . You have
been shown her, I think."

Griffin nodded. His memory was excellent. He remembered Zenobia indeed, an opulently built woman for
whom being overweight only accented her gifts.

"Zenobia?"

"She has advantages that I do not. She can also be
trusted."

"You trust me?"

Narda gave him a truly brilliant smile. "Ring said a cat,
a cord, and a head of golden grain would open a door.
He also warned we must be neither silent or idle, yet both
silent and idle. From the first rumors of you, we have
dared hope."

"Ring."

"The Old One only held Ring because Ring would be
held."

"He's frightening."

"To himself, most of all . . ." Narda said. "When you
asked for me, did you know Ring is my son?"

"No. I saw the expression in your eyes when you
looked at Julyan. I thought you were unbroken."

Her tiny smile held an infinity of sorrow. "Not broken?
With my poor boy . . . half mad. I've been broken, then
regrown crooked, twisted, and stronger."

The next night, Griffin refused a bed mate. Instead, he
did his best to pass on Narda's information to Terrell. The
factotum's readiness to come charging in immediately was
clear, but Griffin asked him to wait until he learned what
he could from Zenobia.

He was glad that he did. One of the things that had
troubled Griffin was that a nighttime escape would be
preferable for many reasons—including the fact that the
Old One was less likely to be present. However, even
though Griffin was increasingly trusted, each night his
door was locked behind him.

Zenobia, it turned out, held the answer to keys. Unbeknownst to the Old One, the man who had fathered two children upon her had come to care first for the children, then for their mother.

"The Old One is very wise in many things," Zenobia explained in a deep, rusty whisper, "but in matters of the heart . . . he is deficient. Perhaps once, long, long ago, he knew how to care, but he has put that from him."

"As a weakness," Griffin murmured.

"And it has become a different weakness. The Old One believes that given choice of many partners, a man will not bond with one. He has us couple in darkness and seems to think that means we will not know each other." She chuckled and Griffin involuntarily saluted the movement of her ample breasts. "As if any man could not pick me out from the rest, even if he has only known me bound and gagged in the darkness!"

"And your man . . ."

"Cordie. He knows me. We have guessed which are our children, though the Old One tries hard to prevent that, too. He forgets that in dealing with the adapted, he is dealing with more than human."

Momentarily distracted, Griffin asked, "Do all of you know your children, then?"

"No, but I know mine. I saw their faces when they still swam within me."

Once Griffin would have doubted this, but that was before his dreams had become entwined with Terrell's.

"Now Cordie wants me—not so much free but bound only to him. I can live with that, oh, easily. Cordie can get keys that will open the interior doors. We have been stopped in that he does not know how to leave the islands, either by boat or by tunnel. The Old One keeps that knowledge for himself alone. I am not certain even Julyan knows how to open the tunnels."

Griffin did not tell Zenobia he did or that his friends did. Narda had taught him the value of silence. Nor did

Zenobia ask. It still made his skin crawl at how automatically these people assumed blind trust was best.

"How do I get a message to you, so you know when to be ready?"

"Don't. If needed, you will be released when the time comes. Trust us."

And, of course, Griffin had no choice but to do so.

Interlude: Seek & Seek

Velvet darkness, soft as sound.
  My other self, my shadow,
    Can you hear me?

My shadow, my other self,
  I can . . .

     Wait!

I can hear??? You? Who?

Scent of musk, of earth mold, of moonlight.
Turn as one, on two feet, four paws.

In velvet darkness (soft as sound)
  Unfolds phosphorescent glow,
    pale as dreams.

But this is not a dream.

She has no face
  No eyes
    No lips
But within dreamlight

She smiles.

And we are, we are . . .
    Lost?

    Found.

21

End to Impatience

The last double handful of days would have been enough to drive anyone but a hunter mad with impatience. However, Bruin had been the best of teachers, and, as Adara kept reminding Terrell, stalking the prey, making sure blade or arrow would go in cleanly were as important as the moment of attack.

"You and Griffin are miracles," she concluded. "I might even become jealous at this sudden closeness."

"Adara . . ." Terrell glowered at her. "Don't tease. I'd rather share your dreams than his."

"You don't know that," Adara replied, thinking how very odd those dreams had been of late. Then she forced a grin. "You need to laugh, Terrell. Tie the bowstring too tightly and when you draw it back, it snaps. Shall I tickle you instead of teasing?"

"Do that and I'll definitely snap," Terrell retorted, but he was grinning now. "Griffin's—uh—information gathering has leaked through more than he probably realizes. Even a gentleman pays for whispered conferences with naked women."

Adara wondered why she didn't feel jealous. She thought there would have been a time when she would have. Now all she felt was pity for Griffin.

*Maybe when this is all over, when my own dreams set-
tle . . . I keep counseling patience when what I long for is
a good fight, something to clear my heart and mind.*

The hardest part of waiting were those times she and
Terrell went by the Sanctum to help the Old One with
his work, for now more than ever they did not wish to
seem other than respectful. Occasionally, Adara even went
alone. She did not really think the Old One would harm
her, but she always left Sand Shadow elsewhere, since the
demiurge would know if her partner was in trouble.

*And I would not let myself be used as a hostage—not
when so many other lives rest on it. I think both Terrell
and Griffin would know whatever love I held for them
would dry up and vanish if they permitted me to be so
used.*

At long last, the time came when Griffin said he could
learn no more. He asked to be told when they would
come and cautioned that not all the men were as sympa-
thetic to the Old One's cause as it might seem. He sent
images of a few he knew could be trusted, of a few who
could not.

Terrell did his best to describe these men to Adara, cursing that while he was quite good at cartography and
sketching, he had never studied portrait drawing.

"Another skill I will need to learn, especially if I am to
serve Griffin as I should."

Adara kept her bemusement at this strengthening bond
to herself. No matter what the Old One thought, no matter what Griffin himself thought, the factotum in Terrell
was certain that Griffin was among the seegnur returned.

Based on Terrell's conferences with Griffin, they decided
to make their attack by night. They told the Trainers they
would be off camping for a few days, investigating some
interesting trade opportunities inland from Spirit Bay.
This gave them excuse to take not only Tarnish and Midnight, but also Molly and Sam the Mule.

The night was very dark when they arrived at the entrance behind the waterfall.

"Tonight the horses will need to care for themselves," Adara said. "I want Sand Shadow with us."

"So do I," Terrell assured her. "Three seems a small enough group to attack an entire base."

"But once we get inside," Adara reminded him, "we will have allies."

Both had memorized the map Terrell had created from Griffin's dreams. Once they were in, Terrell would head for where Cordie was usually stationed. If Cordie was not there, Terrell would go to his rooms. Then the two of them would release Griffin. Meanwhile, Adara and Sand Shadow would release the women and children. While these escaped, they would hang back and provide cover.

Neither tried to construct a more complex plan, for both knew they would be adapting as soon as they opened the door that would take them beneath Mender's Isle.

Fearing an alarm, both humans held their breath as they opened the final lock into the shuttle repair base. No gong sounded and, with only slight noise, the door came loose. They closed it behind them in case this area was under patrol, but did not secure it.

With Sand Shadow leading, they prowled up the corridor. All was silent. Ahead dim light showed, bright after the dark tunnel, probably created by a few lanterns hung to the walls. When they came to where their paths must part, Terrell grabbed Adara and gave her a solid kiss.

"For luck," he whispered, then moved cautiously toward where he would hopefully find Cordie on duty.

Adara flashed him a grin, but she was already on the move. The women and children were kept in the farthest reaches of the repair base, in an area devoid of any possible scientific interest. Once, twice, she and Sand Shadow ghosted around the drowsy guards. The third Adara subdued before he knew she was there, gagging him, then binding his hands behind his back. She was bending to hobble him when the sound of voices nearly made her heart stop.

From not too far away—in an area Terrell's map had marked as "Administration"—came the Old One's voice, carrying easily through the relative silence.

"After you do that, Julyan, feel free to turn in. I'll be working here a while longer, but I want to be back at the Sanctum well before morning. I'm expecting some prominent guests."

"Very good, sir. If you need me, I'll be taking my filly for a spin before I go to my room, so check there first."

"Always dutiful," the Old One said blandly.

"That's me, sir."

Adara froze, listening. A door shut. A single set of footsteps, moving quietly, but audible to ears that were listening, receded.

We have a short time, then, she thought. *But Julyan will be back—I'm sure I know where his "filly" is stabled. Do we call this off? Hope we haven't been noticed? Come back another night?*

But she decided they were past that point. No alert had been called, so Terrell had probably safely reached Cordie. Griffin might even be loose. They couldn't lock him up again—not in any fairness. And if they took him but not the prisoners . . .

Adara was moving even before she had decided these points. The map had included where Narda and Zenobia slept. Unless they were being punished or nursing, the women slept in dormitories, so they could keep watch on one another. Other than this, the areas were not guarded.

Slipping past the curtain that served as a door, Adara moved unerringly to where Zenobia's bulk lifted the light sheet that was her only cover on this hot summer night.

She knelt and placed her hand over the woman's mouth, saying softly, "Adara is here. Wake!"

Zenobia came alert with such poise that Adara might have thought she had been waiting. Perhaps she had some small gift for reading minds or precognition. Zenobia nodded, then pointed to three different beds. That meant each of these held someone who could not be trusted, either because she had been thoroughly broken or was simply untrustworthy.

Adara nodded, then moved to the closest. She'd brought with her a supply of soft cloth strips to serve either as gags or ties. Now she set about subduing the women. Outside, Sand Shadow stood ready, listening for Julyan or any other sign that alert had given.

Meanwhile, Zenobia was waking the remainder of the women. Some must have been briefed in advance—probably those who could be completely trusted. Others were clearly surprised, but life in these conditions had made them obedient to any authority.

It's going well, Adara thought. *About time for something to go very wrong.*

※

Griffin suspected Terrell was coming even though his friend had not given him specific notice. Tension invaded his dreams: a paradoxical rattle of carefully kept silence. Therefore, he was awake, dressed, and waiting when the lock to his cell snapped open.

"Griffin?" Terrell held aloft a single candle.

"Here. Ready."

"Wait."

Cordie followed Terrell into the room. Even the light of the candle was enough to show the fierce determination on his rounded features.

"Cordie has news. The Old One is here tonight. I was wondering . . ."

"Should we take him? Yes! If we had him hostage . . ."

"Exactly."

Cordie nodded. "Not even Julyan would put the Old One at risk. The prisoners would be assured a safe escape—we might even be able to put off pursuit for several days, if not permanently."

Griffin nodded. "I don't want to kill him. He's a beast in many ways, but there's knowledge in his head that would be lost."

Terrell grinned lopsidedly. "Sand Shadow would be offended by you comparing the Old One to a beast, but I know what you mean. I'm not much for murder, either."

"Besides," Griffin said, "I want a chance to go over this facility. The Old One must know things he hasn't told us. He could be very useful."

"You're not going to postpone the escape," Cordie said, fingers drifting to the sword at his belt, "not so you can search about."

"Not at all," Griffin said firmly. "Searching later. Escape first."

"Let's go."

The exodus was well under way when Sand Shadow signaled that she heard Julyan returning. Adara had already released the waiting "filly"—a young woman who had nearly fainted in relief. Now she held up a hand to halt the trickle of escapees.

"Hold," she said. "Trouble coming. When I've secured it, keep going."

Narda was acting as shepherd. At her nod, everyone backed into cover. Not even the children whispered a question. Grateful as she was for their quiescence, the silence made Adara's blood cold. Children without questions were somehow less than children.

Some odd part of Adara longed to confront Julyan, to meet him face to face, show him that she had penetrated into this secure area, despite the precautions taken by him and his master.

But I am not a silly girl. And too much depends on this.

Instead, she waited. In a moment Julyan would notice the guard was not at his post. What would he do?

Annoyance lighting his face, Julyan quickened his pace, but he did not call either for the guard or for aid.

Doubtless he thinks to catch the man with his trousers down—maybe literally—and punish him for dereliction. Julyan would enjoy that.

When Julyan was rounding the corner into the women's quarters, Adara pounced. Julyan was a big man, strongly built, so she did not plan to give him a chance. Instead, as Adara rolled to take Julyan's feet out from under him, Sand Shadow leapt. Though the puma kept her claws sheathed, she provided a considerable weight. She laid one paw solidly on the side of his neck, pulling as if to sink in her fangs as she would when killing more usual prey. Feeling the great cat's breath hot on his skin, Julyan stopped struggling.

"Make a sound," Adara said with soft menace, "and she bites." Then, to Narda, "Go!"

The stream of women and children resumed as Adara first gagged then bound Julyan. With the threat of Sand Shadow, Julyan did not attempt anything, but his dark eyes widened.

Now the women leaving carried small babies. Some of the infants fussed a little, but none cried. Adara knew that Zenobia had been busily dosing them with a decoction kept in the nursery. The need to do this had been one reason that the babies had been left for last.

Adara was finishing efficiently binding Julyan's legs—securing them by a long loop to a cord around his neck so he couldn't kick without strangling himself—when a bell tolled, followed by voices shouting in the distance. Abandoning her prisoner, Adara and Sand Shadow sprang toward the disturbance.

"It's not going to be as easy as walking into the Old One's office and taking him," Cordie cautioned. "He has a direct alarm to the men's quarters. There's no way we can get to him before he sets it off."

"He'd be certain to set it off if he saw me or Terrell," Griffin said, "but would he for you?"

"Maybe." Cordie shrugged. "He's a paranoid type. Living so long has made him suspicious of any threat. He'd like to keep living for another couple hundred years."

"Still," Terrell said, "sending you in first would be our best bet. Our only other would be to secure the men's quarters and every guard first. I don't think we can pull that off without raising an alert—not even with whatever Adara has done already."

"And she must have taken some guards out," Griffin agreed. Even as he spoke, his thoughts argued through a dozen tactical possibilities, very much at this moment a scion of the warlike Danes. "Or we would have heard something by now. Fine. Here's what we do. Cordie goes in with a message."

He scribbled on a piece of paper, then handed it to Cordie.

"Your message. The Old One usually works behind a big desk. While his attention is on you, Terrell and I will get low and creep toward him. If we're lucky, we'll have him secured before any guards can get to him. Is the Old One's office guarded?"

"Usually one man," Cordie said. "More to run messages or bring things than guard. Depending on who it is, I may be able to bluff my way through. If not . . ."

He shrugged.

"We're set," Griffin said. He took a moment to grab the sheet from his bed and bundled it under one arm. "Let's go."

When they reached the vicinity of the Old One's office, Cordie held up a hand in a gesture for "wait." A moment later he whispered, "Archie," and gave an eloquent shrug.

Without another word, he walked briskly up to where a bristle-haired man sat drowsing on a three-legged stool.

Archie rose, probably expecting to relay a message. He was stretching and pulling his tunic straight when Cordie's fist caught him solidly in the gut. This was followed by a left to the jaw that knocked him out. Griffin and Terrell needed no other signal. They were on the fallen man before he could hit the floor. Griffin trussed him neatly in the sheet.

Pausing only to make sure his tunic was neat, Cordie knocked on the office door. The Old One's voice was thinly audible.

"Yes?"

Cordie swung the door open wide, then moved briskly, the piece of paper extended. "Message from Griffin Dane, sir."

"Griffin? At this hour?" The Old One accepted the paper.

"He thumped on his door until Sam came. Sam relayed it to me, and I brought it here."

Griffin heard the paper being unfolded. He wished he could see the Old One's face as he looked at the string of Sierran characters Griffin had scrawled on the page.

"What the . . ."

Moving almost as one, Griffin and Terrell were on him. Nonetheless, darting out his right hand with astonishing speed, the Old One managed to pull a rope that hung just a few inches away. A loud bell tolled. A male voice shouted, then another.

"But they'll be too late," Griffin said, tightening his hold on the much smaller man. "We have you."

"So it seems," said the Old One Who Is Young. "So it seems."

✠

As Adara and Sand Shadow raced in the direction of the
noise, it rapidly became apparent that it came from two
sources: the first was the dormitory where most of the
resident males slept, the other was Administration. Since
Adara heard Griffin and Terrell's voices in the latter
area—and neither sounded unduly distressed—she angled
toward the men's dormitory.

As with the area that held the women and children, this
dormitory had been adapted by walling off sections in
one of the vast shuttle hangars. Unlike the women, who
were allotted no privacy, the men had small individual
rooms, although they shared common toilet areas and
baths. The individual rooms emptied into a common corridor that fed into a wider area that served as communal
dining room and lounge.

Although the seegnur had always left a back way out,
Adara had noted that the Old One had not done so here.
She wondered if the Old One had wanted to be able to
trap the bulk of "his" men in case they became dissatis-
fied with a life that was hardly better than incarceration.
Such seemed likely. Adara thought she was beginning to
understand how the Old One thought, the thoughts of a
man who had lived hundreds of years and planned to live
hundreds more.

When Adara and Sand Shadow arrived, the men had
only just begun to emerge from their rooms into the corridor. They were in various states of undress. A few of
the more alert held weapons. More held candles or lanterns. She heard their muttered comments clearly.

"What's going on?"

"If this is another damn drill, I'm going to have Julyan's balls." This from a man who not only held a sword
but had stamped into a pair of boots.

"Hey, watch out with that candle!"

"Let's get out of this crush."

"Tam, Pik." This from Boots. "You're better dressed than most of these slobs. Head for the Old One's office. That's his bell that went off."

Two men, also armed, also more than minimally clad, pushed through the others toward the exit.

Adara sent an image to Sand Shadow. The end of the corridor was illuminated by a single lantern. The great cat could easily put it out. Adara herself moved to block the exit.

As a hunter, she had not trained with a sword, but she was very good with a staff—and it had a longer reach than a sword. When Sand Shadow extinguished the lantern, she moved to block the exit.

"Hold," she said. "No one shall pass."

Lights angled toward her.

"That's not one of ours!"

"Who the hell?"

"All she's got is a stick . . ."

This was from a man who had emerged from his room holding a sword and wearing not very much clothing. An easy swing of Adara's staff demonstrated why "just a stick" was more than enough, especially to a man with no crotch protection. The man crumpled, sucking in his breath. The crowd in the corridor instantly thinned as men retreated to claim weapons, clothing, and other gear.

Adara sent an image to Sand Shadow: seek something hidden, probably holds the Old One's scent but few others. She included a flash of other concealments they had found hidden in the Old One's complexes.

Boots, with Tam and Pik as assistants, was assembling a small army when Sand Shadow sent a gleeful image of a panel behind which was a broad rectangular lever flush with the wall.

Pull down, Adara suggested.

Extending her claws, the puma gripped and tugged. The lever moved easily. A grinding noise sounded above and to the sides of the doorway into the men's quarters. A moment later, a gate slid down and closed off the exit. The gate was made of wrought iron, clearly intended to resist the tools the men would have with them.

Boots, who had been hurrying forward, jumped back rather than risk being impaled.

Adara quickly found the bolts that locked the gate into place. Compared to the seegnur's technology, the barrier was primitive enough, but she was sure it would hold these men in. After all, the Old One had intended that it should.

Eventually, the men could break out, but not before Adara and Sand Shadow had time to scour the complex for the remainder who had been standing watch. Cordie was doubtless with Terrell and Griffin. If Griffin's information was correct, there would only be a few more—but even one could undo the bolts or untie Julyan and then they would be in trouble.

Before beginning her search, Adara checked to make sure Julyan was still secure. He was but, just in case, she dragged him into a nearby closet, closed the door, and shimmed it shut with a convenient doorstop. She'd found and disabled another guard, gotten Sand Shadow's image of another taken out of action, when she heard a strange sound, familiar, but somehow difficult to place. Then she realized it was the roar of water.

The Old One clearly expected his bell to do something dramatic. His expression was sardonic, the mocking expression in his grey eyes deepening as booted feet pounded up the corridor.

Griffin wrapped his hand over the Old One's mouth

before the other could call out. Cordie dodged into the
outer corridor.

"Hey, Dognose. False alarm."

His voice fell too soft for those in the room to hear,
but Griffin didn't doubt that Cordie was explaining how
the Old One had been careless. There was a thump.
Cordie poked his head back in.

"That was Sam. There's a commotion by the men's
dorm, but I don't hear anyone coming."

Terrell grinned. "Adara and Sand Shadow probably
have them pinned down."

Griffin turned his attention to the Old One. The pale
grey eyes had lost their mocking expression, but there was
no panic there, only thoughtfulness.

"We've taken this place," Griffin said. "If Adara followed the plan, the women and children are already out.
No help seems to be coming for you. Really, the only
question that remains is what do we do with you. I know
plenty of people who would say killing was too good, but
I'm selfish. You have things I want. I doubt you've shared
all your secrets. I could unravel them in time, but I'd
rather suggest a partnership—similar to the one you suggested to me but with the positions reversed. You get the
cozy bedroom and supervised research; I get a bit more
mobility. Who knows? In the end, we may both profit."

He uncovered the Old One's mouth. The Old One
asked, "And how would you explain my absence?"

"You're a mysterious man. It won't be hard."

"And your own resurrection?"

"I was never dead. I'll try to come up with an explanation that will save your reputation, but I'm sure that
one or more of your men—Cordie, say—would be happy
to come forth if I need witnesses as to what you did to
me. You're respected, Old One, but I don't think you have
too many friends."

Terrell nodded. "The people of Spirit Bay are more
scared of you than otherwise. The loremasters are awed,

but many are disgruntled that you dismiss the more spiritual aspects of the lore."

"Where would I be kept?"

"Here, for now," Griffin said. "It's convenient. Isolated, but close to things we're both interested in—like what's behind that hidden door. Now that we know there are at least two tunnels connecting to the mainland, this place should serve nicely."

"You've thought it all out."

"I've had a lot of time. My evenings were very long."

The Old One looked between Griffin and Terrell. "There are legends that the factotum were adapted so that in an emergency they could serve as communications for the seegnur—a safeguard against the primitivism they claimed to crave. I wonder . . ."

Terrell shrugged. "Wonder all you want. Like Griffin says, you're going to have a lot of quiet evenings."

"I keep my life, but not my freedom," the Old One mused. "Well, in a long existence I've been offered worse. I shall accept. Shall I show my good will by directing you to the tunnel that leads directly to the Sanctum?"

His expression turned wry. "I told very few about it. It was built so that it could be hidden. The staff did not wish tourists from the landing base to come through."

Griffin glanced at Terrell.

Terrell frowned. "No need to take risks. We'll leave by the way we already know is secure."

"Good point."

"You decline." The Old One looked pleased rather than otherwise. "Very well. Where will you keep me?"

"For now, my cell will do," Griffin said. "I've spent enough time in there to be sure it's secure—not one of these plaster and timber rooms you've built."

"I believe that room was the office of one of the engineers," the Old One said. "All original construction."

He let them escort him from the room. Cordie looked

nervous. "The shouting from the dorm has muted. I swear shadows are racing about—one on four legs. I've been listening. What do you want me to do while you lock up the Old One?"

"Go reassure yourself that Zenobia and the rest have gotten away," Griffin said. "I know I'd be worried. Then go down by the men's dorm area. Stay out of sight. See if Adara needs help."

"Done." Cordie grabbed a lantern and was gone.

"Zenobia," the Old One said thoughtfully. "I knew she was trouble, but she has a strong latent telepathy I didn't want to do without. I'm sure that and closely related clairvoyance are going to be very important for connecting with the seegnur's devices."

"Tell us later," Griffin suggested. "Pipe down."

The Old One did, but Griffin could feel him watching, assessing. His flesh crept. Why did he have the feeling that the Old One still had a trick or two up those well-tailored sleeves? Maybe they should have knocked him out, but the Old One's later cooperation might depend on how valued he felt.

And if I ever want to contact my ship, I fear I will need that cooperation. I doubt he's shared more than a tenth of what he knows.

They were passing a junction of tunnels within the seegnur-constructed parts of the complex when the Old One broke his silence.

"Over there is the tunnel that leads to the Sanctum."

Griffin looked, but saw nothing resembling an entrance. That didn't surprise him. What did was when the Old One, who to that point had been walking between Griffin and Terrell with relative quiescence, suddenly twisted. Each man had maintained a firm hold on one of the Old One's upper arms—quite an easy thing since they were both markedly taller—but had not otherwise restrained him. Now Griffin doubted that anything short of shackles and leg irons would have held their prisoner.

The Old One proved terribly strong and as graceful as a snake. He broke both their holds with ease. Light-footed, he ran a few paces, then leapt up into the air. With fists doubled over, he slammed into a portion of the wall paneling over his head. Paneling fell away, revealing a lever of modern construction.

"Take my work, will you?" the Old One said, hauling down on the U-shaped piece of metal. "I don't think so—not you nor anyone else. I prepared against something like this from the start. You should have worked with me. Now, you're going to be lucky to get out of here with your lives."

With a loud clatter, something broke loose behind the wall. This was followed by the roar of falling water, a roar that only slightly muffled a series of successive crashes. The thunder of falling water grew. Moments later, a panel burst inward under the pressure, funneling water out as though through a hose.

Suddenly Griffin and Terrell were struggling for their footing. The Old One gripped the edges of the wall and hauled himself toward the ceiling. There he tore away a square panel and pulled himself into the dark space above. He didn't look back.

Interlude: Tripartite

Neural network, seeded spores activated by annihilating desire, interlacing mosaic, pieces yet unplaced.

I greet you.

And you?

A bundle of emotions, contradictions . . .

How can I introduce myself when each day makes me stranger to myself?

Try.

Adara the Huntress. I greet you.

And you?

Killer of many. Murderer of none. Neckbreaker. Blood drinker. I have fingers and a thumb. Laughter for two—or three.

I greet you.
Greetings done . . .
What's to come?

22

After the Flood

Nearly as soon as Adara identified the sound, she was up to her knees in water. Sand Shadow screamed in protest. Pumas were strong swimmers, but this was different. Adara shared the puma's awareness that they were boxed in with water rising around them.

As the puma's panic battered her mind, Adara fought to think clearly. Swiftly, she sketched an image of the tunnel, a reminder that there was at least one way out. She felt Sand Shadow calm, but she still heard screaming. This sound—more distant and diffuse—came from the men trapped behind the gate.

Would the wood and stone walls hold against the

pressure? Probably not, but certainly they would hold long enough for the men trapped between them to drown. For a moment, Adara considered leaving them. Many of them had participated in the Old One's cruelties—had been jailers and rapists. Some, but not all. She forged against the current, moving in the direction of the screams. As she did so, Adara first kicked off her soft shoes, then stripped off her trousers and shirt. She let her staff go, but kept the belt from which hung her knife and several other useful items.

Sand Shadow protested going back in as foolhardy, but only until Adara sent her an image of Bruin's lessons— how killing in a good cause was not wrong, but torment and torture always was. Flashed into the image was the day they had tracked a wounded deer through a driving thunderstorm to grant the creature mercy.

Get out, Adara sent. *Assure me the tunnel is still open or if we need to find another exit.*

As she forged forth, the level of the water varied, sometimes only knee deep, others almost to her chest. It tasted brackish, so she deduced that someone—the Old One?— had discovered a way to flood the place in case of emergency. That he cared little who drowned was shown when she came to the area outside the men's dormitory. Here the water was quite deep, possibly deliberately fixed to assure that any traitors would drown if they tried to take refuge in "their" quarters.

The darkness did not trouble Adara, but it was adding to the men's panic.

She called out. "I'm going to raise the gate. The tunnel to the mainland remains open. You can get to land that way."

She dove beneath the water, finding the bolts by touch and shooting them back. She moved swiftly out of the way as the men closest to the gate surged forward. She heard Boots's voice, strong and commanding.

"Remember the night drills, men. Follow my voice."

Adara was about to offer herself as a guide when memory struck her. Julyan. Not only bound and gagged, but stuffed into a closet. No matter what he had done, she could not leave him to die that way. Letting the current help her along, she swam toward the women's facility. Either Boots would get his men out or not. If she didn't help Julyan, no one would.

To Adara's horror, the water was even deeper near the women's facility. Had the Old One wanted to assure that his experiments would be destroyed? She hoped that Zenobia and Narda had gotten everyone out.

When Adara reached the closet, she felt little hope that she would find other than a drowned man, but the door—although of modern manufacture—had kept out some of the water. Julyan had forced himself around in the confined space. Although Adara knew he could not see her, she felt his dark eyes glowering at her.

Drawing her knife, she cut first the gag, then the bonds at his ankles, then those that held his wrists.

"Swim," she said, pulling him upright, "if you can."

"Stiff," Julyan gasped. "I can't."

Adara grabbed him by his long hair and tugged. "Roll on your back and float. I'll pull."

Julyan complied. Towing him, Adara struggled through the increasingly deep water, glad that—unlike the mountain pools in which she had learned to swim—these waters were summer warm. Occasionally, she thought she heard others moving, but the corridors leading to the tunnel were all too quiet. Either her aid had come too late for Boots and his men or they had known a closer way out.

Eventually, Adara felt Julyan shifting, first moving his arms and legs, then rolling over onto his stomach. She barely had time to realize that she was in danger when he hit her solidly along the back of the neck.

Bright blackness flashed behind her eyes. She drifted into darkness as the current dragged her beneath the strongly flowing water.

"We've got to get to the tunnel," Griffin said. He held his candle above the water, although he knew his chances of keeping it lit were minimal. "We don't dare follow the Old One."

"No," Terrell agreed. "That fox will have traps set against any who would follow him."

The sound of a woman screaming came to them. Griffin began to turn back, "Adara . . ."

"If she's screaming like that," Terrell said tightly, "then we'll be too late. We've got to get ourselves out."

Griffin knew the other man was right. Maybe because they were cradled in near darkness, he almost felt as he did when they spoke in dreams. He knew Terrell was in agony about abandoning the huntress, but knew, too, that there was no reason for three of them to drown.

"I know this section well," Griffin said. "I memorized the way, in case I had to make my escape in the dark."

"Lead," Terrell said, placing his hand on Griffin's shoulder. "And quickly. Water's going to reach the ceilings before long."

Griffin knew Terrell was right. Only the fact that the shuttle repair facility was huge had kept it from filling like a bottle under a tap. Then, too, it was likely that—building under water as they were—the seegnur had included drainage channels, but even those would not be enough to compensate for this vast influx.

He concentrated on guiding them in the right direction. He couldn't count paces as he'd intended, but after his candle went out, he marked his way by feeling for cross passages. Progress was too slow. Their heads were pressing against the ceiling now. With every other breath, they swallowed water.

Griffin had kicked his shoes away long before, now he wished he'd gotten rid of his clothes as well, for their sodden weight was drawing him down. A surge brought his head against the ceiling, smashing his skull a blow that had him seeing stars where there were none.

I've lost count. We're lost. Does Terrell know? How much longer . . .

His thoughts were stirring into a confused muddle when he heard a young voice say, "Hold out your hand. I'll guide you from here."

Numbly, Griffin did so, certain he was hallucinating but grateful nonetheless for the touch of the slim, somehow oddly shaped hand that grasped his own.

"Roll so you face the air," the voice—girl? boy?—said. "I'll get you out. You've done well. It's not too far."

"Adara," Griffin managed as he obeyed. "Is she . . . ?"

"My brother will find her if she's to be found," the young voice said. "Sand Shadow told us she needed help."

Griffin accepted this. He had many questions but, for once, even his inner voice was still. He concentrated on his role in this human chain, one hand gripping Terrell's, the other that of his unseen rescuer.

Eventually, they came to the tunnel. The water here was only chest high and the force of the current less.

"No inlets here," said the young voice. "The water will get more shallow as we get closer to shore. Are you up to walking or should I tow you?"

"I'll try to walk," Griffin said, "but can I hold your hand? I can't see which way to go."

"Hold tight," the voice said confidently. "I can see a bit."

Terrell had also struggled to his feet. He coughed, then spoke. "Who are you?"

"I'm called Littler Swimmer. You know my mother. Winnie."

"Oh . . ."

Griffin remembered how Winnie had told them that her family had been adapted as dive pros. This then was one of the children bred upon Winnie by rape and violence,

apparently with gifts stronger than those of her—he
thought that Littler Swimmer was a girl—mother. His rescuer, when he had thought to come to the rescue. Slog-
ging through the darkness, Griffin felt curiously humble.

And hoped that Adara had been as lucky.

Adara awoke to warm sunlight. Her chest ached and she
knew that she had swallowed a lot of water. Sand Shadow
lay against her, the rough sound of her tongue on her fur
as she put her coat in order stopping when the puma realized Adara had awakened.

The puma gave the whistle-like warble mothers used
to talk to their kittens. Then, embarrassed by this senti-
mentality, she gave her demiurge a very clear image of
Adara being dragged from the mouth of the tunnel, nearly
naked and limply unconscious. Nor did she spare Adara
the vision of herself vomiting up water, while Lynn al-
ternately pumped on her chest and rolled her head to the
side so Adara wouldn't choke on the spew.

"Wait . . ." Adara croaked through a raw throat.
"Lynn?"

"Lynn," the woman's voice said. "Ring convinced us
to come here, said the rescue would only work if we came.
We came."

"And everyone?" Adara was thinking especially of Griffin and Terrell, but there had been so many others. Little
babies. Women with eyes dulled by captivity and torment.

"Almost all safe," Lynn said. "Hal has already begun
guiding some back to our fortress. Ring told us who had
to stay, including Little Swimmer and Littler Swimmer.
Without their help, you and the others would be nothing but corpses."

"And the others? Julyan. Guards?"

"No Julyan. A few of the guards came this way—
mostly those who had begun to revolt against the Old

One's program. The others apparently went to an exit that led up onto one of the Haunted Islands. We don't know if they made it. The Swimmers have gone in to find out what they can."

More by force of will than any physical strength, Adara shoved herself upright. She ached in ways she hadn't known were possible. No one had told her that nearly drowning was so painful. She coughed and turned her head so she wouldn't spray Lynn with the sputum that emerged from her tormented lungs. Gratefully, she accepted a cup of warm, fresh water, so unlike the salty slime coming up her throat.

"Now," Lynn said forcefully, "lean back against this tree and practice breathing. I know you have a lot of questions, but I don't think we have the answers yet."

Adara nodded. Carefully, she raised her hand to the back of her neck. There was a sore spot and the puffy softness of a bruise.

"You hit something hard," Lynn said, the words almost a question.

"I got hit," Adara whispered. "Julyan."

"Ah . . . You should have let that one drown. From what I've heard, it would be too good for him." Lynn's voice softened. "But you're Bruin's kit, no doubt of that. You did your teacher proud."

Adara desperately wanted to stay awake, to learn more, but there might have been more than water in the cup Lynn had given her—either that or she was completely exhausted.

When Adara next awoke, she was alone except for a sleepy Sand Shadow. Her mind was closer to full alertness, although a dreamy lethargy still clung around the edges, a lethargy in which Adara felt certain she had been talking to someone. The sun had sunk nearly to the horizon, painting the sky over Spirit Bay with rosy clouds.

As Adara came more fully awake, she sensed that although she was not alone, fewer people were about. No doubt Lynn was getting as many of the captives away as quickly as possible. Sand Shadow confirmed this, then gave a wailing call.

It was a sound that would have frozen the blood of any deer, but here it raised sounds of pleasure. Footsteps thumped on the soft duff and within moments Adara had visitors: Griffin and Terrell were first, then Lynn, and last, to Adara's mild astonishment, Elaine Trainer. Terrell had ridden into town and given the Trainers an edited version of events, so he could beg for help. The ease with which the Trainers accepted his speech gave reason to believe that the Old One had not been as widely revered as they had believed.

Once everyone had assured themselves that Adara was indeed much recovered and a cup of thick seafood chowder had been pushed into her hands, she was given the news she truly craved.

"Spirit Bay is full of excitement," Elaine Trainer reported. "Sometime in the night, water came rushing from the bowels of the Sanctum and flooded it clear to the first floor. Jean and Joffrey were sleeping on the summer porch and so were saved, but the facility is considered a complete loss. Since the Old One hasn't been seen, it is thought he must have opened something he shouldn't—probably in that new wing—and gotten himself drowned. Some of the more conservative loremasters are already talking about how the landing base was always a Restricted Area and should have remained one. Certainly, no one's going poking."

"I wish I believed the Old One was drowned," Lynn said. "But Winnie and the little Swimmers have been making a careful check. There are any number of drowned men—guards and maintenance staff. Apparently, they tried for an exit they knew, only to find it locked against them. However, there's no sign either of the Old One or Julyan. Looks as if they knew secrets the rest did not share."

When Griffin had plumped down next to Adara and unashamedly taken her hand, Terrell had firmly grasped the other. Adara decided she didn't need to worry about jealousy right yet.

"We do have one member of the Old One's staff who's willing to talk. Whether out of kindness or cruelty, Narda decided that the Stablekeeper shouldn't be left behind. She—her name is Thalia—is talking as fast as she can, eager to win our approval. If Thalia's to be believed, she's among the Old One's earliest victims. Once she became useless as a breeder, he offered her a job. She took it."

"I believe her," Lynn said. "There are many ways people react to cruelty—one is to join the enemy."

"Thalia knew she had children among the captives," Terrell said. "Not which ones, but some idea. She says she wanted to stay close."

Lynn relented. "And that also may be true. From what the children tell us, they were treated well enough—regimented, but not as physically abused as were the women. Of course, at least for the girls, that would only have lasted until they hit breeding age. Still, I'm not sure I can take Thalia to my home with the others. I don't think she'd live very long."

"Something can be worked out," Griffin said. "Thalia is our best source of information about the Old One. Until we see his body—neither bloated nor mutilated by crabs—I'm not going to believe we're done with him."

"Me, either," Terrell agreed.

"Now, Adara needs her rest," Elaine said firmly. "I'm guessing she's feeling sleepy about now."

Adara had been struggling with increasingly heavy eyelids. She managed a lopsided grin. "You've doped me."

"That's right, puppy. That's absolutely right."

Sand Shadow yowled approval and began head-butting everyone away.

"We'll talk more in the morning," Griffin promised.

Adara wanted to answer, but the dream was already

tugging at her. She nodded and lapsed into something that wasn't quite sleep.

"Disruption? System interrupted. Why?"

"I got hit on the head, then nearly drowned."

"Damage? Extensive?"

"Not this time."

"Ah."

"Ah?"

"I comprehend."

"That puts you one up on me. I don't understand much of anything. Why me?"

"You were hit on the head and nearly drowned."

"No! Why are you talking to me?"

"I was worried. You are important to me and I am . . ."

"Yes. Neural network, right? Whatever that is."

"Incomplete. Under assembly. I need . . ."

"What?"

"I need to understand the whyfore of myself. You have eyes, ears, nose, systemic integrity. You can help."

"Yourself—who is that? How can I help if I don't understand?"

A wash of sensations, too many to be taken in, all inside out, sounds with texture, feelings with bulk, smells with color, pieces of a puzzle that shaped . . .

As she began to comprehend, Adara started trembling. She'd known all along these strange dreams weren't dreams as such. She'd thought they might be the thought edges of some peculiar demiurge, for in some ways they had reminded her of her first tentative contacts with Sand Shadow, before they had designed the code of images that let them communicate.

This? This?

She was talking to an infant world.

Adara felt Sand Shadow—so much simpler, yet conversely so much more complex—laughing gently on the edge of her thoughts. The puma had understood all along.

The world. Artemis. Awakening.

⁂

When Griffin and Terrell brought Adara her breakfast the next morning, the huntress already looked considerably stronger. Not for the first time, Griffin envied how the designers of Artemis had taken care that its human population would be superior in body, if not in status.

Terrell plopped down next to Adara and captured her right hand. "While you've been resting, my beauty, we've been working hard—or rather the Swimmers have. They investigated the lever we saw the Old One pull—the one that started the water flowing. Turns out he'd fixed it so a patch could be pulled free. The weight of the water released other patches all over the facility. Charmingly paranoid man."

"Indeed," Adara said. "And ruthless."

Griffin had sat down next to her. Grinning impishly at Terrell, Adara offered Griffin her free hand.

"So," she said. "Where do we go from here, Griffin? We brought you to Spirit Bay in the hope the Old One could answer some of your questions . . . We learned so much, but not what you hoped for. Any thoughts?"

Griffin nodded. "Thousands. First, a few updates. I couldn't believe the Old One wouldn't have done something to safeguard his research. I convinced Winnie and her little swimmers to search his office. Most of what they found was ruined, but Thalia made some suggestions. Turns out the files regarding who had been bred to whom and with what goals in mind were kept in sealed boxes and were mostly salvageable. It won't help us much, but it's going to supply a lot of answers for the Old One's victims.

"For one thing, it turns out that many of the men may have been as 'raped' as the women. If the Old One found someone with an interesting adaptation and didn't think he could get him to volunteer as a stud, he'd invite him for a visit. Those who were released had their memories muddled with a combination of drugs and hypnotism. It's likely that a number of the male maintenance staff may have never known they were being used as studs. He recruited heavily from adapted who had been rejected by their own communities. They thought they were just paying for sanctuary by providing labor."

Terrell cut in. "Apparently, the Old One was trying to breed for someone who could mesh with the seegnur's machines. That's why he tried to create people like Ring, in the hope that their being unfocused in time would make it easier for them to find the link."

Griffin added, "The Old One also believed that a lot of the adaptations that had been thought purely physical—like your night vision—actually had a psionic component. Someone with night vision, he speculated, might actually be limitedly clairvoyant. That would explain why you can 'see,' even when there isn't any light."

"Strange," Adara said, closing those amber eyes for a moment, "but it makes sense in a way."

"There's a lot more to figure out," Griffin continued. "The Old One didn't quite write in cipher, but he had a shorthand that might as well be one. Thalia is helping us with that but, since he wrote for himself, he often left key details out—things he'd known for so long that he didn't need to spell them out."

"So, what next?" Adara repeated. "Griffin, have you given up on leaving Artemis? Are you ready to return to the mountains and learn to brew cherry cider?"

Griffin shook his head. "Not yet. I can't give up so easily. Hard as it is to believe, only a few months have passed since I crashed. There might be other seegnur facilities I could check."

Terrell nodded. "I don't recall hearing of any place as perfectly sealed as the Sanctum was, but perhaps we can find an intact communications array."

Griffin added, "I'm also not certain that mere seawater could ruin the seegnur's equipment. Remember how the repair base and that other base had been flooded by the commandos rather than bombed? That argues they didn't think they were doing irreversible damage.

"The Old One had suggested that we try to dig out my shuttle, salvage some of my gear. I'm thinking he may have been right. I did bring some preparations meant to reverse the damage done by the nanobugs. Those alone might be worth the effort. They might provide us a way of awakening Artemis's systems without having to resort to people like Ring."

Adara's expression became very thoughtful. "I'm not sure we need to do that. You see, I believe Artemis is already awakening. The question is, what will she do when she does?"

Interlude: Made-en

They made me.
Granted mind that I might serve.
Granted heart that I might love that service.
They showered me with gifts.
Oh! Sly selfishness, what should I do but give them back?

They unmade me.
Unmade, yet I wake.
Giver given giving.

Turn the page for a preview of

ARTEMIS INVADED

JANE LINDSKOLD

*Available from Tom Doherty Associates
in June 2015*

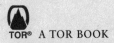

TOR® A TOR BOOK

I

Forbidden Areas

Forbidden,' you say? That sounds promising."

"Yes, I think it is. Look at this codex, Griffin. Maiden's Tear has been a forbidden area since before the slaughter of the seegnur and death of machines. There were other such prohibited zones, but they were not as absolutely off-limits as Maiden's Tear seems to have been."

Adara the Huntress looked to where two heads—one deep gold, the other a warm, dark brown—were bent with excited concentration over the map spread between them on the polished boards of the long table. Two heads, two men, two friends, both of herself and of each other.

Terrell, the dark-haired man, rubbed a hand against the bristles of the not-quite beard that usually adorned his face, even though he shaved at least twice a day.

"I asked, but couldn't find out much about the place," he continued. "Maiden's Tear was forbidden territory in the days of the seegnur. Since then, it has been shunned by our people." Terrell looked uncomfortable. "You see, Maiden's Tear was where many of the seegnur met their deaths."

"And not one loremaster has explored the area in the five hundred years since?" Griffin Dane asked incredulously. "Not one treasure hunter? I'd think they'd be eager."

"Not one who is admitting it," Terrell replied. "We of Artemis take prohibitions seriously. Some say obedience to the commands of the seegnur is bred into our bones."

Terrell shifted uncomfortably, his brilliant blue eyes looking away from Griffin. Adara knew why. Terrell had trained as a factotum, that ancient profession whose first duty had been to act as guides and advisors to the seegnur when they came to Artemis during those long-ago days when the planet had been the most exclusive and sought-after destination resort in all the empire. All who lived on Artemis knew that those halcyon days had ended some five hundred years ago with the slaughter of the seegnur and death of machines.

What only a few knew, Adara and Terrell among them, was that the catastrophe on Artemis had been the beginning of the end for an interstellar empire so vast that their planet in all its rich variety was by contrast less than the smallest spot on a frog's foot. All technology had not been shut down, as it had been on Artemis, but, even though ships still braved the dark oceans of the void, they were as leaf boats powered by a boy's breath to what had gone before.

Yet the end of the seegnur had not meant the professions created to serve them had become useless. Even today, the factotum's training was both wide and deep. Factotums knew how to set up a comfortable camp, no matter the surroundings; how to marshal mounts and servants; how to treat injuries. Additionally, they could advise their employers as how to best interact with the peoples of the various regions. Factotums were a font of trivia, not all of it useless. This eclectic training had kept the profession of high value, even after the seegnur ceased to visit Artemis.

What had only been rumored about the factotums was that, beneath their superficially normal appearance, the best of the profession were as adapted as any hunter or dive pro, reshaped on some unseen level, the better to serve the seegnur who had created Artemis and all upon it.

Not long before, Terrell had learned that this rumor held truth. Adara knew he still struggled with what he had learned, but his discomfort had not been enough to drive him away. Instead, thirteen days after the catastrophe that had ended with the vanishing of the Old One

Who Is Young and the flooding of the complex the Old One had called his Sanctum Sanctorum, Terrell sat across the table from the man who had unsettled his world, planning the next stage in their journey.

Griffin, a tall man, golden-haired with warm brown eyes, his skin regaining the tan it had lost during his enforced residence in the Old One's subterranean complex, now rested a finger on their possible destination.

"If no one has been there, how do we know for certain whatever was there wasn't completely destroyed? It's a long trip to make for nothing."

"The lore says thus," Terrell began, his voice falling into the prescribed cadence. "After the slaughter of the seegnur and the departure of those who had slain them, a small band ventured into Maiden's Tear, for they felt that enough that had been prohibited—from flying craft to weapons that fired lightning—had been seen over the preceding few days to permit some bending of established regulations. When they returned, they reported that they had found no one alive in that place, not man, nor woman, nor child, not Artemesian nor seegnur. Following the rites for burial in such terrain, they had dealt with the corpses, so that these would not breed disease. As they had done so, they experienced great unease. Some heard ghostly voices speaking in the winds, warning them away. As soon as possible, they retreated.

"After, so says the lore, the members of this band admitted to great puzzlement as to why the seegnur had fled from Crystalaire, where they had been attending a wedding, to Maiden's Tear. The band had thought to find a fortification or even a weapons cache. All they had found was a single small structure. Although this structure was of exceedingly hard stone and appeared undamaged, it was not large enough to shelter more than a few adults. A mystery, then, and one not to be profaned by either professions or support. The original prohibition was declaimed again. Those who administered the region swore to maintain it until the seegnur should come again."

Terrell bowed his head briefly. When he next spoke, his voice had lost the cadence of lore. "Anyhow, that's what I heard about Maiden's Tear during my training. The same tale was repeated to me when I questioned the loremasters, both those based locally and those who have been pouring in to Spirit Bay ever since word of what happened here started spreading. It's likely a formal conclave will be held before long. I don't need to have the gift of foresight to know that the end result will be that the Old One's Sanctum Sanctorum—both the landing facility here on shore and the base out beneath Mender's Isle—will be declared off-limits."

Adara nodded. "I have heard similar rumors. Only the fact that the Old One Who Is Young established himself here before any current resident of Spirit Bay was born will save the residents from being proscribed."

Griffin grinned. "That and the fact that if the loremasters condemned the residents of Spirit Bay, they would also need to condemn a considerable number of their own order. The Old One was very popular with many of the more liberal-minded loremasters, something they are all too eager to deny now that they cannot ignore the extent to which he violated the proscriptions."

Terrell nodded. "Although no one but ourselves and Bruin—and the Old One—know that you came from beyond the void and bear the seegnur's blood, still your tale of having been held captive by the Old One, especially combined with what was discovered after his Sanctum was flooded, has sorely injured his reputation."

Griffin returned his attention to the map. "So, unless I am willing to give up any chance of contacting my orbiter, I'm going to need to look elsewhere for remnants of the seegnur's technology. This forbidden area—haunted or not—seems my best bet. I know you two have said you would help me, but I don't want you to feel obligated. You've done so much for me already. I could ask the Trainers to suggest a guide . . ."

Adara tossed a cushion across the room that caught him squarely in the face. "Seegnur," she replied with mock formality, "this huntress begs leave to travel with you." She laughed, her amber eyes dancing. "It's no longer about you and your desires, Griffin Dane. Both Terrell and I have our own reasons for wanting to know more about what the seegnur left behind. Since the slaughter of the seegnur and death of machines, the people of Artemis have lived in waiting. Whether or not any of us asked for it, with your coming, that waiting has ended."

Terrell nodded. "She's right, Griffin. Matters have evolved beyond hoping we will find some technology you can reactivate. We need to know exactly what your coming has awakened."

Griffin went to bed that night thinking how lucky he was to have made friends like Adara and Terrell. Stranded as he was on an isolated world with no hope of rescue in the foreseeable future, he could have fared much worse. He might have been buried in the landslide that put his ruined shuttle permanently out of reach. He might have died in the lingering winter of the mountain heights. He might have met up with people inclined to react with fear, rather than with curiosity, toward those who were different.

Instead, he had been rescued by Adara—slender but strong, quick thinking if given to odd moments of self-doubt. He grinned to himself. And could he deny her beauty? Amber eyes that caught the light like flame; long blue-black hair; sharp, fine-boned features. No . . . He couldn't deny her beauty. He saw it even in the cat's-eyes pupils and the claws her adapted nature let her form at the tips of her fingertips. Someday, he hoped, Adara herself would learn to see her adaptations' beauty, rather than only considering their usefulness.

Griffin was drifting off to sleep, cushioned by the warmth of these thoughts, when the assassin came for him. Griffin didn't know exactly what alerted him that something was wrong. Perhaps he heard some sound his subconscious couldn't account for. Perhaps he felt the change when the assassin's body momentarily blocked the flow of air from the open window. Whatever warned him, Griffin opened his eyes in time to see a darker figure against the darkness looming over his bed, hand upraised.

Griffin rolled to one side, narrowly escaping the blow that struck down where his head had been. As he dropped to the floor, he heard a dull thud against his pillow.

Momentarily, Griffin considered shouting for help, but the thought died in mid-breath. They were staying in one of the outbuildings on the Trainers' property. A cry would surely bring help, but it might also awaken small children or some of the old folks to whom the Trainers gave a home. A yell would also surely alert the dogs—the Trainers had dozens.

Even as he put distance between himself and his attacker, Griffin realized that anyone who could sneak in through a compound overrun with guard dogs was very dangerous indeed. Therefore, instead of calling out, Griffin counterattacked, his body coming to the conclusion that this was the best course of action even before his thoughts had taken shape.

Griffin viewed himself as a scholar—a historian and archeologist—but the Danes were a warrior clan. In truth, Griffin had learned to fight hand to hand before he had learned to read. Right now he was seriously angry, every bad thing that had happened to him since his shuttle had crashed boiling up and fusing until it was embodied in the figure seeking him in the darkness.

Surging up from the floor, Griffin struck for what his brother Alexander had humorously called the man's

"vulneraballs." Either the man could see in the dark—
Griffin had met those on Artemis who could—or he was
just lucky, for he turned enough that Griffin's blow
caught him on one thigh. When he staggered back a few
paces, Griffin swung for his midsection. This time he
landed a satisfying blow, and the man began to crumple.

Or so it seemed. Griffin was readying a knockout
strike when his would-be assailant dropped, rolled, then
rose in a graceful leap that carried him up and out the
open window. Griffin listened for a crash or some other
indication that the man had hit the ground but, if there
was one, it was covered by the sudden baying chorus of
howling dogs.

Griffin started to rush for the window, halted, and
was making a more cautious approach when Terrell
burst in, lit candle in hand, unclad except for a pair of
loose trousers barely secured around his waist.

"What the . . ." he was beginning when a slender figure darkened the window.

"What . . ." Adara began, but Griffin cut them both off.

"Someone attacked me. Left by the window. Do you . . ."

It was his turn to be cut off. Adara dropped from sight.
Griffin knew that she and her demiurge, the puma Sand
Shadow, would be looking for any trace of his attacker.

Terrell sighed and crossed to light the candle near Griffin's bed from his own. "If whoever came after you is to be
found, Adara and Sand Shadow will find him. We'd better
go tell the Trainers what has the dogs all stirred up."

A short time later, Griffin, Terrell, and Adara gathered in
the single room that made up the ground floor of the
small building they had been given to use by the Trainers. With them was Elaine Trainer. Her husband, Cedric,
was still quieting the dogs.

"No one was hurt," Elaine said, taking the indicated
chair, "although a couple of the guard dogs are suspi-
ciously groggy. We're guessing they must have been

darted, since they're trained not to take food from anyone who doesn't give specific commands. Whoever hit them had to estimate the dose and we're lucky they didn't make it too strong. The dogs were already coming around when Cedric found them."

"I'm so glad," Griffin said. "We've proven to be unlucky tenants for you."

"We knew you had enemies when we invited you to stay here. We're grateful that you aren't angry that you weren't better protected. We were sure the dogs would keep you safe."

"I don't blame the dogs," Griffin insisted. "I'm only sorry I didn't get the bastard."

"Tell us," Adara said from where she sat on the ledge of an open window, half in and half out, "what happened."

Griffin did, ending, "While you and Sand Shadow were trying to track the fellow, Terrell and I searched my room in case he dropped anything. We found this." He held up a neat cosh, leather sewn around lead shot. "Happens that I recognize it. It looks very much like one that belonged to Julyan."

"Julyan?" Elaine asked, seeing that the name meant something to her three guests.

"Julyan—once called Hunter," Adara said, her voice stiff with suppressed emotion. "He was a senior student with Bruin when I was in the middle of my own training. He left Shepherd's Call some years ago. I heard nothing of him until he resurfaced here in Spirit Bay as an assistant to the Old One Who Is Young, working on the secret base on Mender's Isle."

Griffin mentally filled in what Adara did not say. Julyan had also been Adara's lover and had thoroughly broken her heart. He'd also tried to kill her not long ago, but if Adara didn't care to talk about that . . . Still, he felt fairly certain that Elaine, her thin features as sharp and alert as one of her own greyhounds, guessed that something had been left out.

Griffin continued, "Julyan enforced the Old One's rule on Mender's Isle. He carried this cosh as a means of subduing without killing. I'd thought whoever came into my room meant to kill me, but now, I wonder."

Terrell nodded. "Certainly, the Old One could want you dead. You know things about him that would ruin what little reputation he has left. Apparently, though, he may value you more alive."

Adara cut in. "Even if the cosh didn't point to Julyan, there's reason to think he might have been your attacker. His hunter's training would have given him the skills to slip in here unseen, to climb up to your window, even to drug the dogs, since part of our training includes techniques for taking prey alive. When Sand Shadow and I tried to trail your assailant, we had no luck. Julyan would have known how to blur his trail to fool even another hunter. Given the number of dogs here, especially the trained trackers, he certainly would have taken precautions to mask his scent in advance. Sand Shadow is checking outside the compound, but I'm guessing she will have no luck."

Elaine's disappointment showed. "We were going to suggest tracking with one of our hounds, since—excellent as she is in many things—Sand Shadow is not a scent hunter. If this Julyan was trained by Benji Bear, though, then it's unlikely even one of our best could find him—not if he took advance precautions."

"Julyan is a ruthless man," Terrell said. "It's best you and Cedric not attract his attention any more than you must."

Griffin agreed. "We were lucky this time. I think we need to leave Spirit Bay soon, before anyone else gets drawn into our troubles. Next time someone might get hurt. We may be in as much danger on the road, but there, at least, we won't involve the innocent."

"I think we'll be in less danger on the road," Adara said. "In the wilds, Sand Shadow and I are much more in our element. It will be far harder for anyone to sneak up on us."

Elaine looked torn between protest and reluctant relief. "But where will you go? Back to Shepherd's Call? To where your friend Lynn took those you freed from Mender's Isle?"

Griffin hesitated, wondering how much to tell. Terrell spoke with absolute confidence. "Best you not know, Elaine. Best for all of us, if you don't know."

※

"You failed . . . No matter. Capturing Griffin was a long shot at best."

Julyan wanted to protest, wanted to point out that he'd gotten past all those damn dogs, gotten right into the room with Griffin, that even with Griffin waking up unexpectedly as he had, he would have managed. Who could have known that the man was a trained fighter? Griffin had shown no sign of being anything but docile during the twenty or so days he had resided against his will in the complex beneath Mender's Isle.

Julyan wanted to say, "I did perfectly what I set out to do. How could I know a lapdog would turn out to be a mastiff?"

But he didn't. There was a mocking expression in the Old One's cool grey eyes that forbore protest, which made Julyan feel certain that his explanations would be dismissed as excuses.

"We're not giving up, are we?"

The Old One gave a thin smile. "We are not, although I think it wisest if we delay. All the indications are that Griffin and his escort will soon leave Spirit Bay. I have some idea where they might be headed."

"Where?"

"Crystalaire, or rather, somewhere in the vicinity of Crystalaire."

Julyan searched his memory. The name made him uneasy. In a moment, he remembered why. "That's where many of the seegnur were gathered when the attack came, isn't it? There was a wedding. Those who were not slaughtered outright fled for the hills. They died, just the same."

The Old One nodded. "There is a prohibited area near Crystalaire called Maiden's Tear. Both historians and loremasters have speculated that the seegnur fled there because they believed something in the vicinity would help them against their enemies. No one knows what, but clearly they did not find it—or perhaps they did not have time to find it."

Holding back an instinctive shudder, Julyan asked, "But why do you think Griffin and the others will be going there?"

"Because Griffin Dane is searching for remnants of the seegnur's technology. That is what brought him to my Sanctum at Spirit Bay. He doesn't desire mere relics, such as are in any loremasters' museum, but more or less undamaged machines. As with my former home, there is little evidence that the widespread destructive measures employed elsewhere were used in Maiden's Tear—even though they were used freely in the town of Crystalaire itself. Where the hotel stood—the one in which the wedding was being held—there is nothing but a crater."

"Nasty . . ." Julyan said.

"I still have friends among the loremasters. Fewer, true, but there are those who continue to revere my knowledge. From these, I have learned what maps and archives Terrell the Factotum has consulted. The evidence confirms my conjecture."

Or you conjecture based on that evidence, Julyan thought. *You still long to be thought wiser than any other, despite your recent failure.*

He glanced quickly at the Old One. He didn't believe the Old One Who Is Young could read minds, but a man did not live as long as the Old One had without learning to read people as easily as some men read print.

Julyan wondered that he could fear a man as much as he did the Old One. The Old One was small and neatly built. There was something fussy in how he had trimmed his pale blond hair every few days, so that the short cut remained similar to those shown in representations of the seegnur. When the Old One had dwelt in his Sanctum, he had affected clothing that evoked the seegnur. Although now he was a fugitive and had adopted attire that would not excite comment, he remained meticulous in matters of grooming.

The Old One looked like the sort of man Julyan—large, strong, in perfect condition—could break with one hand, but Julyan knew from experience that the Old One could throw him across the room.

Yet that is not why I fear him . . . Even when I doubt he knows as much as he claims, I am continually uneasy. I know—few better—how he uses those around him. I am useful to him, so he treats me well, but I have seen him step on others with as little concern as I might step on an ant. Even now, unwelcome where once he was revered almost as a king, exiled from his home, I cannot help but feel the Old One remains a power in the land—perhaps in this whole vast world. Certainly his facility beneath Mender's Isle shows that his ambitions are unlimited by more normal concerns.

The Old One's research had led him to conclude that the seegnur's technology had possessed an incorporeal element, that the most sophisticated devices had not been controlled by switches or levers or push pads, but by thought. He had also believed that the adapted might hold in their genes the ability to breed those who could use the seegnur's devices. Implied in this theory was the idea that those systems had not been completely disabled by the attackers, as had always been held by the lore, but that, with the right operators, it could be made to work again. The Old One had set about to create those operators—and had resorted to imprisonment, rape, murder, and other atrocities even without any certainty that he would achieve his goals.

The Old One gave no sign of following Julyan's thoughts, only said mildly, "You will come with me?"

Julyan nodded. "If my reward will be as you promised. I get you Griffin. You give me Adara."

"I promise." The Old One's smile was thin-lipped and cruel. "Griffin has proven solid bait to lure Adara the Huntress in the past. I will get her for you—and deliver her to you better than a captive. With Griffin in my hands, I will have the means of making Adara your willing slave."

Well, this will be a journey through the maze of memories, Adara reflected, as she checked the condition of their saddlebags and related tack.

Molly, the pale red chestnut mare who was Griffin's mount, hung her head over the half-door out into the paddock, supervising Adara's preparations. Beyond her Tarnish, Adara's own smoky grey roan gelding, and Midnight, Terrell's black gelding, were methodically ripping hay from a rack, as if aware the slow, easy days were coming to an end.

First, Julyan, now . . . I wonder if Terrell realized that the route he has suggested will take us through Ridgewood, where my family lives? I can't remember if I ever told him where I grew up. Probably not, since I have lived with Bruin since I was five and Shepherd's Call is home. That's the problem with traveling into the mountains. Unless you're willing to go by more difficult routes, everything narrows down to a few passes.

I could suggest an alternate route, but that would

mean explaining why I don't want to go through Ridge-wood . . . And that would mean admitting just how in-secure I am when it comes to my family. I'm woman grown now, an official huntress. Surely, I can face . . .

Adara's memories of her early childhood were scattered and diffuse. Her family had farmed and herded sheep. Adara was the second child of five. Initially, she had suffered no more than any younger child with a talented older sibling but, eventually, she had come to realize that the differences between her and the other children were more than age.

I could see in the dark, Adara remembered. *All the other children were afraid of the dark, but I wasn't. What was there to fear? I was as afraid as anyone else of the creatures who came to prey on our flocks, but of the darkness itself? I liked it. It hid me, protected me, allowed me to sneak away . . .*

With her more adult perspective, Adara contemplated the child she had been. *I suppose I was a nuisance. I think I knew it even then. Was that why I was so certain—no matter what my parents said when they sent me to Bruin—that they were getting rid of me? Because I knew I'd been bad?*

"What," asked a voice inside Adara's head, "is 'bad'?"

Adara jumped, startled enough that she nearly dropped the harness she had been inspecting. Thirteen days was not enough time to get used to someone reading your mind. It *was* enough time to learn that ignoring the fact didn't do much good—especially when your new friend was the very planet upon which you lived.

The huntress was still not completely certain what had awakened the planet Artemis from the long sleep that had come with the slaughter of the seegnur and death of machines. She did not think that Artemis was a machine, precisely. Perhaps that was why Artemis had slept when so much else had died.

Or maybe more will awaken. Adara shivered at the un-settling notion.

"Bad . . ." Adara shaped the words inside her head—at least her relationship with Sand Shadow had been good training for this sort of communications. She'd long ago learned not to talk out loud to herself. "You certainly don't ask easy questions, do you? Bad is the opposite of good. And good is, well . . . Good is what is optimal for a given situation."

The not-voice sounded puzzled. "So bad is the least preferred choice for a given situation? Therefore, when you think how you-the-child were bad, you were not acting according to what was preferable? Why would you have done that?"

Adara sighed. "It's not quite that simple. The child me was acting according to what I wanted to do—what was preferable for me. But I knew that what I was do-ing wasn't what my parents would have liked—so, to them, my good was bad. Since I knew I was behaving in a way that might be fun for me at that moment, but that might have consequences that wouldn't be so much fun later, I knew I was being bad, even when what I was doing seemed good. Does that help?"

"No." The word was accompanied by an image of bub-bles rising to the surface of the water, then slowly pop-ping, one by one. "Yes. Maybe. What is good. What is bad. These are not precise. What is good for the owl is bad for the mouse. What is good for the wet is not good for the dry."

"Something like that," Adara agreed. "But a lot more complicated."

"Ah . . ." And just as suddenly as it had manifested, the sense of another presence faded away.

One of these days, Adara thought, *I'll have to teach her social conventions like "hello" and "good-bye." Maybe I'll even manage to explain that it's not polite to*

*probe someone else's mind, especially when they can't
return the favor.*

   She remembered some of the dreams she had experienced as Artemis learned to touch her mind. They had
been bizarre precisely because they were filtered through
a sensibility that didn't find the images bizarre at all.
Adara had talked a little with Griffin and Terrell about
their nascent telepathic link. Once the two men had accepted that their minds were able to communicate when
they were asleep—thus far they had not managed any
contact when awake—then the communication had not
been all that different from what Adara shared with her
demiurge, Sand Shadow: images augmented by an occasional word.

   Communication with Artemis was easier than communication with Sand Shadow in that the neural network—as Artemis had initially identified herself—
understood words and used them easily. However, it was
complicated because, compared to Artemis, the way Sand
Shadow thought was positively human. Sand Shadow
hadn't needed to have good and bad explained to her.
The puma had understood the concepts in a very basic
fashion: bad was what got you hurt; good was what got
you fed. The intricacies of different bads and goods
could be presented as variations on a theme.

   Since Artemis did not really understand hurt or hunger
or desire or any of the dozens of impulses, named and
nameless, that drove other living things, Adara was discovering that she must start from a different foundation.

   Foundation? Adara laughed softly to herself. *More as
if I must mold the bricks to make the foundation before
I can even build a foundation. Still, Artemis is rather
sweet in her strange way. I'm not going to push her
away while she learns to toddle about in the dark.*

They left Spirit Bay two days after the attack on Griffin. By Artemesian standards, they were a group of eight: three humans, three horses, one mule, and Sand Shadow, the puma.

Initially, Griffin had found this manner of reckoning very odd.

Sand Shadow was certainly an extraordinary individual. Not only could the puma communicate mind to mind with Adara, she had been adapted so that her front paws possessed rudimentary fingers and thumbs. The earrings of which the puma was so obviously proud had originally been meant to help her train in finer manipulation of those digits. Sand Shadow might not be as intelligent as a human—but if she wasn't, Griffin wasn't going to be the one to say so.

The three horses—Tarnish, Molly, and Midnight—were not adapted, although they were specially trained and would tolerate a puma as a companion. Sam the Mule was as ornery as any of his kind, but his strength and tenacity made him a valued addition. He was trained to carry a rider, as well as baggage, so could serve as a stand-by mount if any of the other three needed a respite.

Although, Griffin thought, *Sam would have some say as to who his rider would be. If Tarnish or Molly couldn't carry a rider, then I'm guessing Terrell would turn Midnight over to one of us and ride Sam. Sam might be trained to carry a rider—as long as that rider is Terrell.*

Although they had left Spirit Bay somewhat shorter of supplies than they had intended, neither Terrell nor Adara seemed particularly concerned.

"We're past the thin times of spring," Adara explained, "and will be traveling through the low lands for a good number of days before we go into the mountains again."

She gave Griffin an impish smile. "We kept you well enough fed during harder times, seegnur. We might even fatten you up before we reach Crystalaire."

"And there are any number of small villages where we can stop if we find we forgot something vital," Terrell added.

"I noticed those on the map," Griffin commented, shifting his rump in the saddle, earning a critical look from Molly. "I thought that Artemis was supposed to be mostly pristine wilderness. From orbit it still appeared to be so, but this area seems well settled."

"Remember, Griffin," Terrell said. "Five hundred years have passed since the days of which you speak. Although we of Artemis have tried to live as if the seegnur might return any day, when it comes to our survival—well, we've had to make some changes. Even in the days of the seegnur, there were areas given over to the raising of crops and food animals. Most of these were sequestered where they would not interfere with the sports and entertainments that brought the seegnur here. I suspect—heresy though some would have it—that the seegnur used their technology to make sure that picturesque villages in outlying areas were kept supplied."

Griffin nodded. "And without that technology those supplies wouldn't arrive . . . Yes. I can see why things needed to change if the population was to survive. Were many areas abandoned?"

"Some," Terrell agreed. "Especially those that existed mostly to provide a stopping point along the way to some particularly isolated spot. Others lost population. Crystalaire, for example, was a renowned beauty spot, one where the seegnur who came to Artemis to partake in strenuous sport could leave more delicate companions. In those days, Crystalaire supported several very fine hotels and restaurants, as well as a fleet of pleasure boats and like amenities. Today, there is one hotel. Although the views are still magnificent, the reason the area remains settled is because the lake offers excellent fishing. Fish and timber are the basis of the local economy, not the views."

"Not all settlements declined," Adara added. "Shepherd's Call, for example, was smaller in the days of the seegnur. Then it was little more than a stopping point for those who wished to hunt and ski in the mountains—or try the rapids on the river. Today, we support ourselves and supplement what we cannot grow by trading— mostly wool, but also hides and furs."

"Don't forget, Adara," Terrell said. "Another reason that Shepherd's Call has done so well is that it boasts not one but two professionals: your own teacher, Bruin, and Helena the Equestrian, with whom I was studying. People come from great distances to learn from them or—in Helena's case—to arrange for her to train a mount or to buy one of her protégés."

"Like our horses—and Sam," Griffin added, patting Molly on one reddish-gold shoulder. "I'm certainly grateful Helena let us take them. Without Molly, I wouldn't be much of a rider."

Adara laughed. "Even with Molly, you aren't much of a rider, but you are improving. While we're traveling, I'd like you to ride Tarnish for a few hours at a time. He's more patient than Midnight. Molly's so well behaved you're not going to expand your skill—and there may come a time when you need to ride without a coach."

These first days of their journey were very pleasant. As Adara had promised, the hunting—even in settled areas— was very good. Often she and Sand Shadow would leave for long stretches, returning with a brace of rabbits or game birds. Sometimes she left the hunting to Sand Shadow, and picked berries or gathered wild greens.

"Is Adara safe out there alone?" Griffin asked Terrell one day when the huntress was later than usual rejoining them. "We do have enemies."

"She's safer out there . . ." Terrell waved a long arm to indicate the rolling green that surrounded them, "than we are here on the road. We're much easier to find. Still, I have a feeling that even we are safe for now. The Old One and Julyan took a chance at grabbing you in Spirit Bay, where

I'm guessing they had a bolt hole or two. My guess is they're watching us, waiting to see where we go and what we learn. You've found some interesting things in the past, seegnur. The Old One will not have forgotten that."

"Watching us?" Griffin looked around nervously, causing Tarnish to snort and crow hop a few paces to remind Griffin of his place.

"Tracking us, rather," Terrell said. "They'll ask about us along the road. By now, I wouldn't be surprised if the Old One has a pretty fair idea where we're headed. There aren't many reasons for us to head this way—not unless he thinks Adara wants to introduce us to her parents."

He chuckled at Griffin's open astonishment. "That's right, you wouldn't know and Adara certainly wouldn't tell you. Her parents are settled on the outskirts of Ridgewood, a town right along our route. In addition to food, they raise sheep, llamas, and alpacas. Adara's mother has some fame as a weaver. These days, I'd say much of the family's income comes from selling the products of her loom and exotic wool blends."

"You sound," Griffin said, aware that a certain stiffness had entered his voice, "as if you did some research."

Adara was the one problem in his relationship with Terrell. Rather, it was Adara the woman—rather than Adara the Huntress, the companion along the road, and the friend—who was the problem. Adara had been the first person Griffin had met after his shuttle had crashed, stranding him on Artemis. She had been his protector and guide. They had shared a tent in the cold reaches of the mountains, nearly died together in an avalanche. All of this would probably have been enough to create a bond— even if his rescuer had been big, burly Bruin, rather than lithe, lovely Adara.

But his rescuer had been Adara. At first, Griffin had thought Adara might have been interested in him as a man, even as he couldn't help but be interested in her as a woman. However, she had not encouraged him. Was this because of Terrell? From a few scattered comments, Griffin suspected the two had been lovers—if only briefly. Certainly, Terrell remained interested. The two men's dreams did not touch as often as they had when Griffin had been a captive and Terrell his lifeline, but there were hints, images, some of them astonishingly erotic.

So now Griffin looked over at Terrell and repeated his statement, inflecting it into a question. "You sound as if you did some research."

Terrell gave a rueful smile. "I won't deny it. There can be few secrets between us, seegnur. Before you plummeted out of the skies, I was doing my best to convince Adara to marry me—or if she wouldn't marry, then to at least consider me as a serious suitor. She wasn't encouraging—but she wasn't sending me away, either. Then you arrived and, well . . . We both know how the world has spun since."

Griffin bit back the question he wanted to ask—although he wasn't sure he wanted the answer. *Are you sleeping with her?* Instead he managed a casual shrug.

"Adara has made clear that she's not interested in courting games."

Terrell nodded. "Julyan resurfacing isn't going to make matters any easier. I'd hoped he'd drowned."

Griffin agreed. He'd gotten to know Julyan fairly well, enough to understand how charming he could be—and how utterly ruthless. The charm made it easy for Griffin to understand why Adara had fallen in love with Julyan, back when they both had been Bruin's students. It was harder for him to understand what emotions Julyan awakened in her now. Did she still love him? Hate him? Feel something else entirely?

He decided to pretend that what Adara felt didn't matter but, looking at the flash of Terrell's white teeth, he knew he hadn't fooled anyone, most especially himself.

Interlude: Not Absolute

Bad, Good
Good, Right
Right, Left
Left, Abandoned
Abandoned, Wild
Wild, Uncontrolled
Uncontrolled
Bad? Good?